This is a work of fiction. Names, characters, places, businesses and incidents either are the product of the author's imagination or are used fictitiously. Any resemblance to actual persons, living or dead, events, or locales is entirely coincidental.

VESPERS
© 2016 by Sharon Stoker Laurent and Amy Dunn Caldwell

Cover Art: Kanaxa
Editor: Linda Ingmanson
Proofreader: Michael Valsted

ISBN: 978-0-9968099-5-5

VESPERS

HOURS OF THE NIGHT, BOOK 1

IRENE PRESTON
LIV RANCOURT

To everyone who has the courage to take a new path when they need to.

CHAPTER ONE

S ARA'S MOTHER CALLED HIM AGAIN outside of Baton Rouge, thankfully *after* his nav had guided him off of I-10 and onto 12.

"Yes, Ma, I'm awake. I've got plenty of gas. I stopped to eat two hours ago. I'm not texting and driving. I'm not speeding."

After three days on the road, he could predict in what order the questions would come. They both knew the last answer was a lie. They both knew what the next words would be.

"You don't have to do this, Sarasija."

"We've been over this. I'm a big boy. Let it go."

"I don't like you living-in. What kind of person advertises for an assistant in a town three thousand miles away?"

"I'm sure the FBI will be able to tell you after they find my body."

Silence.

"Joke, Ma."

"Not funny, Sarasija. What does this Mr. Dupont do? I can't find him on the internet. Not even a Facebook. I have a Facebook. Your grandmother in Jaipur has a Facebook. Who doesn't have a Facebook?"

"Lots of people aren't on Facebook." Or he had heard some people weren't, anyway. "Rich people who want to be private, maybe. Stop worrying." As if she would. "He didn't even hire me directly, Ms. Alves did. She has a Facebook and LinkedIn and a website. Look her up. And she advanced the money for my moving expenses. It's totally legit, so stop worrying. Maybe my first duty will be setting up his Facebook."

"Who offers a salary so large without even an interview? Did you ever speak directly to Ms. Alves?"

"I was a last-minute replacement. I'm *lucky* somebody left them in the lurch."

Another silence. Then a sigh that said she hadn't really given up badgering him. "Where are you?"

"I'm almost there. I just left Baton Rouge. Ms. Alves wants me to be out at the house by six tonight so she can introduce me to Mr. Dupont and stuff. Hey, maybe she wants to make sure I'm not the axe murderer, huh?"

That line went over almost as well as the crack about the FBI. Ma had no sense of humor about his current adventure.

"It's almost six now, Sarasija." Now her tone conveyed disapproval at his tardiness.

"There was a stalled car on the bridge over the Atchafalaya. I'm sure Ms. Alves and Mr. Dupont will understand." Or he hoped they would, because he'd been trying to reach Nohea Alves for the last hour to let her know he'd be late.

A few minutes later, Ma ended the call the same as all the others. "I miss you already, Sarasija. If you don't like Mr. Dupont, come home. We'll get the money some other way."

Maybe, but Sara didn't see how.

If it were just his father's company, he might feel differently. Saving the company wouldn't bring Dad back. But Ma stood to lose the house, life savings, everything. This job was his only chance to make up for his part in the family financial disaster. No matter how suspicious it seemed, he had never considered turning it down.

Not that he'd ever tell his mother he had any misgivings at all, but he had looked in a lot more corners of the internet than Facebook, and he couldn't find anything about Thaddeus Dupont either. A niggle of doubt tickled his stomach, punctuated by an ominous beep.

Phone, Sara. Just your phone. He plugged in the charger, wedged the phone into a stationary position in the center console next to his travel mug, and jigged both ends until the red charging light came on. Note to self: buy new car charger first thing tomorrow, because this wedging, jiggling routine was a major PIA.

Queuing up a new playlist would require more wedging and jiggling, so he tried the radio. The scan picked up WWOZ out of New Orleans. Badass! He and Nate, his roommate for the past three years, had binge-watched all four seasons of *Treme* over a long weekend. They had downloaded the soundtracks and played them endlessly afterward.

Sara would be living less than an hour outside New Orleans. Nate was already planning a trip down next month. He had some kind of crazy plot to get his work to pay for it. By the time the Natester got here, Sara would know the best places to get crawfish pie and po'boys and jambalaya, not to mention the best places in the Quarter to cruise hot Cajun guys. Louisiana was going to rock, no matter what Ma thought.

The optimism and music didn't erase all the doubt, so he started a game he had been playing with himself ever since he accepted the job—the Deal with Dupont. Maybe Dupont was a University of Washington alum who wanted to give back. Maybe he'd grown up in Seattle and wanted someone from his hometown. Maybe he had decided to hire staff from each state in the union starting in reverse alphabetical order.

There were all kinds of explanations, and all of them seemed perfectly reasonable with WWOZ blasting out Big Easy awesomeness.

He jammed out to Credence Clearwater, the Neville Brothers, and Dr. John. He turned when his phone said turn and tried not to notice the sun dropping lower and lower. Three voice mails, two emails, and a text message. Maybe Ms. Alves had her phone off or couldn't get reception out here in the country. Whatever the problem, they could sort it out when he got there.

Turn left onto Cypress Bayou Road. He was flying fast to make up time. Even with the nav, he almost missed his final turn. The two-lane road, almost hidden in the trees, flashed past the window. He hit the brakes hard, skidded to a stop on the shoulder, checked his rearview, and reversed back to make the turn.

The new road was a lot smaller than the one he had just left. It was also…residential? Nothing like any homes in Seattle, though. The road curved along the side of the Amite River, and none of the houses sat on the ground. Some were raised a few feet. More, many more, were elevated a full story on stilts. At ground level were garages and storage. The area would flood, he realized. Duh. The reality of living in a flood plain hadn't sunk in until he got the visual.

Continue on Cypress Bayou Road for twelve point three miles, his phone instructed. Okay, he had a ways to go yet. Good. Because nothing was wrong with any of these houses, except they weren't exactly in the income bracket he had been expecting.

He checked the clock. After seven. Not good.

The road curved away from the river, and homes became less frequent, or maybe they were clustered down by the water. He passed the occasional mailbox, but the houses they belonged to were hidden in the trees. On WWOZ, Dr. John rasped out some nonsense about a black widow spider. *Kinda creepy, Doc.* Without lawns and structures, the forest closed in around him, blocking out most of the light. The lush, subtropical vegetation he had admired along the highway since Houston seemed less lush and more impenetrable, adding to the spooky swampland vibe.

Ridiculous. It was the same vegetation he had been looking at all day. It was getting darker, because darkness happened when the sun started going down. And maybe he should find a new playlist, preferably something with a nasty beat recorded in the last decade. He reached for his phone, remembered the iffy cord, and punched Scan on the radio instead. Dr. John broke off as the numbers scrolled across the display, then picked right back up as if WWOZ was beaming in on a special frequency just for him.

He hit the power and cut the good doctor off mid-wail just as the road curved again and opened up onto buildings, sunlight on water, and a dead end.

All righty, then. He must have arrived? Except…where? No help from the nav.

He coasted forward to the cul-de-sac at the end of the road, which split into two driveways. On the left was the parking lot for what looked like some sort of extremely rustic convenience store. PINKY'S was hand lettered on a piece of plywood over the door. BEER. SOFT DRINKS. BAIT. SUNDRIES. Wouldn't they be better off up at the intersection with the main road? He stared at it for a second, then decided it didn't matter.

A padlocked chain blocked the drive on the right. A small sign hung in the middle.

13001. NO TRESPASSING.

13001? His new address. The phone sat silently in the console. Maybe the nav cut out? Lucky the road was a dead end, or he would have missed it.

Behind the chain, the driveway ended next to a small metal building. In the tall grass down by the water were the remains of what might have once been a pier. The overgrown grass and weeds growing out of cracks in the driveway gave the lot a neglected air.

No house. No car. No Ms. Alves.

He looked at the street number.

Im-fucking-possible he had the address wrong.

Seven fifteen. He picked up his phone. Maybe Ms. Alves had replied to his email or text.

A black screen confronted him. Great. He gripped the phone between his knees so he had both hands free. Jiggled connection to the phone; rotated the lighter plug.

Nothing.

He stared out the window at the empty lot. What now?

The **OPEN** sign blinked cheerfully at the shop next door. He sighed and got out of the car. The humidity slapped a wet towel in his face as soon as he opened the door. A layer of water condensed on his skin. By the time he had walked the few yards across the parking lot, his shirt was soaked with sweat and his whole body felt sluggish and waterlogged.

Somehow, the sweat was the last straw, worse than the traffic jam on the bridge, the broken charger, and the mysterious dead-end address. He took a determined breath of air that somehow smelled heavy and breathed like mud. Acclimate, he told himself. I will acclimate. What choice did he have?

The bait shop was bigger than he had first thought. Like everything else, the building sat a few feet off the ground. A deck ran the length of the building and disappeared around the side. Along the wall, a succession of large bins promised SHINERS! CRICKETS! WORMS!

Enthusiastic. The impression didn't falter when he opened the door. The little store was packed with so much merchandise, stuff literally hung from the ceiling. He blinked up at the water toys and life vests in assorted sizes. Coolers full of drinks, bathing suits, camping and fishing supplies lined the walls, and a small grocery section held more sundries than he could name—even if he included what appeared to be a stuffed alligator head in "sundries."

Crammed into the valuable wall real estate were signs offering knife sharpening, key-making, crawfish in-season (twenty-four-hour notice) and Jet Ski rental.

"Evenin'. Whatcha looking for, hon?"

"Fuck!" He almost pissed himself, jerked around, then wanted to die of embarrassment. "Sorry. I'm so sorry."

"Well, now, didn't mean to startle you. You okay?"

The woman behind the counter was petite, but he bet she was a force. Her face, framed by snow-white curls, was lined in all the best ways, and her bright eyes watched Sara curiously.

"Sorry for my language." His mother had raised him right.

"You're excused. You lost?"

"No. I mean, I hope not."

"Well, which is it?"

"I'm, uh. I'm supposed to be at 13001 Cypress Bayou Road?"

"You're in the right place. Dupont is next door."

Where? In the shed?

"Is he expecting you?"

"Yes, but I'm late. I'm supposed to meet a Ms. Alves?"

"Darlin', I haven't seen Nohea all week. You sure you got your days straight?"

"Pretty sure. I'm Mr. Dupont's new assistant. I'm supposed to start today, and I haven't been able to reach Ms. Alves to let her know I got stuck in traffic."

"Assistant?" She gave him a funny look. "Well, sure you are. Welcome to the neighborhood, honey. We supply all Mr. Dupont's groceries, so we'll get to know each other." She gave him another assessing look. "You *sure* you have the right day? Maybe you should call Nohea, or, what do you kids do now, text?"

"I've been trying. My phone charger's broken, and the battery died."

"Ah, *puave ti bete*, ain't that the way? Bet you were on the road all day, too."

"Pretty much."

"You look half-wilted. Come on back." She didn't wait for an answer before heading through a door next to the sunscreen display. "I'd sell you a charger, but we're out until the truck comes in next week. You can use the house phone if you want."

Sara trailed her into the next room, which turned out to have a nice bar, a few tables, and patio doors opening out onto a deck overlooking the river. Way more than a convenience store. Did he want to use the phone? His had been dead less than thirty minutes, and he hadn't been able to reach Ms. Alves all day. If she wasn't here already…

"You want a coke? I'm Dot, by the way." She raised her voice. "Bren? You want to get Mr. Dupont's new…assistant…a coke."

"Be right there, Maw-maw. I just—oh—hello." The girl at the register stared, then looked him over with a slow smile. "*You're* Dupont's new assistant?" Her short black hair had purple highlights, and she wore shorts and a Pinky's T-shirt.

"Yep. At least I hope I am. Nothing like showing up late your first day, huh?" He smiled. "I'm Sara. I guess we'll be neighbors for the next year."

Bren threw Dot an unreadable look. "Sara? Well, you're not his normal. What can I get you?"

"Thanks, but maybe you could just give me directions? I don't want to be any later than I am already."

Dot and Bren exchanged another look.

"Someone will have to take you," Bren finally said. "Didn't Nohea arrange to meet you?"

"Yeah, but I haven't been able to reach her all day." *Had* he mixed up the dates? Yeah, no, Ms. Alves had emailed him yesterday confirming his arrival time today. "I really don't want Mr. Dupont to have to wait. I don't want him to think I'm not reliable."

"Well, I suppose I can take you."

Dot made a soft noise under her breath. "It's almost dark, Bren."

"Maw-maw, we have lights. I'll be home in no time. Anyway, taking him will be a favor to Mr. Dupont."

Dot looked as though she would say something else, but Sara headed her off. "Please? I'm already off to a bad start my first day. Can't you help me out?"

"Well, I wouldn't want to inconvenience Thaddeus Dupont, heaven knows. I suppose you can go, Bren, but you come straight back, you hear?"

The next thing Sara knew, Bren was hustling him out the door. "Come on, get your stuff before she changes her mind."

"Get my stuff?"

"Well, not everything. Just grab enough for tonight."

"Wait. What? Can't I just follow you?"

"Ha-ha. Very funny—oh shit. You're serious."

They were at his car, where Bren wanted him to get his stuff because… Oh. The significance of the boat dock address finally hit him. "I can't get there from here, can I?"

"Well, not in that. Cute car, though."

The electric-blue Civic, a sixteenth birthday present from his parents when money hadn't been an issue, was tricked out with Lambo doors, a bass cab, and custom rims. Even after six years and almost a hundred thousand miles, the car was his most valuable asset. He'd just been asked to leave it on the side of the road in the middle of a swamp. He popped the trunk and pulled out the same duffel he'd lived out of for the past few nights. He hesitated, looking at the rest of his luggage.

"I'm sure Nohea will be out first thing in the morning to get you sorted."

"What about my car?"

"No one will bother it as long as you're parked here."

She sounded so sure of herself, he didn't think to question how she could be so positive. Instead, he followed her across the parking lot, through the store, and out the back door. *Rustic convenience store, my ass.* He bet Pinky's had anything you needed out here.

Down by the river, there was a drive-down boat launch, enough dock space for a few dozen boats, and two gas pumps. Bren led him down to the last slip, where a small flat-bottom boat bobbed in the water. Before he knew it, they were headed down river at a steady clip. The noise of the motor discouraged idle chitchat, but Bren fiddled with the radio until she hit a station. Not Dr. John, thank you. Because that shit with WWOZ had freaked him out a little.

Apparently, swamp kids liked Dave Grohl as much as Seattle kids. For a few minutes, his day didn't suck—cruising down the river, listening to the Foo Fighters, on his way to his kickass new job. Bren throttled down until the engine noise settled to a low hum and veered off the open river. Then she veered again, and they were in straight-up swamp. The radio went static, more static, full-on static. Bren tried the tuner, and staticky Grohl returned briefly, then gave up the ghost to WWOZ.

She hit the power button. "I don't know why the radio always goes funky out here."

The loss of music settled over them with the next layer of twilight. The boat slid through the water as Bren navigated through tree stumps, low-hanging branches, and occasional knolls of land. Without the radio, the sounds of the swamp took over—crickets so loud, they should have drowned out the music, the lower thrum of frogs, and the occasional screech of a bird. Apparently, he needed a better soundtrack, because Dr. John tuned in to his head where there was no Off switch.

Bren flicked a switch, and lights at both ends of the boat came on, beating back some of the gloom. Sara forced his fingers to unclench from the seat. Jesus, he'd been admiring the same cypress trees and Spanish moss out the window all day. Except down in it, the scenery seemed less romantic and more…

"What the hell?" He scrambled across the seat. "Alligator! Bren, there's an alligator over here!"

Bren peered over the side of the boat, where dark eyes glided above darker water. "Wow, he's a big 'un. Don't worry, they aren't usually aggressive. I wouldn't do any night swimming, though. You'll have to get used to them out here. Might be more of them than there are us."

Bren sounded so casual, he felt like an idiot. Except, alligator. No. Sorry, he refused to feel unmanned by his fear of a six-foot predator with very large teeth.

"Maybe we should have called Mr. Dupont to let him know we're on the way." He needed to talk. Anything to break the mood and make things seem more normal.

"Eh, wouldn't have done any good. He works nights. Way I hear, even if he's up, he won't answer his phone half the time."

Major distraction, because now curiosity was killing him. The Deal with Dupont—works nights. What the hell did he do all night in the middle of a swamp? Sara tried to figure out some way of pumping Bren for information without coming off like a gossip and couldn't do it. The best he could come up with was "Your grandmother knows him?"

"Well, they've been doing business for a while. I guess she knows him as well as anyone. He mostly keeps to himself."

"You've never met him?"

"I've seen him over at his dock a few times." She frowned. "You know, I could swear I've talked to him, but I can't remember when or what we talked about. Or maybe I'm remembering his father. The land's been in the same family for generations."

"No offense, but are you sure you know where we're

going?"

She scoffed at him. "'Fraid I'll feed your Yankee ass to the gators?"

"Crossed my mind."

She laughed. "I've done plenty of deliveries out to his place. Don't worry, I'll get you there in one piece."

A few minutes later, she made good on her promise as the swamp gave way to actual land. Bren guided the boat up to a long, skinny pier jutting out from a sloping lawn. In the fading light, Sara could barely make out a large structure set back among the trees. Bren steadied the boat while he clambered out onto the pier with his duffel, then peered up toward the house. "I don't see any lights. You want me to come up with you?"

Yes. Except she had promised her grandmother she would come straight home, and he was a big boy. He didn't need someone to hold his hand while he walked a hundred feet to meet his boss.

"He's probably in the back."

"I guess. You sure you don't want me to hang out for bit, just in case?"

"I'll be fine. He's expecting me, and I'll be living here. I mean, his other assistants survived, right? It's not like he's an axe murder." That came out as a joke, right?

"Yeah, no. You're right. They all seem to love the job. I just, what if he's not home?"

"No, she said he expected me by six, so he must be in there. Get home to your grandmother."

"Have it your way." She pushed off from the dock. "Good luck with the new job."

Sara watched the boat disappear into the swamp, then picked up his duffel and started across the lawn. The house wasn't as far as he had thought. The distance was an optical illusion, because a structure that big should have seemed a lot more obvious. Instead, the trees, the wispy Spanish moss, and the hint of fog along the ground combined to deflect the eye until the house seemed to waver insubstantially in mist. Sara got an impression of a steep roof and aged wood, then he was on the long porch running the length of the house without knowing quite how he had traveled the last few yards.

God, it had been a long day.

Tall windows lined the porch, but they were shuttered, so he couldn't see anything inside. The door was heavy wood behind a screen. There was no bell. Why was knocking so much harder?

Sara stood outside, his heart pounding in his chest, and called himself every kind of idiot. Mr. Dupont expected him. This would be his home for the next year. If it hadn't been for a fender bender on an endless bridge, he would be inside right now. He wiped sweaty palms down his pants. Took a deep breath and tapped on the doorframe.

The long wait should have given him a chance to calm down. Instead, his reluctance to disturb the silent house grew. He counted to a hundred, slowly, and then rapped harder.

The third time, he pounded.

After that, he cursed. Quietly, under his breath, in case the door suddenly opened.

He left his bag and walked the length of the porch and through spongy earth down both sides of the house, looking for any hint of light. Nothing. No light. No sound. The utter inanimateness of the building mocked him. He went around to the front. Feeling like a total douche, he opened the screen door and tried the knob. Locked.

Well, that was just…super swell.

A cast-iron patio set occupied one end of the porch. He sank down into one of the chairs, stared out at the water, and took stock of his situation. He was in the middle of a swamp at a house that looked deserted. He had no phone. It was almost full dark. He slicked his hand through sweat-soaked hair. At least he wouldn't freeze.

Down by the water, some of the shadows began to move, followed a second later by the sound of bodies sliding into the water. *Probably more of them than us.* The sounds of the crickets and bullfrogs faded behind a high-pitched whine next to his right ear. A second later, he slapped at a sharp sting against his arm, then another. He looked down to find a visible smear of blood and another mosquito settling in for lunch.

Freakin' perfect. *He mostly keeps to himself.* Bren's words from earlier snuck into the forefront of his brain. Only how the neighbors described every axe murderer ever. *What kind of person advertises for a personal assistant in a town 3,000 miles away?* He propped his feet up on the table and settled back in the chair, too tired to come up with any new explanations for Dupont. *I don't know, Ma.*

The final bit of twilight faded, and living in the city hadn't prepared him for the reality of night. Even straining his eyes, he couldn't see a damn thing. He could hear plenty, though, most of it scary as shit. Yeah, man had invented fire first thing, because this kind of dark ate your soul and left your body for whatever crawled up out of the swamp.

He sat in the dark, cursing his own stupidity for not stopping earlier to buy a fifteen-dollar car charger and trying not to jump at every crackle and splash. He was so focused on the noises in front of him, he completely missed the first signs of life from the house.

He didn't hear the door open or movement on the porch, but suddenly, every instinct screamed to high alert. *Danger.* Way more danger than anything the swamp had served up.

He froze and tried to focus past the sound of blood rushing behind his ears as his heart rate kicked into high gear.

Something was on the porch behind him.

CHAPTER TWO

H EAT AND HONEY. CRIMSON AND coal. A haze of color and sound. The man—for it was a man—stood on the porch as if he had every right to be there. As if I didn't care he'd interrupted Vespers, the evening chant that allowed me to greet him without breaking his foolish neck. As if I'd expected to find him, tall and proud and soft as a yearling buck.

I had no such expectation, and he had no right, and only the luck of the innocent kept me from breaking his neck on principle.

"If you're here to sell me something, I must respectfully decline."

"I'm, um, Sara. Sara Mishra." He scratched his arm, adding an earthy copper note to his honey scent. Blood. "Are you Thaddeus Dupont? I'm sorry I'm late. I was supposed to be here by six to meet Ms. Alves, but there was a stalled car and my phone died and—"

I cared little for his arguments, as long as he left, so I raised my hand, driving my gaze to the bottom of his fathomless brown eyes. He paused, then gave me a nod and kept going.

"You are Mr. Dupont, right? I'm really sorry for being late." He nodded again, uncertain, no longer a yearling buck but a hare, ready to turn and run. "Wait. I already said I was sorry."

His speech lacked a Cajun swing and his rapid-fire heart-beat echoed in my throat, under my sternum, stirring the hunger. He shouldn't have kept talking after I willed him to stop.

"I am Dupont." I spoke because it forced my body to breathe, and breathing gave me something to do besides surrender. His resistance to my will frightened me, adding a dash of cayenne to the craving his presence evoked.

"Awesome. I've only got my one duffel bag." He gestured into the darkness over his shoulder. "Bren over at Pinky's said Ms. Alves would help me get the rest of my stuff later."

What had Nohea done? "I'll call her now." If my *couyon* associate had hired a man to be my assistant, we were all in trouble. I gestured toward the door, inviting the rabbit into my lair.

"I've been trying to reach her all day." His bag was big enough to hold a body. "Don't worry, though. I've got everything I need right here."

Taking one step to the side, I allowed him to enter. Once out of the steaming sable night, his posture straightened, firmed, and he stood tall enough to look me in the eye. I flexed my fingers, rooted my bare feet into the wooden floorboards, refused the impulse to stroke the breadth of his shoulder, the beautiful curve of his ass.

My home was simple enough, two stories, elevated to clear the water, with a deep porch and a pitched roof. A lone candle burned on the desk next to my psalter, providing the scant light my vision required. My furnishings were equally simple: a long low couch bolstered by two ancient club chairs, their leather upholstery buffed beige on the armrests. A kneeler pulled up to the desk. Such art as would keep my mind on the eternal.

"Wow." The northern man with the woman's name—Sara—stumbled over the low table in the center of the room. Large windows overlooked the bayou, glossy and black except for the pool of reflected candlelight. "You must be part bat to navigate this place."

"Here." I switched on the overhead light, an old screw-on fixture holding two low-watt bulbs. His presence made me conscious of the dense humidity enfolding us, mingling our energies through the medium of water.

He rested the body bag on its end, holding it upright. "Where should I put this?"

"Please sit down while I call Nohea." I waved him over to the couch. "I believe there's been some mistake."

He demonstrated the scope of my mistake by ignoring the command to sit. Instead, he eased the duffel bag against the wall and wandered around the room, examining the art, touching, breathing, disturbing my peace. His wide brown eyes spoke of youth, though his proud carriage and the late-day scruff on his chin were all man. Each step he took tightened fear's grip on my gut till the friction sent a completely unwarranted spark to my groin.

I pulled the cell phone from my desk drawer, the hunger clawing at my resistance. Dialing Nohea's number, I breathed the words of a psalm. *Pray for the peace of Jerusalem: they shall prosper that love thee.*

Like David, I yearned for the Lord's strength, to keep from tasting this most succulent temptation.

The call went to voice mail, an exercise in vacuous communication. Nohea had been my business manager for less than two years. She'd inherited the position, and I'd been impressed by her diligence. This error was highly uncharacteristic, assuming it was an error and not something darker.

"So, are you an art historian or something?" Sara caressed a picture's frame with his fingertips. "You've got one of everything here."

So light, those long, trailing fingers. How would they feel on my skin?

"I guess in this one, the pope's telling off some demon."

"Close." Disconnecting the call, I moved toward him, stopping when his honey scent made my mouth water. *Always the hunger.* "It's a fifteenth-century piece called *Saint Wolfgang and the Devil.*" Another step, another shot of desire. "I find it both amusing and an eloquent reminder of the challenges we face."

He grinned at me over his shoulder, his wavy bangs partially obscuring one eye. "You spend a lot of time dealing with the devil?"

So confident. So soft. "Don't you?"

He paused as if my tone had unsettled him. For my part, I took my nerves in hand and dialed Nohea. Again it went to voice mail. "*Merde alors.*"

"Look, your contract was pretty straightforward, but if there's a problem, I guess I can…" He paused again, rubbed his face. "Well, shit. I don't know what I'll do. I can't get to my car without a boat, and there's no way in hell I'm doing it alone at night."

I could have told him he'd face as much danger here than in any swamp. He wouldn't have believed me, for his bravery rose sweetly, like the incense from a swinging thurible at Mass.

Non. I would not give in. As if readying my home for a hurricane, I shored up my internal defenses. I had been the old man in the swamp for more years than anyone around had been alive. Surely this one bright spark of humanity would not be my undoing.

"You won't have to travel at night." An owl's mournful cry rose over the song of the frogs and underscored the tension crackling between us. "I'll phone Bren and ask her to retrieve you in the morning."

His expressive mouth gave up any pretense of a smile.

"And I'll have Nohea write you a reference." His dejection touched me. None of this was his fault. *It's who you are and what you could do to me.* "You'll be compensated for your time."

"Sure. Yeah." He covered his mouth with an open palm. "It's just, I drove all this way, and…"

"I'm sorry." Though Nohea owed us both an apology. A corrosive trickle of anger threaded past the hunger and desire. Recruiting my assistant was her primary task. The position had two main stipulations: a one-year contract offered to a female candidate. For me to live with a man in this isolated place would be a death sentence, for him surely, and likely for me as well.

"Nah, it's cool. I mean, I don't understand, but whatever."

I moved toward the hallway. "Come. I'll show you where you can at least get a good night's sleep."

With a soft grunt, he lifted his bag, the light pad of his footsteps barely louder than mine. I opened the door to the guest room. "You'd be wise to lock the door. The key is on the windowsill."

He brushed past me in a burst of nectar and warmth. "Is there someone else here?"

"No, just the two of us."

The door swung shut. "Effing hermit." The whispered words were loud in my ear, punctuated by the click of the key in the lock.

For the first time all night, he did as I asked.

As a young man, I studied the Word. I worked the land. I joined with my brethren and forced my foolish heart to open so the Rule of St. Benedict could wear away my pride and my selfishness.

Then my first life ended, and I was remade. For some ten years, I indulged in every vice, a soulless being of the night. The White Monks engineered my rescue, and I returned to the Rule. As a result of my effort, the will of God, or sheer dumb luck, I have sustained myself over eighty years, giving the Lord what the Devil once tried to claim.

On nights like this, the effort weighed heavy indeed.

I mounted the steps to the second floor, accompanied by the endless chorus of peepers, ornamented by the whip of a bat's wing, the slop of a diving *caimon*, the scream of a bobcat. To those were added the small sounds a man makes as he's undressing, the soft thump of a shoe, the quick buzz of his zipper, the rustle of fabric pooling on the floor. Even from the upper level, I could hear Sara moving, the soft whir of his breath.

Perfect torture.

No one could breach my sanctuary. The stairs ended in a small landing, with two doors opening from it. In one room, I stored most of the family heirlooms I no longer needed. I spent my days in the other room, if not asleep, then in the somnolent state required by my nature.

Kneeling on the bare wood floor of my inner sanctum, I regained some measure of peace through meditation, then began the chant for Compline. Over one hundred years, I had cycled through the missal, till I could recite the psalms and antiphons and sing the hymns from memory.

He who dwells in the shelter of the Most High, abides under the shadow of the Almighty.

The psalms are the perfect prayer, the rhythm of the words molded and shaped by years of recitation, the way stone steps curve under the persistent pressure of weary feet. The couplets leave space for the breath, carrying prayers aloft where the Almighty can hear them.

This night, I could not fit my will to the shape of the words, and my breath stuttered between the phrases.

The hunger. Always the hunger.

I fought till the sweat beaded across my brow, until the pain of it twisted like a fist in my intestines. Sara had asked about Saint Wolfgang, who faced a warped, insectile demon with a bombastic smirk. I had faced real demons, and while I grasped the Saint's humor, no demon had ever tortured me worse than the man asleep in my house.

Not just any man. With his warm brown skin and his honeyed scent and his steady, even breathing, Sara created a pulse my chanting could not match. At dawn, I would retire. He would wake, Bren would come, and Nohea's error would end.

Halfway down the steps, I realized my failure. I bit down on my lip to keep from crying out, hard enough to taste blood.

The lock on his door was intended less to give him peace of mind than to create a mild deterrent for me, for I could not open the door without first acknowledging my intention. With a gentle nudge, the door swung open, and I again fell to my knees.

This time at the edge of a banquet, one I could not touch.

His breath rumbled in and floated softly out. Keeping a span between my body and the bed, I drank in his beauty. Dark hair tumbled around his face, and his black lashes were long and thick. I had no need for light to see the most minute details, the faded crescent scar above his right brow, a small mole on the tender skin between his jaw and his left ear.

My body's ageless variation on humanity proved still capable of hardening with need. My hands hung loose at my sides, their lack of action requiring more effort than lifting a ton of rock. My own breath rasped, harsh and desperate, leaving me poised on the edge of the precipice. I struggled to find a prayer to keep myself from tumbling into the abyss of heat and sex and blood.

His honeyed scent wrapped around me, nearly tipping the scales. I leaned forward close enough to feel his breath against my cheek. Close enough to see the steady pulse at the base of his throat.

Gloria patri et filio et spiritui sancto…

I landed hard on my heels.

Sicut erat in principio, et nunc, et semper…

Rose to my feet.

Et in saecula saeculorum. Amen.

And fled.

Pounded up the stairs. Reached for the one thing I could do. The only thing that would help.

My cat-o'-nine.

When one possesses more strength than any three men combined and the ability to heal on a dime, any suffering is limited, transient. Regardless, I stripped off my shirt and grasped the leather-wrapped handle. The tails were tipped with lead, designed to tear flesh without the permanent burn of iron. Though the two of them could not be more different, still Sara's presence had called to mind a ghost I would sooner keep buried.

Kneeling for the third time, I swung the flogger hard, setting my back on fire.

CHAPTER THREE

T OO QUIET.
Too bright to still be night.

Where was he? After days on the road, Sara didn't know. There wasn't any traffic noise. Where were the cars?

He rolled over and opened his eyes to the sight of a crucifix on pale plaster. He stared at it, trying to make the mutilated body of Christ conform to budget hotel décor. Where the hell had he stopped?

His brain woke up more slowly than his body, gradually filling in the previous day. He hadn't stopped. He'd made it to Louisiana and the home of Thaddeus Dupont, who had redefined Sara's previous vague definition of the phrase *wealthy eccentric*. The hermit in the middle of a swamp. *Okay, Ma, now we know, thank you very much.* At least he hadn't been chopped into bits and fed to the alligators, so that was something.

He stretched and took further inventory of his surroundings. The four-poster bed was pretty cool. And, damn, his room at home had a memory foam mattress and pillows, but right now he could have been floating in a cloud. Ceilings high enough to feature a big paddle-shaped fan. Dresser. An armoire. An actual antique armoire. His buddy Nate, a massive gay stereotype regarding home décor, would be in heaven.

He was looking around for his phone to send him a picture when the rest of reality kicked him in the gut.

He was freaking fired.

Shit.

He finally found his phone. At least he had remembered to put it on the charger before he passed out. He crossed his fingers and hit the power. And praise the dead Jesus on the wall, his phone lived. An actual signal was confirmed seconds later when it blew up in his hand, vibrating and buzzing like the world was ending. Missed calls, voice mail, texts, emails, tweets and—aw hell—he had forgotten to call Ma last night.

He stared at the barrage of communications from every possible source, all with one message. CALL HOME.

He contemplated the screen glumly and half considered turning the thing off so he wouldn't have to deal with any of it. How was he supposed to tell Ma he'd been fired? She wouldn't care, he knew. She would be ecstatic to have him home. But...

Another buzz as a new text from his big brother appeared.

> Dev: You better be dead, asshole. Ma's
> trying to book me a flight because she can't
> get the Louisiana State Police to take her
> seriously. Pick up your phone.

Trust Dev to text in complete sentences.

> Sara: Dead battery. Sorry.

The phone immediately started ringing. He ignored it and finished his reply.

> Sara: Will call Ma later. Have to go.

Then he turned the phone off. Total chickenshit move. He needed a little space before he talked to anyone.

How could he be fired? He had a contract. Dupont hadn't even given him a reason. Misunderstanding? What misunderstanding? "Your health benefits don't kick in for three months" was a misunderstanding. Give up your apartment and move halfway across the country to not have a job was something completely different. Why the hell hadn't he said something to Dupont last night? He searched his memory for the rest of the conversation. He was to be compensated? Hell, no. Not unless compensated meant the whole eighty grand. Ma needed every dollar.

He rummaged in his duffel for clean clothes. He wanted a shower something fierce, but he wanted answers more. Dupont had some explaining to do. He gave the crucifix another glance as he left the room. Freakin' hermit. The thing was gruesome. Catholics were weird.

When he stepped out into the hall, the silence hit him again. He stopped and listened, trying to decide which way to go, but the house offered no clues. He chose left, mostly because it was familiar. In the room with Saint Wolfgang, he paused. Everything looked as he remembered it except… He pivoted, trying to remember the details of what had happened the night before.

Dupont had found him on the porch. Sitting in the dark outside a locked house definitely counted as a misunderstanding. He had been tired, and scared, and shit, he had babbled incoherently when Dupont startled him. Okay, not a great first impression.

Not a fireable offense either.

Then they had gone inside and…what? Why did everything seem so fuzzy? He remembered Saint Wolfgang, and Dupont saying something about devils and misunderstandings.

Dupont wasn't an old dude, not old at all. If asked to guess, Sara might have said they were about the same age. His dark, wavy hair looked too long and unruly to be remotely corporate, and his shapeless clothes had obviously been chosen for comfort.

The olive undertones in his pale skin hinted at a person who would tan dark and easy but didn't get much sunlight. Tech geek, maybe. If not for his bossy, uptight attitude, he could have been another college kid chilling out in nature over summer break. The attitude added an easy decade, though. And the eyes. Dupont had the most intense eyes.

Funny he couldn't remember their color, but he had been so tired from the drive. What had they actually said? Nohea, misunderstanding, and then somehow Sara had agreed to leave the next day. He'd just accepted that he was going to turn around and go home. He shook his head, trying to figure out why he had done that. Had he actually said he would?

He ran his finger along Saint Wolfgang's frame. He should have allowed another day for the drive down. He was shit for brains when he got tired. Now where had Dupont gone? They needed to straighten this out.

He tried the door on the other side of the room, which led to the kitchen. No Dupont. He found a note, though, propped conspicuously on the counter by the coffeepot.

He picked it up. Damn, dude had some handwriting. He traced the flowing script. Who wrote like that? He skimmed the words, which basically stated he could help himself to anything from the kitchen and Bren would pick him up sometime before noon. *My sincere apologies for any inconveniences.*

Sara read the last line three times. On the fourth, he crumpled up the piece of paper with the pretty writing. *Bastard. You're not getting rid of me so easily.* He took stock of the other items on the counter, dumped grounds from the canister into the coffeepot, and added water. *Couldn't even stick around to tell me yourself? What's up with that?* Milk, juice, eggs, and bacon in the fridge. Bread and fruit on the counter. Cereal in the cabinet. He went for fruit and toast and took them out on the porch.

The temperature outside hadn't yet made it to the energy-sapping, steam-room levels of the day before. There were fans over the porch, and he turned them on. The breeze carried the scent of the wisteria growing up the column on the side of the porch, and the view over the pier was…nice. For a few minutes, he forgot to be pissed.

Then he thought about calling Dev and Ma, and his mood soured again. Did he want to live the next year in the middle of a sweltering, alligator-infested swamp? Hell, no. He had expected to spend the summer after graduation fucking off before grad school, because God forbid any of the Mishra kids left college with anything less than a PhD.

Even after his father's death…

He took another swig of coffee and managed to choke down the last bite of toast over the ball of grief, anger, and shame lodged in his throat. Losing this job wasn't an option.

He stared out into the swamp for a few more minutes, trying to decide what to do. Then he got out his phone and scrolled through the barrage of call-home messages from the night before. Nothing from Nohea Alves. He tried her number and got a message saying her voice mail was full. Not helpful. Also, what the fuck? He added *corporate HR department* to his mental requirements for his next job.

Then he made a decision. Too bad he didn't have Bren's number, because she'd be making a trip for nothing. He didn't want to be a dick about it, but contracts bound both ways. Leaving the premises would send the wrong message. He had a contract. He wasn't going anywhere. It would be easier to stay than try and argue his way back in. Better to break the news to Dupont gently, though. They would be working together for the next year. It would suck if they couldn't get along.

After breakfast, he returned to his room. He wanted to be ready, whenever Dupont showed up. A shower would help, and maybe nicer clothes than a T-shirt and shorts. They were in a swamp. Even if Dupont didn't care how his assistant dressed, Sara wanted to make a good impression. He didn't know what Dupont's deal was. Whatever the misunderstanding, they'd have to sort it out. Dupont needed to understand he had hired an awesome assistant.

He didn't remember the final bit of weirdness from the

night before until his hand touched the bedroom door-knob. Dupont had told him to lock it. And he had, hadn't he? But it hadn't been locked this morning. He had walked right out without thinking about the key at all.

THE MUSIC OF THE SWAMP changed at dusk. The crickets' song faded, and innumerable *grenouille* begin their evening conversation. Their single-syllable words added texture to the night, my signal of safety for leaving my windowless room.

By habit, I rose in time for Vespers to pray. My knees were immune to the unyielding wood floor and my body unaffected by the heavy blanket of humidity. The regular rise and fall of the psalm tones lulled me into contempla-tion.

For the rod of the wicked shall not rest upon the lot of the righ-teous; lest the righteous put forth their hands unto iniquity.

I feared the rod of the wicked had found Nohea. The young man who had appeared on my doorstep identified himself with a woman's name; however, the coincidence was too obvious, too blatant.

Nohea's intelligence had always impressed me, and a mis-take of this magnitude was uncharacteristic. I sank into the moment, pondering the question and shifting the heavy air in time with my breath. How had a man—a young, desirable man—come to be hired as my assistant?

A low tone interrupted my meditation. It sounded again, drawing attention to one of my few concessions to mod-ern communication, my iPad.

The signal sounded a third time, and I rose, swiping the screen and carrying it to my narrow bunk. Skype. Some-one wanted to talk.

I opened the program, hoping to see Nohea. Instead, Brother George glared at me. "I hope I'm not disturbing you." A self-righteous man, his constant judgment was a thorn in my peace of mind.

"I just finished with my prayers."

Some twenty years ago, Brother George had been assigned to be my liaison with the White Monks, a subset of the Dominican Order of Preachers, whose special skills allowed them to directly combat evil. When Satan's children—demons and hellions and fiends—engaged with humankind, the White Monks forced them Below.

According to Brother George, my nature was as tainted as any of the monsters we fought. Communicating with him required every bit of my forbearance. With any luck, the Lord would credit our exchanges against the time I'd spend in Purgatory. Assuming Brother George was wrong. Otherwise, my efforts were wasted, because I'd be going straight to hell.

I rested the iPad against the footboard and used his bombastic opening monologue to remind myself of my pledge. In return for an assistant to satisfy my need for sustenance, I'd serve the White Monks in whatever capacity they deemed appropriate. I couldn't be a full member of the Church; Brother George counseled me in a weekly confession but did not offer me absolution, and when I chose to attend Mass, I received an unconsecrated host at Communion. Though their terms were harsh, if I met them, I stood a chance of restoring my soul.

When it came to beauty, our heavenly Father had dealt Brother George a penurious hand. He had too much nose and too little chin and small eyes peering out from under bushy gray brows. I didn't pay him much attention at all until he mentioned my business manager's name.

"Pardon me, Brother. What did you say about Nohea?"

His thin lips tightened further, and beads of sweat glistened along the edge of his tonsure. "I said, she missed this morning's meeting. Have you heard from her?"

The White Monks provided for Nohea too, my human presence during daylight hours. "She was supposed to be here last evening."

"Supposed to but wasn't?" His unpleasant tone turned caustic. "Sounds like your manager needs a lesson in discipline."

I spoke carefully, sorting through the possibilities, tamping down a moment of regret for sending Sara away. My motivation was too suspect to examine closely. "Nohea organized the transition to my new assistant."

"Yes. We received her contract." Sara's name must have fooled Brother George, too.

"*His* contract."

"His?" Emotions flashed across his face. Surprise. Concern. Glee.

"His." My confirmation caused his smile to broaden, an expression so exceptional on his wizened features, I choked on my dismay. "I sent him away."

"Oh no, Brother Thaddeus. You cannot. The contract has been signed."

The implication in his words rolled over me, hardening my dismay into the walls of a trap. "Then I shall retrieve him." As if that glorious young man was a wallet or a set of keys whose worth was best proven by his absence.

Brother George had been waiting twenty years for me to slip, and from his barely suppressed smirk, he had me. "Perhaps Nohea can assist you." His head gave a portentous tilt, as if the motion could tighten the trap around me. "You have seen her?"

"Mmm." Some residual humanity kept me from giving him a direct answer. All my lifetimes had taught me not to share secrets with someone so *désagréable*.

"Well." Brother George crossed his arms, gloating at me from under his bushy brows. "You have a new assignment, so I'll need both you and Nohea to meet with me as soon as possible."

I nodded, my palms open. "Of course, Brother." Assignments were best given in person, in places where information could not be overheard.

"Notify me when you get to town, and I'll tell you where and when."

My jaw tightened at his high-handed tone, though anticipation beat in time with my pulse. It had been two years since my last assignment. Two years since leaving the river. And now Sara arrived, Nohea proved undependable, and I had an assignment.

"I'll be in touch," I said. "God's peace be with you, Brother."

"God's peace." He reached forward to close the connection as soon as the words left his mouth. Brother George made it very clear I was as much a trial to him as he was to me. I tapped my iPad screen, sending it to sleep, though I did not move right away.

I lost myself in the swamp music. My previous assistant had left a week ago, and now my most pressing concern was for sustenance. Feeding from Sara would have begged disaster. Fear of the possibility had racked me all night, though the twin desires, hunger and lust, had come close to winning through.

My resolve had held, and now I had to move on. A quick search of the house should tell me whether Nohea had been present. I rose, headed for the door, heard a sound.

Footsteps. On the stairs.

Inhaling, I caught the faintest hint of honey.

Sara.

Mon Dieu, j'ai faim. So hungry.

For one moment, I lost control, a very human lapse, where *I want* became the only thing. When I regained myself, I had bent Sara over the banister, his hands scrabbling at my shirt. I shifted away, and his hands flew out, as if he might overbalance. I caught one wrist, his flesh warm, his pulse thudding under my thumb.

"What. The actual. Fuck." He jerked his hand away, then blinked, slowly, rubbing the place I'd touched with trembling fingers. "I wasn't, um"—he paused to clear his throat—"sure you were still here."

"*Je m'excuse,*" I murmured, breathless. I took another step. "Come. We'll eat." Brushing past him, I headed down the stairs. He stayed still, clasping his wrist, the heat of his gaze following me. "Come." I paused on the steep stairs. "We'll talk."

CHAPTER FOUR

SHIT. *SHIT.* WHAT WAS THAT all about? Sara clung to the polished banister as he followed Dupont's implacable form down the stairs, trying not to wind up in a heap at the bottom. The stairs were steep enough to be tricky already, never mind he was still shaking like a leaf. *We'll talk*, Dupont had said. And walked away, cool as you please, as if nothing had happened.

We'll talk? Or had he said eat? *Not relevant.* Because, okay, maybe he shouldn't have surprised the guy. Dupont obviously had expected to be alone in the house, but that didn't excuse... *What?* The details were fuzzy.

He had been downstairs, getting antsier and antsier about confronting Dupont and second-guessing his decision to send Bren back to Pinky's alone. When the noises overhead started, he had kicked himself. Duh. Dupont worked nights, so maybe he hadn't bugged out, maybe he had just been asleep most of the day. After a while, when Dupont showed no inclination to come down, Sara had lost patience. He'd climbed up to the master suite or secret hideaway or wherever. And, jeez, was the guy some kind of miser, or just super conscientious about his energy usage? Again with the lack of lights. The narrow landing at the top of the stairs was dark, and the shifting shadows in the close quarters gave Sara the willies, not to mention second thoughts about invading his employer's privacy.

Suddenly, Dupont had been there, way too close, pressing their bodies together way too intimately. Or had he? Had Sara just imagined that part? Because the next thing he knew, he was falling. He would have fallen, except Dupont's fingers had wrapped around his wrist and hauled him to safety with no more apparent effort than if he were a child. Safe.

He didn't feel very safe, though. His heart was pounding hard enough the gators could probably hear it out in the swamp. He hit the bottom step and then level floor with relief. Dupont turned left, away from the kitchen. Talk, then, not eat. Why had he heard *eat*?

Focus. Breathe. They'd startled each other on the landing, that was all. And Dupont had kept him from falling. Awesome. Not the impression he needed to make. He wanted Dupont to see him as professional and competent, not the body he almost had to clean up from the bottom of the stairs.

He took a deep breath as he followed Dupont into the front room. His boss wore another set of shapeless, baggy clothes. Tech geek, Sara had thought earlier. But Dupont stood maybe six feet tall and Sara only a couple of inches shorter. The strength to catch a grown man out of the air didn't come from sitting in front of a computer all day. And the way the body under the loose clothes had felt…

Keep it professional. He smoothed his damp palms down his side. *And stop zoning out.* He didn't usually have trouble focusing. Maybe he needed some vitamins or something. Or maybe he was just stressed.

He tried to review all the bullet points he had practiced in his head all day. Then Dupont turned to face him. As soon as their eyes met, his arguments disintegrated into chaos. All he got out was "I'm not leaving."

"As you wish."

"I, uh. I mean, I have a contract."

"Yes."

"And if there's some skill I don't have, I can learn."

"Undoubtedly."

"So…" He stopped, not sure what to do since Dupont didn't seem to be putting up any argument. "Uh. Maybe I misunderstood something last night? I was more tired than I realized. Do I have a job?"

Dupont stared at him for a few minutes and Sara tried like hell to organize the bullet points ricocheting around in his head in case they turned out to be necessary after all. It wasn't easy with the guy's gaze boring into his. *Intense.* Hard to think with someone giving you the Death Stare. Dupont seemed to expect something from him, but Sara had no idea what.

"As you say, you have a signed contract. I suppose you must stay," Dupont finally answered. He sounded absolutely put out. Which was ridiculous. He wasn't the one who had uprooted his life and moved across country.

Sara stared back, feeling more and more pissy himself. Even though gracefully accepting victory was obviously in his best interests, at this point, he couldn't let it go. "Was this some kind of test?"

One side of Dupont's mouth twitched. "Someone is definitely being tested."

Had he just smiled? Was this Dupont's idea of a *joke*? The little bump of outrage died an unmourned death as Sara replayed the twitch in his head. Not old. Dupont was definitely not old. And if he ever actually smiled, Mr. Intense would be devastating.

Yeah, he better cut off that line of thinking right now. The last thing he needed was a crush on his roommate, who also happened to be his boss. And who wasn't old. And who absolutely did not look hot in a grim, uptight kind of way.

"So." Better get his mind on business. "I'm here. I'm on the clock. What do you want me to do?"

Dupont gave him another hard look. "Amuse yourself.

I'm busy."

"Yeah? Well, I'm here to help. Hey, Ms. Alves didn't give me much in the way of details. What exactly do we do?"

Dupont looked annoyed. "Did you not say you saw her last night?"

"Nah, she didn't show. We must have gotten our wires crossed somehow. That's why I got Bren to bring me."

"And you haven't seen her today?"

"No. Bren came out, but Ms. Alves wasn't with her. She should have been here to tell me all this stuff, huh?"

Dupont responded by going to his desk and digging around in a drawer, where his phone apparently lived. He dialed, frowned at the screen, then tossed it in and slammed the drawer closed.

"Hey, it's no big deal. I can get the rest of my stuff whenever. Maybe she had some kind of emergency or something. So, you know, here I am, ready to work. And I got to tell you, I'm really curious about what you do out here at night."

Dupont did his Death Stare. "I do contract work."

"Yeah? Cool. What kind?" Because *nighttime contract work* didn't sound ominous at all. Seriously, why did the guy have to be so freaking mysterious?

Dupont stared harder, his gaze boring across the distance between them until Sara swore he could feel it drilling holes through his head. "You ask a lot of questions."

"I do? I mean, yeah, I got a few. Like what do you expect me to do? And why do you live out here in the middle of nowhere? Wouldn't it be easier to live someplace with, like, a driveway? And how old are you? Because you're paying me a lot of money? Did you inherit it? Because what kind of contracting pays you enough to pay me eighty grand a year plus expenses for part-time? Are you a hit man or something? I guess you could do that in the day, couldn't you? And why would a hit man need an assistant? And why do you work at night? And *seriously* are you ever going to answer any questions? Because how am I supposed to be your assistant if I don't know what you do? And—"

"Enough."

The single word brought the word vomit to an abrupt halt. He snapped his mouth shut. *Fuck.* What was he thinking? He stared in horror at his boss. He was fired for sure now.

Dupont looked pissed as hell, but…his lip twitched again before he replied. "Of course you are confused. I don't know why…" He shook his head. "I'm not used to having to answer all these questions. My apologies."

"Ms. Alves does it, huh? And she's not here. I'm sorry. We're kinda getting off to a bad start, but I'm sure it will sort itself out soon. All I really want to know is what you do and what you want me to do. I'm supposed to be here to help you."

Dupont stopped staring at him and wandered over to a window. "I'm a very specialized consultant," he finally said, over his shoulder. "In fact, I only have one client. They are headquartered in Rome. It's more convenient for my business hours to correspond with theirs."

"Mr. Dupont, are you telling me you work for the Church?"

"In a manner of speaking."

"Oh, okay." Well, that was…interesting. Something rather horrible occurred to him. "Uh, you aren't a priest or anything, are you?"

"No." The word sounded heavier than it should, as if there was more to it. Then, *twitch,* "Or I suppose it depends on your definition of *or anything.*"

Sara took a chance and grinned at him. "You couldn't resist being mysterious at the end, could you?" To his relief, Dupont didn't look mad. Encouraged, Sara started to ask again exactly what his duties would be, but Dupont raised a hand, indicating silence. He frowned at the window, then walked across the room and opened the door, where he stood staring into the night.

"Is something out there?"

Dupont didn't respond.

Sara didn't hear anything. They were isolated out here. Used to the noises of the city, at first he didn't understand. It was too quiet. Last night he had been scared out of his mind with all the noises out in the swamp. Tonight it sounded…dead.

He didn't like the word his brain supplied. Whatever was going on out there wouldn't bother them in here. The logic didn't stop the goose bumps breaking out along his skin or the knot forming in his stomach.

"Mr. Dupont?"

Dupont responded by slamming the door and heading upstairs, taking the steep stairs faster than could possibly be safe. He came down even faster carrying…

"Is that a *crossbow*?"

"Stay inside, please."

Sara stood in the middle of the room and stared at the door, ears straining for any sound outside. What the hell required a crossbow? He didn't know how long he stood there, listening to the silence, before he managed to unglue his feet and make his way to the window next to the door.

Outside, Dupont stood on the edge of the porch, staring off into the trees. Sara pressed his face against the glass, trying to see across the lawn. Some kind of animal, maybe. But what animal would be so dangerous Dupont needed to go out after it? They were safe as long as they were inside.

Right?

Beyond the glow of the porch lights, the night was impenetrable. Sara switched his gaze to Dupont, who must have way better night vision, because his head turned slowly as though tracking something through the trees.

He moved in a blur, bringing the bow up and firing in one smooth motion. In the darkness, something screamed.

Cold dread squeezed Sara's heart. *Human.* Human and in pain. He didn't think. He hit the porch running, his one thought to get to whoever had been hit. He'd reached the top step when Dupont's hand caught his wrist, the same as earlier, yanking him backward onto the porch.

He tried to jerk away. "Are you crazy? You shot someone. Someone is hurt out there."

"*Non, non.*" Dupont dropped the crossbow and wrapped both arms around him to pull him farther onto the porch. "It is not human, *cher,* I promise."

Another scream. Sara kicked and squirmed, not caring if he hurt the crazy man holding him. "You shot someone." Sobbing floated out of the darkness, and he began sobbing himself, tears running down his face. "Please, *please,* we have to—"

Hard fingers under his chin forced his face around while Dupont held him in place with one arm. "Look at me. Sara, *look at me.*" Dupont's eyes filled his vision. Eyes with no color, every color. Impossible eyes.

Stay here. Listen only to my voice.

Had Dupont said something? He tried to move. He tried to think. He couldn't look away from those mesmerizing eyes.

Stay with me. I will keep you safe.

Somewhere in the distance, a voice chanted unintelligible words. Farther away, the sobbing stopped and another sound started. Something not human at all. He shivered. Even though it was August and still eighty degrees outside, he was cold all the way to his bones. He sagged against the man holding him. "Mr. Dupont?"

The chanting broke. "Shhh. You must come inside."

He had trouble talking. "What happened?"

"You aren't acclimated to the heat. You felt dizzy. Come inside."

It sounded reasonable. He let himself be pulled into the cool air of the cabin but balked when his boss wanted him to sit and recover. Despite his effort to move away, Dupont insisted on supporting him.

"I'm not an invalid." Except he had never gotten dizzy and disoriented before either. And he sure as hell didn't have trouble remembering things after they just happened. He quelled a sharp jab of fear that the explanation might be something other than *heat*. He took a slow breath and concentrated on a more concrete issue. "What was out there?"

"Just a predator. It's gone now. I promise."

What kind of predator?

He felt slow and sluggish, and before he could ask again, Dupont cut him off. "When you feel better, we'll go into town. We should check in on Nohea. I'm worried about her."

CHAPTER FIVE

I PROMISE.
The syllables reverberated, landing harder than the beat of Sara's pulse against my chest. I held him close, his energy intoxicating me. I hadn't tasted such enthusiasm in years. And now his fear…*mon Dieu.* Ignoring my internal perturbation, I attempted to loosen my grasp. Inhaled his spicy-sweet scent instead. He rocked his head against my shoulder, lungs heaving. So much trust. The motion bared his neck, leaving him doubly vulnerable.

He took a determined breath, and reluctantly, I released him. Without my support, he bent from the waist, propping himself with his hands on his knees.

What had I promised? In the midst of a demonic threat, I promised the screaming wasn't human. On a deeper level, I promised to keep him safe. And I would. My foolish heart always took its vows seriously.

We needed light. Light alone would not keep out the agents of Satan, but it might assuage my new charge's fragile state. I flipped the switch for the overhead fixture, then coaxed the pull chain on the table lamp to function. The weight of Sara's gaze followed me, so I kept my movements slow. The way I'd handled the crossbow had been unnatural, blatant evidence of my inhuman state.

Unbound demons operated by grabbing the first available body, and they hunted in pairs. I'd destroyed one, its mission thwarted. Unlikely the remaining demon would strike again tonight. Unlikely, not impossible. I couldn't be sure.

"We need to leave here," I said.

Sara scratched at a welt on his arm, eyes narrowed as if he suspected my motivation. "I guess."

His confusion gratified me. So far my attempts at guiding his thoughts had been inconsistent. With any luck, he might not ever remember the events on the front porch. I touched his hair. He inhaled in a hard burst of fear.

"I apologize." *Je suis bête.* I'd only intended to draw his gaze to mine. "Do you still want to help me?"

He stood straighter, and his gaze took on more focus. "Yes."

Good. Resilience in a man appealed to me. *Bête.* I stared at the floor, corralling my unruly thoughts. I'd had several lifetimes to learn my own weaknesses, and right now I needed to overcome them all.

Something still held the swamp in a dense silence. "*Allons-y.*" I peered out into the darkness. "Can you shoot?"

"I'm pretty good with a soda popper." He rubbed a hand through his dark hair, as if to organize himself. "Don't know how Team Fortress 2 translates to real life, though."

"It's probably easier to teach you to paddle the pirogue than it would be to fire the crossbow."

"I'm all about the paddle, then," he said. His grin landed like a blow to my gut, my system no longer able to sort one hunger from another.

Any other man would have answered his smile. Keeping my expression neutral took every ounce of my will. Any other man could eat a meal without making it an act of debauchery. "Good. I'm not sure when we'll return, so you should bring your things. There's an old backpack on a peg near the kitchen door." We'd leave as soon as possible. The silence weighed on me, pushed at me, begged me to move with all alacrity.

I ignored Sara's questions, jogging upstairs to retrieve my other weapons: a dagger for my boot, a small sword belted at the hilt around my waist, a quiver of arrows for the crossbow. I also retrieved my cell phone from the desk, mainly as an emergency precaution. The bow itself still lay on the front porch, unless one of the demons had stolen it. The possibility added another layer of urgency.

He waited for me, the backpack over one shoulder. If he was frightened, it didn't show in his expression. He nodded, expectant, even eager, and I stumbled on the steep stairs.

I may have promised, but I'm so extraordinarily hungry.

"Hey." Sara reached for me, walking right into the lion's den. "Are you okay?"

I scrambled away. "Fine." My voice was a pained wheeze. "Let's just…" I pointed at the door.

He took my meaning and led the way. We both paused before I turned the handle, and I cast my senses out. Nothing unusual except the dense quiet. I eased the door open and motioned for him to follow.

The crossbow still lay on the porch where I'd dropped it. In a beat, I had it strapped across my shoulders.

"Why—"

I shushed him with a sharp glare. "The boat is tied up to the pier." I gestured in the direction I wanted him to go. "Watch your step."

"With what?" He hissed the words, an irritable slice of sound.

"Pardon me?"

"Maybe you're part cat, but I can't see shit." He did something with his cell phone, causing it to give off a bright white light.

"Of course." Though the light might attract the remaining demon, the only alternative I could come up with would be to carry him, which would engender another difficult series of questions. White light and speed would have to do.

My pirogue was a long, flat boat with a kelly-green hull and a single bench seat. I settled on my knees in the prow, crossbow at the ready. Sara took the bench seat and the paddle and, with a minimum of verbal instruction, moved us out into the swamp. Moonlight filtered through the cypress branches and swags of Spanish moss, providing more than enough light to see by.

"I don't suppose you could hold up my phone so I can see where I'm going?" Sara sounded as exasperated as my mother on washing day. Of all her children, I was the only one who ever responded to her requests for help, so I bore the brunt of her ire. Despite our current circumstances, I couldn't quite conceal the flicker of a grin. My mother's censure had faded from my memory, and it had been almost as many years since anyone had been honestly irritated with me.

This made Sara a novelty in more ways than one.

A soft ripple in the water behind us distracted me. I could see no benefit to advertising our exact location, so I gave Sara a short nod. "Just paddle. I'll direct you."

"Awesome." The word was lost in a snort, which almost made me laugh out loud.

The silence pressed heavily in my ears, and again I sent out my senses, touching the muddy rot smell and the subtle splash of Sara's paddle. There. Another ripple.

"Veer to the left." Under other circumstances, I would have planted the words directly in his mind, lest we be overheard. We made slow progress, accompanied by the fitful suck and gurgle of another presence in the water. *Caimon*, or something else? Keeping pace. Stalking us.

"So what's the plan?"

Dismay jerked my attention to my companion, tightening the tension across my shoulders. I laid my index finger across my lips, then pointed in the direction I wanted him to take us. His breath quickened, the only indication I'd communicated my fear. I wasn't afraid for myself. Over the years, I'd put down countless demons like so many rabid dogs. I was afraid for this young man, who'd signed my contract and inadvertently extracted my promise of protection. And who'd brought the first hint of humor my life had seen in a very long time.

We slid into the river's current and picked up speed. Soon the neon glare of Pinky's sign gave Sara a point to aim for, and he further picked up his pace. We tied off my boat in a slip near the edge of the dock. I left it with some regret, fairly certain the demon would destroy it out of spite. *Bon rien diable.*

"I don't want to leave my car." His quiet words seethed with determination. I nodded and took hold of his arm, willing to promise anything to keep him moving.

We'd gone about ten paces when a cackling laugh halted our progress. "Brother Thaddeus, you found yourself a boyfriend."

I tightened my grip on Sara and kept moving. "Who is that?" he asked, forming words out of a breath.

"*Le monstre,*" I murmured. I cut left, dragging him off the path and cutting across the grounds toward the parking lot. The demon struck before we reached the gasoline pumps.

"You think you can just walk away, lamia?"

The evil voice raked down my spine.

"I got something to show you, something your lackey left behind."

Lackey? Nohea. I slowed. "Stay behind me," I said, without letting go of Sara's arm.

The demon had started his adventure dressed as an ordinary businessman, though his slacks and button-down shirt were slicked to his body with mud. He'd flipped his tie over his shoulder, and blood was smeared across one temple.

And in his fist, he clutched a clump of hair, sandy brown dreadlocks, bits of flesh still clinging to the roots.

Nohea.

"Run, Sara." I freed the blade from the sword belt at my waist. "Get in the car and drive."

The demon cackled again. "You gonna send that puppy out where we can get him?" He flipped the clump of hair in the air. "Too easy, Brother T."

"What the hell, Mr. Dupont?" Sara didn't run, despite my exhortation.

The demon pulled out a Glock, waving the dull gray handgun around like he couldn't decide which of us to shoot first.

There's an old joke about bringing a knife to a gunfight, but in this case, I called his bluff. I didn't have time to load the crossbow, and the biggest risk was that he'd get a stray shot off at Sara. A shot I fully intended to block, with my body if necessary. Silver wouldn't do nearly the damage to me it would do to Sara.

Keeping my eye on the weapon in the demon's hand, I ran. Light streaked through my line of sight, and each detail impressed itself on my consciousness. Sara's shout. The demon's twisted grin. A flare from the store's rear porch. The Glock's deadly roar.

I leapt, swinging my arms. Making myself a target. The bullet went wide, or at least Sara didn't stop shouting. Then my blade caught the demon's hand. He howled, though not nearly as loud as the unearthly roar coming from my very soul.

We hit the mud together and rolled to the water's edge.

Where a *caimon* watched, all but his eyes submerged.

The demon fought fiercely, digging nails and teeth into my flesh. Even so, within moments, I snapped his pathetic neck. And then…then…

The blood of a human who's been possessed is just as sweet.

The moment overcame any prayer I had of restraint. I bit. And drank. The warm salty life running like a salve across my parched throat, sending pulses of vigor coursing through my body. Laced with relief. Fueling my desire.

A small sound distracted me. Sara, standing only a yard or two away, hands covering his mouth, dark eyes wide.

"Get up here, Sara. Leave him," Dot screamed from the porch.

I rose, a hulking carcass. He backed up a step. *Don't run, prey.* I advanced, lost to all except the need. Blood smeared my face, my hands. We continued our pained dance until he ran into the porch's railing.

"Mr. Dupont?" His ragged whisper teased my senses.

"Dupont, if you don't step away, I'm going to blow your fool head off."

Over the barrel of a double-barreled shotgun, Dot glared at me from point-blank range.

I could take them both. My grin spread slow and easy.

I promise.

The words burst from my core. I stared into the blackness of Sara's eyes, horror overtaking every other emotion.

"Go," I whispered. Shifted my weight. Released him.

Dot lowered her weapon, slow, weary, her expression closing in on itself. "Too close, Dupont."

"*Pardonnez moi.*" *I'm so very, very sorry.* Shaking as if the earth itself rattled underneath me, I stepped in Sara's direction, feeling every moment of my one hundred fifteen years.

"You gonna clean that up?" Dot pointed the gun in the direction of the swamp.

I stared at my blood-smeared hands, wondering if Sara would be willing to make a call. "Brother George will send someone."

I found Sara standing next to a small blue coupe. "My truck is…" I pointed vaguely in the direction of the shed I used for a garage.

"I"—he stopped, swallowed, closed his eyes, his face paler than the moon—"I'm not leaving all my stuff at the edge of a swamp, Mr. Dupont."

I held my breath for one brief, painful second. "Of course." In truth, I was in no shape to drive. He fumbled with his keys until the car chirped and the headlights flashed. I got in without waiting for an invitation.

Before he started the engine, Sara tapped at his phone. "Where…um, where are we going?"

The *caimon* scuttled out of the water, dragging the demon's borrowed body in. "The Garden District. Twelve thirty-seven First Street."

"In New Orleans?"

I glanced at him. His gaze was fixed out over the steering wheel, his face very pale.

"Yes."

He fiddled with his phone again.

"Can you do this?" I asked.

He didn't answer.

"This is what I need you for, you know, as it specified in the contract."

He covered his mouth with an open palm. "Yeah." The word came out muffled. "I might have missed the part where it says you kill people and drink their blood."

Shock deadened his words as effectively as his hand. I gave him time, or gave myself time, really. What could I say? I'd lost control. He'd seen it. *Merde alors.*

After a very few moments, shame—and the fear of yet another demon—drove me to push him. "We need to arrive before sunrise."

"Of course we do," he muttered. "Because vampire."

"We have much to do before we rest."

He did not deign to respond.

A mellifluous voice from his phone instructed us to drive a quarter mile, then turn right. I rode in silence. For the first time in over eighty-five years, mortification over my condition tempted me to walk out into the sun.

HE DIDN'T REMEMBER THE DRIVE along the river and through French Settlement. He used the I-10 on-ramp as evidence they'd made it. After negotiating the merge, Sara risked a glance at his companion. Dupont sat next to him, staring straight ahead and still covered in blood. Sara focused out the front windshield, unwilling to cope. The Deal with Dupont. Yeah, fun game, right?

He probably shouldn't be driving. He shivered despite the heat, a clammy sweat covered his skin, and the taillights ahead of him seemed too bright in the darkness. The rational part of his brain ticked off the symptoms. He was in shock. He should pull over, get a sweater, eat a candy bar, and drink a hot beverage.

He kept driving.

Of course, he might not be in shock. He might be flat-out crazy.

Another glance right confirmed the blood on his boss was real. It had dried around his mouth because… Because. Wow. Finding out the last half hour had been a hallucination brought on by the heat would have been really welcome.

Run, Dupont had said. Except Sara hadn't run from the crazy man who had walked out of the swamp. And he hadn't run from Dupont, even when he returned, covered in mud and blood and death. When he had returned from eating someone.

His mouth was dry. He swallowed. Drove. Swallowed again before he thought he might be able get words out. He had to know. "Did we just kill two people?"

"You didn't kill anyone." Dupont paused, as if judging his words. "But no. At least as far as our understanding goes, the host dies shortly after the possession. I just… de-animate the body."

Possession. He filed the word away for later, along with the distinction between dying and de-animating.

Although far from adequate, the answer calmed the worst of his fears. "I think there's a bottle of water on the floor somewhere, and you can grab a shirt out of the backpack, if you, umm, want to clean up a bit."

He waited while Dupont silently removed as much of the blood as possible. Sara refused to watch while he changed into a clean T-shirt. He didn't want to know how vampire bodies looked. He didn't.

"So, I'm what? Like a Renfield?"

"A stupid term, and inappropriate."

Inappropriate? He stifled a very inappropriate and possibly shock-induced giggle. "What would you call our relationship?"

"Unexpected. Inconvenient." Dupont stopped abruptly, as though cutting off more words. "Why didn't you run when you had the chance?"

A very good question, Mr. Dupont. Sara turned it over in his head. "Would it have done me any good?"

"No." The reply was quiet and without any of the irritation flavoring Dupont's speech in most of their interactions. "I'm sorry. Once you signed the contract we were…bound…in certain ways. It hasn't been relevant in so long, I had forgotten. Usually there is little actual risk, but if either of us were to break it, we would both be more…vulnerable to certain influences."

Still with the mysterious. They were going to have to work on communication skills.

"You couldn't have known the risk when we were attacked," Dupont continued. "I ordered you to go. Why didn't you?"

He didn't know. "My brother, Dev, says I'm too optimistic and I can never believe things won't work out. He sided with my mother about this job. He didn't want me to come here."

"He sounds very intelligent." Dupont sounded irritated again, almost like his normal self.

"Yeah, well, I need the money, and you're my boss. I couldn't just leave you there. Anyway, *dude, you saved my life.*"

"More correctly, I put your life in danger."

"You jumped in front a bullet."

"I would have survived. You might not have."

"Whatever."

He knew there were more questions he should ask. Important questions. Right now he couldn't face prying responses out of Dupont. Or maybe he just wasn't ready for the answers. He reached for his phone and hit a playlist. No WWOZ. Nothing that stank of the bayou at all.

Nicki Minaj pounded out of the speakers, and Dupont winced. Too bad. His passenger had presumably already acclimated to a world view that included vampires and possession. Upside of being the one in shock: he got to choose the music.

CHAPTER SIX

⚜ ⚜ ⚜

THE HOUSE ON FIRST STREET was nothing like Dupont's house in the swamp and everything Sara had expected from a wealthy employer in south Louisiana. An hour earlier, he would have been thrilled. After the excitement at Pinky's, he barely glanced at the double galleries and ironwork. He made the turn into the narrow drive running alongside the house and parked next to the back door.

Dupont left the car almost before it stopped moving. Sara grabbed the pack and followed him. They entered through the kitchen, Dupont muttering something under his breath as he unlocked the door. Not French this time, maybe Latin. Then he went through the entire house, pointedly ignoring Sara.

"If you tell me what we're looking for, I can help."

"Nohea," came the terse answer. "Or anything she may have left us. Maybe a note."

"Wouldn't she just text or, you know, call?" He recalled the lack of modern electronics in the cabin. "You at least have email, right?"

"Of course." Dupont looked disdainful. "But as she has not texted or called or emailed we must search."

"Maybe something happened to her phone," Sara conceded. "Does she come here often?"

"Sometimes. If she was in trouble, she would be safer

here than at her home."

Sara started to ask what kind of trouble she might be in. The memory of the crazy gun-toting guy shambling out of the swamp stopped him. He kept quiet and looked around the room, not sure what would constitute a clue.

An old-school corded phone hung on the kitchen wall. The antique looked as though it had been there since the seventies, at least. Probably a relic no one had bothered to pull down. Sara picked up the receiver and was surprised to get an actual dial tone. "If she came here, wouldn't she have used this?"

Dupont, of course, refused to admit this should have been obvious. "Get the car. We will try her house."

Seemed like they should have looked there first, but what did he know. Maybe there was a secret vampire protocol for this sort of thing. Ms. Alves had probably forgotten to send the memo. Or maybe that was on the syllabus for Advanced Renfield Training.

"Mr. Dupont?"

"Yes?" The irritation was definitely back.

"You, ah, maybe want to change clothes before we go?"

Dupont stopped and looked down at himself. The U of W tee was clean and not a bad fit on him, but his shoes and pants were caked with mud and other...things.

"And maybe a shower? You've got—" He couldn't say it. Sara touched his own hair, and Dupont mirrored the gesture, grimacing as his fingers hit dried...mud. Mostly mud, anyway. "If you don't keep clothes here, we might be close enough in size you can borrow what I brought."

"Yes, thank you. I have clothes." A slight flush darkened his boss's cheekbones, the first hint of an emotion other than irritation he had shown. Or maybe been able to show, Sara realized. He hadn't noticed in the dark of the car, but under the lights in the kitchen, Dupont's skin showed a lot more color than in the cabin. Sara hadn't realized how pale he had been before. Now, despite the scratches on his skin and muck in his hair, he looked healthier, less emaciated. Less *hungry*.

"Give me a moment, please. Make yourself at home." And he was gone, almost quicker than the eye could follow. Vampire. Sara was crazy to stay here, no matter the consequences of leaving.

He told himself he stayed because Dupont had saved his life. He shouldn't leave until he had all the facts about the consequences of breaking his contract. He needed the money. And he was curious about this house, which hadn't been stocked with religious artifacts like the cabin, and which actually freaking rocked. He wandered through the ground-floor rooms while he waited. Polished wood floors, chandeliers, antiques. There had to be advantages to the Renfield gig, right?

He took out his phone and shot a picture of a built-in wet bar complete with a Baccarat decanter and stemware. He sent it to Nate.

> Sara: In a vampire's house in NOLA. Job rocks.

As long as he didn't think about mealtimes, anyway.

"I'm presentable. We can go now."

He jumped at Dupont's voice behind him.

When he turned, he almost swallowed his tongue. In the swamp, Dupont had worn shapeless gray pants and even more shapeless shirts of indefinable color. The U of W shirt hadn't been much better. In the clothes he wore now… *Okay, get a grip, Sarasija.* The man had only put on black jeans and a pretty boring short-sleeve black shirt. Both of which actually fit. He was sure Dupont hadn't styled his hair, either; the messy, tousled look probably came from running his fingers through it wet. But with the healthy new color, the clothes, and the freshly scrubbed look he was… Still the boss. And vampire. Important safety tip.

"Yes?" Dupont's voice broke his train of thought.

"Yes, what?"

"You're staring. Is something wrong?"

"No." His boss's eyes were gray, a shifting color that looked like it wanted to be light blue but couldn't commit. "I, uh, you just startled me. I'm ready if you are."

In the car, Dupont rattled off another address. Sara plugged it into the GPS and spent the short drive wondering why he had never noticed how small his car was and how close the passenger and driver seats were to each other. Dupont spent the drive being a vampire, which meant really-really quiet and still. So how the hell was he so distracting?

Ms. Alves lived a few blocks off City Park in a neat, primrose-blue shotgun house. Sara parked on the street and stared at the house. Midnight had come and gone, but light poured out the windows. Before he realized Dupont had moved, his passenger was halfway up the sidewalk. Sara scrambled out after him.

"Hey—hold up."

"Yes?"

"It's late. Are you really going to go barging in?" From the house, he could hear the sound of a sitcom on TV and men's voices. "Maybe you're overreacting."

"I'm not going to barge in. I'm going to knock."

"Yeah, but—"

Dupont did the quick-move thing again, and Sara trotted up the steps to catch him on the porch. "Mr. Dupont. Maybe she lost her phone. Or maybe, uh, you know, maybe she just isn't taking your calls."

"It's her job to take my calls."

"Yeah, well, as great as you are to work for, maybe she found something better."

Dupont stared at him, obviously thinking the idea over. "No." He rapped sharply on the door.

A minute later, a large black man in sweats and a Saints shirt opened the door. Dupont didn't waste time with niceties. "Where is Nohea?"

"Who?"

"Nohea Alves, the woman who owns this house. Is she here?"

"I'm here with Carl. I don't know a Nohea. Hey!"

Dupont ignored him as he shoved the door open and strode inside. Sara followed, inching past the big dude at the door with an apologetic glance. Someone had put care into decorating the living room. The walls were painted gold and covered with art hung on thin wire from hooks in the molding. Ms. Alves had a taste for bright colors and cubist paintings. Like the house they had just left, the floors were polished wood, but she had added area rugs for more color.

In deference to the narrow design of the room, most of the furniture lined the walls. On the left, two chairs flanked a low bookcase. A flat-screen TV took up most of the space on top. On the right was a long sofa, where a second man, Carl, presumably, sat smoking and drinking beer. Sara had never met Nohea Alves, but judging from the rest of the room, he'd bet his left nut she would have a fit over the beer bottles cluttering the coffee table. Those were going to leave rings.

Dupont didn't even glance around the room. He zeroed right in on Carl. "Where is Nohea?"

Carl didn't look up from tapping out a cigarette on the table. "She ain't here, man."

"Where is Nohea?"

"Hey, man. I said I don't know." Carl flicked greasy blond bangs out of his eyes, then blinked as he looked up. Dupont's expression must have made it clear a better answer was expected. "Letty's in the kitchen," he muttered. "She might know."

The narrow house was bigger than it looked from the street. Sara followed his employer through two bedrooms. Both showed the same attention to design as the living room and the same state of current disarray—overflowing ashtrays, beer bottles, and unmade beds. In the second, a toddler slept, surrounded by pillows.

In the kitchen, Dupont faced off with the final occupant of the house—a skinny woman in shorts and a tank top who leaned against the far counter. She had the same dark copper skin as the baby in the next room, though she didn't look nearly as peaceful.

"Letitia. I thought you moved to Metairie."

"None of your business if I visit my sister."

"And how long are you visiting?"

She shrugged. "Little while, I guess."

Dupont seemed more annoyed than the answer warranted, but he was nothing if not on task.

"Where is Nohea?"

"I ain't her keeper."

"You must know something. Tell me."

Letitia glared at a spot on the floor. "I said I don' know. She got some new girl she sniffing around. She don' come home some nights." She pointed at Sara. "Who's he?"

"My assistant," Dupont said, before Sara could answer for himself. "How many nights?"

Letitia cackled at him. "Not your usual type, is he?"

Dupont ignored the comment. "How many nights since Nohea has been home?"

"A few." Letitia turned a sullen gaze on Dupont. The standoff lasted only a few seconds before the Death Stare won out. She blinked and mumbled, "Not last night or the night before."

Dupont made an irritated noise. "Who is the girl you mentioned?"

They weren't there long after that. The only other information they could get out of Letty was a name, Nikki, who sometimes had gigs at a bar on Frenchmen Street, which was where Ms. Alves had found her. Sara looked up the address and plugged it into his phone. Dupont shook his head. "We should take a taxicab. The car will just be a problem down there."

Then Dupont clasped his hands behind his back and stood at ease, waiting for the cab. Sara took his stance to mean that actually obtaining transport fell under the duties of an assistant. It was the first normalish thing Dupont had asked of him, or assumed of him, so he didn't complain. He brought up his Uber app and then tried to mimic Dupont's waiting pose. He lasted about thirty seconds before giving up and pulling his phone out until their ride showed. Dupont gave the unmarked car a suspicious look but didn't say anything before climbing in.

Without driving in a strange city to keep him occupied, his thoughts wandered to places Sara didn't want them to go. Pinky's dock, mostly. His heart rate picked up a notch. He shifted closer to the side of the car and folded his hands in his lap to eliminate the chance of an accidental brush of his fingers against Dupont's. More worrisome than the tiny shot of adrenaline was doubt about the cause. Fear of the man next to him would be logical. Instead, he saw, over and over in his head, Dupont flinging himself at the crazy shooter, willing to risk himself rather than Sara. It had been too dark to see what had happened next, or maybe the darkness was a product of his mind, protecting him from things he didn't want to remember.

Then, thankfully, they were pulling up outside a club on Frenchmen Street. They paid the cover and made their way inside, only to find out Nikki wasn't on stage tonight. The bartender knew her, knew Nohea too, but had seen neither in a few days. Sara figured it for a dead end. Dupont wouldn't give up.

Sara sipped an Abita and watched a very polite inquisition. For someone so taciturn, his boss had a knack for getting people to talk to him. Instead of demanding answers, he maintained eye contact and questioned the bartender in a calm, implacable voice. The bartender ignored his other customers for the privilege of leaning over the bar and staring at Dupont. Sara suppressed a grimace. *Totally unprofessional, dude.* But Dupont hit pay dirt. Nikki's roommate, Kyle, worked on Bourbon Street at a place called Lafitte's. Maybe try there.

Outside, Dupont scanned the street. "Walking will be easiest from here."

Worked fine for Sara. He didn't need any more close spaces with his boss or quiet moments to think.

Even in the Quarter, the weeknight crowds were sparse, and they made good time. Sara tried to enjoy his first walk down Bourbon Street, but he had been on the road for days, then lost, then fired, then… The shock hadn't worn off, just been pushed to the side so he could keep moving.

He got a confused impression of balconies, bars, sex shops, hurricanes sold out of windows, and dozens of souvenir shops spilling lewd T-shirts, shot glasses, and Mardi Gras masks into the sidewalk under fluorescent lights. Everything was a lot dirtier and more faded than he had imagined, but still infused with some strange magic that made peeling paint and panhandlers a feature rather than a flaw.

Dupont walked fast enough to discourage talking, and Sara had to hustle to keep up. When his phone buzzed a notification, he looked down and plowed full tilt into Dupont.

Shit. Had he just *bounced* off his boss? He stumbled, trying to control his reaction to a solid male body with firm glutes and… Dupont realized his assistant was trying to catch his phone and his dignity, not copping a feel. Right?

"Sorry," he managed. "Are we there?" Stupid. Of course they were. That's why Dupont had stopped. Except Dupont had *completely* stopped and stood staring at their destination across the street.

Lafitte's. The bartender had shortened the name.

"Lafitte's Booty?" Sara couldn't help it. He snickered. *And* it was a strip club. The sign depicted a couple of very fabulous pirates in tight pants who had somehow lost their billowing shirts while playing with their swords.

The whole thing became a lot less amusing when he got a look at Dupont's face. Disapproving was an understatement. *Catholic. Works for the Church.* The religion thing had been sorta funny before. Didn't feel funny now. It felt like judgment.

He tried to ignore the lump of disappointment in his stomach. Just another homophobic straight guy who would probably fling himself in front of a bullet for anyone. Didn't matter. He'd known Dupont for less than forty-eight hours, so his boss's prejudices and opinions could not possibly make him feel this bad. But the magic of Bourbon Street wilted under Dupont's grim expression.

Sara'd had a very bad first day on his new job. It was late. They were standing across from a strip club on a grimy street that reeked of piss and regurgitated rum. "Well? Are we going in or not?"

Dupont, an unstoppable Nohea-seeking missile, visibly hesitated. Asshole. Sara headed across the street on his own. One job all night. Find Ms. Alves. Right, then.

Dupont caught up with him before he hit the door. Sara ignored him and smiled at the bouncer. "Is there a cover?"

"Not for you, sweet cheeks, but I can't do anything about the two-drink minimum."

"Thanks." Sara headed inside, not waiting to see if Dupont had to pay the cover. He headed straight for the bar around the stage and pulled up a chair front and center.

One look at the dancer almost changed his mind. The wee hours of Wednesday morning apparently didn't rate first-string talent, or even second. At least he hoped so. The pimples didn't bother him, or the bad haircut, but the guy looked seriously emaciated. He wore tighty-whities and off-brand running shoes while showing off some extremely Not Hot moves.

Dupont hovered for a minute and then sat down. He

turned sideways, ignoring the dancer. Sara picked up the drink menu. "All tonight's expenses are job related, right?"

"Yes, but—" Thanks to the stunning lack of clientele, their cocktail waiter showed up before Dupont could finish the sentence.

The skimpy shorts and tacky pirate vest were a minor improvement on white underwear and too-prominent ribs. Sara peered through the gloom at the name tag pinned to the vest. "Hi, Brandon. We're looking for Kyle. Is he working tonight?"

"He won't be on for at least another hour." Brandon pulled up a chair and sat next to Sara in a move obviously designed to imply intimacy and generate tips. "I'll be happy to take care of you guys until he gets here."

"We do not require you," Dupont intoned from behind Sara. "We will wait."

Brandon smiled at Sara, maintaining eye contact. Sara wondered if there was a manual. *How to Make Your Mark Feel Special.*

"Sorry, guys. We have a two-drink minimum." He sounded sincerely sorry. Sara bet he made way more tips than the poor dancer.

"We do not want drinks. Go away." Dupont sounded testy.

Sara smiled into Brandon's eyes. "I'll have the Jolly Rogered." He named the most expensive drink on the menu. Strip-club prices. *Suck on that, Dupont.* "Go ahead and bring one for my friend, too. It sounds like just his type of thing."

Dupont made a strangled sound behind him. Sara ignored him, shifted his body to face the dancer, and pulled a handful of bills out of his wallet.

THE JOLLY ROGERED TOOK TWO hands to lift. The drink featured half a dozen colors of layered alcohol garnished with pineapple wedges, orange slices, cherries, multiple cocktail umbrellas, and a flashing rainbow-colored straw. It was also cold and sweet. After hours in the heat, the cocktail went down way too easily.

A third of the way from the bottom, Sara decided he didn't want to be mad at Dupont. He slid a glance at his companion, who hadn't touched his own drink. Could he drink it? Or was he restricted to… Another long pull on the straw killed that thought nicely. Up on the stage, they were being treated to a very up close and personal look at the tighty-whities. No other customers sat near the stage, and Sara had tipped repeatedly and generously. He supposed they were stuck with the dancer for the duration. He hoped the dude bought himself some food, at least. So far, Dupont had managed to pretend the stage didn't exist, despite all the gyrating.

"'m, sorry."

"Oh?" Dupont sounded skeptical.

"You don't have to reimburse me for the tips."

Dupont didn't reply and Sara searched around for something else to say. "How am I different?"

"*Quoi?* What do you mean?"

"Everyone keeps saying how different I am from your usual assistants. What's that about?"

Dupont fidgeted, an action so out of character that Sara noticed despite the lulling effects of the Jolly Rogered.

"Seriously, dude. It's giving me a complex."

"It's nothing." It was obviously *something.* "I usually, that is…my last assistants have been female."

"Oh." Yeah. Of course. Sexy vampire living alone in the middle of a swamp. Of course he hired women. Perv. Sara reached for his boss's glass. No sense in letting it sit there and go to waste.

"Some people have obviously drawn the wrong conclusions."

"I bet." Time to switch topics again. "So, Ms. Alves—you really think she's in some kind of trouble?"

"Yes."

One word. Yes. Great explanation. Sara watched the pretty colors blinking on the straw. They looked a little fuzzy. "How can you be so sure?"

"Sara." Dupont's voice was very gentle. "The…man… at Pinky's had a hank of her hair. He taunted me with it."

Had he? It had been so dark, but…vampire. Dupont hadn't seemed to have any trouble seeing in dim light. Suddenly the yummy, super-gay drink was the wrong kind of sweet.

Brandon picked that moment to rejoin them and ask if they were ready for their second round. Sara looked up at him blearily. "Do you dance too?"

"Nah, my mama would have a cow." Dimples again. "I make plenty of money doing the cocktails."

"Brandon." Dupont's voice, sounding extra rich and plummy. "Brandon, look at me."

Brandon switched his attention from Sara to Dupont. "Yes, sir?"

Huh. Sara hadn't been *sir. Anything for a tip, right, Brandon?*

"We've already had our two drinks."

Good try, Dupont. Minimum meant two drinks each.

"Of course. You're all good."

Really? Brandon had come across brighter than that.

"Brandon," Dupont continued, "Kyle is your coworker. You must have his phone number, yes?"

"Yes." Brandon gave the information up without hesitation.

"Stop flirting with Sara and go call Kyle. See if he can come in early. Send him over here when he arrives."

"Okay, I'll call him now." Brandon hurried off to do Dupont's bidding.

Sara took a contemplative sip of Dupont's drink. Something about the conversation caught on the edge of his brain, then floated off on a wave of rum and whatever else made up the Rogered. He traced circles in the puddle of condensation under the giant glass.

"Dev says I'm too pretty for my own good. He says I'm spoiled and no one makes me work for anything."

"Oh?"

Shit. Had he said that out loud? The words were completely out of the blue. Or were they?

"You don't even smile," he accused Dupont, still thinking out loud, because now he was closer to the elusive bit of flotsam swirling through his rummy buzz. "You just tell people what to do."

In fact, he had been giving Brandon the Death Stare, which was not a pleasant experience. He backtracked through the night, the bartender on Frenchmen Street, Letitia, Carl… "Mr. Dupont, are you putting the vampire whammy on people because—"

"Sara."

He looked up, right into Dupont's storm-cloud eyes. In the distance, he could hear himself continuing to ramble, going on about how compelling random people to do your will with your vampire powers was not cool and what kind of long-term effects shit like that might have on someone's brain.

Sara.

He didn't think Dupont had said the word out loud. He pushed the drink away. He didn't need to drink anymore. He didn't need to worry about Brandon or how Dupont got the information he needed. Dupont would take care of all of it.

Call me Thaddeus. Streaks of lightning behind the shifting clouds and gathering darkness.

Sara's chair crashed over as he jumped to his feet.

"Stop right there. That is not okay, Mr. Dupont."

CHAPTER SEVEN

*T*HAT IS NOT OKAY, MR. *Dupont.*
I stared at Sara. I could do nothing else. *Many a time have they afflicted me from my youth: yet they have not prevailed against me.*

Bad enough we were in a nightclub on the edge of hell. I rarely came to the Quarter, and never to places such as this. For all my remembered shame, this young man sitting across from me offered a greater danger to my soul. Once before I'd given in to an abnormal love, and for all these years, I'd dragged the guilt like the chains behind Marley's ghost. Despite my years of penance, I still carried the weight of another man's corruption. I still carried the weight of his death.

Shock faded, replaced by…humor? *Mon Dieu.* I didn't trust myself enough to open my mouth. I held his gaze, wordlessly apologizing for invading his mind. Wordlessly chastising him for pushing me into such an action.

Wordlessly begging the Lord's forgiveness for my most secret thoughts.

Brandon's return interrupted our stalemate. The waiter surprised me, since I'd given him instructions to leave. I must not have been the only one under the spell of Sara's appeal.

"Kyle'll be here in ten." Brandon nodded at me with his gaze on Sara.

His brother, Dev, was correct. Sara was too pretty for his own good.

They talked. I ignored them as best I could. I needed time to pray, to find a way around this new threat. Never before had a demon come to my home on the river. I'd missed Vespers and Compline and even Matins. It would soon be time for Lauds at dawn. God willing, I'd be in my own room by then. Leaving Sara alone and unguarded and myself vulnerable. Nohea possessed the skills to act as Sara's protector, and my ability to manipulate his thoughts should keep him safe. But Nohea was missing. And controlling Sara's thoughts was *not okay*.

Merde alors.

I didn't notice the new arrival until Sara laid his hand on my arm, his touch warm and light, his face as shuttered as a cabin in a hurricane.

"Mr. Dupont." Sara nodded at the young man standing next to our table without meeting my gaze. "This is Kyle."

Better nourished than most of the others in the club, the young man had the twitchy neediness of an addict in search of his next fix.

"Do you know Nohea Alves?" I asked him. I found it difficult to hold his gaze, at least at first. Then he settled under my control with a soft sigh. Sara made a scoffing sound, which I chose to ignore. "Please sit down, Kyle. I have a few questions."

"Yeah." He sank into the fourth chair at our table. His hair was bleached and spiked, and silver hoops glittered from one brow and from both nipples. "I met Nohé when she hooked up with my roommate, Nikki. She's okay, you know? Kinda weird, but she treated Nikki good." He sniffed hard, rubbing at his nose. "Then she, like, disappeared. Just up and left. Nikki was pretty broken up about it."

This Kyle obviously skated along the surface of his life. It had taken just a gentle nudge to get him to talk. Of course, we could be trapped here all night, listening to his infant traumas. "I've always found Nohea to be very reliable."

"Yeah man, she was, like, classy."

Spare me from young men saying "like." I nudged him again, with my gaze alone this time, which prompted a snort from Sara. He shouldn't have sensed my action, another thing I'd need to ponder later on.

"Nikki said she ran into Nohé coming out of a club with some sketchy dude couple nights ago. Not like her at all, man." Kyle gave his nose another rough scratch. "I'ma have to get to work. You got anything else you need?"

"When did you see her?" Sara's bright comment cut through my pull on Kyle's attention.

I endeavored to reclaim them both. "Be precise."

Kyle's gaze jumped between the two of us. Precision seemed to give him difficulty. "I'm pretty sure it was two nights ago." He stood, blinking hard. "I gotta get my bank and get on the floor."

He left, taking Brandon with him.

Sara filled the silence between us with a hard slurp on the straw in his *bon rien* drink. "Might as well get really, really hammered," he said under his breath.

I had a sudden longing for a glass of bourbon. We'd drunk beer in the monastery, though I'd had nothing alcoholic since 1925. January twelfth, 1925. The warmth, the relaxation, the release had some appeal. I eased back, stretched my legs, and my eyelids slid shut.

No. I jerked upright and grabbed Sara's arm. "What do you hear?" I whispered. "What do you sense?"

I never drank bourbon, and I never fell asleep in public.

"What are you talking about?" Sara's words were crisp despite his befuddled expression.

I half dragged him to standing. "We're not safe."

"Well, by all means, let's get the hell out of Dodge." He took a staggering step toward the door. "It's been a good half hour since you said anything truly batshit, anyway. You were due."

The club was still virtually empty, except for the poor skeleton gyrating on the stage, our two waiter friends, and a bartender.

A bartender who had very dark eyes and a foul odor. Rancid roses. Cheap perfume left too long in the bottle. "Now, Sara. We need to leave now."

"Be nice if we had a car nearby."

I dropped his arm before I snapped it off his body. "Please. If you cannot say anything helpful, *fermez la bouche*." I stalked off, hoping he had the good sense to keep up. And stopped three strides later. I could not let him die.

"Fairmay lah boosh? Did you just call me a cow?"

The rancid rose scent grew stronger. I had no choice. I scooped him up, stifling his squeal of protest with a hand over his mouth, and dropped into the shadows. Roses. Strong enough to make me dizzy. On my own, I could take two demons. Sara's vulnerability was my weakness. I lowered him to the ground. "Get your arms around my shoulders."

"Dude, you're crazy, you know?" He shifted out of my grasp. "Oh wait. Not crazy. Vampire."

We had no time left. The demon bartender came out, aimed toward us, and I could sense his partner down the street. I ducked, put my shoulder in Sara's midsection, and grasped his hips. He flopped over me, hollering a string of curses.

I took off running, knowing the demons would follow. The streets of the French Quarter were narrow and nearly empty of people. Half a block up, I spied an ornate balcony with the French doors open and no lights on in the room beyond. I leapt for it, grasping the wrought iron with my free hand and pulling both of us up.

I thrust Sara into the room. He landed on his butt and immediately crab-walked away from me, his dark eyes huge and his mouth working. I pulled out a small vial of holy water. "Invite me in."

"What?"

No time to explain. I pushed more conviction into my words. "Invite me in."

He opened his mouth. Shut it. "Come in." I stepped across the threshold, sprinkling holy water behind me. Once I had entered a home, nothing could keep me out. The first time, however, required an overture. After locking the door, I faced my assistant. "Listen to me," I said, adding as much persuasion as possible without rolling his mind. "The blessing won't hold them for much longer than the lock on those doors."

"Julio, is that you?" a young woman called from the room next door.

"Oh man oh man oh man," Sara muttered to himself. Short of knocking him out, I didn't know how to make him calm down.

The door opened, silhouetting a young girl in the hall's light. "Who the *hell* are you?"

Short and plump, she wore too much makeup and not enough fabric in her dress.

"Our names are irrelevant. Do you have a car?"

"I'm Sara, and this is Mr. Dupont." Sara found his feet and his voice in the same moment. "We're so sorry to intrude on you. We'll be going now. Have a good night."

"We can't leave her, Sara." I raised my hand to stop his protest. A thump behind me said the demons had reached the balcony. If we left the young woman alone, she was as good as dead. "Miss…"

"Rayna, but I'm not going anywhere with you."

"I apologize for the inconvenience, Miss Rayna. For your own protection, you must accompany us. If you had a car, things would be much more efficient."

"So you're, like, carjacking me from my living room." She grabbed a purse off a nearby bookcase. "And yet somehow I'm going along with it."

She led us down a narrow hallway with overbright fluorescent fixtures and a squeaking floor that had been in place since the year 1820. We followed her out to an alley, where a tiny Fiat sat under an awning. Soon we were loaded in, easing down the narrow streets. Sara sat in back, continuing his litany of complaints, while I kept a lookout for our pursuers.

"Sara."

"Oh man oh man oh man."

"Sara." I leaned over the seat and grasped him by the chin. "I need you to call someone for me." He stopped muttering only long enough to pull out his phone. I gave him a phone number for the monks. "Tell whoever answers I need a representative at my First Street house, and I'll need a team to repair whatever damage happens to Miss Rayna's home."

"Damage to my home!" She jerked the wheel to the right. I covered her hand with mine, calming her so she could focus on the work of driving.

Sara did as I asked as if I had compelled him, though I had not.

"So, we're going to stop and get my car, right?" Sara interrupted my murmured directions to our driver.

"I'll make arrangements for it."

"What?" He threw himself against the door. "That's like, the only thing I own, and all my stuff is in it. We have *got* to go get it right now."

"Where is it?" Rayna asked. "Maybe we can swing by on the way to—"

"Stop!" I all but cracked the tiny vehicle's front window with my roar. "We are going to one-two-three-seven First Street. When we get there, there will be men who will assist us in all we need to accomplish. Until then, we will all sit quietly and let Miss Rayna concentrate on her driving."

The eastern edge of the sky had turned a soft purple, the

first sign of the coming dawn. In the privacy of my own mind, I began the chant for Lauds.

Deus in adiutorium meum intende.

Dominum, ad adjuvandum me festina.

THERE WERE NO MEN AT First Street when they arrived. After his outburst in the car, Dupont had gone into full vampire miff. Or at least that was what Sara assumed it was. His boss had spent the drive venting his feelings via chants under his breath obviously designed to let the other two occupants know he was On the Edge.

Fine. They were now kidnappers. Sara could use some quiet time of his own while he got a handle on the new twist in their evening. Some freakin' answers would be nice. He didn't intend to poke an angry vampire to get them, so question time would have to wait. He couldn't take many more revelations tonight, anyway.

Inside the house, Dupont guided Rayna to the sofa and explained how she had knocked on their door, disoriented and confused. *Creative, Dupont. Missing time. Intruding on strange men. That won't cause any anxiety later.* He didn't interrupt, though. What would be the other option? *Hi, you've been kidnapped by my boss, the vampire. It's my first day. Please don't press charges.*

No going back now. He was an accomplice. Dupont had said he worked for the Church. Maybe they had a pass, like James Bond or something. He knew he was kidding himself, though. His trust in Dupont didn't come from anything his boss had said. Every word out of the man's mouth was batshit crazy. Plus Vampire. A fact he found too easy to forget.

But they had spent their night scouring New Orleans because Dupont believed Ms. Alves was in trouble. Dupont could have convinced Rayna to give them her car keys and forget about them, except he wouldn't leave her in the path of the…men…who chased them. And he had flung himself between Sara and a bullet. Those weren't the actions of a monster.

Plus, they had a contract. Ma needed the money. He'd die before he proved Dev right by abandoning this job. Although, maybe he should have listened when everyone said it sounded too good to be true.

Dupont finished up with Rayna and came to stand next to Sara in the doorway. "The men coming are monks from my order. They will take care of Miss Rayna and retrieve your car." For the first time since they left the Quarter he met Sara's eyes. "I must retire."

Sara nodded. "Yeah."

Dupont hesitated. "Remember what I said about your contract. There are consequences if either of us breaks it."

"Yeah. Got it." Asshole. Why did he keep assuming Sara would be the one to break the contract?

"You are tired. You should sleep also."

Sleep sounded like a great idea. Sara stared pointedly at the ceiling. "You think?"

"I'm only making a suggestion. You may, of course, do as you will."

When he looked at the place his boss had been, he was gone.

He should go to bed. He was fuck-off tired. If he bothered to think about it, he was still sorta drunk and in no condition to think through a lot of these things. Dev would lecture him about his attitude, but some of this he didn't *want* to think through.

He went and sat next to Rayna on the sofa. He patted her sleeping form ineffectively. "It'll be okay. He's not as bad as he seems."

The doorbell rang before he could worry about assessing the truth of his statement.

Three men stood on the doorstep. Two had scary Men in Black attitudes. They stood bolt upright and looked around with sharp eyes in expressionless faces.

The other one, though…

"Hi," the third man said. Though he towered over the other two, his broad face and soft, caramel-colored eyes managed to seem the least threatening. "I'm Brother Michael. We're with Victim Services. I believe you are expecting us?"

"Oh yeah. I'm Sara, the new assistant? Come on in," Sara said as the other two men brushed past him. Michael lingered just inside the door.

All three men were dressed in gray, not black, despite the spooky vibe. Gray slacks and white shirts. Very boring. Michael had added a smiley-face Jesus Loves You lapel pin. The two drones were all business and already focused on Rayna. Michael, though…

The monk took his hand. "I'm so glad you're here." The truth of the statement flowed into Sara on a wave of peace and good vibes. He yanked his hand away, but the vibes stayed with him. He tried to give Michael a suspicious stare. It wilted under Michael's beaming countenance.

You're not a vampire, are you? He still had enough wits about him not to ask out loud. He wasn't sure what Victim Services knew or needed to know about them. The sun was up. Dupont was in bed. And whatever Michael had done hadn't felt intrusive. It felt like *something*, though.

"What the…?" Rayna's screech from the next room brought his focus back to priorities.

Rayna had moved behind the sofa, where the Victim Services reps were closing in on her from both sides. "We're here to help, ma'am. If you would just calm down—"

"*Calm down?*" Rayna shifted her attention between the two men, trying to watch them both at once. "Who are you? Where am I?"

Great. Sara edged into the room and tried a smile. "Hi, Rayna, I'm Sara. Do you remember me?"

Rayna's brow creased in obvious confusion. "Maybe?

Were you in my car? Do I know you?"

"You came to our house," Sara said. Not *exactly* a lie. "You were the victim of a home invasion." *Still true.* "These men are from Victim Services. They're here to help you deal with your ordeal." Hopefully true. He would have to trust Dupont for now.

Rayna didn't look convinced. In fact, she looked like she might take the run-into-the-street-screaming-bloody-murder option. Then her eyes shifted behind Sara to Michael.

Peace and good vibes flowed into the room. The next thing Sara knew, Rayna had settled onto the sofa. Michael had his arm around her, and he was spinning the same nonsense as Dupont, but with a better bedside manner. The narrative was interspersed with *there, there* and *you were very brave* and *I don't know how you're holding up so well.* Sara turned to look at the other two, who seemed to notice him for the first time since he had walked in.

"You're Sara?"

"Uh, yeah. Nice to meet you."

They exchanged a look. "Well, this ought to be interesting." The one with the cowlick gave him a plastic smile.

"Gentlemen," Michael's soothing voice reproved from the sofa. He sent Rayna to the powder room to freshen up and came to stand next to Sara.

"He's not going to work out, Mikey. I don't know what Brother George is thinking," Cowlick said. "This kid has to go."

The other one was apparently mute.

"Hey, I'm right here. If you have something to say about the way I do my job, you maybe want to say it to my face?"

Cowlick ignored him.

"He seems very competent to me." Michael smiled at Sara.

"You know what I'm talking about." Cowlick sounded grim.

"God works in mysterious ways," Michael said serenely. "If he has sent Sara to Brother Thaddeus, I'm sure it is part of his Divine Plan."

Great. Sara tried not to roll his eyes. Michael seemed like a nice enough guy, but Sara wasn't buying into the Divine Plan narrative any more than he was listening to some random guy tell him he had to leave. Why didn't anyone think he could hack this job?

The question stayed with him long after the Victim Services team had left with Rayna. What had Dupont's other assistants been like? Female, supposedly. Which told him nothing. Everyone he met took one look at him and acted as if they were in on some big joke at his expense. Maybe the reason was as obvious as it seemed. If so, he really didn't want to know what reputation Dupont had with his female assistants that made people think he couldn't work with Sara.

Outside, the city was waking. Even on this upscale residential street, the traffic noises were getting louder. With Rayna and the monks gone, he felt detached from any touchstone of reality, isolated in a bubble of solitude while the everyday world went about its business without him.

Not sure what to do with himself, he wandered into the kitchen to retrieve his backpack, and made his way upstairs. Which bedroom? The closed door at the end of the hall spoke for itself. He didn't have to try the handle to know it would be locked. Paranoid bastard.

He picked one of the open rooms at random, too tired to decide if there would be advantages to looking out over the front or the rear of the house. Then he stood in the middle of the room and stared at the bed. He didn't trust Dupont an inch when it came to putting an extra whammy into his *suggestions*, but sleep would be good no matter whose idea it was. Just…

He set the backpack on a chair in the corner and stripped down, trying to concentrate on one action after another.

Shoes off. Socks. Shirt. Normal stuff. Going to bed. And this bed looked a lot better than the budget hotel beds he'd been in while on the road. He hesitated at the jeans.

C'mon, Sara. You're tired. Just go to bed. You can think it all through in the morning.

No. It was morning now.

A door slammed outside, and he heard a car engine purr to life. The neighbors were off to school or work or wherever other people had to be out in the real world. His new world didn't include morning commutes. He was in here with the vampire, where you went to bed at dawn and slept in your jeans in case you woke up and needed to run.

He put everything except his shoes in the backpack, hesitated, then pulled out a fresh pair of socks and put them with the shoes next to the bed. They were expendable if he was in a hurry. Then he zipped the pack, set it on the bed within easy reach, and climbed under the covers.

As soon his head hit the pillow, he was back at Pinky's. *Dupont flung himself forward at impossible speed as the gun discharged…*

Sara opened his eyes. Light, the sound of traffic. He rolled over so he faced the window and the bright sunlight and closed his eyes again.

Dupont, tackling the stranger, rolling with him through the mud…

Sara sat up, unzipped the front pocket of the backpack, and pulled out his phone. Nate, a YouTube addict, had sent links to about a million videos since Sara had left Seattle. He had time for one or two, just to unwind.

CHAPTER EIGHT

HE WASN'T AWARE OF FALLING asleep or being asleep. But some part of his mind knew he dreamed. It had to be a dream, because Dupont was here, and Dupont…slept…during daylight hours. Only it wasn't daylight anymore. It wasn't anything. They were both bathed in moonlight, trapped in a twilight world shifting with ambient light and shadows.

Dupont's gray eyes roiled with reflected darkness. Sara, caught in the eye of the storm, fell into the abyss of his pupils. Then Dupont lowered his head, stealing his last refuge.

Adrenaline spiked in anticipation of the sharp sting of fangs. Instead, the soft touch of lips grazed his jaw, then the column of his throat. Dupont's hands skimmed his body and pulled him closer. The lips on his neck became more insistent. Sara moaned as Dupont suckled and the lips moved lower. *Dream.* There were no jeans to impede his progress, no awkwardness with the bedclothes. Only moonlight. He let his head fall, let his fingers tangle in Dupont's tousled hair, let his hips…

Sara opened his eyes, cursing as a beam of sunlight almost blinded him. He was sweating, tangled in sheets that hadn't existed a heartbeat ago, and aching for a lover's touch on his overheated skin.

He clenched his hands in the sheets, wanting to finish

what the dream had started. Hell. He absolutely could not jerk off to the idea of Dupont going down on him. He tried to call up an image of his last boyfriend. He'd always loved the way Tyler rolled his eyes up so their gazes met while he was sucking Sara off. Before he could fix the memory, Tyler's green eyes bled to gray, and Dupont was on his knees in front of him.

No. Just… Fuck no.

He rolled out of bed, tripped on the shoes and socks he had left next to it, and almost wound up in a heap on the floor as his phone started buzzing. By the time he found it under the bed, the buzzing had stopped. His backpack had fallen to the floor on the far side of the bed, still zipped except for the pocket the phone had been in along with his wallet and keys. Which had fallen out. Complete go-bag failure. Cowlick monk was right. Sara wasn't going to work out.

He pawed angrily through the clothes he had brought, not sure what he wanted. Something lightweight and comfortable, because lack of dress code might be the one upside of this job. The downsides were numerous, including the fact that everyone he met, even his employer, already expected him to fail.

He wondered if Ms. Alves found working for Dupont this challenging. His hand stilled, clutching the T-shirt he had pulled out of his bag.

Shit. Yeah, if Dupont could be believed, things were pretty challenging for Nohea Alves right now. She was in trouble, and they couldn't exactly fill out a missing persons report. Not that Dupont would sit around and wait for someone else to handle things even if they could. He thought of the vampire's single-minded focus on his task last night. Being forced to sleep in the middle of a crisis must drive him crazy.

⚜ ⚜ ⚜

*U*BI CARITAS ET AMOR, DEUS *ibi est…*
The hymn brought me to consciousness, the sweet melody slowly lifting the veil of pseudo-death enfolding me. There were no windows in this room, no way for the damaging light of the sun to reach me. Soon my somber wall clock would chime the hour, and I would begin with the service of Vespers.

And then I would descend to the main floor, ready to ascertain whether Nohea still lived.

I lay still, conscious of the ambiguity in every breath. We called my previous daylight agent "Grandmother," though the term skimmed over several generations. Mayette and I had worked together for over eighty years, until she gave in to an exhaustion no sleep could cure. Mayette had chosen Nohea to take her place, and from the age of sixteen, the young woman had trained diligently.

She had sacrificed much, and she deserved my protection. The thought of her torment at the hands of a demon made her rescue essential.

A sense of urgency fueled my actions. I rose, completed my observance of the Hour, and dressed as if readying myself for battle. My leather pants were supple enough to allow for movement, my shirt had long sleeves to protect my arms, and I chose a jacket made of heavy oiled canvas. Nohea wouldn't approve. She tried to insist my clothing "enter the damned twenty-first century" when we were in New Orleans. I could only hope she'd survive to scold me for my lack of taste.

Prior to leaving my room, I replayed a message on my cell phone. Brother George's nasal voice disquieted me further.

Miss Alves missed another meeting, and you should have already contacted me. The task I have for you has taken on an added dimension. We're running out of time. If you are in any way responsible for Miss Alves's disappearance, the consequences will be severe. I expect word before sunrise, Brother Thaddeus. God's peace be with you.

His blatant threat settled like ice in my belly. For a moment, I contemplated asking for the monks' assistance in finding Nohea. My finger hovered over the key to return his call.

I had not the strength. I turned the phone off and placed it on my desk. I only had a few short hours to learn where the demons were holding her. Instinct told me they were keeping her nearby. I prayed for a similar instinct so I could understand why they'd taken her at all.

I had a theory, and if I was correct, arriving with a team of monks made a boldfaced request for bloodshed. I trusted myself against a dozen demons. The monks—skilled fighters to a man—were still human, and therefore too easy to kill.

My conscience couldn't tolerate the weight of their souls.

The clarity of my decision offset some of the dread raised by Brother George's message. I alone would search for Nohea. I alone would take the risk. Arming myself with my short sword and boot knife, I left my room.

If my home had a name, it would be Dupont's Folly. I'd acquired it in the late 1920s, the result of a game of Bourré gone awry—for my opponent, anyway. I appreciated the symmetry of the house's structure, the simplicity of the double-gallery design. Deep porches faced the street, supported by Italianate ironwork and Doric columns. The front rooms never saw direct sunlight, allowing me to move about before nightfall.

Habit had me stepping slowly down the curved staircase, close to the wall to avoid the creaking boards. I kept the house well warded, though still I leaned toward caution. Pausing at the foot of the stairs, I let my senses reach out. A heartbeat, half again as quick as my own. A buttery baritone voice. The sweet scent of a man.

Sara.

He stood in the arch between the dining room and

the front entry, his back to me, phone against his ear. By focusing strictly on my business manager, I'd squashed any meandering thoughts having to do with my new assistant. Sara brought his own troubles, and I had not had time to deal with them.

Although soon, quite soon, I would be forced to. The meal I'd made of the body the demon possessed would last me seven days, maybe less. Unfortunately, Sara's resistance to my attempts at mental persuasion left me with no confidence he'd allow me to take what I required.

The White Monks provided me with an assistant to lessen my most heinous urge. They might not object to me feeding from a demon-possessed being, but their contract limited me to one living person. If I didn't feed from Sara, I would die. And if I did, I'd very likely take liberties with his body, destroying us both.

Another reason I needed Nohea. Sara had promised the Church a year of his life, and she was a stern mistress. Nohea might find a way out of his contract, though due to his association with me, he had attracted the notice of demons. Even if he should leave immediately, they would still haunt him. As things stood, we were both doomed whether he stayed with me or not.

"We're just going to be in New Orleans a few days, Ma. It's fine." Sara paused, and from the set of his shoulders I guessed his mother might be explaining why his assessment of the situation was incorrect.

"Mostly we'll be staying at his house out on the…"

"River." I supplied the word, making him jump.

"River." He fixed me with a scowl so harsh, I had to stifle a laugh.

He looked tired, no, exhausted, his eyes surrounded by shadow and his hair tangled across his brow.

"Yes, Ma. I will call you tomorrow." He bit his lip, and nearly overwhelmed me with the urge to touch him, to brush my thumb over the indent made by his bright white teeth.

Instead, I crossed my arms. No good could come from touching him, even if I only intended to give him comfort.

My impulse was not so pure.

He stepped out from under the archway, moving toward the big front windows. I could have stood next to him, protected by the overhanging porch, but his hunched posture demanded privacy. Instead, I went into the dining room where he'd set his laptop.

"I will… Um, yes. Tell Dev I said hi." His footsteps approached. "I didn't expect you up before dark."

I touched a key on the laptop, bringing a map of the city into view. "I rise in time for Vespers."

"When?"

I glanced at him over my shoulder. His worn shirt displayed the muscular definition across his chest. Nothing excessive, the planes and angles gave the impression of strength. "Were you raised Christian?"

"Um, Sarasija Mishra? I'm thinking not."

I nodded, conceding his point. "Muslim, then?"

"Hindu, but I don't, like, practice or anything."

He wouldn't. I wondered how many demon battles it would take to change his mind. "Vespers is one of the monastic hours, observed at sunset. I endeavor to chant all the hours I am conscious for." Another flaw in my observance. I would never celebrate Terce or Sext or None, the hours that passed while I slept. I could only hope the practice of many lifetimes would compensate for this lapse.

"Why?"

Scaring him with the whole truth wouldn't do either of us any good. "Did you sleep?" He'd managed to accommodate both my nature and two separate demon attacks. He had to be mentally exhausted, and I fought off another urge to care for him, stifling the impulse. We had no time. Nohea had no time.

"Sure." He rounded the broad dining table, resting his

hands on one of the tufted velvet chairs. Long, tapered fingers. I blinked. *No time.*

"I napped. My brain wouldn't shut down, though. Too many questions." He sat, rotating the laptop so he faced the screen. "You said the demons kidnapped Nohea." He rubbed at his cheek with a quiet laugh, as if he couldn't believe his own thoughts. "Why would they do that? Are they trying to prove something?" His fingers flew over the keys. "Come here."

Reluctantly, I took the chair next to him.

"Like, I'm a college kid, so I don't have a lot of experience with, well, any kind of crime, really, but most kidnappers want money or something, right?"

His laptop screen showed an article with the bold heading, *Abduction & Kidnapping.*

"Not in this case."

"I didn't think so." He raked the hair out of his face, eyes intent on the screen. He changed the view to the map. "You haven't had any weird demonic messages asking for ransom, right?"

I gave him a wry smile. "I have not."

"So why, then? Are they trying to make a point?"

To prove something to me. "In the past, the demons we fought demonstrated a limited range of skills. Few spells will call a demon, and even fewer humans have the necessary power. Most who attempt it are destroyed by their creation, who then run rampant, at least until the White Monks intervene."

I rose and paced the room, my actions fueled by the need to fight. "To be attacked at my home and have them taunt me with her hair…" My fists were so tight, the nails dug into my palms. "This is very unusual behavior."

Sara followed me with his gaze. "So maybe they are trying to make a point. Like, play a game of let's tag the vampire. We can get to him at home, and we can snatch his girlfriend—"

"She's not my girlfriend." Horrified, I interrupted him.

"Whatever." He waved away my dismay. "She must be pretty important to you, or you wouldn't care so much."

"She is…" My only connection to the woman who had been my right hand for eighty-five years. Nohea shared Mayette's greatest gift to me: an utter lack of judgment regarding my abnormal lifestyle. "Yes, Nohea is very important to me."

"So I made a list of what we know." He brought up a new image on the computer.

I made a general sound of agreement, intrigued by the working of his mind.

"We know Nohea's ex-girlfriend hasn't seen her in a couple of days, and we know she never made it out to meet me. This is"—his lips tightened—"well, are you sure she's still alive?"

"Yes." I snapped the word, trapped by a tide of emotion. To recover myself, I stole time with a slow inhale. "Yes, I would have felt it otherwise."

Sara tapped a knuckle against his lips. "Yeah, the mind thing you do."

"Not the same." Dust motes floated near the window, caught by the early evening light. While I had never intended to have children of my own, I had watched Nohea grow up. She might not be my flesh, but she was my child just the same. I wouldn't feel her death in my mind. I'd feel it in my bones.

"Okay, so see, they already hit you at your other place, and if they're really trying to make a point, I figure they'll try something here, too."

"This place is too well-secured. They'd never get in."

"Could they maybe come close? Assuming some bunch of abnormally well-organized demons have Nohea and haven't killed her yet, and assuming they're trying to prove they can get at you, I figure we should start by looking around here."

I nodded, encouraging him to go on.

"I did a search for vacant properties, places the demons could hide someone."

His logic made sense, and I was impressed by how he'd worked things out. He must have seen the confusion on my face, because he continued without waiting for a response. "I looked for empty houses and big open spaces, where they'd have privacy. Like the cemetery, or the big Audubon Park over by the university."

"How were you able to obtain this information?"

"Tax records. Real estate listings. Obituaries. You know, digging around. Come here and I'll show you."

I possessed a rudimentary knowledge of computers, and while I knew such things were possible, his efficiency impressed me. I resumed my place in the seat next to him. "So these Xs…" I pointed to the map of the Garden District on the laptop screen.

"Yeah, houses. I checked those out, though, and don't think they're the place we're looking for."

His words knocked the breath from my lungs. "Pardon? You left? You went outside?" I asked harshly.

Sara raised his hands. "Dude, Mr. Dupont, calm down, okay? I just walked around for an hour."

All my discordant emotions found a focus and I rose, towering over him. He shoved his chair away from the table, his face as pale as milk. Closing in, I grabbed his arm roughly. Anger sang through me, its jagged pitch and drag shredding my last vestiges of calm. "While we are under attack—" The pallor of his face made me regret my word choice. "While Nohea is missing, we need to stay together. I cannot protect you during the daylight hours, so…" The gravity of the risk he'd taken weighed me down. "Until Nohea returns, do not venture outside alone, s'il vous plait."

"Mr. Dupont, you're scaring me." Something—fear?— dampened the sound of his voice.

"You've explained why the demons are likely close by, so you must recognize the risk."

He nodded, gulped hard enough to show the movement in his throat. "I guess I thought the daytime was safe." He stopped, eyes large and dark and locked on my mouth.

For the first time since I'd met this young man, a fracture appeared in the surface of my resolve, wrought by his obvious distress. My body sank into a state of quiet, watching him, ready to pounce. I could take him so easily, indulge both of us, and when we had sated our carnal hungers, I would feast.

Salty warmth poured over the back of my tongue. My own spit. As if sensing my shift into a predatory stance, Sara froze.

I eased off and crossed my arms, both to resist the impulse to tear something apart and an equally strong urge to draw him closer.

"I didn't think it through, Mr. Dupont. I'm sorry."

The quiver in Sara's voice made it plain I'd frightened him.

Astonishingly, my concern was not limited to the threat to my own safety. This boy, this young man, with his impertinence and his quick intelligence and his glowing smile, this person had my promise of protection. I might have failed Nohea, but I would not fail him.

"None of this is your fault, Sara." I gazed into those bottomless dark eyes, willing his belief. The demons—or whoever guided them—were my true target. "None."

Deus meus, ex toto corde paénitet me ómnium meórum peccatórum…

"Go rest, Sara." My hands clenched, the knuckles white. "And lock your door."

He fled, leaving me strangling on my own desire. I reached for the chair he'd vacated, dug my fingers into its velvet cushion.

AT SUNSET, I ARMED MYSELF and called Sara to me. This time, I wanted no misunderstanding. He must stay behind.

"Are you ready?" He clattered down the stairs. "Good. Let's head out and take a look at the places I marked."

His fingertips bounced against his thighs at a rate of three or four taps per second. More worrisome were the shadows around his eyes. I pressed my palms together and rested my lips against my fingers. While I generally preferred to discuss all contingencies before embarking on a mission, maybe he was correct. Maybe this was as simple as getting into the car and turning the key.

Except I would be going alone.

"Your bravery does you great credit, Sara, and I am honored by your loyalty. I must ask you, however, to stay here while I search for Nohea."

"Seriously? No way."

"Listen to me." I laid my hands flat on the table, a deliberate move to keep from grabbing him. "If I'm forced to choose between fighting the demons who have Nohea and fighting to keep you safe, I'm going to lose one of you. That is not acceptable." The possibility ground against my soul. "The house is warded, so please..." I loaded the words with my will. "Please stay inside."

"Sure." Indecision clouded his gaze.

There would be time for discussion later. For now, I had work to do. With a huff, he followed me to the door.

Standing on the front porch, I struggled to find words to reassure him. A sound, soft and urgent, distracted me. I held up a hand. "Pardon." There, again, underneath the quiet rumble of the neighborhood and Sara's overly patient sigh. I stood still, eyes shut to strengthen my focus on one particular thing. Calling my name. "It's her," I whispered.

The tilt in Sara's lips clearly expressed his opinion. I was one *couyon* vampire. "I can find her if I run. Please, Sara, stay inside."

Moonlight and humidity washed over both of us, amplifying his incipient rebellion. "If you're afraid, I can link with your mind, which will allow me to know if you're in any trouble."

He raked his fingers through his hair. "Not just no, but HELL no."

We had no time. Pain threaded through Nohea's insistent call. I pressed my tongue against the roof of my mouth. The pressure and my excitement drew my canines into extended, needlelike points. Ignoring the implications of my action, I stabbed my thumb. A single bead of blood welled up.

"Here." I offered it to him. "On your lips. My blood will strengthen the bond between us without the mental connection."

Too many emotions flashed behind his eyes. "This wasn't in my contract either," he muttered, then drew my hand close and rubbed the blood on his lower lip.

Nohea screamed, though nothing in his expression changed, suggesting my ears alone were acute enough to hear her. "Be safe, Sara," I said, putting as much command in my tone as possible.

Let your powerful arm protect him, Lord.

I ran, listening for Nohea in the wind.

HEAT. THE GENTLE CARESS OF Dupont's thumb followed by scalding fire rushing out from the point of contact. Sara blinked, and the world was reborn—shadows banished, every detail pulsing in sharp relief. Another blink, and darkness reclaimed the street. The fire in his veins subsided into warmth. He touched the tip of his tongue to his lip. Vampire blood tasted of molten copper and mellowed to mulled wine. He licked again, already craving the kick of sensation. The heat settled in his groin, dark and heavy. Dupont.

Sara froze as the images from his dream returned. Dupont's body against his, hard and urgent. He could only hope his reaction didn't show on his face. He cleared his throat, suddenly not sure what to say to his boss, who was...

Gone.

Please stay inside.

Sara found himself locking the door. Halfway through the foyer, he stopped, at a loss as to what to do next. Freakin' vampire powers. He had a right to control his own actions.

Of course, his last action had been to get stupid horny in the middle of a crisis when he should have been pointing out some obvious facts to his boss. Facts like Dupont was being lured into a trap.

Dupont had thrown himself in front of a bullet at Pinky's. He had *carried* Sara away from their attackers in the French Quarter.

And when the time had come for Sara to return the favor, what had he done? Stared at his boss's mouth and let him leave without any backup. *Way to go, hero.*

Disgust at his actions worked better than a cold shower.

He licked his lip again, even though he knew the blood must be gone by now. The burn was addictive. No heat this time, just a sick feeling of urgency. He needed to do something, anything.

Frustrated, he wandered back through the house. He had no idea where to even start. As he passed the dining room, he heard a sharp beep.

Dupont's iPad sat on the table, blinking some type of alarm. The screen activated as soon as he touched it. *No password, Dupont? Really?*

He started to turn away when the words on the screen caught his attention.

```
Brother George Francisco: Why can't I
reach you and Miss Alves? Contact me AT
```

ONCE. URGENT info that is VITAL to your
safety.

Sara reached for the device. *VITAL to your safety* sounded important. And one of Dupont's monks would be really handy for backup. He hit Reply, then stopped. Who was Brother George Francisco? And if Brother George was someone Dupont trusted, why hadn't he already contacted him?

He canceled the reply and stood staring at the screen. *VITAL to your safety*. What if it really was? What if this Brother George had information Dupont needed before he confronted the demons?

The sense of urgency intensified.

Please stay inside.

He hadn't promised. If he had Dupont's vampire powers, he would still be able to follow him. *Screw it*. He had a car, and Ms. Alves must be near if Dupont could sense her. Maybe it was futile, but Dupont had saved his life. Sara couldn't just sit at home when there might be important information Dupont needed and didn't know about.

He ran upstairs and snagged his keys from the bedroom. Halfway through the kitchen, the knife block on the counter caught his eye. Weapon. A weapon would maybe be a good idea.

He pulled the knives out one by one, testing the feel in his hand. Which one? The cleaver looked effective, but the boning knife was longer. The carving knife? None of them seemed right. He yanked open the deep drawer under the counter, with some vague idea he might find something better. He rifled through a tangle of spatulas, spoons, whisks, and other kitchen implements. Nothing. He had the drawer half-closed when something caught his eye.

The leather sheath did not look like a kitchen implement. Hunting knife, maybe? He fished it out and unbuckled the strap over the crossguard. The blade slid free almost before he touched the handle. The weapon settled into his hand like an extension of his arm. *Yes.* The engraving on the blade drew his eye, but he didn't have time to study it. He resheathed the dagger and headed out the door.

NOHEA'S VOICE DREW ME WEST, toward the cemetery. Sara had made a good guess. They had trapped her very close to my backyard. The heavy humid air dragged against my skin and dampened every sound except her voice. Keeping to the shadows as much as possible, I covered the few blocks to my destination.

Less than a block away, I ghosted past Commander's Palace. Wrought iron fixtures spewed light at intervals along the striped awning, the second-story windows glowed, and jazz poured from the restaurant's lobby. Guests strolled up the uneven sidewalks, and valets shuttled cars around the block. Across the street, the white plaster walls of Lafayette No.1 stood chipped and sullen in the moonlight.

There. My destination. A field of charnel houses slumbering in the shadows.

A queenly old oak grew near the main entrance, her crown of branches spreading out across the street and draping over the cemetery's plaster wall. Far enough away from the Palace's crowd for me to make use of it. The gate would be locked by now, so, approaching the trunk, I slowed, then stopped. A car's headlights brushed over me, and I shrank into the coarse and ancient bark. Then, with a burst of speed, I scaled the trunk and used the branches as an unsteady ladder down behind the barrier.

I hit the ground at a dead run, gathering shadows around me. Bisecting thoroughfares formed a cross and divided the cemetery into quadrants. More oaks, magnolias, and moss-draped cypress shrouded the paved paths lined with raised crypts, the above-ground tombs holding the remains of the city's long-departed. Somewhere in the northwest corner, my own grandparents rested, awaiting the return of the Lord Jesus Christ, who would call them out of darkness and into eternal life.

From inside the cemetery walls, Nohea's voice became a booming wail, the sound surging from everywhere and nowhere at once. Impossible to locate the source, but, guessing the demons would know my history, I headed north.

Some of the vaults were separated from the path and the other mausoleums by knee-high wrought iron gates, and none of them were more than five or six feet high. My family possessed such a crypt. Tucked in the corner, under the shadow of a pecan tree, its marble exterior had been mottled by time and weather.

I approached slowly, my heartbeat heavy in my throat. No sign of Nohea. Still, her call drew me. I was close.

I passed my grandparents' tomb and rounded a corner. There. A familiar marker, suggesting they'd studied my history indeed.

A long, low bed of marble occupied most of the space, with a simple headstone at the far end. Leo Killian. The name carved a hole in my belly.

The marble glowed white in the moonlight. Beneath the headstone, bound hand and foot, Nohea lay on the marble slab.

CHAPTER NINE

ON THE STREET, SARA'S DOUBTS returned. What was he doing? He kept driving. The churning in his gut wouldn't let him return to the house. Without any better plan, he headed west, battling the traffic around some fancy restaurant to drive past the cemetery.

No sign of Dupont. He slowed to a crawl and continued down the block, keeping his eyes peeled for…what? Something out of the ordinary? So far, he had failed spectacularly at recognizing vampires, demons, and, hell, werewolves for all he knew.

He should go back. This was useless.

Giving up, he clicked on his right turn signal, then sat at the light, gnawing his lip. The light changed. He pulled into the intersection and turned left alongside the cemetery.

Stupid. Ms. Alves and Dupont weren't in a cemetery. But his eyes were drawn irresistibly to the left as he cruised down Prytania. He touched the tip of his tongue to his lip. The memory of molten copper burned along his senses. Anxiety spiked through him, along with a burst of impatience that didn't make any sense at all.

The shadows behind the next gate drew his gaze despite every rational argument. He was almost past, and calling himself every kind of idiot, when he caught a flash of movement between the monuments.

He stomped on the brake, checked his mirror and reversed for a better look.

A man darted across the central walkway and disappeared into the maze of crypts on the other side.

Dupont.

He shouldn't be so sure. The cemetery had to be closed and locked for the night. No one should be inside. But he hadn't imagined the man, and Dupont wouldn't have had any trouble with the wall.

He parked along the street. As he got out of the car, the lights of a passing vehicle hit him. He looked down at the knife clutched in his hand, and the reality of what he was doing washed over him in a clammy sweat. For a minute, his world wavered. He used to be just like that guy. That guy in the Taurus who was probably going to dinner or out to a show or maybe just home for a night of TV or something else boring and normal. That guy probably worked all day in an office, where his job description did not include breaking into cemeteries.

The gun went off, and Dupont flung himself forward…

He took a deep breath, stuck the sheathed knife in the waistband of his jeans, and dropped his shirt over it before heading down the sidewalk. No sense scaring any residents.

He glanced back down Prytania Street, looking for a way an ordinary guy with no vampire powers could get past brick walls and wrought iron gates topped with spikes. When nothing occurred to him, he started around the perimeter.

And really? The cemetery? Who *did* that? The demons had Ms. Alves. They could have emailed Dupont with any location in the state, and he would have come running without all this melodramatic staging. Some kind of psychological warfare, maybe? Dupont didn't seem the type to be impressed or intimidated by their choice of location.

He was still pondering demon logic when he rounded the corner onto Sixth Street. On this side of the cemetery, the street was dark and deserted. On Sixth Street, he tripped over a section of sidewalk pushed up by the roots of a giant oak. He sucked in a breath, and his tongue swiped his lip involuntarily. *Molten copper on a wave of fear and anger.*

He broke into a run. The gate on Sixth was locked too and just as spiked. By the time he hit the next block, the need to do something had ants crawling over his skin. How had the damn demons gotten in?

He sprinted toward the final gate and his last chance to find an entrance. Half a block and he would reenter the real world with the diners around the restaurant.

Then he spotted it. Some of the spikes in the fence around the gate had been broken off, leaving a smooth bar for a few feet at the top.

Without vampire strength, the boost up took effort. He wedged a foot on the top bar and braced it against one of the remaining spikes. A few seconds later, he stood on top of the nearest vault, gasping for breath.

From on top of the vault, he looked down into the cemetery. No sign of movement. Could he navigate the top of the wall and vaults? Because anything could be in the shadows below. Before he could decide, night disappeared in a blinding sweep of white light. He dropped to his stomach, heart pounding, as the NOPD cruiser inched by. Okay, no staying where he could be seen. He scrambled over the side and dropped into the city of the dead.

He cowered against the wall of the crypt as the shadows settled around him. The twenty-first century ceased to exist, and Sara understood why the demons had lured Dupont here. The sounds of the city were strangely muted. With the thick row of wall vaults separating him from the rest of the Garden District even the cars a few yards away sounded muffled and far away. The spirits of New Orleans pressed around him.

The cemetery occupied a full city block. The wind in

the trees offered no clues where he might find Dupont, so he headed in the direction he had last spotted him, trying to stay off the walkways and in the shadows. After a few fumbling steps, he pulled out his phone. The normal flashlight would give him away in a second, but a red light on his screen might allow him to navigate without tripping over flower urns and curbs. He tried not to notice how creepy the bloody wash looked on the vaults.

Halfway up the block, the wide walkway connecting the east and west gates blocked his path. Sara pressed himself into the shadows against one of the mausoleums and surveyed the open area in front of the gate. There would be no hiding while he crossed to the next section.

On the other side of the wall, a car door slammed, reminding him the real world still existed a few yards away. He could leave, get in his car, and return to the safety of the house.

Dupont pulled him back onto the porch. "It's not human, cher, I promise."

He had a science major. Demons hadn't been on the curriculum.

The gun went off, and Dupont flung himself forward…

Clouds moving across the moon cast shifting shadows until the whole landscape danced in shades of gray. The only sounds were the occasional scratch of limbs against graves and the softer rustle of leaves. He waited for a count of one hundred, barely breathing, eyes and ears straining.

Then he stuck his phone in his pocket, picked a mausoleum on the other side as his target cover, took a deep breath, and ran.

Despite his efforts at stealth, his footsteps echoed off the walls as he sprinted into the open. The pounding rush of his heartbeat behind his ears was louder still. He almost collapsed when he finally made the shadow of the wall.

Safe.

He forced himself to breathe slowly, not gasp for air the

way he wanted to. When he had himself under control, he edged along the side of the building. Only a little farther. Keeping to the shadows, he headed for his next hiding place.

He had barely moved away from the wall when they stepped out of the darkness.

THE DEMONS HAD LEFT NOHEA draped over the flat slab of marble, her dreadlocks flaring out like a gnarled halo. She wore everyday clothing, a pair of black stretch pants and a fitted pink T-shirt, now soiled and torn. I no longer needed my psychic hearing. Her whimpers strafed my heart.

Despite her confounding fear, I covered myself in shade, allowing the scene to settle in my consciousness. The lack of light didn't hinder me, and I searched the gloom for the ones who had most assuredly prepared this tableau for my benefit. I sorted through the steady thrum of pulses from the street, the clatter and whir of vehicles driving by.

Nothing unusual, except Nohea's cries.

She lay flat on her back, knees bent, hands clasped on her belly. Ropes bound her wrists and ankles. There. On her chest. The real restraint was the coil of black. Not blood. The blackness stretched and shifted, and her whimper became a single keening cry.

Serpent.

They'd bound her with rope and tortured her with a writhing snake on her chest.

The pitch of her cry rose. The reptile slid between her breasts and coiled over the bare skin on her throat. I eased forward, gently, silently, aware of the risk to both of us if I displayed myself. Whoever had prepared this tableau had to be watching my response, ready to strike.

A shout froze me in the middle of the path, followed by a surge of fear. Sara. The connection I'd forged with my blood burned hot. Another shout, followed by rude laughter. Indecision kept me rooted. Three men came up the path. Two carried the dark energy of the demons.

The third was my new assistant.

My decrepit old heart surged in a fierce staccato beat, and a single thought overtook me.

Kill.

Kill the demons who had the gall to put their hands on Sara. Who had harmed Nohea. Who had dared trespass so close to the First Street house. My home.

Fools.

Though the effort caused me physical pain, I deepened the shadows around me and held still. My mouth watered. My fangs lengthened. Though killing the two holding Sara would bring me exquisite pleasure, jumping in without assessing the risks could lose me one or both of these fragile humans.

I refused to pay such a cost.

So I crouched, stretching my senses to their limits. The soft hum of rubber on asphalt muddied the erratic beating of frightened human hearts. The snake draped over Nohea's throat raised its head with the tiniest hiss. One of the demons jerked Sara's arm, the humid air dampening his answering snarl.

A heavy darkness down the aisle hinted at the presence of hidden evil.

The snake opened its jaws, revealing a soft gray-white mouth framed with fangs. Cottonmouth. The bite would be unlikely to end Nohea's life, so I considered moving for Sara first. Destroying those two demons would announce my presence and draw any others out of hiding. Could I protect Sara while fighting an unknown number of enemies? Sweet Sara, young, breakable…

Lord, forgive your servant his weakness.

I crouched, poised on the edge of indecision. Though I'd fought the forces of evil for nearly a century, never had the battle felt so personal. Never had the demons shown such daring, or come so close to those I considered my own. Fear lurked in the depths of my heart, an unfamiliar emotion, an added distraction. An indulgence I could not afford.

The demons brought Sara closer to Leo's grave. Sara's gaze sharpened; his posture lost some of its looseness. His stumbling gait took on more coherence. The creatures pulled him along, every step tightening the bands of tension around my chest. Moisture beaded on my temples, between my shoulder blades, and I fought a losing battle with rage. I scanned the area again, trying to locate the others whose evil presence I could sense.

Sara leaned heavily into one of the bodies guiding him, pulling both demons off balance. If he fell, the demons would be on him, and they wouldn't be gentle. His sudden vulnerability drew me to my feet, then he threw his weight hard to the right. He jerked his arm free of one demon's grasp, then smashed the heel of his hand into the other's chin.

This feint allowed him to break free. Instead of running for safety, he leapt over the low fence surrounding the grave. The darkness disgorged two more demons, who converged on him, shouting insults. In their battered business suits, soiled white shirts, and loose ties, they could have been in the victims of a hellish raid on the downtown financial district.

The first of the demons straddled the gate. Sara froze, hand hovering over the snake. With whiplike quickness, Sara grabbed the serpent and flung it at the approaching devil. Fear of snakes must transcend even demonic possession, because the body flinched and cried out, falling over the fence. Sara faced his assailants, his eyes wide and white in the darkness.

One of the demons laughed, a sound even more horrible than Sara's rasping breath and Nohea's weak, whimpering cries.

The demon threw his arms out wide. "All right, Dupont. It's your move."

Dread slowed my heartbeat. Just as I had sensed them, so too must they have recognized my presence. Sara looked around as if he expected me to fling myself from the shadows.

"You're a hard guy to get ahold of, but we've got them both, Dupont. There's no point in hiding now."

The snake slithered out underneath the fence, making the nearest demons shy away. Taking down all four demons before one of them could get to Sara might be beyond even my skills.

What choice did I have?

Dimitte me.

The demons fanned out, circling the grave. Soundlessly, I approached the closest one, slipping my dagger from its sheath between my shoulders.

"Mr. Dupont?" Sara's voice was rough, quavering. The glint of a silver blade shone from his hand. "If you're out there, I've got the one with the bad haircut."

Merde alors. Which bad haircut? They all looked awful.

"Come on, dude. Your little catamite is willing to fight." His voice promising all kinds of depraved pleasure, the demon removed the tie from around its neck and stretched the length of silk between clenched fists. "Let's see what you can do. Or better yet"—he allowed the fabric to drop to the ground and held out his hands, palms up—"join us. We're already part of the same team."

The tension wrapped so tight, I could hardly draw a breath. His words resonated deep within me, dredging up an old pain. My evil nature goaded me every day of my endless life. I lifted my gaze, as if the sodden sky could come to my rescue. Sara stood silent, still, waiting.

"Don't listen to them, Thaddeus." Nohea moaned the words, low and soft.

The demon hurdled the gate with a thunderous laugh,

then fell with an even louder shriek.

"I got one." Sara's yell demanded a response. The other demons closed in, surrounding the crypt. Sara raised his hand, his narrow blade bloodstained. "Mr. Dupont?"

I launched my attack, swinging my dagger in a wide arc. My target feinted and came up swinging. An ancient evil powered his limbs, more dangerous than any weapon. He ran at me like a rampaging wildcat, and soon another of his cohorts joined the fray. Their strategy became apparent: keep me away from the grave. Whichever direction I moved, they bounded in front of me, blocking my progress.

Sara had wounded or even killed one demon, and two were converging on me. I swung my blade again, slicing into a soft belly.

The wounded demon stumbled and fell. My attention distracted, his compatriot caught me with a glancing blow, hard enough to make my ears ring. He came at me again, and I dodged, skidding in the spilled blood.

"Thaddeus?" Nohea's distraught cry pulled me to her. My opponent bulled into me again, harder, fiercer. This time I caught him with a fist square in the jaw. Before he fell, I wrenched his head to the side, snapping his neck.

The one I'd stabbed lay curled in the fetal position, his pathetic whimpers drawing a note of compassion from my heart. The man he'd been had not invited this possession. He'd been torn from his ordinary life and would now be left to die. Making a quick sign of the cross, I reached down and tore off his head.

Something heavy and hard slammed me from behind. "Fool," the evil one hissed, throwing my own word at me. I landed on hands and knees, and before I could respond, he grasped my shoulders and shoved me to the gravel path.

I rolled, dragging him with me. "No." The word came out through a fog of pain and humiliation. He knelt on my chest, pounding my face, my jaw, my throat. I got a grip on one of his wrists, then the other. With inhuman strength, he stretched my arms above my head, tearing flesh and muscle. *This cannot be.* I growled, writhing, fighting for any advantage. He slammed his head at my chin, the impact sending out a spray of blood even as it set off a deep ache in my neck.

Another cry from the direction of the grave told me I had no time to waste. I bucked, jerking my arms and thrusting my hips to knock him off balance.

Still the creature did not release me.

"Mr. Dupont!" Terror ripped through Sara's cry. I rolled, hard. Freed one hand. I regained my leverage and rose to my feet. The poor demented soul hanging from my shoulders, I staggered toward the grave.

There, the leader leaned against the low fence, surrounded by a pool of blood, his despicable presence between me and my charges. Sara held his blade at the ready, and Nohea sat on the marble slab, her hands free, frantically working on the bindings on her feet.

With a mighty surge, I threw off the hands clamped around my neck. The demon laughed, his broken fingers flopping at his side. When he came at me again, I ripped out his throat.

"Why?" I screamed at the fiend Sara had wounded, the only one still alive. "Why bother me now?"

"You're so misguided, Dupont." Kneeling by the low fence, the demon paused and coughed up a gout of blood. "You could be king, but you grovel like a dog." His laugh blew the miasma of hell into my face.

In the face of his mockery, my resolve burned white-hot. "When you return to the pit, tell the one who sent you to leave me and mine alone," I said. "I will not break."

He spat in my face as I snapped his neck.

With a shameful feeling of satisfaction, I let him fall to the ground and made the sign of the cross. Then, in order to give myself more time before I'd have to feed from Sara, I yanked the body up and drained it dry.

CHAPTER TEN

EVERY LIGHT BURNED. THE SCONCES on either side of the big front door, an antique chandelier in the foyer, every table lamp and candelabra and crystal globe on the ceiling. Bright enough to show the veins tunneling aqua through my pale skin, the dark circles floating down to Sara's cheekbones, the myriad small traumas marring Nohea's beauty.

Before we left the cemetery, Nohea had given in to her suffering, allowing me to carry her to the car and spending the short trip home semiconscious. I carried her into the house too, though she handled my gesture with less grace.

"Put me down. I can walk." She grabbed at my shirt. I held fast despite her squirming.

With Sara at my heels, I brought Nohea to the rear parlor, an archaic name for what people in the sixties called a den and current real-estate parlance would refer to as a bonus room. Nohea had dictated a recent refurbishing with deep, oversized leather couches and two fat brocade hassocks. The whole space glowed with light.

Laying Nohea on one of the couches, I directed Sara to an armoire in the corner. "Get me a blanket."

He came over with an armload of folded fabric. "Lift her again."

"Shut up." She flapped her hand in my direction. "Leave me alone, both of you."

Sara's narrow frown brooked no discussion. I lifted Nohea, bringing forth a shout of protest, and Sara spread a heavy quilt over the couch.

"Now down," he muttered, and I laid Nohea on top, reaching for the edge of the quilt to drape over her. Sara elbowed me out of the way and forced a smaller, rougher blanket into my hands.

"Clean yourself up, Mr. Dupont."

For a moment, the searing blast of shame burned brighter than the lights in the room. Sara's tone bore no judgment, and he met my gaze with a frank expectation that I would comply. I wiped my mouth, my jaw, my throat down to the collar of my shirt. I gripped the fabric, forcing it between my fingers and rubbing away the traces of blood. He watched for a moment, then settled the pillow behind Nohea's head.

"Ow, watch the hair." Her voice carried a shadow of her normal attitude, enough to send Sara to the safety of the other couch. He sank down and interlaced his fingers behind his neck in a weary stretch. My two charges. Glancing from one to the other, I vowed no further harm would come this night.

Kneeling beside the couch, I lifted the blanket and ran my fingertips over the dirty clothing covering Nohea's body. She was nearly as tall as Sara, slender and toned, with light brown skin and green eyes. Her breathing was steady, even, and nothing spoke to me of severe damage.

She batted my hand away. "Jesus, Thaddeus, you're tickling me." She tugged the blanket into place. "Who's that?" She pointed a finger at Sara.

"Don't be rude, Nohea," I said, stalling for time. If I had been surprised by the turn of events leading Sara to us, Nohea was bound to be shocked.

For his part, Sara straightened, expression somber. "I'm Sara. Sarasija Mishra."

His words landed like firecrackers, sending Nohea scrambling up against the arm of the couch. "Thaddeus?" The flashing emotions crossing her face—confusion, surprise, and fear—would have been comical if I'd had any room for humor.

"Thaddeus, is he telling the truth?" Nohea drew her knees up and wrapped her arms around them, drawn in tight like the layers of flesh and bone could protect her soul. "And if he is, what the hell are you going to do?"

Sara's gaze jerked from one of us to the other. "What?"

I heard concern, but no real fear. Not yet.

"Can you do this? What am I saying?" Nohea choked out a laugh. "Of course you can't."

Her lack of faith in my self-control chafed me. Nohea pulled herself in tighter, and while I had no real power to influence her thoughts, I willed her to be quiet. *No more. Not now.* We had other things to deal with.

"What's she talking about, Mr. Dupont?" The worry in Sara's voice rose, and he hunched over, elbows on his knees.

Either my attempt to warn her was successful, or Nohea assessed the situation correctly. Instead of giving him a difficult explanation, she pared it down to just a few words.

"I fucked up."

Non. I straightened, intent on stopping her from taking the blame. "Nohea."

"Oh stop." Her attempt at running a hand through her hair ended with a tiny squeak of pain. "I'm supposed to hire girls, and my first big chance to show what I could do ended—" She barked a laugh. "If you want to fire me, Mr. Dupont, I totally wouldn't blame you."

This young woman, the daughter of my soul, had given up any hope of a normal life in order to serve me. She'd just been abducted by demons, still wore the blood and bruises from their attack.

And yet she thought I would blame her. *Deus.*

"Perhaps the demons interfered with you before even the abduction." I shrugged, aware of the ineffectual nature of my reassurance.

The sadness in her smile made me want to weep. "We'll figure something out, boss."

"We will."

"So are we done with our Hallmark moment yet?" Sara still sat hunched on the couch, and his voice lacked its usual bite. "Because I'd really like to know what the fuck is going on."

I put out my hand, hoping to redirect his attention. "You had a blade, *oui*? In the graveyard?"

He shuffled in the pocket of his jeans and brought out a dagger.

Loosening the leather sheath, he slid out the blade. The familiar gems set in the handle were hidden by dark, clotted blood. He stared at the thing in his hand, his expression hard to read. "I really did it this time."

"*Quoi?*"

"I killed…" His voice trailed away, the blade dropped to the floor, and he covered his face with his hands.

Nohea and I exchanged glances. "It'll be okay, Sara," she said. "I freaked right out the first time I tangled with a demon, and tonight I'da been in a world of hurt without you."

He nodded, hunched over, still hiding from us. I rose and picked up the blade. Taking a moment, I went to the kitchen. There, amidst the familiar tile and the little-used appliances, I sliced my own palm and dripped blood into a mug. When I had collected a few mouthfuls, I carried it to the parlor.

Nohea had her eyes closed, and Sara still hid from us. I knelt down near the couch where she lay and shook her shoulder. "Here."

"Oh." She met my gaze, her dark eyes growing turbulent with emotions I couldn't identify. "You didn't need to—"

"I did." I took one of her hands and curled it around the porcelain. "Come, Sara." My tone brooked no disagreement. "We should allow Miss Alves to rest." To my relief, he rose from his seat.

"Thaddeus?" Nohea fixed her attention on the mug.

I could offer her scant comfort. "Drink it. You'll heal faster."

After a long moment, she raised the glass and tipped it in my direction. The tremble in her lips made her smile a lie. "*Salud.*"

I nodded in relief. I had cared for one of them. Now to repair the damage done to the other.

Wordlessly, Sara followed me out of the parlor and up the stairs. As we trod the groaning risers, his silence bore down on me. Sara was never quiet. I chanced a glance in his direction. He met my gaze for the briefest moment, then turned away.

Pausing several steps from the top, I made a more obvious effort to look at him. I did not yield when he tried to pass me. While he glared out over the banister, the color in his cheeks rising, I replayed the events of the evening.

"You brought down a demon." One of many events weighing on him. "Where did you get the dagger?" Only one weapon in the house would separate a demon from the host, and he'd managed to find it.

"On my way out the door." He paused, his lips pressed thin. "It burned, you know? The stuff you put on my mouth."

The stuff. My blood. "I'm sorry."

He shook his head as if nothing I said would make a difference.

"Whatever, Mr. Dupont." He ran his tongue over his lower lip. The shock of desire forced me to join him in gazing over the banister. "Like I said, I was headed for the door, and I grabbed it out of the kitchen. Figured a weapon might come in handy."

Sometimes this house surprised me. I kept the ritual dagger locked in a drawer in my room. By rights, I should have chided him for leaving the house, but the distress in his face kept me quiet.

I stepped aside so he could pass, and we progressed to the upper level. Sara went down the hall to the guest room, glancing at me before entering. "So, what Ms. Alves, um, Nohea was saying…"

Merde alors. "*Oui?*" Fists clenched, I vowed to answer whatever question he asked.

"So…" His tongue again, just the tip, pink and moist against his darker lip. Something in his face softened, and his sleepy eyes got heavier. "Why is my sex a problem?"

He gave the word *sex* an infinitesimal lift, as if even in saying it he'd guessed the reason and been surprised. His cheeks warmed, adding a hint of pleasure to his reaction.

I found I could not speak. He'd plunged us both straight into a *caimon*-infested swamp. Yes, I'd promised an answer, and yes, he had a right to know. The heat of his stare warmed me in a way I hadn't felt in fifty years.

Though I honored my pledge of celibacy now, it hadn't always been so. The monks held my lone chance at salvation. I could not bear to take the risk.

Without any apparent conscious decision-making on my part, I covered the distance between the two of us, stopped only by his sharp inhale. I pressed my hand to the wall, nails digging into the flocked paper. He stood still, breathing fast and shallow, his scent enticing me to go closer.

"Your s-sex"— I did not stutter—"is not the problem. My response to it, however, is."

I could no more meet his eyes than I could have flown to the moon. His heartbeat should have chased me away. The brush of his breath against my throat should have driven me into my room.

"Not a problem to me," he whispered, the words tickling my skin.

He had to be reacting to the events of the evening, pushed too far to have any sense of self-preservation. My heart, a long-neglected organ, throbbed in response to his closeness. Slowly, as if he might flee into the night, I raised my arm and rested my hand against his cheek.

Just as slowly, he turned and pressed a kiss into my palm.

Extending my arm would have taken no effort at all, wrapping my hand around his neck, pulling him into my body, taking his lips and then—when we were both breathless and flushed—plunging my teeth into the pulse at the base of his throat.

My body roared its desire.

I could not.

Must not.

No.

I backed away, as feeble as a revenant in a crypt. "Again, I must apologize. There are lines we must not cross." Or risk a cost too high for either of us to pay.

The muffled thump of my door swinging shut punctuated my retreat. Alone in my room, I fell to my knees.

For thy name's sake, O Lord, pardon mine iniquity; for it is great.

Crawling, for I no longer had the power to stand, I sought out my one source of help, my harshest recourse when my transgressions were great.

Still on my knees, I brought the discipline from the leather case beneath my bed. The handle was sturdy, fifteen inches wrapped with braided leather, an easy grip, one I'd become well-acquainted with. I let the falls trail across my thighs, then stripped off my shirt.

I welcomed the lash's pain, sought out its oblivion.

Anything to counteract the need.

CHAPTER ELEVEN

SARA WOKE UP IN A room filled with sunlight. It was late. Or early. Depending on if you were on Real World Standard Time or Vampire Saving Time.

He rolled over and stared at the ceiling fan over his bed. Okay, last night had happened. Cemetery, demons, Ms. Alves. Dupont.

The Deal with Dupont.

Yeah. Dupont was…

Sara scrubbed his hand over his face, unwilling to grapple with the questions that inevitably followed the conclusion of that sentence.

Dupont was attracted to him.

And Sara, like an idiot, had let him know the attraction went both ways. He rolled out of bed, willing to focus on anything except…

Ah, hell. Dupont was his boss. It was a really bad idea.

He headed for the shower, still trying not to think. Because…vampire, demons, a beat-up Ms. Alves. There were a million issues demanding brain cells. But he didn't hear the mocking laugh of the demon who had captured him. He didn't see Ms. Alves's bruised face.

He heard the slight hesitation in Dupont's voice. He saw the flush along the vampire's cheekbones as they stood in the hallway.

He turned the water up to scalding. He occupied himself with hygiene and normalcy and shoving anything else firmly to the back of his mind. Fifteen minutes later, he was as clean and normal as he was going to get. Normal being a highly subjective term.

He poked his head cautiously into the den. "Ms. Alves?"

She didn't answer, and he had the sudden, horrifying conviction she had died in the night. Alone. Of her injuries. Because he and Dupont had dumped her on the sofa and left her so they could go ogle each other in the upstairs hall.

He hovered in the doorway, heart pounding, unable to see over the back of the sofa but afraid to go around and check on its contents.

"Ms. Alves?" It came out a whisper.

"Jesus. What time is it?"

He jumped, hand flying over his mouth to muffle a scream.

"I, uh…" Okay, not dead.

"Well?" A head appeared, to go with the grumpy voice.

"A little after noon."

The head disappeared. "Why am I awake? After last night, you'd think I'd get to sleep in."

"Sorry, I just… I wanted to make sure you were—" Not dead. "—okay. I'll come back later."

"Wait." Heavy sigh. Rustling on the other side of the sofa. Then the head reappeared, a shock of short locs springing out wildly from around a grumpy, burnt-umber face. "Never mind. I'm up. Come on in, Sara."

He ventured farther into the room.

She swiveled, watching him intently as he came in and sat on the coffee table in front of the sofa so he was at her level.

"You should rest. You shouldn't move too much until we've had a doctor check you out."

She narrowed her eyes at him. "Uh-huh. Sara, what did Mr. Dupont say happened to me last night?"

"Well, he didn't really *say* anything. I mean, we found you in the cemetery, and Mr. Dupont fought the, uh…" *Demons*. "There was a fight. Then we brought you back here. Are you in any pain?"

"No," she said slowly. "I'm okay. And you were at a fight in the cemetery last night?"

He was getting seriously worried about how her captors had kept her pacified while they had her. Drugs could have long-term effects. Or maybe she had hit her head. She was obviously confused this morning.

"It's okay," he said. "Just, you need to rest. Does Mr. Dupont have a doctor I can call for you? You know, some-one, uh, discreet who uh, knows your situation? I mean, I assume you don't want to go to the emergency room or anything? Or I can drive you if you do."

Nohea stared at him. "What situation?"

Okay. Wow. He had to get her help. "You know, what with Mr. Dupont being what he is and the thing with the people who had you being not exactly people and all." Okay, that didn't even make sense to him. Maybe he wasn't coping quite as well as he had thought with the whole creatures-of-the-night thing. He started to fidget under Nohea's intent gaze.

She finally blinked. "Sara, are you telling me you remem-ber everything that happened last night?"

He blinked back. "Uh, I *think* so. Only, you know Mr. Dupont, with the whammy? I mean I *told* him he had to stop, but I think he keeps trying anyway."

Her mouth dropped open. Her face showed dawning horror and then…

Then she started laughing.

"Ms. Alves?" Was she hysterical? He tried patting her shoulder. She batted him away.

"Whammy?" She gasped it out between howls of laugh-ter. "You *told* him? Oh, honey, I just bet." She rolled over onto her side, clutching her stomach and laughing so hard, she could barely get words out. "How did he take that?"

She dissolved into more laughter, and finally Sara couldn't help grinning. "I guess he's used to getting his way?"

"You might say." Nohea finally got herself under control. She stared up at him from the cushions, humor fading as quickly as it had come. "God, we're fucked."

"Hey," he protested. "We won. We kicked demon ass last night." He was pretty proud of that, not counting the whole getting-taken-prisoner part. Not counting the thing where he was still rolling with the punches and trying not to overthink the cost/benefit ratios of his new job.

"Ms. Alves?"

"Shit, honey, call me Nohea. We don't have what you'd call a formal work environment around here. Leastways I don't. You never know what stick Thaddeus is going to get stuck up his butt."

"Is it always like this? I mean, are we always in danger?" He ignored the way his stomach clenched at the idea. Every job had its downside, he reminded himself. But New Orleans was not going to be nearly as much fun with demons popping out of the woodwork.

"No, it's…" She trailed off and sat up. "No, it usually isn't like this at all. Or at least it hasn't been."

"Great," he muttered. "Just my luck to show up in time for the fun, huh?"

Nohea looked as though she barely heard him. "How many demons did you count last night?"

"Four, unless there were some I didn't see."

"A pair is normal, but things don't usually go down like that. We hunt them. And they're dumber than mud. Even if they decided to make a move on Thaddeus for some reason, coordinating last night's shindig would be outside their skillset. I think."

"What do you mean you *think*?"

"I mean I've never seen them do anything on this scale since I've been working for Thaddeus."

Sara eyed her, suspicious. "Which is how long, exactly?"

She picked at the blanket over her knees, not looking at him. "Depends on how you count. Officially, I guess about a year."

"Oh. Well, a year is…" When you were in college, a year was a long time. But in demon time?

"*You* were supposed to train *me*," he accused. "Don't you know anything?"

"I know stuff. My family has been working for Thaddeus most of a century. Anyway, assistants don't need training."

"So has anybody else been kidnapped to lure him out before?"

"I don't know."

Sara stared at her, frustrated.

"Look," she said. "It was just my grandmother. She's been with him since, I don't even know how long. She knew him when he was human and after Thaddeus was turned he trusted her to look after him during the day. That was back before the White Monks found him. She and Thaddeus were always paranoid about all kinds of things."

"Yeah? Well, maybe you should call and ask Granny what we're dealing with here."

"Can't. She died, uh, just under a year ago."

"Oh." *Shit, Sara, way to go.* "Sorry. I didn't know."

"How could you? Anyway, her death was pretty sudden. I guess maybe she would have told me more stuff if she had known she wouldn't be around. I didn't—I mean, I called her my grandmother most of my life. Only she turned out to be my great-great-great-aunt. My real however-many-greats grandmother was her sister. She and Thaddeus worked together most of her life."

Sara stared at her. "Great-great-great? But that would make her…" He stopped. "That would make Mr. Dupont…"

"Yeah. She could remember seeing the first car in French Settlement."

"Flippin' vampire," he muttered. "Should have known. How old are you?"

"Me? I'm twenty-eight."

"So, what's with your family? Are you witches or were-wolves or elves, or something? Because you didn't look so hot last night and you're pretty perky today."

"What? No. We're just people. Do I look like an elf?"

"How should I know? I still don't know how to spot a demon or vampire. It's not like they all have the same tat-too." He paused. "Do they?"

She snorted. "No. No tattoos. Demons smell like shit, though." She made a gagging noise. "Worst part of being kidnapped." Her hand went to her head, and she fingered the fuzz of new hair covering the bare spot amongst her dreads. "Second-worst part. Motherfuckers messed with my hair."

"So what's with the longevity and the healing?"

"Vampire blood. Tastes like shit, and it's a nasty little addiction, but it has its uses."

He hadn't thought it tasted so bad. He sucked at his lower lip, then realized Nohea was doing the same. "Is *that* what Dupont gave you last night?"

The thought of actually swallowing blood turned his stomach a little.

"Yeah. Plus the effects build up." She gave him a level stare. "Don't take any if you don't need it."

Great. He had about a million more questions, but Q&A time was interrupted by the peal of the doorbell.

Nohea started up, wrapping the blanket more firmly around her soiled and torn clothing. Sara waved her down. "I'm dressed. I'll get it."

"Don't let anyone in."

Great. Paranoia all around.

He peered out onto the front porch and found a kid of no more than eight or nine. He cracked the door open. "Can I help you?"

"Are you Mr. Mishra?"

He nodded. Who knew he was here? The boy was cute. Big brown puppy-dog eyes blinked innocently out of a thin face a shade darker than Sara's own skin. Sara scanned the street, didn't see anyone else, and deemed it safe to step out as far as the porch. A kid-sized bike leaned against the porch, presumably the boy's ride. He hoped like hell demons couldn't possess little kids, because there was no way he could stick a knife in this child.

"Brother George says to tell Mr. Dupont and Ms. Alves he doesn't have any openings in his office hours today. He will be at St. Mary's tonight after sundown."

"Oh, thank you." What the hey? Did no one in Louisiana know about email?

"Brother George says to tell Mr. Dupont he prays for Mr. Dupont's soul without cease."

Sara resisted rolling his eyes. "That's very kind of Brother George," he managed instead. "I'll tell Mr. Dupont."

"Brother George says to tell him those exact words."

"Got it." Sara fished out his wallet. How much did one tip pint-sized bike couriers? Five? Ten?

"Thanks, mister!" The kid snatched both fives out of his hand and took off on the bike before Sara could move.

Ten was good, then.

He turned around to find Nohea standing in the foyer behind him.

"Weird." She strode forward and peered out the window as kid and bike disappeared around the corner a block up.

"What? Do messages normally come by owl?"

"Courier pigeon," she deadpanned.

"Ha. Ha. Who is Brother George, anyway?"

"He's, for want of a better term, our boss. Contact with the White Monks, anyway. When they have a demon problem they can't solve on their own, they call us in."

"Oh. He doesn't have a phone?"

"Yeah, a messenger is pretty unusual. Maybe because the

demons broke my phone and he couldn't get me the past few days? And the boss is asleep and bad about checking his messages even when he isn't. George gets pissy when Thaddeus doesn't jump fast enough for his liking. I don't get the St. Mary's part. Normally we go to his office at Loyola. He's going to be in the neighborhood. Why doesn't he come to the house?"

"There's a demon-hunting department at Loyola?"

"Of course not. The White Monks are Church black ops. The job is his cover. He has some bogus research position over there."

"Wait a sec. Brother George Francisco?"

"Yeah, that's him."

"There was a message from him last night on Mr. Dupont's iPad. It's why I went to the cemetery. He says he has some urgent information."

"There you go, then. He's annoyed if Thaddeus is out of touch for two minutes."

"So what should we do?"

"Eat."

"Eat? What about the urgent information?"

"I'm starving. Asshole demons didn't feed me. I wouldn't worry too much about George. Everything is urgent, according to him. Anyway, there's not much else we can do until Thaddeus is up."

Some of Dupont's paranoia must have rubbed off onto Nohea, because she vetoed going out for food or even ordering in.

"I was looking forward to Louisiana food, you know," Sara complained as they scavenged canned soup and frozen biscuits. It wasn't the worst meal ever, but with all the restaurants in this town, he was sure they could have done better within a few safe blocks of the house.

Later in the afternoon, they kicked back in the den while they waited for Dupont to wake up. Nohea had showered and changed into clean clothes from one of the other spare bedrooms. She flicked absently through the channels on the TV while Sara made up fun anecdotes about his new job to email to his mom. *He really does want me to set up his Facebook page,* he finished up. *Tonight we're meeting a client at a local historic church, so stop worrying. What could be safer than a church? (And don't worry, I'm not converting.)*

Okay. He'd have to remember to set up some kind of Facebook page to show Ma. He hit Send.

"Hey, does Mr. Dupont show up on camera?" Because Ma would want to see a profile picture.

"Yes, he shows up on camera. You can ignore most of what you think you know about vampires. Most of that Hollywood stuff is bogus."

"But he can't go in the sun. That's real?"

"He doesn't burst into flames or anything, but he starts turning red pretty quick, and it hurts him. I'm not sure how long he could last before he got to a point he couldn't heal. And it's almost impossible to wake him up during full daylight."

"Ha! See—this is the kind of thing I expected from my Renfield training."

Nohea choked on her Coke mid-swallow. "Renfield training? Jesus, Sara."

"Yeah, I mean, one-year contract. Seems like it would be easier to just have a manual to get us up to speed. You ought to be used to all the..." He trailed off as something she had said earlier came back to him. "Wait a minute. Why don't assistants need training?"

Nohea evaded his eyes. "What did Mr. Dupont tell you?"

"Dupont hasn't told me diddly. He just... Oh. My. God. He does the whammy on them, doesn't he?"

Nohea remained silent, which was answer enough.

"That's just..." He shook his head. "*So* not cool."

"Look, Sara, he's trying to protect them. For the most part, the less they knew, the safer they were."

"Yeah, but..." It sounded good, but something about the

explanation was off. "If they don't know anything, how can they, you know, *assist* him?" Vampire Assistant seemed like a job requiring full knowledge of…vampires.

"Well, he doesn't have them do much. I mean, they take his daytime messages and…stuff."

"Because he can't work voice mail?"

And the salary. No one paid eighty grand for someone to take messages. Not even a vampire.

His heart started pounding. Not racing, not yet. Just pounding until it was the only sound he could hear.

He was an idiot. Because vampire.

Pound.

"How often does he need to eat?"

Nohea didn't answer.

Pound. Pound.

"I'm not his assistant, am I?"

Pound. Pound. Pound.

A rush of saliva.

"Sara."

He turned to Dupont, who had appeared in the doorway as though summoned by his thoughts.

Pound-pound. Pound-pound. Pound-pound.

He was hungry again. And, and… He shook his head, trying to clear the rush of sensation. He pointed a finger at his boss, pleased when it didn't shake.

"I. Am. Not. Food."

CHAPTER TWELVE

⚜ ⚜ ⚜

SHOCK CAN ACT AS A balm, deadening the senses, protecting the heart. Mine still beat, slow, heavy with dread. "Pardon?"

"I'm not food."

Sara's words carried echoes of rage and fear, slicing through the layer of stupefaction. I stood in the doorway to the rear parlor, unsure if I should stand and fight, or flee.

All I am to you is food. Another voice, this one a memory brought up from the depths of my being. An occurrence I'd put behind me, a period in my life over which I refused to brood.

The sun slipped a filmy reflection under the overhanging porch, though outside the light would be bright as daggers. My nostrils flared. Sara smelled fresh and clean, spicy and furious.

I was nigh on desperate for a taste.

"I don't know what kind of game you're used to playing." Straightened to his full height, Sara commanded my attention. His underlying trepidation demanded it. "But I am not here to be your lunch."

Surprise faded, replaced by an agonizing frustration. His bravado appealed to me, while his fear entranced my predatory nature. All the while, the contrast between his dark hair and his warm brown skin and the faint salty scent of his sweat drove me near to distraction. After so many years of feminine companionship, his masculinity undid me.

My alternatives formed an elegant trap. All my choices led to death.

Matching his stance, I winced at the pull on the freshly healed skin on my back. He'd brought up unwelcome memories and now offered me a direct challenge. I could tell him, of course, explain the true nature of his commitment to me. An exercise in futility, as I had no intention of making him fulfill the role. "This subject is not open for discussion."

"What? Because I signed your damned contract, so I don't have any say?" Sara's outrage turned his eyes to obsidian and ignited the heat in my veins.

We had no time for an argument. I froze my feelings, locked them away. *You're always so cold, Thaddeus. Do you even care about me?* Another young man, one with white-gold hair, his eyes carrying a familiar pain. "Enough." Unsure of whom I was addressing, I kept my voice modulated and shoved down the apparition along with my memories. "There's no reason for you to be upset, Sara. I won't—"

"The hell you won't." Nohea surged between us, her fierceness breaking the link between our gazes.

Merde alors. "Nohea."

My attempt to censor her was wasted. She held up her palm, stopping me with a toss of her head. "I don't know what you're thinking, but we got to get this sorted out."

"No." I wrenched command away from her. "What we need to do is arrange a meeting with Brother George. He's been—"

"He sent a messenger." This time, Sara interrupted me.

"What?" I glared at him until it became apparent he wouldn't—or couldn't—speak while under my scrutiny. I crossed my arms and rolled my eyes up toward the ceiling.

"There was a text on your iPad last night, and today this kid came by..." He repeated the message, complete with the implied threat, *I'm praying for your soul.*

Sara finished his recitation with a shrug. "Does he always send juvenile delinquents around when he wants to talk to you?"

"No. We use Skype."

"Skype?" He blinked once, slowly, and rolled his head like he had a kink in his neck. "Of course you do."

His tone held enough mockery to raise my ire. I brought my hands together and pressed my fingertips to my chin, mimicking the act of prayer. "I will contact the Priory, if you will both change into…something more formal." I gave Nohea's garment—either a long shirt or a very short dress—and bare legs a hard stare.

They glanced at each other, and then at me. Neither responded, and I was struck by a twinge of something new. Jealousy. Their eyes had had a conversation I could not follow, their youth speaking a language my spirit couldn't translate. For the first time, I noticed music in the background, music they'd been sharing, played by an unfamiliar band.

"I assume you are well enough to see him tonight?" I directed the question to Nohea, though in reality I meant both of them.

Another glance. Another discussion that excluded me.

"Sure." Nohea nodded at Sara. "You want him to go too?"

"I don't want to leave him here." Unguarded. Unsafe. "We can arrange for an escort while you and I meet with George."

"It's okay. Seriously." Sara dropped onto one of the overstuffed couches, as if this exchange had drawn off all his energy. "I can just stay here." He patted the leather surface. "Me and the ghosts."

One ghost. *You've been closing me out for years, Thaddeus. I want someone I can grow old with.* I cleared my throat, willing the phantom away. His loss had left me broken, vulnerable to the entreaties of Brother George's predecessor. "Our ghosts will not protect you from a demon, Sara. We'll stay together until this situation is resolved."

"In more ways than one, *Mister* Dupont," Nohea snapped.

I bit down on an equally caustic response. "I'll contact the Priory and let you know what time we'll need to leave." With a final nod, I left them to their youth and their budding camaraderie. I left them to prepare myself for an audience with the good brother.

I left them to the ghosts.

AS A CHILD, I ATTENDED Mass with my family. Mother would march us up the front steps of the cypress church by the river. Our neighbors in the village felt obliged to ensure our compliance with this basic tenant of the faith. The habit became so ingrained, I believed the world would crash to a stop if Mother and Father had not led the five Dupont children up the center aisle every Sunday.

Attending a church in the next town over would have been unthinkable. The words, the rituals, the beliefs were the same, but we were raised with a vague suspicion *others* might pervert the perfection of the Mass. Even after one hundred years and countless hours spent in prayer, I still couldn't quite suppress a twinge of discomfort at trespassing on someone else's sacred space.

Nevertheless, I stifled my uneasiness and asked Sara and Nohea to prepare for an eleven o'clock meeting at St. Mary Assumption. Brother George would be attending Ordination, a long service saturated with tradition. He'd left instructions for our meeting, and I endeavored to communicate a sense of urgency to my companions. I did not want to be late.

I readied myself with a shower, clean clothing, a stiletto blade strapped to my thigh, and a second, shorter blade in my boot. The latter were likely unnecessary precautions; however, on reaching the dining room I saw I was not alone in my concerns. Nohea sat at the table, clad in skintight black clothing, her weapons hidden but a twenty-foot bullwhip hanging from a belt on her waist.

I frowned, unsure of how to approach my list of concerns. "We are meeting Brother George at a church."

Ignoring me, she wrapped a scarf over her dreadlocks. A lace veil would have been better, but at least she'd covered her head. Tucking the loose ends in, she deigned to acknowledge my comment. "And so?"

"You appear to be dressed for battle."

"It's all a battle until we figure out what the hell is going on."

She had a point, so in lieu of a lecture, I took advantage of an opportunity. "Before Sara comes down"—I paused, selecting my words carefully—"how did you fall afoul of the demons?"

Giving the scarf one final twist, she faced me with squared shoulders and a firm jaw. "Yeah, I should have said something sooner." Her gaze traveled to a spot above my head. "I was out in a club Saturday night." She bit down on her lower lip. "I saw a couple dudes, well, demons, sorta lurking."

"On Bourbon Street?" In response to her glare, I covered my mouth with my palm to stifle any further interruptions.

"Yeah, they came in about a half hour after me. I knew something was up, because the whole place felt funky." The heat in her gaze faded to embarrassment. "I shouldn't even have gone out. I should have just gone over to the River House to get things ready for Sara."

The name brought her to a stop. She crossed her arms, uncrossed them, and shook her head. "I am so sorry, Mr. Dupont. I seriously never realized Sarasija could be a guy's name, and my stupid mistake has put you in a shitty position."

I moved fast, too fast for her to protest, and put my hands

on her shoulders. She jerked away from my touch.

"I've known you since you were a child, Nohea Alves, and I believe in my soul you would not have done this deliberately." I let my hands drop but did not move away. She'd always been too hard on herself, and she had my forgiveness, whether she would accept it or not.

"Thank you." The words were grudging, loaded with disbelief. "Those demons were talking shit, you know? About all the ways they could hurt us." She gave an exaggerated shrug. "I only had a stiletto with me, so I told them to get the hell out." She coughed into her hand. "Then one of them pulled a gun. A gun, Thaddeus."

Lips pressed tight, she took a deep breath before continuing. "Before I knew it, they marched me out of there like some kind of dumbass kid. Said they'd shoot the place up if I didn't go with them."

"You have my deepest apologies, Nohea. Never should you have suffered in my service."

Her eyes grew glassy, and she rubbed them hard. "I knew what I was getting into. Who the hell gives a demon a gun anyway?"

We shared a moment, till the squeak of Sara's footsteps on the stairs caught my attention. "Would it be possible to, ah…" I gestured to her outfit, particularly the whip.

She huffed a laugh. "I guess so." On her way out the door, she passed Sara. "I'll be quick." She gave him a conspiratorial smile, distracting me with another sliver of envy.

Her departure left the two of us with an awkward silence.

"Here." I handed Sara the blade he'd brought to the cemetery.

He let it sit in the palm of his hand, brows drawn together. "I thought we were going to a church." His royal-blue short-sleeved shirt played up his coloring, and his jeans were disturbingly snug across his thighs. I might have objected to the denim, if not the fit, except his smile had an edge, as if a mistimed word would shatter him.

"Do I have to carry this?" He closed his fingers around the leather sheath.

"I hope not." I wondered how much else to say. The truth would have to suffice. "It's a ceremonial blade, and I keep it locked up in a safe."

The edge in his expression tightened. "But I found it in a drawer."

"I'd say it found you, sweetie." Nohea wore one of Mayette's old dresses on top of her black clothes, and she had looped the bullwhip around her waist as a belt. On Mayette, the flowered housedress had been cheerful; however, in the present context, the poppies splashed on white cotton bore a close resemblance to blood.

Clearing my throat, I stifled my thoughts. "The blade's virtue is its ability to sever the connection between a demon and its host."

Sara's dark eyes widened.

"I cannot account for how you came to find it, but please keep it now."

He hitched his shoulders and stuffed the blade into the pocket of his jeans. It was a small thing, but powerful, and as a last resort, it might just keep him safe.

And his safety had become very important to me.

"Would you like to drive, or shall I?" I asked Sara, using my most conciliatory tone.

His scowl didn't lighten at all. "I looked on a map. This place we're going is all of seven blocks away."

I won his incipient argument with a single word. "Demons."

"So we better just drive." Nohea patted him on the shoulder. "Though, meaning no disrespect, Mr. Dupont, you haven't driven the T-bird for what? Twenty years?" She headed for the kitchen door, where a stone path led to the driveway running along the side of the house. At the end of the drive was Mayette's 1979 baby-blue Thunderbird.

Sara stopped a few feet away. "Where'd you get that

antique?"

"My grandmother." With a huff, Nohea brushed past both of us. "Give me the damn keys."

"I'd prefer you had both hands free, Nohea." In case we needed to fight.

Nohea tossed Sara the keys to the Thunderbird. "You can drive the boat, then."

We parked the car on Josephine Street at eleven p.m. The streetlights were bright enough to hide the stars, though the moon had not yet risen. The air was dark and heavy, and men in clerical collars crowded the road.

"Are you guys going to tell me what's going on?" Sara turned the engine off, but none of us moved to leave the vehicle.

The Thunderbird's black interior held on to every particle of heat, baking us even with the windows open. "Sure," Nohea said.

I shot a glance over my shoulder, locking her in my gaze.

"Brother George says he has a project for us." My answer cut Nohea off before she could take the conversation in an undesirable direction. "Once we know more, we can come up with a plan." Both for the good brother's project and for the rest of our lives together.

After a period of general socializing, the good fathers and brothers cleared the street. A row of spotlights shone up the sides of St. Mary's Gothic brick façade, a wrought iron fence surrounding the church and its adjacent buildings. Our destination was the welcome center, a lower, more modern building next door to the church.

My phone chirped, our signal from Brother George. "Let us go." I climbed from the passenger seat, the others following my lead.

"Come here, Sara my love." Nohea's words were light, but her tone was deadly serious. She positioned Sara between us, walking just ahead of us both.

Sara snorted. "What, are you guys Mom and Dad?"

I didn't respond to his jibe.

The humid air carried the chemical smell of old pavement. We crossed Josephine Street and let ourselves in the gate. A novitiate waited for us, his white cassock flaring over the bulk of muscles across his shoulder. These young monks were taught to fight.

"Brother George is in room one-oh-four," he said.

"Fine. Will you be waiting out here?"

The novitiate nodded, fresh-faced and eager to please.

"This is my assistant, Sara. He'll wait in the lobby." I drilled the young man with the fullest extent of my will. "See that no one bothers him."

Sara could well refuse to wait for us in the lobby, but I had no better ideas. Leaving him with an admonition—both verbal and nonverbal—Nohea and I went in search of Brother George.

The lobby itself was a narrow space smelling of cleaning solvent, mildew, and humility. Room 104 would have held the same odor, if the sharp bite of an arctic freeze had allowed for any scent. The furnishings were simple: a desk, several folding chairs, and a grimacing Christ on a carved wooden cross on the wall.

The air conditioner rasped and wheezed, and Brother George peered out through the window's louvered blinds.

He turned, giving me an unpleasant smile. Another man sat in one of the gray padded folding chairs. He gave the impression of height and of power, and his frank curiosity held a great deal more sincerity than Brother George's grin.

His presence brought me to a halt.

"Thank you for joining us, Thaddeus, Nohea." Brother George took a seat behind the desk, his military precision at once threatening and reassuring in its normality. "Please sit."

I took one of the folding chairs, while Nohea chose to remain standing near the door. In the year we'd worked together, I'd had few opportunities to learn her patterns. Seeing her in her grandmother's dress brought that home. Mayette didn't fight. She would have taken a seat at my side and used her canny wit to press my advantage. Nohea had nerves of iron and a deft hand with the whip, and she'd asked me to leave her room to maneuver.

The presence of the other man heightened my tension. In all the years Brother George and I had worked together, this was the first time he'd brought in someone new.

"This is Father Patrick Kendall." Brother George gestured to the other man. "He's from the Dominican Provence house in California."

The man half rose, offering his hand. We shook, and Nohea waved from her position near the door. I hoped she was listening to ensure Sara's safety in the lobby.

"Father Pat is here because of some trouble they've been having in the Bay Area."

"There've been a series of incidents, and we believe the source is beyond human capability." His weathered voice matched the creases at the corners of his eyes, and his hair was long enough to brush the top of his collar.

"So, demons?"

Though I had no reason for my misgivings, I didn't quite trust his affable nod.

"Exactly," he said.

My eyes narrowed. Evil events in California, no matter how heinous, were not my direct concern. *Unless Brother George had other ideas.* Regardless, I stayed silent, allowing them to bring the problem to me.

"We have reason to suspect a single entity is behind it all," Father Patrick continued. "And there's a suggestion this entity has moved its operation in this direction."

Brother George jumped in with a single tap of his blunt index finger. "We have seen an increase in fiendish activity of late." He tipped his head in the direction of the doorway. "Miss Alves's difficulties being the most flagrant example."

"If you have any more information on her situation, please tell us." I spoke through gritted teeth. "I intend to exact some measure of revenge."

"No, Thaddeus," Nohea murmured.

Yes. I shot her a quelling glance, and returned my attention to the priest. "So you think we should prepare ourselves for some kind of reign of terror because a malignant entity has taken up residence here in New Orleans."

"A malignant entity or their representative," Father Pat said. Brother George's lips thinned, and he glared at the other cleric.

Father Pat was either oblivious or he possessed affability of steel, because without a pause he continued, "We haven't worked out all the details, but I guess that's really your job, anyway. Figure out what's going on and then make it stop."

CHAPTER THIRTEEN

SARA SNUCK A LOOK AT Dupont, checked the list on his screen, and tried to stop drumming his fingers against his thigh.

Did he have the nerve to ask?

They were in the den. Sara sprawled across the couch with his laptop, and Nohea slumped in an overstuffed chair with her feet propped on the coffee table while she read something on her tablet. Dupont sat in a wingback chair, well away from the window where a glow of late summer sun still illuminated the wall above the heavy curtains. He held a copy of something called *Uniformity with God's Will* in actual paper book form. Maybe God's will didn't include slouching, because Dupont's posture remained perfect as he read. Still, the vampire was the closest to relaxed Sara had seen him. He might not get a better chance.

Sara glanced at the list again. The day after the meeting with the monks, he had been jumpy as all hell expecting demons around every corner. Three days later, with no demon attack and everyone confined to the house to appease Dupont's paranoia, tension had given way to boredom. Also, he was tired of being the only one who didn't know stuff. The internet was crap for vampire research. If he didn't ask, how would he ever learn?

"Umm, Mr. Dupont?"

Dupont didn't look up. "Yes?"

"Can you, like, turn into a bat?"

"*Quoi?*" The book jerked so violently, Dupont almost dropped it. He turned a shocked face to Sara. "I'm sorry, what did you…"

"Can you turn into a bat?"

"No." Dupont lowered his eyes back to his book.

"So, not smoke or a wolf either?"

Dupont placed a ribbon between the pages and set the book on the table next to him before turning to Sara. "Not smoke, nor a wolf," he agreed mildly. "Why do you ask, please?"

Sara almost couldn't answer because, Dupont… Dupont's eyes were dancing and a little smiled played around the corners of his mouth. And, God, Sara had never appreciated how tense his boss normally looked until now.

"I want to know about vampires," he managed. "And you're the only one I have to ask."

"Can you not consult your—" Dupont made a vague gesture toward Sara's laptop.

"Well, yeah. But there's more stuff than I could read in a lifetime and no way to tell what's real and what's bogus."

"Very well." Dupont settled back in his chair and met Sara's gaze over his steepled fingers. "What do you wish to know?"

Sara blinked at him, at a loss, then remembered he had a list. He scanned it, wondering what to ask next. His eye fell on the perfect question. No bat, wolf, or smoke. He schooled his face.

"Mr. Dupont, can you fly?"

Sara bet he couldn't, but flying was the most outrageous thing left. The thing most likely to provoke a response.

His reward was a deepening of the grooves around Dupont's mouth and the appearance of tiny, unexpected laugh lines at the corners of his eyes. Sara held his breath, waiting for an actual grin. Dupont's self-control won out.

"I must confess," he said gravely, "I have not tried."

"Perhaps, in the interest of science, one night you could…?" Sara let the sentence hang.

"*Naturellement.* We must try at once. What greater good could my ancient bones serve than the advancement of human understanding?"

Dupont's expression had smoothed out to absolute deadpan. Sara gaped at him. He was kidding, right?

Dupont stared back, an expression of mild interest on his face. "The roof would be high enough, perhaps? As soon as it is full dark?"

"Uh." Dupont wasn't *serious,* was he? What the hell had he started?

A thunk to his right distracted him. He glanced over at Nohea.

She had dropped her tablet and was biting her lip so hard, he expected to see blood. When she noticed him looking, she lost it and dissolved into giggles. She pointed at Sara. "Your face."

He glared at her.

She kept laughing. "Oh, that was priceless, Thaddeus. *The roof.*"

Sara jerked around to Dupont and…there it was. A real smile.

His heart stopped. He met Dupont's eyes, still framed by those tiny crinkles at the corners. One heartbeat. Another. Somehow, his heart beat differently, faster or slower or more wondrous. More exhilarating. More terrifying.

"The roof?" He tried to glare at Dupont too, but his mouth insisted on curving up at the corners.

"Perhaps not," Dupont said. "I am sorry, I should not have teased you. You could not know."

"I'll let it slide, this time."

"It is natural for you to be curious," Dupont said. "If you have other questions, I will endeavor to answer."

Sweet. "Um, okay. Well, you have crucifixes in every room out in the cabin, and we were in a church the other day. Aren't crosses supposed to burn you or something?"

"They do not." Dupont's tone turned serious. "It is a good question. Holy water does not harm me either. It is one of the reasons I hold hope for my immortal soul."

"That's good, then, right?" He didn't follow up the immortal soul reference. Catholic stuff. Google would be sufficient for research on one of the world's major religions.

"So, we don't have to worry about crosses or holy water. Is there anything that does hurt you?"

He looked up when Dupont didn't answer right away. Oh. Crap. Maybe he had been insensitive. "Never mind," he said hastily. "You don't have to answer anything you don't want to."

"Silver." Dupont sat very still, not giving anything away. Except how to hurt him. "Silver burns if it touches my skin, and it saps my strength even in close proximity. The wounds are slow to heal."

"Right." Sara tried to keep his voice matter-of-fact while he processed how much trust his boss had just shown him. "No silver. Thank you, Mr. Dupont. That's important to know."

He had a million questions, but Dupont had withdrawn subtly after the silver revelation. The goal was information, not making Dupont feel like a freak. Catching another glimpse of his tentative smile suddenly became way more important than finding out how new vampires were made.

Sara was checking his list for something innocuous, when Dupont cocked his head to one side. "Excuse me. Brother George summons. We can continue when I return."

"Did you hear anything?" he asked Nohea after Dupont left.

"You can mark vampire super-hearing down as real. If his iPad is on, he'll hear it even on the other side of the house."

"Oh, hey, you could answer some of these questions."

And he could avoid putting Dupont on the spot again.

Nohea snickered. "Want to know if I turn into a bat?"

"It was a legitimate question."

"Are you high? How would that work?"

"How do vampires work?" he countered.

"Huh. You got me there."

"So, you ever see him suck anyone dry?"

"No! God, you're bloodthirsty. He's careful. He wouldn't hurt anyone."

"I've seen him drain two demons, which is almost the same."

"No, it isn't. I've never even seen him make a living person woozy. You see how he is. You think he's not in complete control when he eats?" The words were confident, but she stopped abruptly after the last sentence and made a show of turning her tablet on.

Sara watched her poke at it while he considered her words. "How do you know? I mean, maybe he's whammied you to forget."

"Doubtful. He doesn't mess with my memory. It was one of the things Gran insisted on. She said if we were going to look after him year after year, we had to know what was going on, and we had to trust each other. She said sometimes there would be things we didn't *want* to remember, but those would be the memories we needed the most."

"Yeah, but if he did whammy you, you wouldn't know, would you?" He had somehow gotten stuck on this line of reasoning. And he had started keeping a log of what he was doing every hour. Mostly nothing, an entirely different problem than why he was keeping track. So far, he hadn't found any missing time.

"Well, he said he wouldn't, so I guess I trust him." She gave him a sharp look. "If he told you he won't, he won't. He's… I give him a hard time, but he's not bad. He didn't ask for this either. He's doing the best he can."

"Feels like he's always in my head."

"The calling and stuff? I think he forgets he's doing it half the time. The accidental pushes, too. He's not wiping memories, though. I mean, think about it. If he were wiping, you wouldn't know he had done any of that shit."

"I guess." He wasn't just worried about the calling. Dupont had become a nightly costar in his dreams, and they were the type of dreams that made *his dreams* and *shared with Dupont* an important distinction. "I'm tired of not knowing if I'm hungry or he is."

"Wait? Say what now?" Nohea put the tablet down.

"Ever since he did the thing with the blood, it's like we've got an open connection. Sometimes I can't figure out what's me and what's him."

"You're telling me you can read Thaddeus?" He had Nohea's full attention, and she looked pissed. "How much blood has he been giving you?"

"None. Well, only the once. Just a tiny bit the night we went to get you at the cemetery. He said it would let him know if I was in trouble. Shouldn't it have worn off or something? It's not permanent, is it?"

Nohea stared at him until he started to get worried.

"What? What did he do to me? Am I stuck like this?"

"Hell if I know. The better question might be what did you do to him? I'm pretty much an expert on the effects of vampire blood, and I've never heard of what you're describing. What he has with me is a one-way street for the most part. Unless he's pushing, I don't get more than maybe knowing what direction to look for him. I sure as fuck don't get our emotions confused. Are you sure it isn't your imagination?"

"No," he whispered. Because he wasn't *completely* sure. Except he mostly was.

"Maybe don't take any more blood until you figure it out," Nohea advised.

No shit.

He could feel Dupont upstairs right now. And he almost always knew when he woke up in the afternoon. First there would be the barest spark of awareness buried somewhere deeper than his physical senses. It would grow almost imperceptibly, surfacing until it became a concrete buzz. By the time Dupont came truly awake, Sara would be so accustomed to the extra sensation, he could almost forget about it.

Which reminded him… "It's still light when he wakes up. Shouldn't he sleep until sunset?"

"He's always up before Vespers, and don't ask me why. It's just the way he's programmed. It'll take more than death to keep him from chanting Lauds, Vespers, and Compline every night."

More Catholic words. Sara made a mental note to look them up. Catholic rituals would be a concrete line of inquiry—better than this random-questions method. He figured he should get as many answers as possible, though. If self-Renfield training was what it took to be a full member of this team, he intended to ace the course.

Nohea didn't seem enthusiastic, but kept answering as he went down his list.

Yes, he could cross running water. No, he didn't have to sleep with dirt from his grave. No, he didn't *have* a grave. Garlic, surprisingly, was a real thing and made him break out in hives.

He was getting to more and more obscure vampire lore when he realized he hadn't followed up on something more pressing.

"You never explained why it's a problem I'm a guy."

"Gay vampire," Nohea said, as though she had explained something.

"Yeah. So?"

Nohea started laughing. "Honey, it's the one damn question you haven't asked. *That* part is true."

"I still don't get it. Girls taste better? If he's gay, he wasn't screwing them or anything, so what's the deal?"

"Sara, he's a monk, right? A *Catholic monk.* And, let's just say, eating is…a very physical experience."

It seemed as though he was still missing something. "Did the girls mind? Before he, you know, made them forget?"

"No. No, they did *not* mind. Jeez, haven't you watched *any* vampire movies?" Nohea threw her head back and moaned. "Oh, *oh, Thaddeus.*"

"Nohea." The voice from behind him didn't sound pleased.

Shit. How had he missed Dupont coming down again? You'd think whatever connection they shared would kick in a few times when it was useful instead of just when it was annoying and embarrassing.

He turned around to face Dupont, who stood in the doorway, looking about as comfortable as you might expect for a hundred-year-old monk who had just watched his coworker fake an orgasm.

"The act is…" Dupont looked completely flustered. "I take every precaution. I hold them in the highest regard for their sacrifice. I don't defile their bodies in any other way. And they don't remember it later."

"Yeah, but…" How did he even address this? "They don't remember it? Dude, that's *worse.*"

Dupont's face closed down, and he did his Very Still thing. "I must eat. Unless you prefer I die. I have considered the option, but in my condition, I do not know if self-termination would be considered an act of sacrifice or a mortal sin. Despite the peccancy of my nature, I still hold hope for my immortal soul."

Sara blinked. Mortal sin? What was this bullshit?

"Okay, so you have to eat. Ever consider finding some willing food?"

"What do you recommend I do? Place an ad in the *Picayune*? Or maybe just ask politely? Please, Sara, will you offer me your life's blood?"

Dupont had closed down his emotions. At *life's blood*, the dam burst, and a flood of, hunger and…*longing?*…hit Sara. And his own response… *Thaddeus.* "I…" He stopped, swallowed. Because he had almost said yes. *Yes, if you ask I will provide.* Were those his thoughts? Or just a new kind of vampire seduction?

"It can't be hard," he said instead. "Why don't you go to one of those vampire clubs?"

"*Qu'est-ce que c'est?*"

"Vampires are hot, Mr. Dupont. There are whole clubs who cater to vampire groupies. They're packed with a bunch of Goths and emos pretending to be vampires. I think some of them even bite each other and drink blood and stuff. You could blend in, find a willing donor, and no one would ever even know you were the real deal. They'd be into the, umm, side effects of feeding, too."

"Disgusting." Dupont looked shocked. "It is not a condition to be envied. No, I will not participate in such perversion."

"Well, I guess we're back to square one, then."

"Have *you* attended one of these clubs?"

Dupont looked so disapproving, worse than at Lafitte's Booty. Sara wanted to say yes out of perversity. Vampire clubs were probably full of people who were looking for meaning and human connection, just like everyone else.

"I'm not into biting and blood," he said instead. Except around Dupont… *Thaddeus.* Nohea's act replayed in his head. Her carnal tone, the thought of Dupont's mouth on his neck, and his own dreams mingled to produce a reaction far from revulsion.

Dupont, already a statue, seemed to stop breathing at his words. And he looked pale, almost as pale as he had out at the cabin before he had fed on the first demon. He was hungry, Sara realized. And, according to Nohea, he hadn't chosen this path.

"I don't want you to die." *I want you to smile again.* Looking at Dupont now, he almost doubted his face was capable of such an expression. "We'll find a way."

"I had a way. The monks have prayed upon it and decreed our previous method is the best solution. But you are here now, which makes the situation complicated. I will try to find an alternative. If I cannot, you have my word I will not force myself upon you."

"And my memories?"

"As safe as your body."

Sara narrowed his eyes at the wording. Before he could challenge Dupont further, Nohea broke in.

"Guys, we have demon activity."

"Where?" Dupont demanded.

"About time," Sara said.

Nohea checked her phone again. "Frenchmen Street. The monks aren't sure what happened. There's lots of sirens and smoke, and they want you to check it out."

Sara patted his pockets. "Let me get my keys."

"Wait." The command in Dupont's tone brought Sara and Nohea to a halt.

They both glared at him.

"I will go alone. Sara, you will stay in the house. Nohea, you will stay here and make sure he is safe."

"Why do I have to stay here?" *Seriously?* Days of waiting, and now something was going down, and he was still confined to the house?

"Thaddeus, are you sure?" Nohea reasoned.

"Yes. If this event is related to the others, they have discovered my greatest weakness. I will not allow them to harm my people. They have already taken you, despite your skills, and Sara would be no match for them."

"Hey," he protested. "I did okay in the cemetery." After he had gotten captured. "I got away. And I stabbed one of them. *And* I'm not *yours*. I'm my own person. I get to decide things for myself."

"You will be safer here," Dupont insisted.

When he started to argue more, Dupont turned the full force of his gaze on him. "We will not discuss this." Dupont's voice did the thing where it sounded like someone had turned up the reverb. His eyes flashed lightning and the pupils expanded until Sara felt himself falling into the storm. "You will both stay in this house until I return."

Sara found himself unmotivated to move until the door slammed behind Dupont.

"Manipulative asswipe." He turned to Nohea, who looked stunned herself. "You can't tell me that was an accidental push."

O CLEMENS, O PIA, O DULCIS *virgo Maria.* The closing phrases of the Salve Regina floated like ribbons through the blackness of my mind. I blew along St. Charles Avenue, keeping under the cover of trees where possible, slowing to human speeds on blocks where the sidewalks were open to view. The air was dense with humidity, traffic was sparse, and in moments, I crossed under the Pontchartrain Expressway. I entered the stretch of office buildings and businesses separating the Garden District from the French Quarter.

I was not weary. My hungers were controlled. Three nights closed in with Sara's brilliant curiosity and need and Nohea's insistence that I *do* something had worn away my patience. Hiring a cab might have endorsed the illusion of my humanity, but I'd inhabited this body for over one hundred years, long enough to recognize when even my exquisite self-control needed a release.

So I wrapped myself in shadows, and I ran.

Closer to the Quarter, the street narrowed, and I slowed my pace. The streets were crowded from some music festival or other, though the endless party atmosphere had transformed into something tense and brittle. People walked quickly, their heads down, or they stood talking in small groups, soon breaking apart and streaming on. I crossed Canal Street, walking even slower, allowing myself to hear what the humans were saying.

Frenchmen Street…bomb…Frenchmen…Washington Park… blood…police…Frenchmen…dead.

I headed for the river, to Decatur Street. The closer I got to the location of the attack, the crowds thinned, as if the great wave of escape had already crested and only the stragglers remained. *Frenchmen…blood…killed.* They did not hinder my progress, these shameless individuals who had come to indulge in humanity's oldest vices. Instead, they'd witnessed one of its oldest evils.

Merde.

Two blocks away, the fiery flash of an emergency vehicle's lights bounced off some of the city's most famous jazz clubs. Yellow tape had been strung across the entire street. Still wrapped in shadow, I hurdled the tape, my hunter's instincts engaged. This calamity had to be a piece of the puzzle Brother George had set me to solve. I wanted—no, needed—to find the cause. As yet, I could not find a link between the events in California, Nohea's capture, and the scream of sirens on Frenchmen Street, but I would.

I would.

A pair of policemen strode down the center of Frenchmen Street, causing me to duck into the entryway of a café. They both wore short-sleeved black uniforms, and they both had the overdeveloped musculature that suggested too much time in the gym. I ignored them, my attention diverted by the turbulent activity a block away.

Not until the policemen had almost reached the café doorway did I see the utter blackness of their eyes. *Demons.* Surprise gave way to a burning need to fight, couched in a sense of rightness. Their presence confirmed my hunch. I held off from an immediate attack, hoping they would give away information I could use.

That pause proved to be my undoing. They separated, one heading to my right, the other to my left. I lunged to avoid being trapped in the doorway. Something pulled me up short. They'd carried a chain between them, links of silver preventing my escape. They wrapped the restraint around me and drew it tight.

"Leave off," I snarled, endeavoring to put up resistance despite the drain on my energies. They each grabbed one of my elbows and propelled me forward, the silver making it difficult to resist.

"Too bad, old man," one of the demon cops mumbled. "Come along quietly and no one will get hurt."

I flexed my shoulders, testing the strength of the chain that ran like a band of fire around my body. Since they hadn't killed me outright, I allowed them to drag me away, waiting for an opportunity to escape.

They led me to the French Market and found an unlocked door, further evidence they'd planned ahead. Long and narrow, the Market took up two city blocks. At this time of day, the building was deserted, the rows of merchandise tables covered with gray drapes. The walls could be opened, and a large skylight ran down the center of the tall wooden ceiling. Even if every window had been opened, the place wouldn't be free of the stench of human effluvia coming up from the river.

They marched me up the center of the main aisle, stopping abruptly enough to make me stumble.

Neither of them said anything, though the one on my right tightened his grasp on my elbow till his nails broke the skin. Frustration warred with a persistent curiosity. Their intent could not have been to kill me or I'd already be dead.

Standing still for half a dozen heartbeats, I sensed another presence, one marked by a foul smell stronger than the river and more powerful than the demons flanking me. Unseen hands touched my shoulders, setting off a surge of revulsion. The man—person—being—wrapped his arms around my body. "Ah, damn, I've waited so long for this."

His grip tightened painfully; his fingers clawing at the fabric of my shirt. I tried to turn my head but one of the cops brought out a knife and held it to my throat.

"Let's behave now." The evil permeating the voice distorted the sound. "Wouldn't want you to suffer any permanent damage, Brother Thad-dee-us."

Surprise held me still, heart beating fast. He sang the vowels of my name, though he should never have known it. I tested the air, and under the appalling stink of demon I found a trace of earthier things. Blood. Sweat. Piss. This person behind me was human.

"Bad scene over by the park, you know? There's at least four ambulances," the man continued. "Couple of fire trucks, at least a dozen cop cars." He rubbed his hands over my chest. "And all for you. You're warmer than I thought you'd be. You know that?"

How did he know my name, my nature? I flinched, and the demons on either side of me tightened their grip. They had me at a disadvantage, so I would play for time. "I'm flattered you would think so."

"Oh, I know so." His nails raked my skin. "I believe some friends of mine gave you an invitation, didn't they?"

The foul smell roiled in my gut. "What do you mean? Who are you?"

"Stop living like a damned hound and come join us."

"I'm afraid I must decline." My voice remained well modulated, despite my fear.

A siren tore across the heavy night air. He released me, leaving a tainted shadow wherever he touched. "Your call. See, we set a bomb off tonight, and while there's a bunch of blood and some people who're definitely going to need to be stitched up, nobody died." One of the cops growled, as if they'd been disappointed with this outcome.

"Won't be able to say that again. And from now on, every time somebody dies in this town, you'll have to wonder if it was because of you." The unseen voice retreated. "Last chance, Thaddeus. Whaddaya say?"

Loading the words with all the command at my disposal, I asked him again, "Who are you?"

"Come on, now. You can do better than that." He took a few more steps, his feet shuffling over the concrete floor. "Your hoodoo don't mean shit to me." His unhinged vibrato trailed over the places he'd touched. "Gentlemen, bind his hands and leave him. Oh, and don't forget the lasso. We'll need it again."

The cops did as he asked, forcing my hands to the small of my back and pinning them with a tight band of plastic. I fought them with as much strength as I could muster, anger locking my hands into fists. This person had treated me like a pawn in a game. That alone should have filled me with fear. Instead, rage burned in my belly, bright and hot and fierce. I would not join in a covenant with evil, even if he should make good on his threat.

Doubt slithered beneath my declaration. *No one should have to die because of me.*

The demon policemen loosened the chain. I whirled toward the one on my right, giving the other one a chance to slam me from behind. Without my hands to break my fall, I landed hard, my temple taking the impact. By the time I recovered from the dizziness, they were gone, all three of them, the pungent odor blown away by the breeze off the Mississippi River.

Struggling to my knees, I took a moment to mentally flagellate myself. So arrogant. So stupid. Bitterness swelled with each passing thought. How had I let myself get caught?

I had fought demons for years, decades even. Most were easily overcome, the bodies they possessed limited to human strength and quickness. A few had injured me, whether through luck or, in rare instances, coordinated effort.

Never had they caught me off guard, and never had they

shamed me. I had spent too much time in contemplation and too little in preparation.

I would change.

With my vow in mind, I struggled to my feet. The strap around my wrist held firm despite my efforts to break it. Rather than remain exposed in the center of the room, I ducked between the tables to reach the far wall. Outside, the shouts and wailing sirens continued, though I judged there was no one nearby. And though I had a few hours till sunrise, the hint of light in the east tightened my tension.

I found a door I could not open. My numb fingers could not grasp the handle. There. The final degradation. The human in me longed to sink down and offer the Lord a prayer for salvation.

The monster inside preferred to tear the limbs off the first fiend I crossed.

Even if I could force the door open, what then? Run home with my hands bound? I strained against the strap, forcing my fisted knuckles together to gain leverage. I took a deep breath, and another. Then, filling my lungs with air, I jerked my arms apart with every bit of strength I could muster.

I succeeded only in sending trickles of blood down my fingers.

Dawn crept closer. I forced aside the panic, wrapping myself in the words of this evening's psalm. *Unto thee lift I up mine eyes, O thou that dwellest in the heavens.* If the monster was too weak, maybe the monk could find a way.

Despite the tightness of the band, I allowed my fingers to relax, sliding my palms together. The blood made a lubricant, and while the psalm's antiphon repeated in my mind, the ball of my left thumb slid free of the band. Still attending to the ancient words, I brought my thumb and fifth finger together, and slowly worked my hand out of the restraint.

Amen.

Barring any further obstacles, I had time to reach my First Street house. Not running this time, but walking. Taking the time to identify possible safe hiding places, if I should need to avoid the sun, and to contemplate an opponent who had the power to call up demons and bend them to his will.

I continued my deliberations all the way to the house, stopping when I reached the second-floor landing. A muffled thump from the direction of Sara's room brought me to a quick stop, sending a flash of tension through my gut. A well-modulated voice through the door. Short, punchy phrases.

"Draw. Move. Slice."

Being accosted by a stranger at the scene of a bomb blast had disturbed me. Knowing Sara might be hurt filled me with terror. I had the door open before my mind formulated a plan, and well before my eyes could take in the scene.

Sara, stripped to the waist, his tawny brown skin damp with sweat, dark hair scattered over his chest. He clutched a blade in his right hand. His laptop sat open on the desk. His cheeks flamed, though I could not be sure whether the cause was embarrassment or exertion.

"Mr. Dupont!"

His voice cracked like an adolescent boy's, and I struggled to make sense of things through a sea swell of relief.

"Mon Dieu." I made to close the door.

"It's okay." He took a step in my direction. "I was just, um…" He glanced at the knife. "Practicing."

I must have looked perplexed, because he continued without waiting for my response.

"YouTube." His confident nod at the laptop distracted me more than the computer screen. "Watching videos on how to fight with a knife." He tipped his head, staring up at me from under his bangs.

Relief allowed me to bark a laugh, though the flash of

emotion across his face stifled me. I had not intended to embarrass him. "Well." I wiped away my smile with an open palm. "I could perhaps"—I stopped, cleared my throat—"help you."

"No, you don't—"

"*Bien sur. Ici.*" I pointed across the room. "Show me what you have learned."

"Come at me."

I raised my arm in a mock-aggressive stance and lunged toward him.

"Like this." With faltering steps, he avoided my thrust, slashing at my forearm. "And like this."

If he had connected, he might well have succeeded in disarming me. "Good." I gave him a look of encouragement. "Now, again."

I struck, he swiped, I grabbed, he spun, and despite my intentions, he ended up pressed against me, his back to my front. His warm, salty, bare skin just inches from my lips. He stiffened. I froze.

Lord, I am not worthy…

I lurched away. "*Pardonnez moi.*"

To his credit, Sara laughed. He flipped the knife on the bed and followed it, lying propped on his elbows, knees spread wide enough to be an invitation. "Whatever, Mr. Dupont. I can keep going with YouTube."

My cheeks felt uncharacteristically hot, and my heart, which had held steady throughout the night, now raced like a rabbit eluding a fox. "Nohea possesses the skills you need." My voice broke on the word *need*. *Gah*. Seventy or eighty years had passed since I last felt so flustered.

"Sure." Sara's chuckle faded. "I'll ask Nohea."

"She is very well trained." I wanted to leave before I could do any more damage.

Sara stopped me. "So did you find the demon activity?"

I paused with my hand on the door frame. "After a fashion." I found myself relaying much of the event: the bomb, the scene in the market, and the offer. I left out the threat.

"You mean you think some ordinary guy is working with the demons?" Sara sat straighter, reaching for his laptop. "I don't know why I think that sounds so crazy. I mean, a week ago I didn't know vampires existed."

He'd adapted to my life with gratifying speed, and admiration layered over the thicket of emotions he brought out in me.

His eyes narrowed. "Keep your thoughts to yourself, dude, unless you want to come over here and show me some real appreciation."

How did he do this? At times his accurate guesses came dangerously close to reading my mind. Even though he had his laptop in his lap, I knew good and well where he'd have me begin. "Again, pardon me." I took a step into the hall, for the first time wondering whether I'd be able to resist him if he made a deliberate play for my attentions. "It's time for Lauds, and then I'll contemplate ways of finding a human with enough power to control demons."

"Wait." Sara fiddled with his computer. "How do you get a demon to appear?"

"To control a demon, a man must be bold, intelligent, and spiritually powerful." I sniffed, remembering the stink from the market. It smelled like shame. "The man I met tonight might be in league with the one we're after, though it would take someone like Father Patrick to have the necessary skills."

"Did you just accuse a priest of calling up demons?"

I laughed at his incredulous expression. "Maybe."

"You're killing me." Sara shook his head. "I meant to ask whether it takes eye of newt or something, because we should maybe start with places you can buy supplies, you know?"

"I suppose. Nohea is more likely to know the details than I am."

"There's always the internet, too. I'll dig around a little and make a list while you chant, then email it to you. What's your email address?"

I gave it to him, and he laughed again. "AOL? Who the hell still uses AOL?"

And with that, I took my leave, curious what this bright, charismatic young man would come up with next.

The hunger outweighed my desire for him by only a feather.

CHAPTER FOURTEEN

THE ALLIANCE BETWEEN MY TWO associates could yet be our undoing. Nohea's contact at the Priory had notified her of possible irregularities at an abandoned hospital, irregularities that stank of demon. They'd called despite no real evidence, a clear indication of how nervous the current situation made the White Monks.

Sara and Nohea used the insubstantial nature of the suspicions to coerce me into allowing them both to come. They argued I should not have to face another fight alone, and while I disagreed in principle, I yielded to their demand. Nohea might have felt the need to make up for what she saw as her own errors, and Sara? Well, I'd seen his bravery, and since the report suggested New Orleans' finest surrounded the building, in all likelihood the area would be free of anything truly dangerous.

Now the three of us hunkered down in the parking structure on Tulane Street. Inside the old Charity Hospital, we hoped to find something to explain how someone had raised such a powerful evil. They spoke in muted whispers, while I pondered how I would ensure everyone's survival.

For although I understood the importance of finding the source of the current tumult, my own program had expanded to include the safety of both Nohea and Sara.

Light flooded the lowest floor of the abandoned hospital, and black-garbed policemen created silhouettes in the glare. The monolithic structure had been deserted since Hurricane Katrina, and according to Nohea's contact, some manner of devilry had taken up residence.

"Somebody reported a light in the window about eight floors up," Nohea said. "No one's supposed to be in there at all. Shouldn't even be power to the building."

I overheard her quiet comment without difficulty. Two single-story structures flanked the hospital's front entrance, surrounded by chain-link fencing and palm trees.

"There are too many cops for a damned light, and if the power was off, it's back on now." Sara reached into his pocket, likely for the blade he still carried. "Does anyone else think trying to get in there is crazy?"

"Maybe." Nohea's tone did not lend itself to further questions. "There must be something more serious going on."

"We need to find out if there are demons involved," I murmured.

And if they were. If they were…

While still a student at St. Joseph Abbey, I'd been transfixed by the case of the Axeman, a fiend who murdered numerous people in their beds. Later, when I was a young vampire sworn to assist the Church, the brothers encouraged me to study the Axeman's crimes. The creature had gone so far as to write a letter to the newspapers, identifying himself as a demon and promising he'd never be caught.

Fortunately, his boast proved inaccurate. He'd been brought down by the predecessors to Brother George and his associates, and the benighted man who'd called the thing from hell had not survived. The story of the Axeman had involved one man and one demon. If this old building truly housed a being with the power to call up multiple demons, one who was willing to do so in public, all the police armor in the city would be worthless.

Nohea glanced at me over her shoulder, trembling with

a fierce energy. "What's really going on in there? Looks like they're searching floor by floor."

Rows of windows covered the building's façade. A light flashed a level above the floodlights' glare. "We'll avoid them." I scanned the hospital's roofline through the garage's open window, shades of dark on black. "If there are demons present, we need to find them before the policemen do. Coming down from the top would improve our chances."

"Gramma never told me you could fly."

I didn't reward her sarcasm with a reaction. The U-shaped building took up most of a city block. The grounds were cordoned off with chain-link fence, and the windows were many and regularly spaced. "The spotlights are focused on the lower floors. If we could get above them, we stand a chance of avoiding attention while we search for any danger. You've trained in climbing, *ne c'est pas?*"

"*Bien sûr.*" Nohea's tone was boastful.

"And you, Sara?"

Strands of dark hair fell across his forehead. "Did you just ask me if I could fly?" His glare was nearly as hot as Nohea's, though his eyes held a note of embarrassment.

"Of course," I murmured. "There must be a rear entrance. Let us go, then. Stay close." I could not fly, nor could I carry a grown man up the side of a building. At best, I could cast a subtle shadow and control the minds of most men. Those skills would have to be enough to conceal us. The old hospital was enormous. Surely we could avoid discovery.

To have any chance of preventing further carnage, we'd have to try.

There was more activity at the Route 10 end of the building, so we headed the other way. We paralleled the chain-link fence, walking single file, avoiding a pair of policemen with a quick dodge into a cluster of palm trees. They slowed, stared hard long enough to raise my stuttering heartbeat, and kept moving.

"How many cops are there altogether, do you think?" Nohea made no more noise than a phantom.

I touched her elbow, nodding at the corner of the building where the shadows seemed the thickest. "Hard to say. There's a door."

Traversing the yard made us vulnerable, though we moved quickly and kept to the shadows. Our destination: a pair of wide glass doors, marked with the red light. Emergency. Sara stepped up to the glass. The doors didn't move.

"Damn," he whispered.

"Didn't bring my lock picks, boss." Nohea rested a hand on the coiled whip hanging from her hip. "How do we get it open?"

Before I could respond, a harsh light flared behind us. "Police. Don't move."

Merde alors. No amount of shadow would conceal the three of us from the glare.

"Go, Thaddeus," Nohea said. I ignored her command. I couldn't hide us all, but I could influence the policeman who approached.

"I'll get him to open the door, and on my signal, you two head into the building. Try to get up higher than the light, and I'll join you." I glanced from Nohea to Sara. Her faint nod, almost a twitch, confirmed her understanding.

The black-clad figure strode forward, his gun drawn. I positioned myself in front of our merry band. Sweat ran between my shoulder blades, a disconcerting reminder of my own weakness.

"Y'all can't be poking around out here." His voice carried a West Texas twang.

"Pardon. If you could lower the light, I'm sure I can explain our situation." Layering my tone with command, I gazed directly at the policemen. "We don't mean to cause trouble."

He did as I asked. "Go on now, get out of here, or we'll have to arrest you."

As soon as I could look into his eyes, I caught hold of his spirit. "Open the door for us, *s'il vous plais*."

My target's eyes widened, a bare flinch. "Okay." He took a couple steps in our direction. Behind me, Sara gave a sharp intake of breath.

"Do it now," I said, exerting even more influence. We had no time to deal with doubt.

The Texan walked over to a touch pad beside the entrance. He keyed in a combination, and the doors slid open. "Just lucky they haven't changed the code."

"*Merci.*" I raised a hand, and with a gentle wave of my fingers, I wiped the memory of our encounter from his mind.

We stepped through the doorway. About eight feet back, a second set of sliding doors slid open, cued by our motion.

To the right was darkness. To our left, a dim red light spelled out the word Exit. Sara pointed in that direction. "Bet those are stairs."

"Be easier to find a damned elevator," Nohea grumbled.

Sara took a tentative step forward. "We'd cover more ground if we separated."

"No." My response was immediate and absolute.

Nohea nodded, her mouth tight. "Be reasonable, Thaddeus. This is a big-ass building." She brought out a small penlight. "Let me and Sara take this flight of stairs, and you go on down the hall with your X-ray vision and find another way up."

Sara headed for the exit sign. "We'll be fine, Mr. Dupont. We'll stop on every floor and see if there's anything, you know, weird."

I could have insisted he take some of my blood so I would sense his danger. The grim line of his jaw kept me quiet.

"If you don't hear us scream, we'll rendezvous on the top floor." Nohea spoke with such absolute confidence, I couldn't undermine her faith with my protest. Against my better judgment, they headed up the stairs, while I went in search of another route.

I found a hallway branching off from the main entrance, and several hundred feet down, a dim red bulb marked another stairwell. The approach of a team of policemen made my decision easy. They entered the stairs behind me, so I made haste, and soon their heavy breathing faded.

On the fourth floor, voices came at me from above. Reinforcements. I slowed my pace. I could stay still, gathering shadows to conceal my presence. I could make a mighty effort to run past the onrushing policemen, moving faster than they could see.

Or I could leave the stairwell and find a window. Climbing the outside of the building would take scant effort and with any luck, I'd have a better sense if Nohea and Sara were in trouble.

I'd take my chances on the fifth floor.

With a heavy shove, I opened the door. Once I was out of the stairwell silence fell heavy around me, except for the distant burble of traffic. My heightened senses are a gift, as is the ability to sense the energies humans ignore. This time, however, the air carried nothing more than humidity. No taint of demon weighted the heavy air.

I took slow steps down the hall, heeding any evidence of human occupation. In the absolute silence, I could hear the creak of my leather shoes and very nearly the slow beat of my heart. With no time to waste, I opened the door to the first open room, endeavoring to ignore my rising tide of anxiety. I entered, kicking up little puffs of dust with each step.

"Bless my peepers. Look who's here."

I came to a sharp stop. I'd never expected to hear his voice again. There. Lounging against the window, his boxy jacket unbuttoned with a flower in the lapel.

Leo. The man who'd given the darkest days of my life some semblance of normalcy. Leo. The last man who'd cleaved me from my vow of celibacy.

Leo.

Though I'd never been able to say the words, I'd loved him.

"You're here?"

"Always were the gumshoe, weren't you?" He trailed long, ghostly fingers on the windowsill. "I'm here."

I blinked. Hard. Half convinced I'd fallen under the influence of some evil. "Why?"

"Good question." He crossed his arms, his crisp white shirt falling open at the throat, pale curls tumbling over his brow. His eyes were the clear blue of an early summer sky, a color I hadn't been permitted to see since before his death in 1934.

"I was just floating along, somewhere between heaven and hell, and something jerked me on over here."

I pressed my palms against my cheeks, disbelief warring with an emotion I had no desire to examine. "Why now?" I whispered.

"I guess it's because you're dizzy with a dame." He chuckled, shifting to rest his hip on the sill. "Though in your case, it's not a dame, is it?"

Shock dampened anything else. My feelings for Leo had run the gamut from infatuation to deep affection to despair. Once I had loved him, and then I'd lost him.

I'd never forgiven myself for his death.

But the man in front of me wasn't that wasted, disconsolate Leo. This man was bright, teasing, fueled by an endless supply of humor.

"This is the first time you've allowed me to be here." His expression changed to one of solicitude. "Do you remember, Thaddeus? Do you remember what we had?"

He took a step in my direction, and my muscles locked between the desire to hurl myself at him and the desire to run away. I froze, and he moved closer.

"You always were sort of spooky." He reached out, close

enough to touch.

I flinched, and he dropped his hand.

"We used to be something, and I have to say it has hurt me to see you so lonely." Sincerity warmed his pale blue eyes, carving tracks in my spirit.

"I haven't been—"

Leo waved a lazy hand. "Nuts, Thaddy. You went whole months where the only person you talked with was that dried-up old biddy, Mayette. The man I knew had a certain appreciation"—his gaze raked me—"for masculine company."

My cheeks heated, verifying his words.

"You deserve more than a falling-down old house in the swamp." He reached toward me again, stopping before we actually touched.

If he touched me, what would I feel? The spectral brush of ghostly fingers? Or the torment of my own imagination?

"I am at peace with my choices, Leo." His answering laughter raised my ire. "I'm able to contribute something to mankind, and my needs are met."

His grin heated an entirely different part of my anatomy. "Not *all* your needs, Thaddeus Dupont." Then he closed the gap between us, soundlessly, so close I could have leaned down and pressed a kiss to his lips.

I didn't want to. I couldn't hear him or smell him. He wasn't real, and even if his pulse raced as quickly as my own, he wasn't Sara.

"There is still blood in those veins, pally." Close enough to touch my cheek, yet I couldn't feel the brush of his breath.

I eased away. "Leo."

"You don't have to live like a hermit. I know for a fact you've got choices."

A shiver floated over my skin. Not fear, not yet, but disquiet.

"You could take your young Asian friend up on his offer. There's a beast in your soul if you'll just let him out." He faded away, his grin down to one dimple. "And if you do, you can join us." His smile grew cold, colder, frozen in hate. "You will join us."

He disappeared, and dread flooded my soul. Join us? My only recent offers had come either from demons or a man in league with them. Had they somehow conjured this specter from my past? The silence flowed around me, accentuating the strangeness of the situation. Had Leo really spoken to me? Chills still crawled all over my skin. In all my years, I'd never before seen a ghost, and echoes of this vision gave off a miasma of evil.

I had tarried too long.

The windows were double-hung, single-paned panels of glass with sturdy cement frames. The walls were constructed of brick and mortar, and up close, they gave off the smell of decay. The span between the top of one row and the bottom of the next required me to stretch to my full height. I managed to find finger- and toe-holds in the crumbling mortar. Reaching the top floor, I pried open a window, sending up a cloud of dust when I landed on the linoleum floor.

Voices. I settled into absolute stillness.

"You know what I think?" Nohea's question filled me with relief. "If they've made it this far up, there're no demons here."

I headed in the direction of the sound, holding my breath for the response I prayed would come.

"Yeah."

Sara's voice. *Deo gratias.*

"I mean," he continued, "we saw that crop circle, or whatever you called it, in the other room, so they've probably been here, but…"

There. Up ahead in the hall. "Sara. Nohea."

I felt their spike of fear in my throat, under my breastbone.

"Damn, Thaddeus," Nohea snapped. "What are you sneaking around up here for?"

"We'll share stories later." Faint, far-off footsteps pounded. "We can't risk further entanglement."

At the opposite end of the hall, a bare red bulb gave me hope for a second stairwell. I pointed it out to Nohea, then took Sara's arm. "Are you all right?"

"Next time you want to do some B and E in a building surrounded by SWAT troops, I think I'll wait in the car."

His smile gleamed through the semidarkness, reassuring me and yet, for one critical moment, distracting me.

The door under the red light flew open in a blast of sound and light. "Freeze! Police!"

Nohea disappeared into an empty room, but Sara and I were caught. Four men surrounded us, weapons drawn. Looking Sara in the eye, I spoke directly into his mind. *At the first opportunity, follow me.* I hoped this situation would be an exception to his *not okay* standard.

I surveyed our opponents, keeping Sara close to my body. One of the police began a barrage of questions, most aimed at ascertaining why we'd left a light burning on the eight floor and what we'd done with the two missing cops.

I chose not to respond, and Sara followed my lead.

No one noticed Nohea creeping out of the room where she'd hidden. Her whip held loosely, she caught my eye. I tipped my head in the direction of the closest door. She nodded.

Don't get caught.

She nodded again, then reared back, and with an almighty yell, she cracked her whip overhead and dove out of sight. A gun went off, but I'd already dragged Sara out of the hallway and into a room. Smashing my fist through a window, I lifted him in one arm. "Hold on."

I launched us down the side of the building, with none of the precise care I'd used on the way up. I kept Sara between me and the brick. If I fell, I'd give him something to land on. Though my energies were taxed, I cast a blanket of shade over both of us.

My biceps strained and the old cement tore the skin from my fingers, yet I kept moving, dropping from one story to the next. The closer we got to the ground, the louder the voices and brighter the lights.

Mr. Dupont?" Sara broke my concentration.

We were two floors from the ground, and men were shining spotlights up the side of the building, though they had not discovered us yet. "Yes?"

"Working for you…" He gazed deliberately over my shoulder. "Well, it's never boring."

His lips curled in a devious grin, those lips I longed to taste. Acknowledging my desire on the heels of Leo's challenge left me with a feeling I'd need to examine later.

When there weren't men aiming industrial can lights in my direction.

I dropped the last few feet to the ground, landing lightly, wrapping both of us in as much shade as I could generate. Sara stood between me and the brick. Every one of my joints hurt, every muscle ached. Exhaustion frittered away at the edges of my vision. Then Sara tipped his chin, and my entire awareness locked on to his mouth. I wrapped my arms around his body, telling myself it was so we could both move at my speed.

Merde.

His lips parted, as if he sensed my turmoil. Tearing myself from the energy throbbing between us, I surveyed the area to make sure I wouldn't lead us into another circle of guns.

I saw a path.

We ran.

"YOU'RE NOT SO BAD, MR. Dupont." Nohea's grin gleamed in the moonlight. Our brush with disaster had lightened her mood. For my part, I offered up a brief prayer, grateful the three of us were safe in Mayette's old Thunderbird, our rendezvous point.

Sara and Nohea sat in front, and I stretch my aching legs across the rear seat. "Thank you. You showed remarkable resourcefulness in escaping on your own."

"And that Indiana Jones thing you did with the whip rocked." Sara's grin had a manic edge. "You totally need to give me some lessons."

With one hand on the wheel, Nohea guided us through traffic, away from the hornet's nest we'd created at the old Charity Hospital. "On further reflection," I said, "perhaps we should have delayed our exploration until the police presence had been reduced."

Nohea burst out laughing.

"Ya think?" Sara snorted. "Did we actually accomplish anything?"

My encounter with Leo sent a chill across my heart. "Another offer I cannot accept."

Something in my tone must have caught their attention, because they both turned around.

"What?" I stared at them, keeping my expression blank, reluctant to describe the visitation. "Nohea, watch the road."

She slowed the vehicle to a crawl. "Only if you tell us what's going on." Behind us, someone honked. "Damn."

"I have reason to believe someone has been plundering my past." I silently begged them to defer asking for details.

My associates exchanged glances. Sara shrugged, and Nohea answered him with a grimace. "All right, then," he said, "besides your cryptic allusions, Mr. Dupont, did we learn anything?"

Maybe he expected to pull the details from me in private.

Sara continued, "I mean, we found the crop circle thing, where you said someone had been doing something."

Nohea snorted. "So close, brainiac. One of the rooms

on the eighth floor had a circle of power on the floor and enough bad energy to make me sick for a week."

"So how's this for a hypothesis? Someone used a big empty building to conjure up demons and then dragged us into it." Sara leaned against the headrest.

"No way." Nohea increased our speed. "No way one guy could be doing all this on his own. It would take a committee."

The Axeman did it, and he boasted of his crimes in public. I shifted in my seat, examining the implications of Sara's theory.

"I overheard a couple of the cops talking," Sara said. "I guess the first two who went in to investigate the lights have gone missing."

That brought me to the edge of the seat. "Missing policemen?" Who had possibly been possessed by demons? No one person could acquire the power needed to control a demon-inhabited body for more than a little while. But if they did…

Fear knotted my belly, only to be burned away by anger. Whether these events were caused by one person or many, whether they were linked or the result of a random streak of horrendous luck, the demons had attacked my home and my friends and my past. I *would* stop them.

With much to ponder, we all kept to our own thoughts. We arrived home in time for Lauds, and the quiet in my room had never sounded so sweet. I stripped, and in the dim light of my bedside lamp, I inspected my body for damage. My fingers were healing, though the strain in my muscles would linger until I had properly fed. On my knees, I chanted the Hour, fighting through waves of exhaustion to finish the prayer.

CHAPTER FIFTEEN

⚜ ⚜ ⚜

"TELL ME AGAIN WHY IT'S my job to feed him." Sara was irritable and taking it out on Nohea while they waited for Dupont to come home from yet another demon deanimation mission. They were in the den again, same as every night, and both of them were about sick of each other. Since their excursion to the hospital two weeks ago, Dupont had been adamant Sara not risk exposure to the demons. Worse, Nohea must stay home to *ensure his safety*. Babysit, Dupont meant. As if Sara couldn't be trusted to sit home alone and not open the door to strangers or stick a fork in the toaster.

He tossed a throw cushion into the air, trying to see how close he could get it to the ceiling fan without connecting. Two weeks of house arrest had him ready to climb the walls, especially on nights when Dupont responded to the monk's calls. Tonight he was particularly antsy. His connection with Dupont, fickle at best, faded almost completely with distance, so he had no way of knowing if the nerves were justified. All he got was a vague pull *north* if he concentrated. He was just stir-crazy, he told himself.

"Crap, I'm not pulling out the damn contract again. Feeding's the part about providing meals consistent with the client's nutritionally mandated diet."

"I read that bit. I figured he was gluten-free or vegan or something."

"But you didn't *ask*."

"It would have mattered if I asked? *Really?*"

"Yep. There's a form letter. Sorry, we've awarded the position to another applicant. It's very polite. You should always make sure you are clear on the details of a contract before you sign, you know."

"Yeah? You read the whole iTunes TOS, did you?"

"Bite me, snack-boy. You're going to have to suck it up and do your job eventually."

"Why? He's getting a steady diet of demon victim. We don't want him to get fat."

"One…the demons won't last forever. And two…I don't think they're good for him. He hasn't said anything, but he doesn't usually have to eat this often, and yesterday morning I heard him throwing up. Those bodies are decaying. How would you like to eat rotten food?"

Great. So now he got to feel guilty. He was the victim here. He shouldn't have to feel guilty for not wanting to be eaten by his boss. "So why don't you feed him?"

"Because, ewwww. Why don't you kiss your brother?"

"Well, he's not your brother, so why don't *you* just suck it up and take one for the team?"

"You've been in a mood all night," Nohea said. "I'm going to get some sleep. Yell or something if a demon comes knocking."

Sara ignored her. He picked up the remote and flicked though the channels on the TV. The problem was, the idea of Dupont biting him hadn't seemed as bad lately. Sometime in the past couple of weeks, the thought of Dupont's mouth on his neck had stopped being something to avoid at all costs and started being something he fantasized about right along with Dupont's mouth on other parts of his anatomy. Mostly, he was irritated that Dupont still hadn't asked. Really asked, not his *please, Sara* sarcastic bullshit. And he still treated Sara like a pet. One of his *people*. Screw him. If he wanted to be that way about it, he could starve.

Only not really, because Sara had been serious when he said he didn't want him to die. Dupont, as far as he could tell, was a freaking hero out fighting demons and saving the world every night. Except Dupont didn't see himself as a hero at all. He seemed think of himself as a half step removed from the monsters.

Sara, meanwhile, had proved himself completely useless at tracking down anything that seemed relevant about demon summoning. He had, however, spent hours chatting up some very unusual people on internet forums. Some of them were way too serious about some very sketchy hobbies, but by and large he didn't think they knew any more than he did.

And while he sat home and tried to separate drops of fact from oceans of fiction online, the demon attacks were escalating. At least the latest ones had been just demons. They felt like taunts, jabs to keep Dupont out every night and test his strength. Unless the vampire was keeping details to himself, there hadn't been any more clear demands or direct messages.

He checked his phone. What time was dawn today? Dupont was really pushing it.

Ten minutes later, he found himself pacing. He peered out the window. Still pretty dark, but he thought the sky had started to lighten in the east. *Where the hell are you, Dupont?*

No clear response from his built-in Dupont magnet. On impulse, he headed toward the back of the house, then dithered in the kitchen with no clear purpose. He checked the time again. Maybe he should get Nohea.

The door slammed open, then closed. Dupont was home but…

"Jesus, Mr. Dupont. Are you okay?" Sara took a step toward the man, who sagged against the door. His clothes were a bloody mess. Deep, half-healed slashes ran down one arm and across his chest.

"I am fine. Thank you for your concern."

He didn't look fine, though. And for the first time since Sara had known him, he didn't sound fine either. He sounded winded and tired and in pain, and to top it all off, he was shut down completely. He was standing six feet away and not leaking a trickle of emotion. Sara had taken some comfort in the connection the last few nights, thinking he would know if Dupont were in serious trouble. But looking at him now… Sara lost it.

"You arrogant dumbfuck. You are not invincible. I'll stay here if it makes you feel better, but next time, you take Nohea with you."

Dupont stared at him coldly. "Nohea will stay here to protect you. I do not require assistance."

"The hell you don't. You are missing a sleeve, which makes me think you were almost missing an arm. You need backup."

"I am going to retire now. Please do not leave this house."

"Why is this your job anyway?" Sara yelled. "What did these stupid monks do before they had you to fight their battles?" He was talking to himself. Even running, he barely made it to the bottom of the stairs before Dupont disappeared at the top. "Mr. Dupont. Mr. Dupont!"

His boss paused and looked down at him.

"I, uh…"

"Yes, Sara, what is it?"

"You're hurt. Will you be okay? Do you need to…?"

Dupont raised one eyebrow. "I heal."

"Yeah, but you must have lost a lot of blood and… If you're too weak, I'll…" He swallowed. Maybe he could.

Dupont wasn't at the top of the stairs. He was so close, Sara could smell the hint of cypress and loam that never seemed to leave him, even here in the city. Dupont's gaze met his, and…hungry… The need wrapped them together as Dupont's mind touched his. Sara barely noticed the wash of saliva, the gnawing pain in his stomach. He couldn't speak. Couldn't move. Couldn't care. Dupont's hand didn't move at vampire speed; it rose in slow motion. Sara had all the time in the world to change his mind, step back, and walk away.

Cool fingers grazed his neck and traced a delicate path along his carotid artery. His heartbeat thudded into a slow rhythm, pumping life and warmth through his body. Instead of the expected rush of sensation, a slow seduction of heat coursed through his veins until it consolidated in his groin. He stopped breathing and waited for Dupont to move, draw him closer, and replace that gentle touch with mouth and fang.

Dupont's eyes flashed silver, then black, then settled to gray. "I have eaten, thank you."

Sara stood in the vampire's house at dawn and stared up the stairs at the empty landing, wondering if the ache in his chest was his own or the echoes of another man's pain.

⚜ ⚜ ⚜

THE POET WROTE THAT HOPE is a thing with feathers. I'd kept the image for decades after I could no longer watch the flight of a sparrow across a pearl-blue sky. I had held on to hope far longer than anyone expected, grasping it with a grim and unceasing determination.

Until the moment I reached my room and closed the door.

I ached. No, I burned. The gouges down my arm split and wept, sending the muscle into spasm. I fell onto my bunk. My rosary hung over my bedpost. For once, the heavy black beads offered me no comfort. Yet I tried.

Ave Maria, gratia plena, Dominus tecum.

The memory polluted the lines between the prayers. Nohea's tidy shotgun house, torn asunder.

Benedicta tu in mulieribus, et benedictus fructus ventris tui, Iesus.

Two men, anonymous, laid out on the floor, their throats cut, their blood sprayed across her pristine walls.

Sancta Maria, Mater Dei, ora pro nobis peccatoribus...

Nohea's sister, Letty, naked, wanton, eyes black as pitch. Holding the child, the only creature in the house still living. The baby's tearstained face nuzzled at her mama's neck.

Her mama, who was dead and possessed by a demon.

"Brother Thaddeus." The fiend's voice rasped through Letty's lips. "So nice of you to drop by."

"Begone, oh minion of Satan!" I threw as much power into the words as I possessed. The one who wasn't Letty only laughed.

"Come on, sweetcakes. Since you too stupid to eat what's right in front of you, I've got a petite snack for you over here." She held the baby out, an offering, if I was fool enough to take it. The child shrieked.

"No!" I cut her words off with a roar. On a breath, I sprang, reaching for the child.

Demons work in pairs, and before I got hold of the small, soft body, the hidden one charged. She tossed the baby aside, and the battle began in earnest. The fight was short and bitter, and I suffered much.

The baby's wail gave me oblique encouragement, and in the end, I prevailed. Despite the horrendous circumstances, I felt a sincere gratitude when I phoned the monks to make arrangements for her care.

...nunc et in hora mortis nostrae. Amen.

The waiting nearly cost me my soul. Standing in those bloody rooms with the motherless child, in more pain than I'd experienced in decades, I could have so easily succumbed. The hunger crawled out and beat me with my own weakness, until I had to place the child on the porch and lock myself inside.

To come home to an offer of succor. A frightened, uncertain offer, laced with guilt and anger. A thing I wouldn't—couldn't—take.

I prowled my room, chased by words I dreaded, a realization I couldn't bring myself to make. There. It nudged me, and in a fit, I flung my rosary hard enough to smash the beads.

Guilt landed a solid hit to my chest, folding me in half.

Letty died because of me, because of my ignorance and arrogance. I neither joined the demons, nor did I exterminate them, and now Mayette's grand-niece was dead. The weight of my culpability dragged me to the floor.

And so, hope left me. What was the point of my labors if they ended in the death of those I cared for? I'd had only a rudimentary relationship with Letty, but I owed Mayette for her years of service to me. I owed Nohea for those tasks she'd been willing to take on.

Yet it was not in me to give up either. Crouched on the floor, I inhaled and nearly gagged on the smell of the gore splashed over my clothes. A shower. Maybe the water could wash clean more than my skin.

I staggered into the bathroom and ripped off my clothes, throwing them into a pile. With a flip of the handle, the water poured over me, hot and strong. Though the cleansing virtues might have been limited, the water melted away my reserve, freeing the sobs that racked my body.

I stayed until the sobs faded and the water ran cold, and then I stayed longer still. In the glacial chill of the stream, I found a sort of peace, and I was reluctant to shatter it by turning the water off.

Then other hands did it for me. The water stopped. The shower curtain's metal rings squealed.

"What the hell, Mr. Dupont?"

A hand grasped my wrist. So warm.

"Thaddeus?"

I was beyond caring who or why, numb to everything but the steady, slow beat of my heart.

"Come out of there. You can't…"

I allowed myself to be led. Unseen hands toweled me off, brisk over my back and belly, where the rough fabric licked like flame. More gently over my damaged arm. Even so, I winced.

"Jesus, Thaddeus. What happened?"

Answering the question would disrupt the oasis of calm I'd managed for myself. "*Rien.*" *Nothing.*

"Right, well, let's get you into bed, okay?"

Unseeing, I allowed myself to be led by those soft, warm hands. The shivering started by the time we reached the hall.

"Shit."

We entered my room, a space I recognized by feel as much as by sight.

"Here. Sit."

My shin barked against the edge of my bunk, and I complied with the instruction. The hands returned, prodding my shoulders till I lay stretched out, shivering from deep in my core.

"Flippin' bath towel's thicker than this blanket," he muttered. "Don't move, Dupont. I'll be right back."

I faded into blackness and out of time, until the shivering stopped and I came to. I lay naked, a soft pillow under my head, a thick blanket covering my body.

And I was not alone.

Sara. The top of his head tucked under my chin, his bare body pressed against mine. The soft huff of his breath brushed my knuckles where my hands were clasped across his chest, his skin smooth and warm. He slept, which allowed me a moment to think. With a slight effort, I'd be able to find his neck with my lips and finally, finally settle this hunger.

"Do it," he whispered.

So. Not asleep. I shifted, loosened my grasp, brushed away his dark hair to bare more of his neck. He stretched in response, giving me greater entrée.

With a groan of defeat, I curled around him, pressing my lips to the skin covering the thick band of muscle running to his shoulder. A kiss. He stilled in my arms.

"It's okay, Thaddeus."

He sounded shy but not uncertain. I still had a choice, though on some level I'd made this decision the night I'd let him into my house on the swamp. I bared my incisors, making a small slice in the skin, nowhere near the artery. Blood beaded up. The scent hit me first, the warm, dull copper salt scent. I licked it away with the flat of my tongue, leaving behind my saliva to take away his pain.

His flavor—rich, complex, delectable—tested my resolve. So easy to make the cut deeper, find the artery, and drain his tractable young body dry.

I did not.

Another slice, in the same track as the first. Another line of bright red beads. Another taste, and this time I rolled, pulling him with me. He lay sprawled on his back across my chest, and I wrapped a leg around his thighs to pin him. His weight, his heat, and the intoxicating flavor of his blood combined to fire desires I had long kept banked.

His head lolled against my shoulder, and I lapped again and again, savoring every taste. As the cut sealed over, I had more attention to give to other appetites.

So did Sara, apparently. He grabbed my wrist firmly, the grip that had been so careful during my distress now giving no quarter. With a directness I couldn't imagine, he brought me to his shaft.

My eyes slid shut as I closed my hand around his silky heat. So familiar. Completely new. After so much death, God help me, I desired the intimacy of knowing a living soul. Of knowing this man, above all others. The notion of sin lost its power in the face of so much need.

I stroked him, profoundly pleased to find it was his turn to shiver.

"Yeah, that's it." He arched against me. "Keep doing that."

I shifted onto my side, sliding him down onto the bed, never letting up on the rhythm I'd established. Rising up, I hovered over him, only now meeting his gaze.

He smiled, giving me the profound gift of his affection and trust. I was too moved to return the smile. Instead, my gaze caught on his beautiful mouth, and I lowered myself for a kiss.

While his blood had been rich and complex, his mouth tasted clean and pure and joyful. I teased his lips with my tongue. His hum of pleasure reverberated through my chest, and at his encouragement, I rose higher, covering his body with mine.

I thrust against his thigh, my own pleasure making me grip him tighter.

"Damn, Thaddeus," he whispered against my chin, his voice tight, and I could feel his need almost as well as I could feel my own. I flexed my hips hard once, twice, then shifted over so I could grasp both our cocks at once. Our foreheads pressed together, I began bucking against him in earnest.

"You are so beautiful." I gasped the words out, too far gone to control my tongue. "You've brought such joy to this house and to my life."

He writhed underneath me. "Aw, man, don't talk to me like that. You're gonna…" He bit down on his bottom lip, trapping the words inside, yet his eyes smiled.

I barked a laugh, and the heat that had been building for weeks broke loose in a maelstrom of pleasure. With a cry coming straight from my soul, I shot against him.

"Dupont." His answering yell gave me scant warning before he climaxed. Still reeling from my own, I endeavored to hold him till his body relaxed.

With the meager common sense I had left, I took one of the towels from the floor beside my bed and wiped us both clean. His deep, even breathing suggested sleep, but I felt warm and vibrant, suffused with life. Regret would set in, hard, and I dreaded it.

For now, I wallowed in something as simple as sharing my bed with another human being.

A man for whom my regard had reached new levels.

"I'm thinking a bed of nails might be more comfortable than this thing."

Sara's dry observation made me chuckle. "I have no need for luxury."

He rose up on an elbow. "There's luxury, and then there's, like, basic comfort." He scooted closer, resting his head against my shoulder. "You're a piece of work, Dupont."

"As are you, Sara Mishra. As are you."

"You going to tell me what happened yesterday?"

The light in the room dimmed. I'd lost track of time, had missed chanting the hours. No, I would not willingly discuss those painful events. "Later, when Nohea joins us."

"I'ma hold you to that."

For my part, I was willing to simply hold him.

CHAPTER SIXTEEN

NO DREAMS.

Sara woke spooned in Dupont's arms. He waited for morning-after panic to set in, *because he was naked in bed with his boss.* Panic didn't seem to be happening, even though this morning they had done a lot more than be naked together. Should he panic because he wasn't panicked?

He stroked a hand along the arm hooked over his body and took stock of his situation. Dupont had bitten him. A shiver of pleasure ran though him at the memory. Dupont had bitten him, and he was…okay with that? Yeah. For now, anyway. What else?

Unwilling to examine his own emotions too closely, he focused on the man next to him.

Vampires weren't cold. Body temp seemed a bit lower than seemed normal, but not cadaver cold. Nothing like the chill emanating from him when Sara found him in the shower. Of course, in Dupont's case, it might be because he kept the AC vent closed and the room was stifling.

Sara glared at the vent twelve feet over his head. He hadn't paid much attention to his surroundings earlier, and he kinda wished he weren't getting an eyeful now. If the rest of the house epitomized Old South luxury, this room… He didn't have any words for this room.

Except for the crown molding still vainly attempting to

add some flair to the ambience, the room might as well have been a cell. A particularly gruesome crucifix (how morbid were Catholics, anyway?) hung on otherwise bare white walls. The only furnishings were the bed (narrow and hard), the ugliest armoire on the planet, a plain wooden chest, and a single small table next to the bed. Dead bolts had been installed on the door. The overall effect was beyond austere. Taken next to the rest of the house, this room was a punishment.

The bed itself had to be the most uncomfortable thing he had ever slept on, including wilderness camping with Dev, who had a knack for picking the rockiest places to pitch their tent. The sheets had obviously never heard of fabric softener or whatever else made his own sheets not scratchy. And Dupont's blanket, if it could be called that, must be as old as Dupont. He rubbed the thin material between his fingers, comparing it to the plush thickness of the one he had brought from his own room. He shoved both of them off. Dupont probably didn't need the extra warmth anymore, despite the slightly cool skin.

Sighing, he wiggled out of the vampire's embrace and propped himself up on one elbow to look down at the man next to him. *Jesus, Dupont. What goes on in that head of yours?*

Dupont didn't answer the silent question. Even in sleep, his face remained stern, but the lines around his mouth were more relaxed and the tension around his eyes had smoothed out. Sara touched the still face gently. So self-contained. Always the hero and protector. Who took care of him when he was hurt or alone? Sara tried to remember Dupont's rusty smile when they had teased each other about flying, or to picture his face last night, abandoned to passion. The moments of pleasure were brief treasures drowning in a sea of self-denial and duty.

Sara smoothed the hair from the vampire's face, ran his thumb along the seam of Dupont's mouth, and finally gave in, and pressed their lips together.

No response. Well, duh. Vampire.

If he had thought about it beforehand, he would have assumed being in bed with a sleeping vampire would be hella freaky. Like cuddling with a corpse. Dupont wasn't dead, though. His skin remained supple, not stiff and cold. Sara checked for a pulse, not too surprised when he couldn't find one. On impulse, he rolled Dupont onto his back and pressed an ear to his chest. He almost gave up, because magic, before he caught a faint thud. Almost a minute later, he heard another. Satisfied, he sat up.

He was dying to test what it would take to get Dupont awake at this time of day. After the way he had found him this morning, though, he figured it was better to let him sleep. He checked Dupont's arm and chest, frowning over pink new skin. *Too close.*

He got out of bed and tucked the scratchy sheet around the still body. On his way to his room, he evaluated his own health. He was O-negative, which meant he gave blood on a regular basis. He didn't mind. He enjoyed knowing he could do something so small and save lives. But he hated the light-headed feeling afterward and the weakness that sometimes lasted into the next day. He *really* disliked the guilt if he missed his regular donation schedule. It sucked when a gift became an obligation.

Maybe Dupont hadn't taken much, because he felt pretty damn good today. He grinned to himself. Maybe that part didn't have anything to do with the blood loss. Dupont was freakin' intense in bed.

So, to recap his night, opening a vein for Dupont was easier than donating to the Red Cross. Oh, and he was now sleeping with his boss. Bad idea? Maybe, but compared to moving across country to take a sketchy job offer, finding out his boss was a blood-sucking vampire, and breaking into a cemetery to fight demons it seemed a pretty minor workplace indiscretion.

Also, Dupont did too much alone. He needed backup. No way was Sara getting distracted into forgetting that. And he still hadn't found out squat about demons. Google sucked ass for serious paranormal investigations. Or maybe he just didn't know the right questions to ask, which rendered his usual outstanding Google-fu useless. Time to try a new tack.

He tracked down Nohea in the den sipping coffee and watching CNN.

"What do we know about demons?"

"Good morning to you too, Sunshine."

"Yeah, yeah. It's afternoon, you know. Demons?"

"I know how to kill them. What more do we need?"

"I'm trying to track down who might be raising them. The internet is worse for demon information than vampires." He was sick of spinning his wheels tracking down unverifiable bullshit on the internet. They had almost killed Dupont last night. Somebody needed to do something before they succeeded.

Nohea didn't look encouraging. "I dunno. You're talking Vatican stuff. They have all types of archives. You're looking at some heavy research. Why don't we ask the monks here whatever you want to know? Or check their website. Didn't I give you my password last week?"

"Because the monks seem happy to sit back and point Mr. Dupont at the problem. How do I get to the Vatican archives? I'm good at research."

"Seriously? You're going to go digging through two-thousand–plus years of monk stuff? You won't even know where to start. Isn't your degree in flower arranging or something?"

"*Molecular botany.*" He glared at her. "I have a *science* degree. What's so hard about research?" He eyed her athletic form. "What were you, a volleyball major? No wonder you couldn't figure out I was a dude before you saw me."

"MBA." She smiled evilly. "I went to Tulane, little boy."

"Oh." And it was his family all over again. Everyone was an overachiever except Sara, the spoiled baby, who had partied his way through his bachelor's degree with grades good enough to get into grad school but nowhere near what he would need for a full ride. Without six to eight more years of study and a few more letters after his name, a molecular botany degree got him only slightly more career opportunities than his high school diploma. He wouldn't have to flip burgers. Probably he could be a manager at McDonald's.

Some of what he felt must have shown on his face, because Nohea relented.

"Okay, bring your laptop. The White Monks have a special section at the Vatican. You should be able to set up an account with my credentials. And for the record, I didn't have a lot of time to do the usual background stuff, but I checked your Facebook when I got your application. Who's the *girl*, in your profile pic?"

"I don't..." Sara stopped and thought back. "Oh. That's was my sister, Aahna. Pictured with *me* at my graduation party."

"Well, thanks for that."

"Sorry, I didn't know you were going to base my employment on my Facebook profile."

"Not your fault," she said grudgingly. "Now, Vatican. You might ask Brother Michael if you need access to any areas requiring higher-level access."

"Not Brother George?"

"Stick with Mikey."

Sara filed that away for later. Dupont didn't seem to want him around Brother George either.

Nohea typed the address into his browser and slid the machine back to him. "I never bothered with the Vatican site. Knock yourself out. Don't forget you're me if you interact. Better yet, don't interact. God knows I don't."

"Why can't I get my own passwords?"

"We don't want to explain why you need them."

Something else to explore later.

The local website looked as though it had been designed in 1995 and never updated. The Vatican site was slick, at least the home page. Sara used Nohea's codes and filled out the log-in registration. In minutes, he had accessed an account prefilled with all her information. He spent a minute poking through it. They listed her as a non-clergy associate operative. Like a civilian contractor, he supposed.

"I set you up an account in Rome."

"Yay."

And, wow. In addition to the archive area, the Rome site had forums, classes, a newsletter, even apps. "Why haven't you ever logged in here?"

"For what? I told you—that's Church stuff. They have their job, I have mine. Hey, did Mr. Dupont see any action last night?"

"Yeah, he was pretty beat up."

"Well? What happened?"

"I don't know. Mr. Dupont wouldn't talk about it. Said he wanted to wait for you."

"Okay—guess if he has anything to tell us, we'll find out in about half an hour."

It wasn't okay, though. The reminder of how Dupont had looked this morning hit his good mood hard. Sara cast a glance up at the ceiling. Dupont was up there. He could tell he was awake, but so far no chanting, no shower, nothing. Just a vague ache. Maybe he should have stayed up there so Dupont didn't wake up alone.

"What the hell is with his room, anyway?" he asked. "I get minimalist, but, *damn.*"

Nohea finally showed an interest in the conversation. "What were you doing in his room?"

"He, uh, I told you, Mr. Dupont was in bad shape."

"Sara." Nohea grinned. "By any chance, have you been doing *your job*?"

"Well, you know, contract."

"Uh-huh." She took a closer look at him. "You call him Mr. Dupont while you're *fulfilling your contract*?"

He didn't answer, but he could feel the blush heating his cheeks.

"Oh my God, you do, don't you?" She cackled, "Yeah, I can see him getting off on it, too. All right then, congratulations on being alive. I guess I can cross one worry off the list."

"Wait a minute, you were worried I'd *survive*?"

"Not too worried. I mean he's never hurt any of the others, but you're a special snowflake for sure, and he's been bottled up for a long time."

"Nice," he muttered. "Have some respect. Mr. Dupont risks his life, and everyone takes it for granted." He glanced upward again and rubbed his chest absently.

"What does he do up there? Besides the chanting, I mean?"

"Monk stuff." Nohea shrugged. "Prayers, meditations, whatever."

"But…he's up there for *hours* sometimes. And, I heard—" He wondered how to explain the noises. "I don't think all he's doing is praying."

"Sara, he's old. I know you look at him and you see a guy not much older than yourself, maybe. I've known him all my life. He's always looked the same. Since I was a little girl, he's looked as he looks now. For me, he's not a hot young guy. He's my great-great-great-aunt's friend. And he's not human, or not completely. He has his own coping mechanisms. Whatever he's doing up there and out in the bayous for years on end, I let him do it."

"*DEUS, IN ADIUTORIUM MEUM INTENDE. Domine, ad adiuvandum me festina… Deus, in adiutorium meum intende. Domine, ad adiuvandum me festina… Deus, in adiutorium meum intende…*"

Vespers. Sara had learned the name of this one.

As words floated through the house, he realized he had been waiting for the prayer to start. He had become accustomed to having the rhythms of his day set by Dupont's voice as he called out to his God. He didn't want to admit he actually looked forward to it. Still, the cadence and timbre of Dupont's song were an unexpectedly beautiful start to their evenings.

Tonight's interlude raised the hair on the back of his neck, though. Dupont always infused the beginning phrases with a certain intensity, but tonight the words were a lament. Sara concentrated, trying to remember the translation. *Deus, in adiutorium meum intende.* A cry for help? He'd never noticed the repetition before.

The sound cut off. Cutting the chant short? He glanced at Nohea, who looked just as freaked as he felt.

Seconds later, Dupont appeared. Sara glanced up, suddenly nervous to face his boss after their night together. One glance and his unease consolidated into a ball of fear in his stomach. The passionate man who had held Sara in his arms and called him beautiful was gone. Even the monk had disappeared. In the doorway stood the vampire.

"Boss?" Nohea took a step back as Dupont ignored Sara and glided toward her, inhumanly blank and cold.

He wasn't cold. Only an iron control allowed him to appear so. Sara's control wasn't as refined. He thought he might pass out from the darkness. Black wings beat at the edges of his vision. He bit the inside of his cheek, concentrating on the small physical pain to distract him from the trauma roiling off Dupont.

"Mr. Dupont?" He should have made him talk this morning. Or stayed tonight and done it when he woke up. He shouldn't have left him to sink into whatever emotion gripped him now. "Thaddeus?"

"I'll speak to Nohea now, please, Sara."

He glanced at Nohea, who gave a tiny shake of her head,

eyes never leaving Dupont.

"Go ahead, then. Tell me." Her voice wavered, as if she already knew it would be bad.

"The activity near City Park last night." He paused and held out a hand to Nohea. "Nohea, my dear, please sit down."

She shook her head and backed away another step.

"I regret there was damage to your home. The monks will make restitution."

Dupont was naturally reticent and secretive, but when he had something to say, he rarely beat around the bush. And right now, he wasn't cold; he was brittle. Sara could feel him ready to crack into a million pieces from whatever he didn't want to say.

Nohea must have felt it, too. "Just say it, Thaddeus."

"Your sister, Letitia, is dead. I am sorry for your loss."

Nohea sucked in a breath, and she sagged inward as though absorbing a blow. "How?"

"Please sit down."

"I don't want to sit down. I want to know what happened."

Dupont recited the details, how the demons had lured him to Nohea's home. How he had found the house full of blood and bodies and Letty. How he had been forced to kill her to dispatch the demon.

He sounded calm, unemotional, but the conduit between them was wide open. Sara reeled with Thaddeus's worry for Nohea, fear that he couldn't protect the people closest to him, and disgust at his actions. Over it all, with every heartbeat, throbbed suffocating, all-consuming guilt.

"I am sorry. If there had been another way…" He trailed off.

"You did what you had to, Thaddeus." She took a deep breath. "Was she…did she…?"

Dupont seemed to understand what she meant. "I was as quick as possible, but it was…not pretty. I'm sorry, I do not know how they overcame her, or if she—" He stopped when Nohea shook her head.

"I don't want to know. She… I know she wasn't always the best person. I don't need to know if she made it easy. We weren't…" Nohea's voice cracked, and she cleared her throat. "We weren't close. I tried, after Grandma found her and brought her home, we both tried. She lived with her father's family for so long, and we didn't know how bad things were with them. We tried to help her, but she never—"

"I should have known," Dupont cut her off. "I should have protected her. I have failed you and Mayette both."

"Thaddeus, I don't want to believe she…" Nohea looked anguished. "You barely knew her. I'm her big sister. I should have been able to help her instead of begrudging her the money, or the spare room, or—"

"Nohea, do not torture yourself. You did all you could. And perhaps she fought. I sensed a power residue. More than I would expect from the demons alone."

Sara didn't understand what a residue had to do with anything. Dupont didn't feel confidence in the statement, but he obviously meant to comfort.

Nohea must have understood him, and she seemed willing to take the words at face value. "She was trying. I know she was trying. Since she had Angelique, no matter what happened, she always made sure the baby was safe."

Sara saw the second the realization hit her. She broke. Nohea broke. She collapsed, curling down into a crouch, arms over her head as if she expected a blow. "Angelique," she wailed. "*Angelique.*"

Dupont knelt next to her at once. He picked her up and carried her to the sofa. "*Non, non, cher.* Not the child." He stroked her hair. "She is safe. I am sorry I could not save your sister, but the child is safe. I am sorry. I should have told you before. I am a monster. I did not think." Over and over until the words penetrated. "She is safe, the baby is safe."

If anything, Nohea sobbed harder. "Oh, thank God, thank God. My baby."

Gradually, she calmed. Then, she went very still. "Thaddeus?"

"What do you need? Anything."

"Thaddeus, where is Angelique?"

"Do not worry, child. She is safe with the monks."

"Oh, okay." Nohea sounded confused. "Who has her? Are they going to bring her here, or do we need to go pick her up?"

"I'm sure you may visit her when our situation is more stable."

Nohea sat up. "What do you mean, visit her?"

"You cannot go home. The monks will make arrangements for her."

Nohea stood up. She stalked across the room, then turned to face Dupont. "The monks will make arrangements for her? No. I'm her aunt. *I* will take care of her."

Dupont rose to face her. "It is not appropriate. She needs a wholesome atmosphere. You will allow the monks to decide what is best."

Then the shit hit the fan. Nohea, who had taken the news of her sister's death in as much stride as could be expected, went ballistic.

"You listen to me, old man. Angelique is my niece and the closest thing to a child of my own I'm ever likely to have. She just lost her mother. She doesn't belong with a bunch of dried-up old men in a monastery. She belongs with her family. Now, *get her back.*"

Sara would have sworn Dupont was guilt-ridden enough to do anything Nohea asked. Instead, he went stubborn. "This is no fit environment for an innocent. The monks will provide for her well-being." He used his holier-than-thou monk voice when he said it, which did nothing to smooth the situation over.

"Tell me where she is, or I will stake you myself."

Wow, Nohea had actually snarled the words. Sara always thought that was just an expression. And where the *hell* had she pulled the knife from?

An intervention was obviously called for. Sara stepped between them. He faced Nohea and tried to look sympathetic and nonthreatening. "Let's just take a minute, okay? The important thing is she's safe. We can work out the details later."

"The important thing is she needs her family."

"Right." He thought of the tiny form nestled carefully among the pillows in Nohea's bed. And yes, if she were his niece, he'd be going nuts. "But, Nohea, Mr. Dupont is right. We're not the safest people to be around right now. What's more important? Keeping her with you? Or keeping her alive."

"He's the danger." Nohea pointed the tip of her blade at Dupont. "If I take her and get away from him, we're both better off. She's of no interest to them except by association to him."

"Maybe," Sara said. "Are you willing to risk her life on that? You know he would come for you both if they took you, and we have to assume they know it, too. How confident are you that you could hide her? And for how long?"

"Let the monks care for her," Dupont said. "They can provide for her better than we can."

Sara wished he would shut the hell up. The murderous gleam in Nohea's eye said she was a step away from solving the problem by killing one vampire, thus eliminating the threat to herself and Angelique as potential bait. Dupont either didn't recognize the danger or welcomed it. Death by angry aunt. Suicide without the sin. Sara doubted the stubborn ass had considered what the aftermath would do to Nohea.

"You know it's not his fault. You said he didn't choose this."

The knife blurred past Sara's head.

It missed him by a good margin but almost parted Dupont's hair. Dupont didn't flinch.

He didn't flinch at the curses either, and they were as deadly as the blade embedded in the far wall.

When Nohea wound down, she snapped at Sara, "Get your laptop. You're smart. Figure out what the fuck we're dealing with."

Her phone buzzed, and she yanked it out of a pocket. "Fuckers," she snarled. "You are just what the doctor ordered. Come along, Thaddeus. We've got action."

"You will stay—" Dupont started.

"The hell I will," she yelled. "We are eliminating these bastards if we have to empty out hell to do it."

Dupont tried again. "Sara's saf—"

"Mr. Dupont." Sara used his softest voice. He smiled, because Dev was right, sometimes a smile got him what he wanted. Then he looked up at the ceiling, away from Dupont's storm-cloud eyes. "You keep telling me they can't get in here. I will stay here, where I am safe. Either you take Ms. Alves with you, or we all go and she can try to protect me while I fling myself at a demon."

CHAPTER SEVENTEEN

FOR ONCE, I WANTED A fight. *Bon rien diable.* I could find no outlet to my howling frustration. The monk's information, usually so accurate, led us to an abandoned warehouse. Some few youths posturing on the sidewalks outside scattered when Nohea threatened to summon the authorities.

We returned to First Street in awkward silence, neither of us willing to speak of our earlier discussion. Nohea still vibrated with emotion. For myself, I revisited my failures.

Brother George and Father Patrick had asked me to find the source of the current devilry. Now, due to my incompetence, the evildoers had struck too close to me. As Sara would say, that was *not okay.*

My own attempt at humor left a bitter taste behind.

At the First Street house, I retreated to my room. Chanting the psalms was insufficient to soothe the pain in my soul. Still on my knees near my bed—the same bed I'd shared so joyfully with Sara—I waited for the storm in my heart to calm. Questions burned through the peace of my meditations. I could not believe more than one person possessed the power to call up and command demons without themselves being destroyed. Yet it was also difficult to accept so many evil events could happen independent of one another. In many cases, I was the common thread. Why? And where did the man from Frenchmen Street fit in?

The Lord's eye might be on the sparrow, but my trust had been shattered. Sequestering myself would help nothing. This eve, I did not possess the fortitude to offer more than the most basic prayers. St. Michael held the scales, and I burned with the need to hasten someone's final judgment.

The need to *do* something sent me down the stairs to the main floor. I found Nohea in the foyer. She knelt on an orange mat, her forearms intertwined and fingertips pointed at the ceiling. Between the stillness of her posture and her dark clothes, she could have been a shadow. She gazed at a point beyond where I could see, and I left her to her meditation.

Sara sat at the dining table, hunched over his laptop. "Oh, hey Mr. Dupont." He spoke without raising his eyes from the screen.

"Thaddeus." My cheeks heated at the memory of why he deserved such intimacy. "Please, call me Thaddeus."

I earned a small grin.

"Gonna take some practice."

I rested my hands on the chair next to his. The laptop screen showed the exterior of Nohea's house, surrounded by bright lights and television news crews. The faint buzz of an announcer's voice grew slightly louder when Sara slipped a plastic nubbin out of his ear.

"I'm hoping the yoga helps her get some sleep," he said, nodding toward the foyer.

"Ah."

Again a small grin, this one holding sadness. To my shame, I had to struggle against the memory of the sweetness of those lips.

"I've been thinking…" I forced my focus to the sober newscaster mouthing words on screen. "All of these events, they're public. Nohea was left in a cemetery, a bomb went off in the French Quarter, a simple light in an abandoned building involved the SWAT team—"

"And now this." Sara shut off the newscast. "We're on all the major networks."

"Hmm." I tapped the top of the chair with the side of my fist, trying to jar loose an idea.

"Dude's probably hiding out in the bushes, watching it all," Sara said in an undertone, bringing a different image to the laptop screen. Black-and-white. Small print. Columns.

"What's are you doing?"

He made the image larger. "Missing persons reports." His fingers glided over the keys. "I figure the possessed bodies gotta be coming from somewhere. I'm just sorting through to see if I can find a pattern."

Astounded, I pulled out the chair and dropped into it. "How?"

"Google can find anything in the public record."

I squinted at the screen. "And did this Google find anything useful?"

"Not yet." He laughed softly. "You know, we could go wander around Nohea's neighborhood and see if there really is anyone hiding in the bushes, *Thaddeus*."

His use of my name flattered me, but no. "The monks are attending to Nohea's affairs. I assure you, if they find anything suspicious, they will tell us."

"What if they miss something? It won't hurt to take a look."

"Your safety—"

"My safety would be significantly improved if I had a vampire to protect me." He caught me with his warm brown gaze.

"Sara." He did not understand.

"They're reporting that Nohea's gone missing, too." He finally turned to his screen. God help me, I almost agreed to his mad suggestion just to have his eyes upon me once more. A poor protector I would be if I gave in so easily.

"It's unfortunate the authorities arrived before the monks could complete their work."

My statement brought on a quick glance and a raised eyebrow. "The monks would have cleaned everything up?"

"They would have tried." His scornful snort brushed against my damaged soul. "As it was"—I kept my voice even by force of will—"they had time to eliminate the most flagrant evidence of supernatural involvement."

"So is she going to call somebody?"

"Soon," I said. "The monks will do their best to smooth this situation over, and the Church will provide her with a lawyer if needed. For now, it is best if she is as invisible as possible."

"So the monks"—he gave the word *monks* a scornful emphasis—"can clean up a crime scene but have no clue who is doing this."

"*Non.* They have tasked me with finding the source, and I do not know where to begin." I looked away, unwilling to face the disappointment Sara must feel at my failure.

"Could be any nutjob," Sara muttered as he worked. "I don't know how they expect you to know any more than they do. Nothing about the attacks gave you any ideas?"

Despite my shame, I spoke the truth. "I believe all these events are linked, and I believe I am the commonality."

His fingers stilled, and he turned a shrewd look toward me. "What if the guy on Frenchmen Street is the one who's raising the demons?"

Again, I must disappoint him. "I think I would have sensed the power."

"Okay, then." He gnawed on his lower lip. I held his gaze and tried to ignore the movement and its inevitable effect on me. "So either the city has had the worst run of luck in forever, or there's a pack of super villains with a grudge against a vampire."

If a single source—either an individual or a group—had that much power, surely I would have felt it. "Regardless, we need to work faster. Too many people have died," I said.

"Yeah. That."

⚜ ⚜ ⚜

YEAH, THAT? BRILLIANT RESPONSE. SARA turned to his laptop and tried to focus on the screen. Everything looked like gibberish, maybe from the distraction of watching Dupont in his peripheral vision. Next to him, the vampire sat stewing in his own guilt. What crap. Some madman or evil cult or something had targeted him, and instead of offering him their support, his stupid *order* had shrugged their collective shoulders and told him to go solve his own problem. *Great way to treat the victim, assholes.*

Sara was trying to step up, but demons and criminal profiling were outside his area of expertise. He and Nate should have binge-watched *CSI* or *Criminal Minds* instead of *Treme*. Or maybe *Buffy*.

He tried to think like a cop and came up blank.

He snuck another peek at Dupont out of the corner of his eye.

This morning had been… When they had…

Was it all part of the vampire diet? He wished he had someone to ask, because he hadn't felt like food. Sex with Dupont hadn't felt like doing his job or offering comfort or even a casual thing with the hot guy he lived with. The experience had been…

They were going to do it again. Per their contract. Even without the contract, he would want to. He'd never met anyone like Dupont, someone so dark and so good at the same time. Last night had been inevitable on Sara's part.

And Dupont hadn't mentioned it. Well, of course he *wouldn't*, because the timing had been… Did he regret it? Had he simply given in to hunger? Sara had felt Dupont's hunger gnawing in his own gut. He wouldn't blame anyone for seeking relief. And the bite… Sara shifted in his seat and pictured the periodic table. The visual did nothing to distract him from the memory of Dupont's lips on his skin.

He keyed up another missing persons report. He couldn't read Dupont right now, probably because his own emotions were jamming the connection. He hoped Dupont, *Thaddeus*, couldn't read him either. They were supposed to be tracking down a killer. Dupont would never lose sight of priorities to indulge in a juvenile relationship discussion.

His hands stilled on the keyboard.

What did the police always say? Not just in crime dramas, on the evening news. They looked first at the boyfriend or husband. Thaddeus implied someone wanted to prove something to him. Everything pointed to the motive being very personal. Even if it wasn't literally one guy raising demons, someone had to be in charge.

Sara stared over the screen, his mind distracted from missing persons. Mentally, he walked himself through both of Dupont's houses. He had been in every room except Dupont's bedroom out in the swamp. "Don't you keep any photographs?" He didn't think he had even seen one of Nohea.

"It is safer for everyone if I do not." Dupont shifted in his chair, but when Sara turned to look at him, he did Very Still. Then he sighed, "Eventually there were only pictures of dead people. I put them away."

Oh. "I'm sorry."

"Why did you ask?"

Because he was an insensitive dick. He wouldn't insult Dupont more by lying to him. "I wondered if it might be someone you know. Why else would they be trying to get your attention this way?"

He felt like shit saying it.

Dupont shook his head. "I promise you, one person would not have the power. Even they did, I spend most of my time on the bayou. Few people still remember my existence, and I can think of no one alive who would go to these lengths on my behalf."

"Hasn't there been anyone else who"—*did he really have to ask*—"you might have been, umm, intimate with? Someone who might not have wanted to let go?"

"I have been with the monks for over seventy-five years."

Wow. Okay. He tried to wrap his head around what he thought Dupont had just said and failed. *Seventy-five years?*

Then he remembered. Vampires and demons. And Dupont hadn't actually said there hadn't been anyone. He had said one person couldn't do this. He looked at Dupont's Very Still face and couldn't ask. What were the chances Dupont had some crazy ex from almost a century ago stalking him?

"Did you always want to be a monk?" he asked instead.

"*Want* is perhaps not the term. I desired to live a godly life, and the Rule of Benedict offered a clear path. I did not wish to marry. The Church offered opportunities to further my education I would not have had otherwise. When I look back at my time at the abbey, I remember tranquility. Those years, my life were as calm and ordered as I wished. Although," he said wryly, "I am sure much of the serenity is a product of nostalgia. I believe my teachers considered me a fractious disciple."

Sara tried to picture Dupont in a monastery. Way too easy. He wanted to ask what had happened, but couldn't quite get the words out. Dupont spoke while Sara hesitated, "What about you? Nohea said you have a university degree. What did you study?"

"Molecular botany. I only have a bachelor's degree."

Dupont frowned. "Botany I understand. I am sorry, I have not kept current in the sciences as I should. Explain molecular botany, *s'il vous plaît*. What work would you do?"

Sara shrugged. "Research, most likely. Maybe medical research or environmental science. I hadn't decided." Probably why he had never taken his studies very seriously. "The University of Bonn has a great program."

"In Germany? Will you continue your studies there?"

Not likely. "Maybe I should have taken a few classes in German, huh?" Or maybe forensic botany, which paid for shit but might at least be useful now.

A line appeared between Dupont's eyes, and Sara could see him struggling with the subtext.

"I don't know if I'll go back. The degree… I had to pick something, you know? And when I thought about the things I enjoyed doing, all I came up with was puttering around in the garden with my dad. We had the next best thing to an orchard, with all kinds of weird Frankenstein fruits and stuff from splicing hybrids. Only, garden putter-er's not exactly a career. I picked the botany pretty much at random and added the molecular part to keep Ma and Dev off my back. The classes weren't any harder and *molecular* sounds impressive."

There. He had admitted to Dupont his total failure as a human. No goals. No five-year plan. The only reason he had a one-year plan was their contract. And now he would get the same look from Dupont he got from Ma and Dev whenever they had these little talks. His sister, Aahna, at least, had the decency to be a goal-oriented, type-A personality in another state and not nag him when they Skyped.

"And your father is also a botanist?"

"Was." Did this part ever get easier? "Was, not is. I mean, no, not a botanist. He isn't anything, he's…" Why couldn't he spit it out? "He was an entrepreneur. He started and sold almost a dozen companies before he died last year. Gardening was a hobby."

"Losing a parent is hard. You must miss him very much."

Dupont didn't keep pictures, because everyone died. "Yeah. Losing people is always hard." Especially the one person who had been excited about his botany degree.

"You will find your calling," Dupont said. "You are young. You have plenty of time. There is no need for you to commit to a path now if you are unsure."

Sara blinked at him. Seventy-five years with the White Monks. Seventy-five years of saving the world instead of drifting through life wondering what to do with himself. How old had Dupont been when he committed to his path? How old had he been when he became a vampire? He didn't look any older than Sara did now. He had been a student, too. Then someone had ripped away his expected future. Except the course of Dupont's life had been disrupted far more brutally than Sara's. It had been done in a way guaranteed to separate him from everyone he cared about. And instead of giving in to despair, Dupont had become a hero.

Sara looked at the documents on his screen. It would be nice to feel he was doing something worthwhile, at least.

"Hey, if you want to get your iPad, I'll send you this spreadsheet I'm making, and you can help me plot these addresses on a map. I'm trying to get home and work addresses, plus last place seen for everyone missing the last six months. I don't know if it's worth anything, but it's better than sitting around waiting for the next attack." At least they could feel they were doing something.

They worked together the rest of the night. Sara's eyes blurred, and his back ached. Then he would glance at Dupont working beside him. He remembered Nohea's face when she learned of her sister's death. He thought of Angelique, alone with strangers, and he kept working.

"I must chant Lauds." Dawn. Dupont's voice already sounded drugged with fatigue. "And you need rest."

"Go on up. I'm almost finished here."

Almost turned into another two hours. He added the last addresses to the map, color-coded for home, work, last-seen. Hours of work. He hit Full Screen and stared at the map full of dots. He might as well have thrown darts at it.

So much for being useful.

He dragged himself upstairs to find Dupont's door closed. They hadn't talked.

⚜ ⚜ ⚜

I DIDN'T REMEMBER CRAWLING INTO BED, and when awareness returned, it came in the form of a different kind of warmth. Velvet skin. Sweet sweat. A heavy arm across my chest.

Sara.

I stiffened, my vision dominated by his welcoming smile.

"What?" I couldn't form a more complete question.

He rubbed his palm across my chest. "Hi."

His slight figure held me down, though I would have had no difficulty pulling away. Where was the strong, dedicated monk? I should have thrown Sara out of my bed and out of my room. I should have called Brother George to arrange for a confession.

Maybe the late-day sun sapped my resolve. I inhaled, ready to raise my objections to his presence, but his scent—warm honey and salty sweat—drove all thought of protest away.

"So I've been thinking, since the missing persons reports didn't show us much, we need to find a different angle." He spoke lightly, as if I wasn't trapped in a horrific internal quandary. "And a few days ago, I did me some research."

"Oh?" The word was more of a gasp.

His sly smile hinted he guessed at the discomfort caused by his body pressed against mine. "First I looked up ways to raise demons, which, what a bunch of crap, you know? Even with Nohea's access codes, the Church archives are a mess." He stroked my throat, toying with me, playing.

When his hand encountered the still-healing scars on my chest, he paused. "Damn vampire." He grimaced as if something had made him angry, though I didn't understand why. "Anyway," he continued, "when I got tired of chasing my tail on the monks' website, I turned to the Bible."

His tone still held too much humor for me to take him

seriously, but I allowed him to continue.

"Do you believe everything in the Bible?" This time, his voice carried more weight.

Because he didn't appear to be mocking me, and because I enjoyed the rough burn of his hairy thighs against mine, I answered him perhaps more seriously than I otherwise would have. "I believe the Bible holds the truth, in the abstract if nothing else."

I let him ponder my statement while marshalling a few arguments. "You see, you could argue the natives who inhabited North America occupied a corner of the Garden of Eden, at least until the arrival of those explorers who had eaten from the tree of knowledge, and brought their weapons and their diseases and their ideas." The sharp intelligence in his gaze undid me. "You see? Truth, but also fable."

He scooted closer, and I wrapped my arms around him reflexively.

"Thaddeus?" He nuzzled my neck. "Is it a sin to eat shrimp?"

Ah. Leviticus. I rubbed my cheek against the top of his head, for once indulging in a purely physical sense of affection. "I've had over a hundred years to come to terms with my perversion, Sara, and I tell you in truth, my greatest transgression is the breaking of my vow of celibacy."

"So?"

Explaining the consequences to Sara would ruin the spirit of the moment. Instead, I rolled us both over, hovering above him, mad for a taste of him. It had been years, decades even, since I'd wanted to possess a man so fully, and if this was going to be my end, I wanted it all.

I lowered my head, breathing hard, and kissed him.

*P*ERVERSION. THE WORD WARRED FOR attention with the sight of the scars. How hurt did a vampire have to be before he didn't heal completely? Then the pressure of Dupont's mouth on his overrode both thoughts. Sara opened his mouth and sighed as Dupont's tongue took possession. He could worry later. They were both alive now. Better than alive.

He angled his head and arched into Dupont. He hadn't expected the shrimp discussion to yield such immediate results. Or maybe, as usual, he had no idea what was going on inside Dupont's head. Having an intermittent live feed on the man's emotions was less helpful than one might think, especially since Sara still hadn't gotten a firm handle on which of them was broadcasting what at any given time.

He kept his eyes closed, avoiding Dupont's gaze. He slid their tongues together, trying to remember why he had been worried about coming in here. They hadn't talked about sleeping arrangements. The door hadn't been locked, though. And after yesterday...

Dupont shifted his hips so more than their tongues could get friendly.

Talking could wait. When he had climbed into bed with Dupont, he had stupidly left on his boxers, and now they were hindering full appreciation of the moment.

And maybe they were on the same wavelength right now. Dupont had his thumbs under the waistband, and Sara lifted his hips and squirmed out. Dupont pushed them aside so they were skin to skin. Sara ran his hands along the vampire's arms, over his back, into his hair.

He would never mistake the feel of the man in his arms for anyone else. Dupont's body, not yet warm after his day sleep, slid along his like cool satin. *Shouldn't be a turn-on.* But *should* had nothing to do with it. Sara's skin burned in all the places they touched. He wrapped his legs around Dupont and held him closer, more than willing to warm him up.

The arms around him tightened. Vampire arms, strong enough to crush the life from his body. Their hold was reverent, as if he were something precious. Dupont's mouth left his to trail kisses over his cheek, his temples, his eyes, each touch a tiny benediction. Cool kisses on burning skin. He didn't need or deserve adoration. He was only a man who wanted a man—not the vampire or the monk, but the man at the heart of them both.

As if reading his thoughts, a cool hand cupped his hip, then slid around his thigh, lighting fires in its wake until he burned with need. Dupont's finger circled his hole and ripped away the last of his restraint. He moaned, aware of two things. They weren't nearly close enough, and he was going to combust when Dupont got inside him. He pulled his legs in closer to his chest and bucked against Dupont, hoping to inspire some urgency.

Dupont took his time, as focused and deliberate in this as in everything else. His kisses wandered lower, grazing along Sara's jaw, nipping at his ear, sucking on his neck.

Sara angled his head to offer better access. Finally. The biting had been amazing. They could do that again, no problem. Instead, Dupont moved lower, sucking on Sara's nipples and sending zaps of sensation straight to his dick, maddeningly trapped between their bodies.

It seemed he'd spent an eternity in a haze of need before Dupont was poised over him again.

Then, without warning, everything went sideways.

"Tell me to stop."

The words didn't make any sense, but the stillness in Dupont's body did.

Sara's eyes flew open, meeting Dupont's. The conduit opened, and he fell into the storm.

"Tell me to stop." Far away, the words came again, whispering through the power of the vampire's gaze.

Sara stared at Dupont, angry he would use his power now. Like the leaking emotions, Sara had never figured out why the whammy worked sometimes and not others, but he doubted he could resist a determined effort when they were this connected. He gathered his own will anyway, ready to fight the command…until he realized he didn't have to. They were just words. Weak, insubstantial words, struggling to find their way through the waves of need cresting on the real power. He smiled. "Not a chance in hell."

Dupont's eyes closed. Breathing heavily, he rested his forehead against Sara's. "I am unprepared, and I would not hurt you more than I can help. Let this be our salv—"

"Nah," Sara managed. He tried for cool, but his voice came out so breathy, he'd have to rely on Dupont's supernatural hearing. "I was a Boy Scout."

He reached back awkwardly and fumbled on the table next to the bed. The shorts had been a cop-out, but he hadn't been stupid enough to come into this bare little room again without lube.

Dupont seemed like he still might be gearing up for second thoughts. Sara wrapped his arms around him and rolled. Coming to his knees over Dupont, he flipped open the bottle and slicked up his fingers. When he met Dupont's eyes, a big wave of shy hit him. Lots of guys got off on watching their partner prepare themselves. Of course, lots of guys weren't hundred-year-old monks. He bit his lip, still committed, yet suddenly too self-conscious to reach around and oil his own ass. But, hey, with the beauty of lube, application wasn't specific to Slot A or Tab B. He scooted backward until he straddled Dupont's thighs instead of his hips.

Dupont didn't make any move of encouragement, lying vampire-still beneath him. Stubborn as usual. *Iron will* sounded hot in genre fiction but was a pain in the ass in real life.

It wasn't as if Dupont wasn't turned on, too. Evidence to the contrary bobbed between them, daring Sara to test Dupont's resolve.

Dupont himself looked hot as hell, laid out naked on the

narrow-ass bed under Sara. His skin was moonlight and shadow, a Frenchman's version of vampire pale. His lips were swollen from their kisses, and a dark flush stained his cheeks.

He looked carnal, and wicked, and nothing like a man too holy to fuck. Despite the stillness of his body, lightning still sparked in his inhuman eyes. Sara met his gaze deliberately as his hand took Dupont's shaft in a firm, sure downstroke.

"*Merde.*" Dupont arched off the bed.

Oh God, so hot. The power to make Dupont respond, the look on his face…

He slicked his thumb across the head of Dupont's cock, and Dupont clutched at the sheets. Iron will. Sara grinned. If Dupont tried to whammy him now, he bet it wouldn't be to make him stop.

Before he could finish the thought, Dupont's hands were on his arms, pulling him roughly forward. He forgot about whammies and iron will as their mouths met again. Kisses, even Dupont's, weren't enough now. He could feel what they both needed behind him, hard and slick and already so close. A little help would be nice, but not necessary. Dupont didn't need to stress himself, Sara could take care of this for them both. He adjusted his body and impaled himself on Dupont.

The universe went still for one white-hot second. Dupont's eyes were wide, startled, then the lightning struck.

Combustion.

Dupont was everywhere, between his thighs, in his body, in his head. He was open, invaded, possessed. Hands on his hips set the rhythm, as Dupont drove into him. Concepts of *his* and *mine* became meaningless. There was no separation. No Sara. No Dupont. Only the storm, building to an inevitable peak.

They had moved. Sara couldn't tell how, only that somehow they still had one more barrier to breach. Lips grazed his neck. A final penetration, then even their hearts beat as one. Their shared pulse pounded through him. His body erupted in starbursts and lightning. And his soul found… communion.

HE FLOATED IN A WARM blanket of white noise. Somewhere, his conscious brain knew Dupont had withdrawn and they were less physically connected. Dupont's warm arms embraced him, holding him carefully, no longer one body. Dupont's lips touched his neck again, soothing laps over the wounds on his neck, then gentle caresses on his face. Something seemed wrong. Reality still hummed too fuzzily for him to make sense of any of it. He tried to drift into the white noise. Something sharp and discordant pulled him back. Dupont's hands on him, so gentle, but…bursts of guilt and fear.

With an effort, he cracked one eye open.

"Thaddeus," he managed. "Stop worrying. You were amazing, but I'ma take a nap now. We can discuss the shrimp again later."

He let his eyes drift closed again. He should get up. Thaddeus would be doing Vespers soon and he should get back to demon research. Thaddeus and Nohea seemed sure one person couldn't control so many demons, but Sara couldn't shake the feeling that they were missing something. The attacks didn't feel like some deranged cult targeting a vampire. They were way too stalkerish in tone. He let his mind roam lazily through the conversational threads he'd started on the monk forums. Mostly, they confirmed what Thaddeus and Nohea had told him. The problem with demons was they *couldn't* be easily controlled. Except for the urban myths a few of the guys had thrown out, obviously to mess with the new guy on the forum. Really scary End of Days stuff with demons raised by madmen using some mythical book no one had ever seen.

Supposedly Brother Guillermo was going to be on

the forum tomorrow with a recent sighting of the book. Sara wondered how far they were willing to take the joke. Because really, if a book like that existed, the monks wouldn't be hiding in offices at Loyola, they would be on the news every night right next to Seal Team Six.

CHAPTER EIGHTEEN

THE SHOP WAS DARK, DUSTY, and crammed with implements of the arcane. It smelled of incense and black magic.

"These voodoo shops are all tourist traps." Nohea squinted at a burlap doll in the dim light. "Made in China. I don't know why I let you talk me into this. If Thaddeus wakes up before we get home, we're both in trouble."

"Shhh, they'll hear you. Have you got a better idea where to look for eye of newt?"

"Do you even know what a newt is?"

Sara ignored her. They weren't here for newt. He had an idea if he told her what they were really tracking down, he wouldn't have gotten out of the house. He hadn't spent eighteen hours on the internet yesterday to lose this lead now.

He inched toward the rear of the store, hoping Nohea would remain interested in voodoo dolls and love potions. No such luck. She stuck right to his side. He gave up and headed for a display counter manned by a pasty Goth chick who looked as though she might expire under the weight of her ennui and piercings.

Sara tried a smile.

She stared back, unimpressed. "Yeah?"

"We're looking for"—he consulted his phone—"graveyard dirt. Bone from a black cat. Milk from a black cow."

The girl didn't bat an eyelash. "Sure."

She rummaged around on the shelf behind the counter and returned with a small bone and a baggie of dirt. The milk was in the cooler next to the Red Bull and a few more love potions.

Nohea snorted. "Yeah, right. Looks like dirt from anywhere, bone from anything, and Kleinpeter's in a mason jar. C'mon, Sara. Let's go."

"Nice tats. I really like the one on your neck." Sara tried the smile again. "I'm pretty sure this spell from the internet is bullshit. Maybe you could point me to something more authentic?"

"Spell books and grimoires on the far wall. Take your pick."

"Do you have Weyer's *De Praestigiis Daemonum*?"

"We specialize in voodoo." Still the bored voice, but her eyelid gave the barest twitch at the title. "Down here, most people want *Le Veritable Dragon Rouge*."

"I'm looking for a specific translation of the Weyer." Sara pulled up an image on his phone and turned it around so she could see. "It's twentieth century but claims to be a translation of a longer, unabridged version of the original work. I heard a rumor a copy came through here."

The girl sucked the bar through her lip in and out a few times.

"You seem pretty knowledgeable." Sara let his gaze flick to the ink on her neck again. "If the store doesn't have a copy, maybe you could tell me where to look. It would really help me out."

"Look, your friend is right. This place is for the tourists, and you seem like a nice guy. Get a copy of *The Red Dragon*. It makes a great souvenir. No one wants Weyer."

"I do," Sara said softly. "I really, really do. Just tell me if you've seen it or know anyone who might have."

The lip bar went in and out a few more times. "Not here," she finally said. "My boss might know. He's big into all those rare translations and shit. You could try our Gretna store. They have a better selection, and the manager over there does the ordering." She picked up the bone, dirt, and milk and started putting them away.

"I'd still be happy to buy those," Sara said.

"I'm betting you don't really need these. But if you do, you should get them from the Gretna store."

"Thanks. You've been awesome." Sara gave her another big smile, on the house, because it never hurt to be nice to people.

"Whatever." The corners of her lips ghosted up when she said it. "Watch yourself, pretty boy. Black magic isn't a party game."

NOHEA WAITED UNTIL THEY WERE outside. "One. We are not going to Gretna. There's no way we'd make it home in time and, two—what the hell was all that? Eye of newt, my ass. You didn't even ask for eye of newt. What's this prestigious domino thing?"

Sara unlocked the car and climbed in. He looked up the address of the Gretna store while he waited for an unhappy Nohea to walk around to the passenger side. Then he started the car.

"We have plenty of time to make it to Gretna if we leave now. The nav says it's, like, ten minutes across the river. And not prestigious domino, *De Praestigiis Daemonum.* It's a book written by a sixteenth-century demonologist. We're not looking for a regular copy. Weyer only published a fraction of what he knew. Supposedly, there's a special copy that includes a lot more stuff he didn't want to fall into the wrong hands."

"What stuff? And why do we care?" Nohea asked suspiciously.

Sara waited for her to fasten her seat belt and pulled out of their parking spot before he answered. "How to raise demons."

"Shit," Nohea scoffed. "There's a million spells for raising demons. Your stupid graveyard dirt thing could probably summon a lower-level one. It can't be very hard. That's why we got work. Dumbasses raising demons all the time, and then we got to go deanimate them. We're not worried about the raising. We're worried about this coordinated crap they're suddenly doing."

"So hear me out. I'm not just talking about raising them. I think Weyer knew ways to raise demons and not wind up possessed. Maybe even something simple enough a novice could use. How to raise and *control* demons."

Nohea grunted. "What makes you think someone's doing that?"

"Okay, check it. You and Mr. Dupont keep saying demons travel in pairs, right?"

"So?"

"Well, why would they do that?"

"They're demons. Why do they do anything?"

Sara ignored her. "And your monks on the Vatican forums knew this one as soon as I asked. Because you're right. Demons aren't hard to raise. Or at least the bottom-of-the-rung ones aren't. In fact, they are ridiculously *easy* to raise. They *want* to get summoned. Except then you have to do something with them, right? Like, you could stick one in a chicken, but what good is a possessed chicken?"

"Are you going somewhere with this?"

"So instead, you stick them in a human body so you can send it around to do your dirty work. Except that's more of a problem, because the type of person who would do that type of thing is sort of a creep, obviously. And if you have what the monks call *stains on your soul*, or whatever, you're more susceptible to demon possession. So then, you have to either be really, really good at magic rituals, or when you summon the demon, it hops right out of your handy human sacrifice and into you."

"Fascinating." Nohea sounded bored. "Still only one

demon."

"Yeah, except then you have two human bodies connected ritually, and the first demon turns right around and summons a buddy."

"And then someone calls Thaddeus, and we get work. What's your point?"

"There was more than a pair of demons in the cemetery. And they were organized. Someone's calling them and controlling them. The monks only knew of four cases like this in the past two hundred years. One of them was some mass murderer called the Axeman right here in New Orleans, and no one ever found out how he did it. Two of them were done by some huge cult of satanists who pulled power from over a dozen practitioners at once to control just one demon."

Nohea was quiet for a minute. "And the other one?"

"Uh, the records are sketchy, and you understand I wasn't actually allowed to *see* them, but…monk myth says someone had a copy of the Weyer and uh, they had to call in monks from all over Europe to take down the last demon."

Nohea grabbed his phone out of the center console and scrolled through his pictures. She barked out a laugh. "This? God, you're gullible. This is a spiral notebook. The fucking graveyard dirt was more authentic."

"Maybe. All I know is that notebook showed up for sale recently and was purchased almost immediately by someone from one of the occult shops in New Orleans. And then almost every record of it disappeared."

"So how come you know about it, then?"

"I got lucky." His big research breakthrough had come by accident, and no thanks to the Vatican archives. He suspected he needed higher clearance than anyone he knew possessed to find anything useful there. He had struck up a few chats with some of the younger monks on the forums, though, who had entertained him with horror stories as well as anecdotes of the type of bogus reports they had to sift through on a daily basis. Sara hadn't taken them seriously at first. Screw with the new guy, right? But then they had started talking about a crazy report from the States recently. Someone claimed to have a partial translated extract from the expanded *De Praestigiis Daemonum*. It had popped up in California and then again in New Orleans. Dead end, of course. But imagine the chaos if it had been real.

Except, Sara thought, someone was raising demons in a whole new way in the same places this nonexistent copy didn't exist. And there seemed to be no record of the original offer for sale or even any chatter about it. Seemed like the kind of rumor all the occultists would be in a tizzy over.

It had taken him hours to sift down to a single vague comment buried in an obscure forum and more hours to hack some dude's cloud account to find the picture. Dude himself had gone as missing as references to the grimoire, which was ominous as hell and which Nohea didn't need to know.

"If it's bogus, it won't hurt to go check out this shop."

Nohea muttered something about him not being the one who would have to explain to the boss why his breakfast had been in Gretna instead of on First Street where it belonged.

Sara headed across the Mississippi and followed his GPS to a nondescript strip center stuffed full of family-friendly options: discount clothing store, Mexican restaurant, sub shop, pet supply. He checked the GPS again, then the center's pylon sign out by the road. The place they wanted was listed right under the nail salon.

Inside, the store didn't look anything like the shop they had just come from. Instead of voodoo dolls and love potions, the stock was heavy on candles, crystals, and books. One whole wall was dedicated to apothecary jars of dried herbs. New Age music and fluorescent lights added a reassuring normality to the whole setup.

The only employee in sight, a woman about his mother's age, was with another customer, so Sara wandered over to the book section to browse. At his side, Nohea sneezed, then sniffed.

"Place smells funny."

He started to ask what she meant, but then he caught it, too.

"Incense?" he wondered aloud. "Or maybe the herbs." Except herbs and incense were the top layer of the funky olfactory cocktail and exactly what you would expect in an upper-end shop where ladies in Lululemon and diamond earrings bought books on aligning their chakras.

The sneezy part hid somewhere underneath.

"Rancid patchouli," Nohea said. "Damned hippies always gotta bathe in the stuff."

"Probably," Sara agreed. He tried to take shallow breaths. "Thanks for pointing it out. Before you sneezed, I didn't even notice. Now I can't un-smell it."

Nohea wandered over to a jewelry display while Sara continued to browse the books. At the counter, the clerk managed to tack a "focus candle" and a "cleansing tea" on to the sale. She didn't look like a hippie—too professional. She looked like a bank manager or real estate agent. Maybe a lawyer.

She wrapped up at the counter and headed for Nohea. Sara caught something about a bigger selection at Walmart right before Nohea's eyebrows hit her hairline. The woman didn't wait around for a response before approaching him. He noticed she angled her body so she could keep watching Nohea, though.

"I'm so sorry to keep you waiting. I'm Missy. What kind of books are you interested in? I'll be happy to make a suggestion." The pitch came with a smile and oozed sincerity.

"Hi." Sara offered up his own smile, which didn't want to stick despite the woman's helpful attitude. She didn't look like a Missy. "Is the manager around? I'm looking for something a unique, and I heard the buyer for this shop might be able to help me."

"I'm the manager, hon, and the buyer, too. What are you looking for? I'm sure I can order it in if we don't have it."

Sara didn't know why he hesitated. Missy seemed way more eager to please than the chick at the tourist trap. "Weyer's *De Praestigiis Daemonum.*"

"Which translation? We have several in stock." So helpful, but something unsettling lurked in her gaze. Sara suddenly wished he had let Nohea talk him into going straight home.

He reluctantly pulled out his phone. Because that was what they were here to do. And because they were in a nice, well-lit store in the middle of suburbia. He wasn't afraid of a flippin' manager in a strip mall. What could *Missy* possibly do to them?

The bell over the door chimed just as he handed her the phone. *Safety in numbers.* He had *not* just thought that. He glanced up at the person entering the shop.

O-kay. Not another soccer mom. The panhandlers down in the Quarter looked cleaner than this guy. He watched as the fellow headed straight for the wall of herbs. *Not the kind you're looking for, buddy.*

Missy followed his gaze. Whatever reaction he had expected from her, it wasn't the one he got. She gave the newcomer a brief glance, then returned her attention to his phone.

"Oh, honey. Someone's having you on. I saw this same picture going around a while back. It's a hoax or a scam."

"I'd still like to find it," he insisted.

"I have access to several rare editions on consignment from private collectors. Let me show you some of those, if you want something unique."

"I'm kinda set on this one." Something about this place was getting to him. Or maybe Missy knew more than the friendly smile let on. "I have it from a reliable source it came through here at some point. If you don't know about it, can you tell me who does?"

"Who did you say sent you?"

Sara thought of the tourist shop. Goth chick hadn't smiled at him once. "I'm sorry. I don't recall the name at the moment."

Goth chick hadn't given him the willies either.

"Mis-see."

Sara and Missy both started at the sound of the voice. Nohea appeared at his side, hand hovering over her hip like she might actually pull a weapon right here in the nice neighborhood mall.

How the hell had the other customer snuck up on them?

"Miss-see." he said again, singsonging her name on boozy breath.

"Yes, Mr. Goutard?" Missy's smile faltered.

"What seems to be the prob-lem?"

"N-no problem. We don't have the item this gentleman needs."

Wow. *Mister* Goutard? Had Missy *stuttered*? Sara took a closer look at the bum. His clothes were wrinkled and filthy, and he *smelled*, but… Tommy Bahama shirt and Mephisto sandals? Dude either knew some excellent thrift stores or he wasn't as down on his luck as he seemed.

When *Mr.* Goutard turned his gaze on him, Sara revised his opinion. Maybe Goutard's problems had nothing to do with money or lack of shelter. The light in those eyes said someone might be home, but home was in a whole different universe. Goutard's gaze flicked between Sara and Nohea. "Raising *de*-mons? How fun."

"No." Sara figured he better shut down any *fun* Goutard might be imagining. "It's just a curiosity for our boss's collection."

Goutard's eyes did the tennis match thing again—back-and-forth-back-and-forth, like he couldn't decide if Sara or Nohea was more interesting. "Boss?"

"Hey, if you don't have it, no worries. I'll just tell him we hit a dead end."

"I'm sure Mis-see can help you locate it. She's very resourceful." Goutard had somehow inched closer, and some of the singsong quality dropped out of his voice. Sara took a step away, trying not to gag. Piss and… Nohea sneezed.

"I'm sorry, I just realized the time. We'll stop in another time, okay?"

Goutard's hand clamped over his arm. Sara froze, every instinct on high alert. But Goutard just smiled. "Of course, take my card. I'm a collector myself, you know. Maybe your boss would like to talk shop?"

Sara managed to take the card that had appeared in Goutard's other hand. "Sure. I'll pass your contact along."

"My name is Marc. You can call me any time."

Sara took a step back, relieved when Marc released him. "Thanks. I'll let my boss know." He took another step, unwilling to turn his back on the crazy eyes while they were too close.

Then he and Nohea were out the door. Not running. Not quite. But not strolling either.

They didn't speak until they were in the car and on the road.

"What the fuck was that?" Nohea sounded rattled.

Sara replayed the scene in his head. Maybe he had over-reacted. Maybe the dude was just eccentric. Maybe he had come straight from doing some work in the yard. Maybe… He couldn't explain the smells. Tracking black magicians induced paranoia. They weren't looking for a harmless hippie with incontinence issues. "He creep you out too?"

"Yes," Nohea said tersely.

"You think he's involved?"

"I dunno. He seems kinda whack. I'm not sure I would trust him to summon a cab without fucking it up, much less a horde of demons. Couldn't hurt to keep an eye on him, though."

"I'll see what I can dig up about him online."

"You do that, Slick, but he's not our biggest problem right this second."

"I wouldn't so much call it a problem as—" He broke off as Nohea gestured out the window. "What?"

"Time."

"I was just making an excuse to leave."

"Time, Sara. You promised me we would be home in plenty of time."

He glanced at the clock in his dash, then the shadows on the road. Oh. "We still might make it."

Nohea didn't even bother answering.

"I'll take full responsibility. It's me he'll be mad at."

No answer.

"My contract only stipulated evening hours. He can't keep me a prisoner."

Sigh. "Just get us home. It's not me you need to convince."

Outside, the sun inched lower toward the horizon.

CHAPTER NINETEEN

✦ ✦ ✦

I AWOKE TO AN EMPTY HOUSE and chanted Vespers in the company of my own thoughts.

Some very distressing company.

I had asked—nay, begged—Sara not to go off on his own, and I could only hope he'd persuaded Nohea to accompany him. Together, the two of them could overcome most any danger.

Except, perhaps, an angry vampire.

The night before, he had not left my side, allowing me to indulge every one of my carnal urges. I had luxuriated in his blood and his sweat and his spunk. The taste of his lips. The taste of his cock.

The sodden taste of guilt now wrapped around me like a python, squeezing the breath from my lungs.

Alone, I had nothing to shield me from my own failings. My actions might have put my own salvation out of reach, but I might yet save him from himself. I would put a stop to our relations right now. I must.

The longer he was gone, the more his absence provoked me. At the first squeal from the kitchen door, I called to him. *Sara.* I may have neglected to use words, because I considered bawling someone's name a poor use of my time.

My foot landed on the bottom step, setting off a familiar creak in the joists, and the kitchen door slammed open so hard it rattled the glass.

"Mr. Dupont."

"Oui?" I kept walking. "Meet me in the dining room, *s'il vous plait.*"

He trotted along behind me, muttering a string of colorful and unfamiliar curses. At some point, I would ask him the meaning of the term *shitweasel.* Even Nohea hadn't used that one in my hearing.

I pulled out a chair, too angry to sit. Sara fumbled for the light switch next to the door. To her credit, Nohea sidled in beside him.

"Look," he said, "I know what you're going to say, but you need to remember the rules."

He smacked the switch, and the crystal chandelier centered over the table bloomed with light. "Rule number one: I am not part bat, so the lights need to be on."

Sara planted his hands on his hips and glared at me from the doorway, obviously determined to bluff his way through this confrontation. I acquiesced with a gentle nod.

"Rule number two." His eyes flashed like black lightning. "Stay. Out." His nostrils flared on an inhale. "Of." Lips so tight they could trap the words. "My. Head."

"Je m'excuse." I gestured to the seat across the table. Nohea sat, keeping her head down. Sara did not.

Fists on his hips and elbows wide, he glared at me. "You wanted me to stay in the house, so I took a damn babysitter with me. There was something I needed to do."

"Oh?"

Nohea spoke up, her expression grim. "He had to go find the prestigious domino."

I kept my arms loose at my sides so as not to conflagrate the energy sparking between Sara and me.

"Damn." Sara's fierce scowl did nothing to calm the situation. "It's the *De Praestigiis Daemonum,* Nohea, but hey, if it'll make you feel better, let's just call it the domino from now on."

De Praestigiis Daemonum? Merde alors. "Why are you

looking for the…domino, as you say?"

"I guess you've heard of it before." Sara shot a glance at Nohea. "What do you know about the *Daemonum*?"

I stared him down. "I believe I asked you a question first."

His jaw hardened as if to lock the words inside. I gave no quarter, refusing to break away from his gaze. He inhaled hard, nostrils flaring. I raised my chin.

"Oh, for fuck's sake." Nohea jumped to her feet and interjected herself between us. "We're trying to figure if it's possible someone's controlling the demons. Sara"—she put a hand on his shoulder—"figured the domino book might contain the right kind of spell."

"A unique copy of the *Daemonum* was recently purchased, and we need to talk to the person who bought it."

So. His terse delivery let me know we'd reached the heart of his argument. I'd heard of the *Daemonum*. The Brothers spoke of it with the same level of respect a modern military officer granted a nuclear warhead. Deadly. The kind of weapon you unleashed only when you wanted to land the final blow.

Sara and Nohea had gone searching for the owner: foolish, fragile children playing games with an asp.

He shall cover thee with his feathers, and under his wings shalt thou trust: his truth shall be thy shield and buckler.

"Could y'all sit down? Please? Before one of you spontaneously combusts?"

Locked in a stare-down with Sara, I did not acknowledge Nohea's entreaty. Still, I yielded, taking a seat at the dining room table. Sara did not, his arms crossed, jaw tight with a harsh determination.

I would need to be careful, because I had the sense Sara could be unyielding if he set his mind to something. "I think I would not willingly handle the *De Praestigiis Daemonum*. Anyone coming into contact with such a thing would be unalterably changed."

Thou shalt not be afraid for the terror by night; nor for the arrow that flieth by day;

Nor for the pestilence that walketh in darkness; nor for the destruction that wasteth at noonday.

They certainly did not fear the pestilence contained in this ancient, evil book, or they would have run the other way. "I must ask—"

"Oh hell no," Sara snapped. "You are NOT going to tell us to leave this one alone. We're not children."

Ironic he'd used the same word, as if he had entrée to my thoughts. Standing before me, so strong and proud, he was anything but childlike. To my mortification, my body responded to him, the heat building into a desire I could never again indulge.

I attempted to calm both of us down. "No good can come from this implement of calamity."

"I don't want the stupid book. I want to know who bought it." He crossed to the table, planting his knuckles on the wood and looming over me. "Listen, you're the one who said the power to call up demons and make them do what you want is extraordinary, and the *Daemonum* is the only thing I've found promising that kind of power."

His defiance irked me, and I stood, looming over him. "What would you do if you found this person?"

Again, Nohea wedged herself in the middle. "Could y'all knock it off? He's got a point, Mr. Dupont."

"Hell, yes, I—"

"Shut up, Sara." She shoved both of us back a step. "Listen, I've had a bad feeling about this all along, and the shop out in Gretna—"

"You went all the way to Gretna?" I exploded. They'd taken a terrible risk. "What if something had happened? I wouldn't have known where to look for you."

Nohea rolled her eyes at Sara, who answered her with a glare. Slowly, with much contradiction and talking over each other, their story came out. While not completely mollified, by the end, I had a new respect for Sara's technological skill.

We all sat at the table; Nohea, the child of my heart, and Sara, who had become so much more.

"So I figure he must have been making them at the hospital." Sara brushed the hair from his face, his lips holding their normal almost-smile. "And then he dragged us down there to show off or something."

Leo. I should confess to the visitation, but shame held my tongue. Leo Killian represented the one time in my life when I'd truly been divorced from the Church. I had gone too long without speaking of him to begin now. The words were grounded in shame.

Nohea tapped the table with one fingernail. "Assuming you're right, where's he making them now? They don't seem to be stopping."

We knew so little. Frustration tainted my every breath. "I suspect whoever is behind this will leave us further clues. Their goal appears to be to get me to join with them."

"Well, they sure are targeting you," Nohea said.

"Yeah." Sara nodded. "I was kind of out of it, but didn't the guy at the cemetery say something about that?"

"As did the man on Frenchmen Street, so if they're targeting me, I'm the one who should deal with them." Even as I spoke, I could sense the mutiny from both of them.

"Oh hell no." This time, Nohea stood, arms crossed, her jaw tight. "I will concede running around on our own might not have been the smartest thing ever." A sharp look from her killed Sara's protest. "But we're in this game too, and you *will* let us help."

I looked from one to the other. Both so young. This was my fight, and if anything happened to either one…

Yet Sara had discovered the *Daemonum*, and Nohea had proved herself to be quite capable during our search of the hospital. I clasped my hands. *Lord, though your will and wisdom exceed my comprehension, if you should take one of these from me, I would be hard-pressed to find understanding.*

"In the future, I will accompany you on these searches."

Nohea shrugged. "That's fair."

Sara nodded.

Later, Nohea retired to the guest room. Sara and I still stood alone in the foyer. His posture was more relaxed, though his eyes were wary.

"You should get—" I said.

"Do you need—" he spoke over the top of me. We both stopped. He dropped his gaze to the floor with a small smile.

"It is time for Compline. I must pray." I took a step toward the stairs. "You should rest."

He stopped me with a hand on my arm. "I could come with you."

The invitation in those few words made me light-headed.

"I'm sorry, Sara." I could not continue the kind of physical relationship we'd shared. Already my transgressions were great, and to carry on would bring him down to the pit with me. "Good night."

Sadness washed over me. Sadness and the deepest regret I'd ever known. I took the stairs at a measured pace, away from his roiling emotions, heading toward the peace of my small room. I had not secured his promise to stay away from the *Daemonum*. I would. Later. After the music of the psalms had reordered my thinking.

There shall no evil befall thee, neither shall any plague come nigh thy dwelling.

TWO DAYS.

Two days of avoiding Sara, comforting Nohea, and waiting for the next disaster to fall. I kept mostly to my room. Waiting.

Shirtless, I knelt on the floor, psalter in hand. The prayer for Vespers moved me one more step along the path of the Psalms, as worn and well-loved as any in my life. Tonight the words offered faint comfort, for each step brought me closer to giving Brother George my confession. Beyond that, my future was too dim to see.

Sara and Nohea moved around the lower level, their footsteps and the clink of silver on china adding a counterpoint to my chant. Their voices rose in a brief and vigorous discussion. Music started, muffling the rest of their talk. They'd become friends, my two charges, and while I valued my relationship with each of them, I listened for Sara.

Every laugh. Every murmur. Every breath.

The evening heat wrapped around my bare shoulders, the leather-covered psalter sticky against my palms. I'd spent much time pondering my own weakness, and it weighed on me heavier than the humid air. Someone had targeted me, putting my closest associates at risk. I'd been charged with finding who, and so far had failed. I'd had a hundred years to acquire enemies; bodies I'd deanimated to rid them of demons, young assistants who might remember more of my feedings than I'd intended.

Leo, who'd never forgiven me for denying the one thing he wanted.

Before this, the monks had used me as a weapon in the fight against evil, offering me the chance to redeem my own soul. I might have eventually found redemption had I not broken my bond by indulging with Sara.

Warm, handsome Sara, whose intelligence and enthusiasm lightened my burden, even as his physical presence drove me to distraction. I shifted, the floor hard under my knees, my body rebelling against the supplicant posture. Over the course of my meditations, I discovered an unalterable truth.

Even knowing I would soon face Brother George in confession, with my very uncertain fate hanging in the balance, I would do it again. If Sara came to me and offered the solace of his physical affections, I would welcome his embrace, though it should seal my fate and drive him down the path of sin.

They say our God is a loving god, and though I tried with all my soul, I couldn't see it.

I'd nearly completed the chant when the bright bleat of a telephone rose above the music. Nohea answered. The music cut off. "Is he up yet?" Her voice carried above the music. "Mr. Dupont?"

Sara gave an indistinct answer. How would he know when I awoke?

Footsteps pounded up the stairs, so I pulled on a cotton shirt. Catching me half-dressed would embarrass us all.

I opened my door before the knock. Nohea stood right outside. "Did you hear that? Brother George says they have a problem at the abbey."

"I didn't, and what sort of problem?"

She shook her head, still out of breath from her run up the stairs. "We gotta get over there now."

I acquiesced, even going so far as to ignore my doubts when Sara agreed to stay behind. He said he had some work to do on the computer, and though his uncharacteristic compliance made me suspicious, I didn't question him. Nohea's grim spirit overrode all other concerns.

While I dressed, I had Nohea seal the doors and windows with holy water, reinforcing the wards of protection. She'd dressed for battle, all in black, with her whip hanging off one hip and a blade strapped to her thigh. I was similarly, though less conspicuously, armed. After locking the kitchen door behind us, I laid a hand on the frame, offering one last prayer for Sara's safety.

"Come on, Thaddeus." Nohea headed for the door. "Dude is in full geek mode. He's not going to look up from the laptop before we get home."

She led the way to her glossy black Dodge Challenger, and I followed, grateful to have time to prepare for whatever we'd have to face.

"Brother G sounded upset." Nohea's sharp comment interrupted my meditation.

I straightened and cleared my throat, willing myself to be present in the low-slung vehicle, cool air blowing from the vents, freeway passing though I had no recollection of leaving the Garden District. "He gave you no clue as to the source of his distress?"

She shrugged, flicked the turn signal, and aimed for an exit. "Nope. Just said you needed to see the chapel at the abbey ASAP."

Within moments, we'd parked in front of St. Joseph Abbey, a monastery and school for boys. The main building had been constructed well after I left school, a simple mid-century structure, boxy and plain.

On the south end of the property stood a much older chapel, built shortly after the monks took up residence. As a young man, this place had shaped my faith as much as the texts I'd read and the sermons I'd heard.

While the words were stored in my mind, in my heart, there were other memories embedded in the stone and wood. Ninety-year-old memories, from the last days of my human life.

A cluster of men stood at the main entrance to the chapel. Weak light shone down from the sconces on either side of the darkened door, casting them in an ominous shadow.

They turned as a group in the direction of my car, a collection of pale skin, dark clothes, and hard eyes.

"Guess we won't be sneaking in," Nohea murmured.

"Apparently not." I climbed out of the car, and Nohea followed.

"Mr. Dupont," a voice called out. A tall man separated himself from the rest and came across the lawn to meet me. "Thank you for coming."

He reached out, and after a moment of surprise, I clasped his hand. He was younger than I expected, barely older than Sara, and though his features were mild, his body spoke of power.

"It's bad in there," he said.

Brother George jogged out of the darkness. "Let's not waste time." His gaze snapped from me to Nohea. "Jordan and his friends did an initial exploration."

"Yeah, the narthex is a mess, and we didn't get far into the nave." The young man, Jordan, squeezed his hands into fists. "There's a lot of smoke, and some surface damage, and"—he swallowed hard, staring off into the night—"they've got Brian."

"One of our senior recruits." Brother George gestured toward the young men waiting by the door. "They've already begun their training, and I've asked them to assist you."

Students from the abbey, being asked to fight God only knew what. There were four of them altogether, and each radiated grim determination. I could not ask it of them. The very ground should have spoken to me of safety. Instead, it cried out of loss, of pain. Of evil. I scrambled for every piece of information I could gather, even as my heart turned to stone. "Your friend, is he still alive?"

Jordan's breathing gave a little hitch. "We think he's been…possessed."

Domine Jesu Christe.

Nohea bounced on the balls of her feet, ready to fight. "What else did you see?"

Both Brother George and Jordan startled, as if they'd only just noticed her presence.

"There are others, strangers, also possessed," Jordan said. "We counted eight, maybe as many as a dozen. It was hard to tell because of the smoke."

Father Patrick strode out of the new building, talking on the phone. He'd likely been charged with keeping civil authorities at bay. He waved at Brother George, who gave me a grim look.

"We've got a team of monks on the way, but I'm not sure this can wait. Jordan and the others are top-notch." George inclined his head toward the altar, his expression as hard as stone. "Can you bring him out?"

"Your student? He's possessed."

George's stony expression grew colder. "Then at least we'll have a body for his parents to bury."

A body. All that would be left of this young man. He could have been me if I'd run afoul of a demon instead of a vampire, or any of these others who were ready to risk their lives. So much life and faith destroyed. How many more deaths would be laid on my soul?

"I'll do this, but I won't risk these others." I gestured at Jordan and his fellow students.

"Even you can't take on a dozen, Thaddeus. Just get it done." With that, the brother jogged over to Father Patrick, his black robes flapping like the wings of a crow.

He'd left me with kids. Students. They might look like men, but they were children, foolishly ready to face whatever horror hid in the chapel. Nohea brought out a blade from a sheath strapped to her thigh. She wasn't much older than the others, and this would be the first time her training would truly be tested.

Every fiber of my body demanded I face this alone.

As if he could sense the direction of my thoughts, Jordan stepped closer. "Brian's like my brother."

The others crowded around: a redhead, a blond, the third with skin so dark, his eyes glowed. They looked at me expectantly, obviously committed to the idea of fighting this evil. If my skill failed in the face of this challenge, then my mysterious opponents won.

Ave Maria, gratia plena, dominus tecum. With that brief prayer, I commended us all to Our Lady's care. "You're all armed?"

Though they could have barely begun their training with the White Monks, they each brought out handguns and the deadly hunting knives typical of the order. I nodded in approval. "All right. I'm going in first, and Jordan, you and Nohea bring up the rear. Watch out for each other, and don't lose sight of the way out. If I give you a command, even if it's to leave the fight, you must do it. Now let's go."

Murmuring their agreement, they all made the sign of the cross and followed me.

The chapel seated fewer than one hundred people. Just past the narthex, rows of pews marched along a center aisle, stained glass lined the walls, and black smoke filled the sanctuary.

The white marble interior had been marred by vandals, with black gangland scrawls in the vestibule, the crucifix broken and upended and splashed with blood.

My ancient heart stuttered.

A young man stood in the transept. His arms were extended and lashed to the splintered end of the crucifix, his white jersey stained with blood, his eyes glowing coal black with demon fire. Those eyes cut through the clouds of smoke billowing around him. I froze, shattered by a bone-deep recognition. The novice could have been me a hundred years ago, or any one of the young men standing at my side.

Nohea jabbed me in the ribs. "Mr. Dupont. Hey, wake up."

Inhaling hard, I rubbed my eyes and struggled with my composure. God possessed the ability to rise above the desecration of the physical structure, though the rage running hot and clear through my veins assured me I would not. I gestured to either side of me. "Spread out."

The four novices did as I asked. Their bravery inspired me, and with Nohea at my right hand, I started down the center aisle.

"There you are, Thaddeus." The young man's voice made the hairs on the back of my neck rise. "Wasn't sure what it'd take to get you invited to this party."

A foul odor permeated the place, and the young man leaned into his bindings, stretching forward to a dangerous angle. His lips curled and twisted, as if his true soul was desperate to escape. The evil energy built until it became a palpable thing. My only response was to move toward him with steady, determined steps.

"Come and get me!" the young man cried, the words both plaintive and mocking.

Rage transmuted into something darker, and in my mind, I stood at the place where hopelessness meets despair. With a long, shuddering breath, I stared into the abyss. Only the knowledge that if I succumbed, so would the young people beside me kept me from falling.

No more innocents would die on my behalf.

The chapel doors slammed shut behind us, and with a rush like a gust of wind, every candle in the place flared to life.

"Well, look at you." The young man's voice throbbed with misplaced desire. "So handsome. And I've seen how you watch him. You just love the taste of that young cock, don't you?" The energy around him coalesced, making it difficult to see or even think straight. The only one of my senses not overwhelmed was my hearing, where the young man's taunts landed like blows.

No more would die.

Anger and determination squared my shoulders. I took several more steps down the central aisle.

"Oh, he's coming. He's coming. He's coming." The tortured boy's voice rose in a mockery of lust. The anger in me curdled to a deep, abiding despair. For a moment, my focus wavered, losing myself in the maelstrom of light and smoke and evil.

"Thaddeus!" Nohea's cry jerked me into the present. *What?* This was too dangerous for her, so I opened my mouth to command her to leave.

And closed it again when several figures stepped out of the darkness.

Eight of them, or were there twelve? More? Shadows kept moving, clad in business suits and day dresses, average in the extreme. Their one commonality was their pitch-black eyes. The figure on the cross reached a crescendo of exhortations, crudely mocking me.

So much death. One of them, a balding man in a crisp white button-down and trim jeans, raised a heavy black handgun.

"Who the *hell* keeps giving guns to these idiots?" Nohea muttered. The balding demon jerked his hand in her direction and took a shot.

I dove to intercept the bullet. Too late.

"Fuck." Nohea hit the ground at the same time as one of the stained glass windows shattered. She popped up with her whip in one hand and a tiny pistol in the other.

"Get down," I barked, crouching between pews and gesturing at the others to do the same. She scuttled up next to me, and the four novice monks spread out. Noise from the front of the church indicated the demons were on the move.

"You stay near the door and get out of here if things go badly," I said.

"Thaddeus, don't—"

I grabbed her wrist hard enough to make her stop. "You *will* leave here alive."

Her chin jutted forward, as if it took all her self-restraint to keep from arguing with me. Something in the front of the room crashed.

"Aw, come on, Brother Thaddeus. It's no fun if you hide." The poor soul taunted me with a voice broken by madness.

Then all hell broke loose.

And explosion lit the high altar, as if the hosts in the monstrance had convulsed in a ball of fire. The demons rushed us, and the young man on the cross screamed.

I had no time to think or to feel. A woman came at me, swinging a heavy gold candlestick. Right behind her, a muscular man swung fists with practiced accuracy. I was faster and stronger, but we were outnumbered.

The demon fired his gun again, and this time, Nohea's whip answered with a high, sharp crack. She screamed like a Valkyrie, throwing herself at a man who had to outweigh her by fifty pounds. He went down with a well-aimed kick to the gut, and she finished him off with a bullet.

The novices were all engaged, fighting with these men and women who could have been ordinary members of the congregation. The redhead had taken shelter in a confessional, firing his gun at any of the demons who came within range. The black man and his blond friend were fighting in tandem on the south aisle, and Jordan had taken a position near the doors.

Two more demons converged on Nohea, and though my instinct was to help, I found myself surrounded. Four? Five? Six? I lost track of the number. I fought them, their fists and their grappling hands, their errant kicks and the weapons they'd created out of holy objects. I shut down my lingering humanity and brought them down, one after the other, tearing out hearts, breaking necks.

For the first time, truly, letting the monster take over.

Finally, I faced the demon with the gun. He stood next to the cross, the only one left, a rictus grin twisted over his face. Nohea leaned on Jordan, clutching her right arm close to her body, her gaze as sharp as the blade she'd pulled from the sheath on her thigh.

Injured? *I will destroy them.*

The young man on the cross chortled. "I could make him bend over for you."

"Take him out, Thaddeus." Nohea's tone brooked no argument.

"Aw, he's not going kill you, Thad-dee. We just wanted to prove a point," the possessed one shouted.

As if on cue, the one holding the gun, who had once been a balding man dressed in expensively casual clothing, brought the weapon to his mouth and pulled the trigger.

Blood and tissues sprayed out from the remains of his head.

Nohea's scream echoed in my ears. I ran for the cross. For a moment, I could not recall my task. The heat, the smell, the frenzied energy paralyzed me.

A simple rope had been wrapped around the young man's wrists and looped through the jagged, broken end of the crucifix. Even knowing the demon-possessed must die, I could not kill a bound man. I lifted the rope, freeing him.

"Oops." He snickered. "Didn't they tell you? If you kill me, the whole place blows."

"All of you, get out," I yelled at the top of my lungs, hoping the others obeyed me, unable to look away from the possessed soul.

"Come on, Thaddeus." His tongue made an exaggerated circuit of his lips. "You know you want some."

Without giving myself time to think, I grabbed his sneering face and snapped his neck.

The rumble started before I reached the last pew.

"Get everyone out. The curse on this place…" I found I couldn't go on. Whoever or whatever had instigated these events had no regard for human life.

The rumble increased to a roar. Squinting, I attempted to force my vision to stay in the present and ignore the tumult of darkness surrounding us. Black scrawls on white marble, brick-red blood. Fire. Heat. Stench.

Scooping up Nohea, I shoved Jordan and his friends ahead of me and ran through the doors. "Move. Move. Move!" Urgency carried my voice beyond Father Patrick and Brother George, and others picked up the refrain.

Men streamed away from the chapel. The rumbling increased till it shook the marrow in my bones. I stumbled on, screaming, "Go."

The sound cut out, leaving us in an echoing silence. One voice yelled, "Hey!" and an explosion rocked us all. White-hot fire blew out the chapel doors. Shattered glass flew for yards in every direction.

The force of the explosion damped the sound of the screams. Priests and monks lay in the dirt, some on their hands and knees, injured or simply terrified.

I'd landed on a sword plant, its broad, spiny leaves scratching my ribs and spine. Nohea curled in a ball at my side. More failure. Sirens shrieked through the night. My very bones ached.

What am I to learn from this, Lord? You've given someone the power to harm those closest to me. To what end?

To what end?

My faith, which had sustained me for over one hundred years, felt as damaged and empty as the blown-out chapel. I had been taught to turn the other cheek, but this?

Non.

Nohea struggled to her feet, still clutching her arm. "We got to get out of here." She tossed her head in the direction of the oncoming police vehicles. Blood covered my hands. Not my own.

Getting to my own feet took effort. "The car." I scanned the scene, noting Jordan and the other young monks. They were all on their feet. Alive. Taking that as a small consolation, I headed toward the car.

Father Patrick caught me. "I believe this proves my fear." He waved a hand at the smoking remains of the church.

His fear? I nearly laughed. If these events were related to the events in California, I'd be damned if I could see how. I shook my head and staggered to the car. Until I'd meted out my revenge, Father Patrick's fear could wait.

CHAPTER TWENTY

SARA CLICKED HIS LAPTOP CLOSED, stood up and stretched. Marc Goutard was not an unfortunate homeless man. He was the owner, or co-owner at least, of a chain of New Age and occult shops which had been founded by his mother. As far as Sara could tell, Ms. Goutard had retired, leaving Marc in charge.

No wonder Missy had stuttered. Nothing like having a smelly, crazy-eyed, not-bum for a boss.

He revisited the idea of Marc as their demon-summoner—but the only link he could come up with was the dubious Weyer translation. As Nohea had said, summoning demons and not getting yourself eaten by one probably took a certain attention to detail. Mark didn't seem to fit the profile.

On the other hand, he hadn't come up with any other clues. The Weyer was literally his best lead, and Marc's chain of voodoo shops were the dead end of the trail. The small company didn't attract a lot of media and internet breadcrumbs, which meant all he could find were their public-facing websites and a few reviews.

The Goutards' private lives, theoretically more interesting and useful, were locked behind privacy filters. The elementary hacking skills he had picked up courtesy of a techie roommate his freshman year didn't extend to breaching accounts set up with decent passwords and more than a passing nod to security.

After hours at the computer, he had exactly zero new info. Modifying a new app for his phone was his big accomplishment for the day. Maybe he should have gone with Thaddeus and Nohea, but the last thing he wanted was to sit on the sidelines again while the adults talked. So much for being more useful here at home.

He spent a few minutes stalking his friends and family back in Seattle via social media, then realized he had somehow missed a string of messages from Nate, who, crap, was coming this weekend? He checked his calendar, and sure enough, this weekend. Nate was interning at his uncle's law firm and had somehow convinced them to send him to a convention in Atlanta, then scheduled his flight with a layover in New Orleans. Sara stared at the excited string of messages, depressed.

Nate was coming. Just like they planned. And, no way could Sara spend a night out partying on Bourbon Street.

Feeling like a total loser, he typed in a reply.

Sara: I can't go out. I have to work. ☹

No immediate response. So he would get to feel shitty later, too, when Nate got his text.

He went downstairs, looking for a distraction. Maybe if he cleared his head, something new would occur to him. The old house seemed as though it would be a treasure trove of odds and ends from Dupont's long lifetime, but whatever personal items Thaddeus might have collected over the years, he didn't display them here. Except for the den and their bedrooms, the house might as well have been a hotel.

He considered using the opportunity to poke around in Dupont's room. Did he have that right? The parameters of their relationship were still too vague for him to be sure. Anyway, what would he to poke into? The chest and armoire together weren't big enough to hold one season of his own clothes. He was unlikely to find anything but

Thad's limited and boring wardrobe.

He wandered aimlessly, until he remembered Nohea saying Dupont had some vintage jazz records stashed somewhere. After a fruitless turning out of the entertainment center, he expanded his search to the less-used, formal parts of the house. A pretty walnut cabinet turned out to be a tube radio and record player combo. Sara stroked a reverent hand over the polished wood. He found the records in a matching box next to it. Mint condition 78 RPMs. He barely breathed as he lifted each one out. Kid Ory, Louis Armstrong, Jelly Roll Morton. He wondered if the record player still worked and if he dared try a few out.

Bessie Smith's "Backwater Blues" was crackling out of the old player when he found the picture.

Two men—one light, one dark. The old black-and-white photograph fell out of a Jelly Roll Morton sleeve. Thaddeus and… Jelly Roll's "Black Bottom Stomp" seemed appropriate for the golden man with him. He sat in his shirtsleeves and suspenders, a cigarette in one hand and a champagne glass on the table next to him. Dupont stood behind him. There was nothing remarkable about the pose—nothing to suggest intimacy. The bottom dropped out of Sara's stomach anyway.

The period looked '20s or early '30s. Thad wore a suit. Nothing like the bland clothes he favored these days, though. Plaid, Thad? Plaid jacket and a bow tie?

Not even nerdy plaid. He looked fashionable. Nothing in either man's attire suggested austerity or restraint. Nothing in the way Thad looked at his companion suggested either of them were monks.

"Backwater Blues caused me to pack my things and go…"

Shut up, Bessie.

Sara stared down at the photograph, grappling with the emotion gripping him. He had never been jealous before. He wasn't now. He had no reason to be jealous. He and

Dupont had known each other only a few weeks, and their relationship status was…undefined. Anyway, this man, whoever he had been, must be dead and gone.

Yet Dupont had valued him enough to abandon his cabin in the swamp, his morbid religious symbols, and his servitude to the Church. Devotion was evident in his gaze. For Sara, he wouldn't even give up the discomfort of his narrow-ass bed.

Bessie's song had ended and been replaced by the erratic hiss of the needle bumping the inner ring. Sara ignored it, not in the mood to value any of Dupont's few possessions at the moment. He turned the picture over.

Thaddy and Leo 1929.

Even the handwriting was dashing. Swell. And what kind of nickname was *Thaddy*? It didn't suit Dupont at all.

He began methodically returning the records to the box. Halfway through, a car pulled into the drive. He took out his phone, peeled back the case, and stuck the picture in behind it. Then he finished putting away the music and went to see what Dupont and Nohea had been up to.

Dupont blew past him in the hall without stopping.

Fine.

He turned to Nohea.

"Not now." Her face looked grim, and she cradled one arm to her chest.

"But—"

"I said *not now.*" She followed Dupont upstairs, and a minute later, the door to her room slammed.

So he didn't get to know whatever had happened with the monks. Because why should they tell him? He wasn't a real member of the team. He was just a steak that had gotten uppity.

He rubbed his chest, vaguely aware the swirling mess of emotions wasn't all his. And screw that, too. He hadn't signed on for this kind of psychological trauma. He was the victim of an unsafe working environment. Except there were no OSHA regs to cover emotional spills from your boss.

He stomped into the den. Where there was still nothing to do.

Dupont's chants started up. Sara pressed his hands over his ears.

When he couldn't block out the sound, he plugged his phone into the entertainment center and scrolled though his playlists. Drowning Pool ought to do. He cranked the stereo system in the den to full volume. And he *raged*.

For about two minutes.

Then he got a grip. Sort of. Enough to realize the chanting had stopped and Dupont was *really* in a state. Not semi-catatonic as Sara had found him in the shower. But… agitated.

Whatever Leo and *Thaddy* had together was in the past. Sara was here now. Even if no one wanted to admit it, he belonged on this team. They needed him. Thaddeus needed him.

Upstairs, he knocked softly on the door. "Mr. Dupont?"
Silence.

"Mr. Dupont? Can I come in?" He tried the knob, not too surprised to find it locked.

He leaned his forehead against the door. "Thaddeus?" He tried to reach through whatever bond they shared. As usual, it defied logic and conscious control.

Without warning, the door opened. Off balance, he pitched forward, straight into Dupont's arms.

"What do you—"

"I'm sorry I—"

They both broke off.

Up close, all the messy emotions boiled down to the physical. The whiff of cypress, the arms holding him steady, the press of their bodies together, Dupont's lips in his hair. For the first time in days, Dupont didn't ignore him or push him away.

Sara froze, afraid to make a move. His arms were trapped between them. He let one finger touch the cool skin above Dupont's shirt.

"Sara."

He couldn't tell if the word was a warning or encouragement. The residual anger stirred, then twisted into a fierce want. He was here now, not Leo. However Thaddeus viewed his vampire nature, he couldn't always be an island. This thing happening between them was more than survival and more than a job, and backing off was not an option.

He finally decided on the one thing he could not be faulted for trying. He breathed in cypress and male. Shivering with need, he tilted his head, offering his neck.

Dupont went still. Then, "I do not need…"

Sara touched skin again, pressing his point home. "You're cool. You need to eat."

"I—" Dupont cleared his throat. "It will not stop with your blood."

"You need to eat." He was afraid to say more, afraid of being pushed away. For the first time, afraid Dupont avoided their intimacy for reasons other than blind obedience to Church doctrine.

The pause lasted long enough for him to realize something. He didn't have a crush. He wasn't just sleeping with his hot boss, he was… Falling for Dupont would be a really bad idea.

The gaping maw of despair in his stomach wasn't concerned with this logic.

Or maybe it was all vampire magic.

His thoughts terrified him so much, he almost pulled away when Dupont took his hand and turned toward the bed.

"Come."

He allowed himself to be led, to be pulled into Dupont's lap, where he discovered plenty of evidence his physical affections, at least, were returned. He couldn't guess at what Dupont felt. The energy churning between them was too tangled to unravel. He could hear his own heart thudding in his chest, and he didn't want to think anymore. He wrapped his arms around the cool body, pressed close, and offered his neck again.

Soft lips brushed his throat. Thad's fangs touched flesh with an imperceptible scrape, like a needle drawn gently across his skin. The tiny discomfort was followed by the soothing lap of Thad's tongue as he accepted the gift. Sara clung to him, gasping as his body responded as though it were being used in an entirely different way. Magic. And maybe something else.

He didn't care. Dupont held him carefully, but Sara could feel his tremors. He pressed closer, wanting more than careful.

Instead, Dupont lifted his head.

"No." Sara sealed their lips together, and Dupont gave in, opening his mouth and letting his tongue make promises about the way they would be together. Sara twined closer, cock straining against denim. He needed skin. His fingers found the buttons on Dupont's shirt. He had the first one undone before his hand was captured and held firmly in place.

Damned control freak. He nipped at Dupont's lip, getting a muffled growl in response.

Dupont cupped the back of his head, and before Sara knew it, he found himself cradled with none of the good bits touching at all. Dupont was *soothing* him.

His over-sensitized body rebelled at the idea, and he damn sure wasn't ready to turn his brain back on either. He twisted his hips, rubbing against Dupont in a way he couldn't possibly ignore. "Thaddeus." He wasn't above begging if it got him what he wanted. "Thaddeus, *please.*"

Dupont's arms tightened. "Ah, *cher.*"

The kiss held all the passion Sara could have asked for. The hand at his fly tormented him for the few seconds it took Dupont to deal with the button and zipper. Sara surged upward into his hand, not trying to hide his eagerness. He wrapped his arms around Dupont's neck and moaned into his mouth as Dupont milked him. *Brain off.* He fucked himself into Dupont's hand, refusing to think about anything but here and now. Physical affection counted. If he wanted more… Dupont's thumb slicking his own fluids over the head of his cock provided exactly the distraction he needed. He teetered on the brink in seconds. *Not yet.* He needed to stay safe in sensation a little longer, not to analyze, not to think.

He tore his mouth from Dupont's. "Wait. Slow down… Thaddeus… *I'm not…*"

Dupont ignored him, and Sara stopped caring as bright light destroyed thought and the rest of the universe in a blinding flash.

He slowly drifted down to earth and into Dupont's arms.

Nice. Lazily, he walked his fingers up Dupont's torso and began with the shirt buttons again.

Dupont shifted his hold and stood, lifting him as if he weighed nothing.

Sara snuggled closer to his vampire as they headed down the hall. "Good," he managed. "M'bed is better."

After Dupont set him down, Sara arched against the pillows and smiled up at him invitingly. Proper bed. Finally.

Dupont dropped a kiss on his forehead and walked out of the room.

Sara's brain froze.

What the hell just happened?

He stared up at the ceiling, trying to process the fact that Dupont had just taken his blood, jerked him off, dumped him in his own room, and left.

His emotions, still riding the orgasm, felt hazy and remote. Then the pain seeped in, tinged with a dull despair and a throb of anger.

Which would be more pathetic? Bursting into the room down the hall and causing a big fat gay scene? Or lying here crying like a baby?

His only consolation was not being upset alone. His on-again-off-again Dupont-o-Meter registered a slew of unhappy. Well, duh. Dude hadn't even busted. He must be all kinds of uncomfortable.

Served him right.

Down the hall, the odd, rhythmic noises started again. Sara strained his ears. *Monk stuff,* Nohea had said. But what?

The pain intensified. His or Dupont's? What a crap superpower. Why couldn't he get something useful out of this deal? X-ray vision would be awesome right now.

More irritating noises. And then…the pain leveled off, replaced by something suspiciously like euphoria.

That was definitely from Dupont's end of the feed. On Sara's end, it translated into outrage. Was he in there getting off *by himself?* Didn't his stupid Church teach that turned him into a werewolf or something?

The outrage propelled Sara out of the bed and down the hall. He didn't stop to consider Dupont's door might be locked.

It wasn't.

He came to a skidding halt in the middle of the room. Took one look at the scene in front of him, then lunged for Dupont's arm as it brought down the whip.

HE LANDED HARD AGAINST THE wall with Dupont's hand at his throat.

"*Merde!*"

And he was free. Sara sucked in air, trying to recover from the shock of the impact.

Dupont had retreated to the far side of the room.

They stared at each other warily. Dupont looked… embarrassed, guilty…*wrecked.*

"Are you hurt?"

Am I hurt? This so wasn't about him. His gaze slid past Dupont to the crucifix on the wall. A shrine to suffering. Blood and pain. And Dupont no less bloody. Sara couldn't see his back anymore. His memory helpfully supplied the image—ribbons of skin laid open in a deliberate mutilation of flesh.

"Sara. Answer me, *cher*. Did I injure you?"

"No." He suppressed an inappropriate urge to laugh. "I'm fine." *Lie.* He wasn't injured. But he might never be fine again because… "Why?"

Dupont's gaze slid away. "I attacked you," he said to the floor.

"No. Not that. Why—" He scrubbed his hands across his eyes, as if he could erase the sight. "Why would you—" *Torture yourself.*

"It is a form of penance."

I've had over a hundred years to come to terms with my perversion.

"Penance for what?" But he knew the answer.

Perhaps Dupont had some inkling of his thoughts. When he spoke, he skirted the issue. "I am vampire, an unholy creature. There can be no end to my penance."

"Yeah? Did you choose to be a vampire?" He held his breath, because if Nohea was wrong, he had just lost this argument.

"Perhaps the fiend was drawn to me because…" He trailed off. "I could have chosen to die. Instead, I clung to life."

"Congratulations, you have a survival instinct like every other human on the planet. Before you had to choose between life and death, did you want to be a vampire?"

"*Non.* It is a torment."

"Why would you need penance for a condition you have no control over?"

Dupont stared at him. "I am a monster. I survive on the blood of innocents. Surely that is enough."

"I'm no more innocent than you, and my blood is a gift. If you want to thank me for it, you can start by not bleeding it out five minutes after I give it to you."

"You had no choice. I have bewitched you."

"No." He answered without thinking. The certainty settled over him as soon as he said it. "No. I knew what I was doing, and I offered it freely, the same as I would for any person who needed it to survive. Try again, Thaddeus. I won't participate in your martyrdom."

"I am an unnatural creature. I die as the sun rises each day. There can be no greater evidence. My soul is forfeit, and God has turned his face from me."

"You don't die. I checked. Your heart doesn't stop while you're asleep. So maybe God doesn't hate you so much, after all."

Dupont's gaze flew up to his. It broke Sara's heart to see the hope in it, but it lasted only a second. "There is still the hunger."

"Okay, so you're…altered. Different. Whatever. It's not as if you go around kicking puppies and sucking babies dry every night. You're a good person. God's lucky to have you on his side. According to your Church, he must have let this happen to you for a reason."

Dupont shook his head, stubborn to the end. "I have sinned, and I am unrepentant."

Unrepentant? "Yes," Sara mocked. "You are so *unrepentant,* you just tore your back to shreds with a fucking whip. Stop pretending, and say what you mean. You weren't in here doing *penance* for eating to survive. You're literally beating yourself up over what we did together afterward. And you didn't even allow yourself to enjoy it." He was shouting. Nohea could probably hear him down the hall, and he didn't give a rat's ass.

"It is a sin."

"Not for me. Or should I be in here next to you with a whip?"

"*Délivre-moi!* Never say such a thing. You are young and a h—" Dupont broke off, but not before Sara figured out what he had almost said.

"Heathen? That's what you were going to say, wasn't it? It's not my fault because I'm a heathen and a child who doesn't know any better?"

"You have not had the benefit of a proper education. I have failed in my duty to you. The sin is mine, not yours."

"Let me tell you something, *Thaddy*, I'm proud to be a heathen. I *choose* not to believe in your uptight, asshole god. Also, you are not the first man I've fucked. Or did you think I just slipped and fell on your dick with that bottle of lube? I like who I am. I'm exactly the way your *god*, if he exists, made me."

Sara slammed the door on his way out of the room, but paused at the top of the stairs to shout one more point over his shoulder. "And find someone else to be your goddamn donor. I wouldn't want to corrupt you with my heathen blood and unnatural desires."

CHAPTER TWENTY-ONE

THE NEXT DAY, TWO BOXES were delivered by courier. The first, Sara expected.

"You'll show him how to use it?" He handed the phone to Nohea.

"Or you could show him yourself." She turned it off and set it next to her own.

When he didn't answer, she sighed. "You two are more trouble than you're worth. You know that, right?"

"Just show him how to use it, okay?" They had decided on an iPhone since Dupont could transfer his limited iPad skills. "It's ridiculous not having a good way to reach each other. And, oh yeah, did you know the phone in the kitchen works?"

"No shit? I wonder what the number is. I mean, I must pay the bill, right?"

"With oversight like that, I'm totally fudging my expense reports."

"Seriously, though. You're going to have to talk to him and work things out at some point."

Probably. He wasn't ready to talk to Dupont yet. He was still angry. And hurt. And...stuff. He wanted Thaddeus to come to him. He didn't have much experience staying mad at people, though. It required effort.

Sara got up and left the den. Consequently, he was nearest the door when the second courier rang the bell.

"Who's it from?" He peered out through the half-closed door. Paranoia was catching.

The courier squinted at the label. "I dunno, man. You know someone in India?" He hoisted up the box so Sara could see the front.

Daadi? "Yeah. Where do I sign?"

He wrestled the oversized box up to his room. Yay, Daadi! His grandmother always had a knack for sending the right thing at the right time, and apparently he wasn't too grown up for her to send him a care package for his new job. The last couple of days had been shitty. He could use a pick-me-up.

He pulled out the letter on top of the inner box first.

> *Sarasija —*
> *Do you remember our storytimes together when you were small? They have been much on my mind lately. You were the only one of the children who always wanted the old stories instead of Harry Potter or Lemony Snicket.*
> *You are an American and your father's son, but I hope these items will still bring you comfort, even if it is only in memory of our times together.*
> *Stay safe,*
> *Daadi*

Daadi always had the best stories. Thanks to her, his make-believe world had included asuras and rakshasas. One of his favorite stories had been about the rakshasa Vibhishana. Daadi's stories were probably the reason he hadn't run screaming the first time he had seen Dupont vamp out.

What had she sent him? He pulled out half a dozen individually wrapped boxes from the big box.

After the first two, he figured it out. Daadi had sent him everything to set up an altar? She knew he didn't practice.

He pulled out her letter again. The words *comfort* and *safe* jumped out at him. Odd words to choose. Or maybe not. Even Dev, as atheist as their father, didn't ignore Daadi's hunches.

What could it hurt to set up the altar? If nothing else, it would be a welcome change from all the crucifixes. And it would probably annoy Dupont.

The last thought decided him. He located the west wall, shoved one of his nightstands against it, and began setting out his gifts. It would take only a few minutes. He would send a picture to Daadi, and it would make her happy. Tweaking Dupont was just a bonus.

As he unpacked each item his hands slowed. These were not new artifacts chosen at random. She had sent pieces from her own home. He recognized the little copper water bowl and the incense stands. In the end, it took him almost an hour to get everything arranged so it felt right. Only the murti of Durga in the center of the altar looked new. His mother's altar at home contained Saraswati. When they performed pujas at home, they were always to Saraswati. But Daadi hadn't sent him Saraswati. She had sent him Durga.

A chill chased down his spine. His grandmother had wished him safe and sent him Shiva's wife, a slayer of demons and destroyer of evil.

It was almost time for Vespers. Down the hall, Dupont moved around in his room, preparing to honor his Catholic God.

He wasn't really Hindu, Sara reminded himself, and his grandmother would never know if he used the altar. Her choice of Durga was probably a coincidence.

He picked up the copper bowl and went down the hall to fill it with water. In the kitchen, he snagged a banana, then hesitated. He needed fresh flowers. The porch couldn't really be considered leaving the house, he rationalized. Still, he listened carefully to make sure Dupont stayed upstairs as he plucked a few hibiscus blooms from the front beds.

In his room, he approached the altar. He didn't know the correct ceremony for Durga. Wasn't it complicated? He thought most people went to temple to do pujas to the goddess Durga. They required a priest. Or maybe that was only during the Navratri. He considered looking up a ritual on the internet, but it seemed wrong to read at the altar. Instead, he began the basic puja he had done with his grandmother as a child.

A few minutes later, his own voice provided a counterpoint to Dupont's chant. After finishing, he sat in silence. He had not performed a puja in years. He was surprised he remembered even a simple ritual. And he had forgotten how clear his mind felt when it was done. Did Dupont feel like this after his chants?

Absently, he smudged a bit of kumkum onto his forehead before he got up. The smell of incense still surrounded him, bringing back memories of home. How many times had he watched his mother at her altar? He missed her. And Dev. And Aahna. He wondered what had happened to Dupont's family. He never mentioned them. Perhaps if you were alone, a god, no matter how cruel, was a comfort.

He supposed he was going to have to talk to him. He couldn't allow the self-flagellation to continue, and he doubted he was going to convince Dupont to stop by yelling at him and issuing threats.

His thoughts were interrupted by a soft buzz from his phone.

Dev: Call me when you get a chance.

He had avoided calls from his family lately. Hard enough explaining he worked nights and slept most of the day, and *not* explaining what his job entailed was easier by email and text.

He hadn't talked to Dev in weeks. Suddenly, he wanted to hear his brother's voice.

The first words out of Dev's mouth put an end to that.

"What do you mean you restructured your mortgage?"

Sara asked. "You mean you took out another loan? I thought you were saving for Jenna to take maternity leave. I thought you said it was more than you could borrow against the house, anyway."

"We got the house reappraised and juggled some other assets and realized we could do it. I thought you would be happy."

"I told you I would get the money. It's why I took this job."

"But now you don't have to." Dev's voice stayed calm. "If the job doesn't work out, you don't have to worry. You can come home."

"While you drown in debt."

"Don't be so dramatic. I have a good job with plenty of opportunities for advancement. We'll cut back on a few things."

"Why couldn't you just trust me to do this?" He was breathing hard. Of course Dev got the money. Perfect Dev. He had probably never expected Sara to contribute at all. He sounded as though it was no big deal, but if it had been easy to get the money, he would have done so months ago.

"Sara, calm down. It's not a matter of trust. We're all worried about you down there. You never answer your phone anymore, and you won't even tell us exactly what you do. We just want you to have options."

"I don't need options. I have a job. I'm *fine*."

Silence from the other end of the phone.

"What about grad school, then? If you don't want to come home now, you can put the money you earn toward going back to school next fall."

"Or I can pay Ma back for my last two semesters, which was money she never should have spent anyway."

"She doesn't want money from you, Sara."

"I didn't even have a job, Dev. She kept paying my rent and my credit card bills. How do you think I felt when I found out she might lose the house, the company, everything? Dad wouldn't have wanted that."

"Dad would have wanted you to finish your education. He would have supported what she did just like Aahna and I did. We didn't pay for a thing. They supported us until I had my PhD and Aahna was out of medical school. They bought Aahna's condo so she wouldn't have to worry about rent while she did her residency. Whatever we needed, Dad was always there with his checkbook. We want you to have the same opportunities."

"You didn't need Dad's checkbook. You had scholarships and so did Aahna. If I hadn't fucked off half the time, I wouldn't have had to rely on you and Ma to pay my way."

Silence. Because there was no arguing with the truth.

"Are you sure you're okay?"

"Yes, Dev. I'm fine. I am an adult with a job, just like everyone else. Why can't you accept that?"

"Okay, okay. Just… If you change your mind, you can come home."

"I'm not coming home."

"And if you were in trouble, you'd tell me?"

"I'm not a baby. Believe it or not, I can take care of myself."

"I miss you, little bro."

Sara hung up on him. Then felt like shit. But he couldn't talk to Dev anymore right now. He tapped a message into his phone.

Sara: I'm fine. Hug Ma for me.

He flung the phone on the bed and paced the room, his peace from the puja completely shredded. What the hell did Dev think he was doing down here? Why did everyone still treat him like a child who needed to be coddled and protected?

If you were in trouble, you'd tell me?

He wasn't in trouble.

Vampire, his conscience whispered. *Demons.*

Well, he was handling all that, wasn't he? Demons and

vampires were part of his job. Which he wasn't quitting to run home to Mommy and Dev.

A thought occurred to him. He headed down the hall and banged on Dupont's door until it opened.

"Let's get something straight."

"*Oui?*"

"I'm your assistant. You pay me to assist. Anything else is on my own time. I'm not feeding you or fucking you for money."

Dupont's eyes went black.

Sara spun on his heel and headed back to his room. Behind him, he heard Dupont's door click shut softly. Asshole. Of course he couldn't slam it like a normal person.

His laptop, sitting on the dresser, mocked him. *I'm not feeding you or fucking you for money.* So what was he doing to earn his keep?

He grabbed the computer and settled himself on the bed. He opened the folder with his notes and meticulously went through everything he had learned. When he finished, he was at the same place he'd started. No clues except the Weyer. No lead on the Weyer except Goutard.

He rummaged around until he found the card Marc had given him. He could call. Was that risky? He didn't really want the dude to have his number.

He stared at the Facebook profile still on the screen. The cover image showed a view of the gulf from the deck of a boat, presumably Marc's. The profile pic was one of the voodoo dolls from the store in the Quarter.

Next he checked his own profile. What had he said about himself recently? Not much since he had moved to Louisiana, he noticed. Mostly close-up selfies with vaguely happy captions designed to convince his family he was okay. A picture of one of Marc's voodoo dolls with a chirpy comment about sightseeing in New Orleans. No mention of Dupont by name. He had never listed his phone number or address, so that was okay.

He chewed on his lip for a few minutes, considering his options. Goutard knew something, and Sara needed to know what. He figured the Goutards had been the brokers for whoever bought the Weyer. Unfortunately, Marc hadn't posted a copy of the sales receipt, complete with buyer contact, on his Tumblr.

His finger hovered. Screw it. He clicked "Add friend." Marc was probably just a local shop owner who could benefit from a few sessions with a good psychotherapist. Even if he were something more, they needed to know, right?

> Sara: Hi! Remember me?

His gut churned after he sent the message, but he ignored it.

Dupont appeared in his doorway later. He hovered awkwardly before gliding into the room. The vampire moves got more pronounced when he was upset. Sara felt himself giving. They should talk.

"Sara, I know—" Dupont stopped at the altar. "What is this?"

"My version of a crucifix." He didn't add, *look—NO BLOOD AND MUTILATION.* Because they were going to talk, right?

"Ah." Dupont frowned at the altar for another minute, then resumed his circuit of the room without comment. Finally, he came to a stop next to the bed. "You are still angry."

Sara shrugged.

"Nevertheless, as your employer, I must ask your cooperation in a certain matter."

As his employer? "Yeah?" Sara narrowed his eyes at Dupont. "What?"

"I must have your word you will not pursue this cursed grimoire."

"The *De Præstigiis Dæmonum?* You mean our *one* clue?"

"It is too dangerous."

"Okay," Sara agreed. "I'll stop looking for it if you stop hunting demons. Except, oh, wait—you can't, because now they are hunting you."

"The demons are my concern, not yours."

"Not true. I'm your assistant. By definition, you are my concern. If the demons are your concern, the transitive law of vampire assistants makes them my concern, too."

"Yes, I am vampire. As you have pointed out, even such a creature as I may be a tool of Our Holy Father. You are yet a mortal and vulnerable to their foul intent. I must ask you to let me handle them."

"I can help."

Dupont crossed his arms over his chest. "Do not make me issue a command."

Sara crossed his own arms and glared up at his boss. "Don't make me ignore it."

The silence stretched out. Sara wasn't sure what he would do if Dupont really did try to resolve the issue by the force of his vampire powers.

To his surprise, Dupont was the one who ended the standoff. "I do not wish to compel your obedience."

"Thank you."

"But I must ask you to take reasonable precautions."

"Depends on what you consider reasonable."

"Next time you want to investigate, you and Nohea will wait until I can accompany you."

"Dude, you can't keep me locked up in this house day and night." Dupont's eyes went stormy at his tone. "I promise not to go off on a fishing expedition again without telling you," he compromised.

Dupont looked like he wanted to argue, but when he spoke, it was to say something different. "I'm sorry this job is not as you might have expected."

The words surprised a laugh out of him. "Not as I might have expected. Yeah, you can say that. I'm glad I'm here, anyway."

Hey, they were talking. And Dupont was treating him like an adult, not threatening to lock him in his room or whammy him for his own good or anything.

Then Dupont ruined it.

"If I could free you from your contract, I would do so."

Sara wanted to hit him. *Adult*, he reminded himself. "Not you, too. I'm happy with the job, thank you." He honored his commitments and their relationship had moved beyond the scope of a legal document. At least on his end. Did Thad still want to replace him?

"If something were to happen to me," Dupont continued, as if he hadn't been interrupted, "you will receive your full salary, and Nohea will make sure you are able to return to your family with no consequences from our… association."

Sara opened his mouth, ready to argue about Dupont making assumptions and decisions for him. What came out was "What's going to happen to you?"

"It is only a precaution," Dupont said.

"You're full of shit. You've been in danger since before we met. Why are we having this conversation now? What's going to happen?"

"*Whereas ye know not what shall be on the morrow*," Dupont shot back in his most supercilious monk voice. "Try not to worry, Sara. Whatever the future may bring, I will see you are taken care of as we agreed."

"What are you not telling me?" Shouting again. Great. He had thought they were going to get through a conversation like adults.

"*If the Lord will, we shall live*," Dupont quoted non-reassuringly as he glided out the door.

So Dupont proved no more willing to trust him with his troubles than Sara's family had been. And he bet Dupont wasn't worried about the banks calling in some loans.

DUPONT HAD COME BACK LATER to let him know the monks had discovered another demonic disturbance. He and Nohea were going to investigate. *"You will stay here?"* Sara hadn't answered. He had already promised to stay at the house while they fought demons. What more was there to say? Nohea had come up next, obviously sent by Dupont. She didn't say anything, just watched him for a minute, muttered something under her breath about boys and their snits, and headed down in a snit of her own.

Sara had spent the night doing property searches. Because, what? They were going to go search every location the Goutards owned? If this were a movie, they would find the stupid grimoire open on someone's desk the second place they looked.

He printed up a list of all the properties anyway, because he had nothing better to do.

He checked Facebook. Marc hadn't responded to his friend request or message. Another dead end.

Then he chain-streamed YouTube until he fell asleep with his clothes on. Too soon, he woke up with his heart pounding from dreams he didn't remember.

He stared around his room groggily, wondering what time it was. Daylight. Noon at least, judging from the sun. Dupont must be asleep. Sara's phone vibrated on the nightstand, probably what had woken him. He untangled himself from his sheets and laptop, which had put itself into power-saving mode.

```
    Nate: I'm here, bro!
    Sara: ...
    Nate: Where are you?
No fucking way.
    Sara: Didn't you get my message?
    Nate: What message?
    Sara: Shit. I'm sorry. I thought you
  didn't respond because you were pissed.
    Nate: WHAT MESSAGE?
```

Sara: I'm out. Gotta work.

Nate: No way. You're ditching me? Call in!

So tempting. He hadn't promised Dupont he wouldn't go out at all, just that he wouldn't follow leads on his own. Nothing had happened when he and Nohea went out before.

Sara: Bro, I live in.

Nate: :(:(:(

Sara: I'll see if I can get off later.

Maybe he could convince Nohea to go with him for a couple of hours.

CHAPTER TWENTY-TWO

NOHEA WAS NOT WILLING TO go with him. Sara tracked her down in the kitchen, where she stood at the counter, chopping a pile of onions, celery, and bell pepper.

"Normally I would…" She shook her head. "Thaddeus is right. It's too dangerous right now. I'm sorry. Maybe you can talk him into taking you tonight, but he's going to hit the roof if you aren't here when he gets up."

Maybe you can talk him into taking you. His mood, already shitty, took another dive. He was a grown man. He didn't need a babysitter to meet a friend for drinks.

"He's got his weekly thing with Brother George tonight too—so probably better to wait until he comes down instead of hounding him as soon as he gets up."

Sara didn't trust himself to speak.

"Hey, you've been complaining about not getting any good New Orleans food. I got groceries delivered for etouffee. Why don't you invite your friend over here?"

"I think he wants to see the Quarter."

She shrugged. "Just a thought."

He left her to her massive pile of smelly vegetables.

He couldn't settle. He tried upstairs, downstairs, *on* the stairs.

Those were pretty much his options.

God, he was sick of this house. He was sick of worrying

about creatures he hadn't known existed two months ago. He was sick of asshole vampires who thought they knew better than everyone else. He was sick of everyone making decisions for him. He was sick of feeling useless. He was sick of being protected and people not telling him things.

The last point stabbed an icepick of tension straight into his brain. He sat on the stairs, drumming his feet up and down, with absolutely nowhere for the stress to go.

His phone buzzed.

    `Marc Goutard accepted your friend request.`

He went still, then jumped up and pounded up the stairs for his laptop.

He opened Facebook and checked his messages. Nothing. *Okay, Marc, what have you been up to?*

He had no idea what to look for, but any distraction would do at this point. Except Marc's timeline turned out to be a wasteland—at least for the past few months. There were a few random memes with disjointed comments attached. A rant about potholes.

A blurry picture of what might have been a goat. More memes.

A notification showing Marc had changed his profile pic—the voodoo doll. This was useless. Sara clicked on PHOTOS, more because it was there than out of any hope Marc's online albums might contain a clue. No stone unturned, he reminded himself. Easier than B and E at random Goutard holdings around the city and less likely to get him arrested.

He clicked through the folders. Pictures of strangers at random gatherings. Football games. Mardi Gras parties. Birthdays. No Satanic Cult Christmas Party album with the attendees conveniently tagged. There were pictures of Marc before he had gone full Derelicte, though. Sara enlarged one of him in on a golf course. Still Tommy Bahama, but in a clean rich-guy-looking-casual way. Still the long hair, but a good cut. Huh. Cleaned up, dude was actually kinda hot.

Except *no*, he couldn't unremember the smell.

Something about the picture nagged at him. He scrolled down and opened more folders, looking for images of Marc specifically. A picture from a wedding finally slid the connection home. Marc—hair cut short and styled, smoking cigars and drinking champagne with the other groomsmen.

Without the hair, he looked…

Sara pulled out his phone and peeled back the cover. His hand shook a little as he slid the picture out and stared straight into laughing eyes identical to Marc Goutard's.

WELL, HE HAD FOUND THE connection to Dupont. He resisted the urge to tear the picture into tiny shreds.

He got up and paced the room, telling himself it wasn't true. Dupont's handsome blond ex hadn't raised a demon army to stalk him.

He caught sight of himself in the mirror as he paced.

Too pretty for his own good. Yeah. That was him. If you liked brown hair and brown eyes and brown skin. If you preferred pale skin, golden hair, and blue eyes, maybe he was just…brown.

What had happened to Dupont's lover? Was he a vampire too? Sara tried to remember what time it had been when Marc had shown up at the shop. Still daylight. But Dupont got up before sunset, so who knew if sun was relevant.

He forced himself to sit down and compare the two pictures.

In the end, he had to admit he didn't know if they were the same person. There were differences. But comparing a single ancient black-and-white to a lot of full-color digital shots left a lot of room for error. Even if Marc was a perfectly normal human, the resemblance was too big a coincidence to ignore.

He was going to have to ask Dupont.

It was the last thing he wanted to do. Because what if Dupont confirmed all his suspicions?

He was still stewing in doubt an hour later when his phone buzzed.

Nate: Sara! I had hurricanes!!!

Great, Nate was drunk and alone in the French Quarter.

It sounded so…*normal*. Getting drunk on Bourbon Street and maybe losing your wallet and having to call in all your cards. Spending too much on drinks and tips because you were flirting with the bartender. Having a world-class hangover the next day. Maybe missing your flight and getting in trouble with your boss.

All of it sounded so much better than vampires and demons and getting in trouble because you were tracking down a cursed book. Way, way better than asking your boss, who you might have fallen a little in love with, if his hundred-year-old ex was alive and stalking him.

Nate: I can't find my Amex.

Sara: Where are you?

Nate: afjldijrr

Nate: Your friend's too drunk to text. He's at Lafitte's Booty. What do you want us to do?

Sara: On my way. Don't let him leave.

He hesitated after he picked up his keys. Nohea and Thaddeus both thought it was dangerous out there. But it was broad daylight. He would be in a public place, not inside a walled cemetery in the middle of the night. And he could take the knife, just in case. He fished it out of the drawer of his nightstand and stuck it in his waistband. Feeling more confident, he headed out.

Nohea was still in the kitchen, so he used the front door and abandoned his car. He squashed a flare of guilt as he sprinted for the streetcar. He had his phone complete with the new apps he had installed for all of them. He would

check in later. Nohea would be pissed, but he could probably, okay maybe, still be home by the time Dupont got up
and noticed he was gone.

Or not, he thought as he opened the door to the Lafitte's
Booty. Because he was an adult and could make decisions
for himself about whether to leave the house alone.

"Sara!"

And whether to have a drink with a friend.

"You're here!" Nate drunkenly threw an arm around
him and held his phone at arm's length. "Damn, bro—
smile. Everyone thinks you died or something. Gotta
commemorate."

A second later, Sara's phone buzzed as the picture popped
up in his feed.

```
    With Sara at Lafitte's Booty. Arrrgghhh!
    Booty! ded
```

"Interesting how you can suddenly work your phone
again."

Nate just gave him the same shit-eating grin that had
gotten him out of almost every scrape ever. At 6'2" with
a burly build and a ready smile, he looked like a cross
between a Viking and a happy blond teddy bear. Most
people saw the fun-loving attitude and missed the sharp
mind behind the endless jokes and pranks. "One drink,"
he said. "C'mon—you're already here. You didn't think I
would leave without seeing you, did you?"

One drink. And Nate. The feeling of *normal* was more
intoxicating than the alcohol. Sara nursed his drink and let
Nate catch him up on all their friends in Seattle and life
as an intern in his uncle's law office. Mostly a lot of very
inappropriate stories about lawyers and clients. Then he
had Nate empty out his pockets to make sure he really did
have his Amex. Also his driver's license, cash, hotel room
key, and the boarding pass for his next flight.

"I can't believe we're both in the French Quarter and
you won't come party with me." Nate sounded more wor-

ried than annoyed, though. "Your boss must be kind of an ass if he won't let you off for one night."

"We're sort of in the middle of a big project right now. It's just bad timing."

"One night, bro." Nate gave him another not so drunk look. "And no one ever hears from you anymore. Everything okay down here?"

"Yeah, the job's just a little more intense than I expected, is all." Just a little. "Hey, I'm sorry our plans fell through. I'll make it up to you if you make it back down here another time, but I gotta get back now."

Sara paid both their tabs, gave Nate directions to the voodoo shop to pick up some souvenirs for his little sisters, and reluctantly left the bar. Playtime in the real world was over. He checked his phone, relieved to see he hadn't missed any urgent messages from Nohea. He had left the bedroom door shut, so maybe she thought he was just pouting. Deep in his chest, he felt the tiny shift that told him Dupont had started his ascent into wakefulness.

He should probably catch a cab himself, if he wanted any chance of getting back before anyone noticed his absence. Instead, he walked toward Canal Street and the streetcar, unwilling to give up this tiny taste of freedom quite yet.

He noticed the smells first. Rancid roses on the left. On the right, piss and… He stopped walking and turned.

"Hello, my new friend. Remember me?"

Hawaiian shirt and crazy eyes. Sara knew he didn't have a chance, but he pivoted and ran. He fumbled his phone from his pocket as he fell, knocked into an alley by a tackle he never saw coming. The knife in his waistband dug into his back as they overpowered him.

CHAPTER TWENTY-THREE

SARA'S CONVICTION PLAYED UPON MY doubt. For some eighty years, I'd adhered to a few simple guidelines: chant the hours, use my heightened physical capabilities to destroy evil, and suppress my unnatural inclinations, by force if necessary.

Now everything had been upended. I rose early on Saturday, my mind in turmoil. For years, I'd labored to redeem my immortal soul, and now a base sin had destroyed my hope. I should confess my sin, even though the penalty would be severe.

Domine Jesu Christe, my doubts persisted. If the monks destroyed me, who would avenge the death of those innocents? Who would discover the source behind the evil touching so many in my life?

If I did not confess, however, I would never be able to resist the temptation provided by my young assistant. He might not acknowledge our desires were wrong, but I could never supplant my own morality with his. Though my own morality looked as worn and shabby as my ancient Psalter.

Either way, I faced destruction.

Sunset turned my windows amber, and the air was thick with humidity. I paced my small chamber. Such ego. Such conceit. To imagine that I alone could stop the demons. To dare think I alone stood between Sara and a lifetime of depravity. He was young. He would find someone else.

Pain sliced through me. *Non.* I stumbled at the thought of Sara touching a woman. This was…jealousy? *Merde alors.* I must make my confession, for by laying my sins on the altar of Christ, I would find peace. Though my faith had been shaken, it was the one avenue I knew, the only resource I possessed.

After prayers, I waited in my room for Brother George's call. There was no point in seeking out the others. Nohea would be tending to her own affairs, and Sara didn't speak, still locked in a frozen rage. The distance between us, in age, in philosophy, in earthly experience, was too great to be overcome. He did not understand what drove me and, *salve me,* I did not understand him.

I dressed well, as a show of respect for my confessor. My shirt was old, made of finely stitched linen. My trousers were linen too, though heavier and dark blue. Music played somewhere downstairs, happy music, songs about love and life and joy. I combed my overlong bangs and said a passionate prayer that Sara would come through this unscathed, and by holding myself to my own standards, I would set him free.

I owed him that much, this young man who had brought the icy winter in my heart to a brief and glowing spring.

The chime announcing Brother George's call came both too soon and much too late. I propped the iPad where we could see each other and greeted him. He told me the police had not, in fact, found a gas leak under the chapel, and I gave him such news as we had about our investigation. Our conversation petered out, the way it will when one or the other participant has something they don't want to say.

When I could put it off no longer, I inhaled sharply and began.

"Bless me, Brother, for I have sinned. It has been one week since my last confession, and these are my sins."

I started with easy things, how I'd omitted chanting the hours when I had other obligations, and moments when I'd been impatient or rude. I told him how I'd failed to find the source of the demon attacks, and how I'd lost myself in the last fight, becoming wholly the monster.

For his part, he let me speak, murmuring soft words to encourage my disclosures. When I'd exhausted all my lesser transgressions, I told him about Sara, how I'd fed from him, and the natural consequences of my feeding. Even more, I told him of my feelings for Sara, how much he meant to me, how his smile could light me up from across the room. Once I started, the words came easily, for though Brother George and I had had a somewhat fractious relationship, in this instance, I spoke directly to my God.

Wash me thoroughly from my iniquity, and cleanse me from my sin. I finished, said the closing prayer, and waited. For a long while, Brother George said nothing. He looked away, as if he had someone else in the room with him, offering him counsel. In all my years with the White Monks, I'd never asked what would happen if I broke my contract, yet I would soon find out. I half expected him to be exultant at finally getting rid of me.

After another long moment, he cleared his throat, his fist brought to his mouth. "Thaddeus." I could just see the tops of his knuckles where he'd crossed his hands on his desk. "As you know, I am not empowered to offer you absolution for your sins. For that, you'll need to make your confession to a priest." He picked up a pen and scratched a note on the pad on his desk. "As your contact with the White Monks, I can tell you—"

Footsteps pounded up the stairs, then the door to my room burst open. "Thaddeus." Nohea's voice clanged with barely suppressed panic. "Thaddeus, they've got him. They've got Sara."

The world can turn on a breath. One moment, I'm begging forgiveness for the carnal nature of our relationship.

The next, I'm ready to commit any sin in order to save my lover.

"Brother Thaddeus, what is it?" Brother George's tone of voice should have brought me up short. Instead, I rose. Nohea rested against the door's frame, breathing heavily.

I spoke to the brother, my confessor, my link to the White Monks, as if he was a servant to be dismissed. "I need to leave you now."

"Dupont, you—" His voice rose, as if he could compel my behavior.

"I will be in contact." I closed the connection and powered off the iPad, my movements methodical, deliberate, as if by doing so I could maintain a measure of control over these circumstances.

"Nohea, we will need to prepare." She nodded once, sharply. I didn't care how she knew he'd been taken or by whom.

"Tell me what you know."

"Our new phones are linked, and he sent out an emergency call. I don't know what the hell he was doing out of the house." She stopped, shut her eyes, bit down on her lower lip. "I was in the kitchen and didn't hear anything until my phone alarmed."

"You have weapons here, *non*?" She nodded a second time, covering her emotional response with calm. "Get them, and I'll meet you downstairs."

"I'm sorry, Mr. Dupont. I swear I didn't know he'd left."

I waved her off. I'd had the chance to compel Sara's behavior and had let it pass. This was as much my fault as hers. "Be quick." She left, her footsteps pounding down the stairs. I changed clothes; dark pants, a close-fitting shirt. Blades at my wrists and ankles, with my sword belted across my shoulders. One last, desperate *ave*, and I left my room.

Nohea had armed herself. I stood on the landing at the top of the stairs, for one moment allowing myself to feel the awful surges of emotion. Fear, certainly, along with anger. Anger at Sara for making himself vulnerable. Guilt for anything I'd done that prompted him to leave. Moreover, a white-hot rage at a nameless, faceless evil for taking what was mine. Though they burned deep in my belly, I forced those feelings away. I needed a clear head, unencumbered by distracting emotions.

I slowed my breathing and closed my eyes against the faint glare of the late-day sun. Where was he? I could not sense his presence. *Benedictus Dominus Deus meus, qui docet manus meas ad praelium, et digitos meos ad bellum.* I begged my Lord to strengthen my hand for battle, and to keep Sara under the shadow of his wing until such time as I could save him.

Nohea had yet to appear. If I stood still much longer, the sheer force of my anger might burn through my restraint. I ducked into Sara's room, hoping for a hint, some sense he still lived. His laptop was open on the small table he used as a desk. I touched one of the keys, and an image appeared on the screen.

A familiar image, though one with disconcerting differences.

Leo.

I sat heavily on the bed and brought the laptop closer. Leo, except *non.* The program didn't look familiar, though I'd heard Nohea and Sara mention Facebook. This man, though. Marc Goutard. Who was he? He had Leo's white-blond hair and extraordinary cheekbones. His mouth, too pretty for a man's. His dark eyes should have been sparkling with laughter.

"I think I can track him." Nohea stood in the doorway, peering at her phone. "We just barely set up the GPS thing." She swiped her thumb across the screen. "Yeah, it's forty—"

"Forty-six-hundred Perrier Street," I whispered. Leo's family home. "I am familiar with the address."

She'd pulled a black cap over her dreadlocks, exposing

every nuance of her expression, and though questions danced close to the surface, Nohea didn't ask them. She pocketed her cell phone without any comment whatsoever. "Should we drive over there, or would it be easier just to walk? It's a couple miles."

I could cover the distance at a run faster than she could drive. Or I could at full dark. "If we take the car, we can leave now."

She gave me an assessing look. "Let's hit it."

Some ten minutes later, we were parked in the shadow of an old oak, though twilight had settled in, reducing my risk of injury. We didn't speak. For my part, too many memories clotted my mind, distracting me from the situation at hand.

With a forced sigh, I pushed the past aside and reached out with my senses. Nothing from Sara. "The main entrance opens into a hallway running along the outside wall of the house." I shifted in the soft leather seat, eager to begin, dreading my first steps. Before anything, we needed some semblance of a plan. "There's a living room and a dining room off the hall, and it ends at the kitchen."

Nohea gazed thoughtfully at the house. "Did you used to live here?"

"No, but a…a friend…" Lived here, and died here. *Leo.*

"There's a story there somewhere. But"—she rubbed her open palms on her thighs—"maybe this isn't the right time."

I couldn't imagine confiding in Nohea under any circumstances. "No." Leo had been a victim, of his nature, of his upbringing, and of me.

Despite all we'd shared, he'd ended up beaten near to death by those who abhorred our love. In the end, his family brought him home, where he'd lingered before departing this earth.

I'd kept vigil in secret, leaving his side to hide during daylight and at night to destroy the monsters who'd killed him. Oh yes, I was very familiar with the layout of the Perrier Street house. If *le monster* held Sara, beautiful, bright Sara, it would tear a wound in my heart.

"There's bad shit in there. It's making my skin crawl." Nohea's murmured observation startled me. "Thaddeus, will you promise me something?"

"What?" I glanced at her, but she stared resolutely at the house.

"If things go crazy in there, you gotta take care of my baby, okay? I don't want her brought up by a bunch of priests."

Her baby. Her niece Angelique. Her last connection to her family.

"I am confident you'll come out of this, and we will retrieve Angelique from the foster family caring for her."

Her small smile flickered and died. "I appreciate your support, but…"

"All will be well, Nohea. Your phone gave us a warning, and so we have the element of surprise. We'll go room by room, floor by floor, till we find Sara and get to the person behind this." We were walking into a trap, and while I believed we would come through these events alive, we might not be unscathed. Reassuring Nohea settled my own nerves and left me better able to concentrate.

Her smile extinguished, Nohea opened the car door. She hung her whip from her belt and stretched, her trim figure a shadow in the twilight.

The white house had a minimum of the gingerbread trim found on Victorian-era architecture. Even in the darkness, the grounds appeared neat, the shrubbery pruned, and the lawn free from weeds. One light burned in the front window.

I climbed out of the car more slowly, beset by memories. When I'd last stood on this lawn, the wisteria didn't reach the top of the fence, and the lilac tree by the front walkway had been too small for me to hide in its shadow.

I hid there now, searching for any hint of Sara, planning our next move.

"Should we knock?" Expressionless, Nohea allowed the barest inflection to communicate the joke.

I pressed my index finger to my lips. She shrugged, and at my wave, she dropped a step behind me. If opening the door triggered another unfortunate event, I didn't want her injured.

Before turning the handle, I listened. The main floor possessed the somber air of death, with none of the subtle squeaks or urgent whispers to give away anyone waiting for us.

Opening the door, I endeavored to step over the threshold. Something, a solid, cool, and utterly invisible something, stopped me.

"What?" Her hand landed on my back, as if she'd had to stop herself from running into me.

The foyer was visible, but I could not cross in. "I do not know." I ran my hand over the smooth, unseen surface. I'd once had permission to enter this home, and even the passage of eighty years could not disavow my right. "You try."

I stepped aside, and Nohea walked through the door.

"Oh, for fuck's sake. Is this a vampire thing?" She faced me, her hands notched on her hips.

"It shouldn't be." I pushed harder on the obstruction without success.

"All right, then. I hereby invite you, Thaddeus Marcelle Dupont, into this residence at forty-six-hundred Perrier Street." With a florid gesture, she waved me in.

The surface did not give, and my foot could not pass the doorstep. *Merde alors.* I ground my teeth to keep from crying out in frustration. Giving the doorjamb a final smack, I stepped away.

"Hey, Thaddeus." Nohea came out onto the small front porch. "Where the hell are you going?"

"A moment, *s'il vous plait.*" We were not facing a *vampire thing.* This was magic, pure and simple. Now how did I fight it?

"Don't you know some prayer or something?"

Did I? I knew hundreds of prayers, though I could not imagine the Catholic Church had ever anticipated the need for a vampire to break through a ward. In old Tolkein's world, I could have said "friend" and entered. Whoever set this prohibition, though, knew I was no friend.

To steady myself, I began to recite one of the earliest prayers I'd learned, the Our Father. *Pater noster, qui es in caelis…*

I repeated the prayer three times, the way I would following confession.

"Thaddeus, come on. We don't have time for whatever it is you're doing."

I straightened following my third recitation, endeavoring to keep my mind clear and my spirit peaceful. "Invite me in again."

I strode up the front walkway, and this time when I attempted to step into the foyer, the invisible force melted away and I entered.

"Oh." Nohea jumped out of the way. "You did it."

"Perhaps." Prayer could be a powerful tool. We'd never know if Nohea's invitation worked, the house had given up, or if my frame of mind had disguised my vampire nature. Leaving the conundrum behind, I refreshed myself with the layout of the main floor. "You check the front room, *s'il vous plait,* and I'll look in the dining room next door."

The front room, where Leo had lain for three weeks before his physical body joined his spirit. I'd watched him, every breath and heartbeat, torn between the desire to savor these moments and to do the thing that would set his spirit free.

No, I lacked the courage to go to the front room myself. Despite the darkness, we dared not turn on a light. My vision was sufficient to navigate, and the soft glow of her phone's display guided Nohea. Moments later, we reconvened in the hall. Nothing. The most notable attribute, beyond the heavy silence, was the appalling smell.

Nohea met my gaze, her hand covering her nose and mouth, the gray light of her phone casting her eyes into shadow. "What is it?" she whispered.

The rooms were pristine, a perfect preservation of some indeterminate historical period. The attention to detail would have been admirable under different circumstances. Worse than anything down by the Mississippi River, the smell captured the sewer, bright, acrid urine, and brimstone, strong enough to make my eyes water. Something awful had overtaken the heart of this place, the miasma of evil spreading out into every particle of space.

There. Underneath the layers of perversion, the faintest hint of Sara's life force.

"He is here, though I do not know where. For now, I suggest we stay together." I pitched my voice low, though I had no sense of anyone listening. If anything, the house radiated a weird attitude of confidence, waiting for us to discover its secrets.

We explored the kitchen, which had been modernized since Leo's death, white porcelain and chrome over a dark red floor. All the while, I kept my ears tuned for any sound, most particularly for the steady beat of Sara's heart.

Nothing.

From there, we moved to the small bedrooms in the rear, the old servants' quarters. They were empty, though in the second bedroom, Nohea's gasp broke through our stealth. She stumbled across the room to the bed, where a figure lay wrapped in a blanket. "Jesus. Look at this." She crouched low, swiping at her phone to bring up the light. "It's like a mummy."

Her voice broke the lock surprise had on me, and I crossed the room in a blur. *Not Sara.* Someone, some other poor unfortunate soul, lay dead on the bed. Dried bodily fluids soiled the pristine bedding. They'd been there a while, months from the look of it, features locked in a grimace of pain.

"Don't suppose we should call the cops yet," Nohea murmured.

Non. "Let us go upstairs." Making the sign of the cross for the repose of this disturbed soul, I led Nohea from the room. "Whoever is here had to have heard us out front. Have your weapons at the ready."

The narrow stairway led to a landing at the second floor. All the bedroom doors were closed, the smell powerful enough to make concentration difficult. I strode over to the closest door. Empty, absolutely vacant, the room's glossy wood floor gleaming in the moonlight.

"*Merde.*" We had no time to waste. Sara was in danger, and a sense of urgency gripped me so tight, I struggled to breathe. In all my long life, I had become accustomed to putting myself at risk. Involving others, Sara and Nohea and the unfortunate child, created a new touchstone for fear.

When the wicked, even my enemies and my foes, came upon me to eat up my flesh, they stumbled and fell.

I called upon the Lord as a tenet of my faith, though he promised only to keep his eye upon the sparrow. He might will my allies to fail in their efforts to defeat this evil, or that I should fail in protecting them. My task was not to wish for the Lord to make everything perfect, but to trust that any outcome reflected his perfect will.

If this was a test of my faith, then I was perilously close to failing.

Nohea touched my shoulder. "You said there's a third floor, right?"

I tamped down my internal distress. The memories of this place combined with my fear for Sara's safety to bind me tight.

"I think it's coming from there." She pointed straight up.

"Agreed." Three more doors opened off the landing. Each could conceal a horde of demons, though I did not believe they did. The quiet was too absolute. I nodded in the direction of the stairs. Nohea unhooked the whip from her belt and led the way.

We stopped on the narrow landing at the top of the stairs. The single door throbbed with the energy behind it. She met my gaze, as strong and direct as any man.

"Let's do this," she said, and flung open the door.

Light. Searing, scalding, white light. The sound of a thousand cannons all firing at once. I felt Nohea's scream and the motion of her arm as she cracked her whip, but my senses were overwhelmed. I could not move except to cover my face and crouch low. I took a sharp blow to the head, and a flash of pain brought me to the floor. Confused, I struggled to rise. Another blow. Everything went dark.

CHAPTER TWENTY-FOUR

✦ ✦ ✦

"**F**OR FUCK'S SAKE, POUR WATER on him or something. Wake him up."

The petulant words brought me to an unwelcome consciousness. The skin on my face burned from the bright lights, and my head throbbed as if the beating had gone on for longer than I realized.

I cracked open my eyes, keeping my body still and my breathing regular. The light, no more than an overhead bulb, burned my skin. I sat in a straight-backed wooden chair, my hands bound with something slender and tight, my feet tied to the chair legs. The room felt crowded, the awful smell overloading my faculties.

Dominating everything else, the vulgar voice, alternately threatening and cajoling.

When I returned to myself, I raised my head. The scene rocked me harder than the blows. The room was larger than I'd expected, the high-pitched ceiling following the roofline of the house. Large spotlights, now mercifully dim, had been positioned in the corners of the room. Nohea lay slumped along the wall, blood trailing from her nose and around her mouth. Positioned across from me, Sara.

He stood on his toes, hands suspended from the ceiling, his head lolling to one side. Broken. Bruised. Blood streaked his face from a cut across his brow. Unconscious or nearly so.

The ghostly form of Leo had an arm around Sara's waist. On the other side of him stood the man whose picture I'd seen on the laptop, now flesh and blood and raging insanity. The two demon policemen kept guard, still in their crumpled uniforms, their regulation weapons drawn.

Who was this man who could create ghosts and allow his demons to preserve their possessed bodies long after they should have fallen into rot?

"Welcome to the party." He extended his hand. "I'd offer to shake, but…oops, you can't." His laugh burned beneath my skin, even as I struggled to recall why I recognized his voice.

Leo distracted me by trailing his fingers down Sara's throat. Sara's eyes were closed, and he shivered. These fiends had beaten him, and somehow I would have revenge.

"As lovely as this one is, Thaddy, you haven't taken any better care of him than you did of me." Leo leaned close enough to flick Sara with his tongue. Sara flinched as if he'd felt the ghost's action. Impossible, though my eyes proved me wrong.

A tiny thread of anger grew into something stronger. I had not fed in days, but to offset any bodily weakness I fortified my grim determination with fear and frustration. My weapons lay under a window, driving home my failure. Next to them was another small pile of items. Sara's cell phone. A wallet. The dagger he'd taken from my house. At least he'd attempted to protect himself. I found that small gesture surprisingly consoling.

"So you know the guest of honor, and you know Leo, of course, but we haven't been properly introduced." The man approached, his mocking smile fueling the fire Leo had kindled. Giving nothing away, I tested the strength of the strap binding my wrists. The infinitesimal stretch gave me hope.

The man must have noticed. "Won't do you any good. We trussed you up with the newest handcuffs from NOLA's finest." He bared his teeth in a grin. "I'm Marc, by the way, the one you've been avoiding." He was also the source of the smell, the root of all the evil energy in the room. The man from Frenchmen Street.

"Avoiding?" I prompted.

Marc crossed his arms, his smile as slick as an oil spill on the Gulf. "I have asked you several times to join me, and you have so far declined my invitation."

One man, the source of all this trouble. Impossible to contain so much power and not fly apart. Yet here he was, flanked by a pair of demons who should have fallen to rot days ago and a ghost who shouldn't exist at all. He paused as if waiting for me to protest. I held my tongue.

"See now, I figured you needed to see what I'm really capable of. Your monks are fine and all, but I've got better toys."

"So it would appear." I inclined my head toward Leo.

Leo caressed Sara's chest. "This would not have happened." His hand made a claw, and his beautiful lips twisted. "If you had just turned me." He raked his hand down through fabric and flesh.

Sara gasped, though he did not move.

More blood. More pain. I lurched against the bindings. Marc's grin widened. He'd given solid form to a ghost. *How?* He must have the *Daemonum*.

I thrashed against my bindings and the police aimed their weapons. Not at me. At Sara and Nohea.

LIKE HIS BODY, SARA'S CONSCIOUSNESS hung suspended, his mind touching reality but not grounded in it. He had no idea how long he had been in this room. Long enough to lose feeling in his hands and for the ache in his arms and shoulders to have pushed him past pain and into dull acceptance.

The air was rank with heavy, cloying incense over another, fouler odor. The fumes filled his nasal cavity, seeped in through his pores, and mingled with the pain to push him toward oblivion. He resisted the temptation to sink fully into comforting darkness, but the reasons for making the effort were harder to hold on to with every breath.

Others surrounded him. Two were men, though no longer human. Against his eyelids, their shadows moved like marionettes between lapses into resentful immobility. One had tackled him, he remembered. Rot doused in roses. The other had held his head, pinched his nose, and forced something sweetly noxious down his throat.

Another presence hovered nearby, so wavering and insubstantial, Sara thought he had imagined it until cold fingers had touched his skin. The chill they left went deeper than flesh but was nothing compared to the revulsion that had gripped him at the moist touch of an icy tongue.

Everything was confused. Nate. Demons. Dark. Light and noise. Voices. He couldn't keep the sequence straight. The only constants were the ungodly smell and Marc Goutard.

Marc's mad eyes chased him deeper into the fog. The gray washed out his tan face and dreads and replaced them with hollow cheeks and tousled curls until only the cold cerulean fire of his eyes remained burning out of the new face.

Sara had retreated another inch into the fog until a sharp line of pain yanked him back toward consciousness. The pain was followed by something more compelling. Anger. Anger and burning conviction of purpose.

Marc's laugh skittered along his spine.

He ignored it and concentrated on the other thing, the anger that shone holy righteousness through the fog.

Thad was here.

He began to struggle toward consciousness.

BLOOD RAN DOWN SARA'S DENIM pants, and his eyes were closed. Alive? I stared hard at his chest, his belly, looking for a telltale motion.

"You let me die here, Thaddeus," Leo said. I could not respond, for he spoke the truth. From the time he'd discovered my secret, he'd wanted this dark gift. Again and again, I refused him. "And now my descendent will have my revenge."

"That's right. See, Leo's my great…oh, I don't know how many greats…uncle." Marc Goutard waved a hand at the policemen, and they lowered their weapons. "Quite a few years ago, now, I found his diary up here, and it gave me all kinds of ideas."

I had difficulty regulating my breath. I could only imagine what Leo had recorded in his diary and what this twisted man had done with the information. Properly groomed, he would be the spitting image of Leo. But while Leo had been angry that I would not make him immortal, he had never been as deranged as the man before me. Goutard's eyes turned a demonic black and the pulse of evil quickened.

"At first, I thought I'd force you to give me what you denied Leo, but then"—another laugh burrowed into me like a swarm of chiggers—"I learned a new trick. I can call demons, as many as I want, as often as I want. Two? Four? Seventy-seven? I can do it."

The attic room heaved at his declaration, the force of his excitement ringing through the space.

"So now I really don't need you." He brought out a ritual blade, long and curved, the hilt carved from ebony. "And you know what? You deserve to be punished for all the unhappiness you've created."

He approached Sara, who either did not sense his intent or was long past caring. *Domine, non.* I applied more of my strength to breaking the strap around my wrists. Either the binding was too tight or I lacked the discipline required to slip one hand free.

"Get the candles." Marc waved his arms, and one of the cops set four tall candles around Sara, along a circle of chalk on the floor. He lit them, and Marc raised the athame over his head. "I've been saving this summoning for just the right host." His whole body gave a twitch. "I got a super demon for Sa-ra."

Catching Sara's throat in his grip, he began a foul chant. Sara never opened his eyes, though his lips tightened as if he fought whatever was being done to him. The chant grew louder, carrying with it an echo from someplace far beyond this world.

If Sara had the strength of purpose to fight, I could do no less. *Dimitte me.* Yielding to the only real weapon I had, I let go and set the monster free.

*T*HAD WILL NEVER LET YOU *hear the end of it if you die here, so wake up, dumbass. Open your eyes.*

But Sara couldn't. He was lost in limbo. He clung to Thad's anger, the one thing he knew to be real.

When the chanting started, he welcomed it. Another link to reality. He strained toward the sound.

Open your eyes.

More voices calling into the dark. Then, from some-where in the fog, an answering throb.

Everything he was went still. Something was in here with him. And here was inside his own head. That couldn't be good.

His soul wanted to shrink, to curl into a protective ball and hide. He didn't think he had the luxury. Whatever waited out there wasn't going to give up and go away.

He turned in the fog. Where was out? *Wake up!*

Movement, or whatever he had just done, was obviously the wrong answer.

It was coming. He could feel darkness hurtling toward him, eating the fog as it went. It would eat him when it got here.

Then it was too late.

There had been no discernible source of light before,

but abruptly, the gray fog dissipated and utter darkness descended. Black so dark it seemed to take on substance and texture. The chanting had stopped.

Thad was gone.

Sara floated in a formless void.

The black pressed around him, squeezing as if he was a balloon that could be popped.

He struggled to breathe against the pressure. His lungs refused to fill. Consciousness began slipping away. *Not real.* He stopped struggling at the realization. None of this was happening to his physical body. The pressure retreated, as if confused. Then it gathered into an angry intelligence, and the real battle began.

Sara had called Thad's mental powers an invasion, but now he realized the absurdity of the claim. The vampire's touch on his mind was a nudge, a suggestion, a gentle persuasion. Thad had never compelled him. It had always been a seduction.

The thing he faced now had no such subtlety. It beat against his mind. It battered with blunt force, ripped with claws, stabbed with sharp knives. It didn't care what damage it did, because it didn't intend to leave. It was cleaning house to take up residence.

And it was winning.

He could feel the alien presence seeping into the cracks in his sanity.

He was going to die. He would never see the people he loved again. And the last thing he had done was yell at his brother and fight with Thad. He hadn't even properly honored his grandmother, assembling her gift only to annoy Thad. Now his vampire would die too, trying to save him.

The cracks were getting bigger. Images flashed through the darkness—memories—his life. He crouched inside his mind and held tight to everything important—camping with Dev, summer afternoons outside with Dad, his mother at her altar, stories with Daadi. And Thaddeus. Such a short time, but so many memories of Thad. The stern, dedicated monk. God's warrior. His impossible eyes and cool touch. Most importantly, his rare smiles. *I want to see you smile again.*

Why had he fought with Thad? He tried to hang on to Thad's smile as the slideshow continued, faster and faster.

Daadi-Thad-Aahna-Dad-Thad-Nate-Ma-Thad-Nohea-Thad

Thad-Thad-Thad

CHAPTER TWENTY-FIVE

THE ROOM FILLED WITH FOUL smoke, and I thrust my hands apart, tearing flesh in the process. The strap gave way. I roared, rising to my feet. The chair fractured underneath me. Goutard waved his blade in crazy arcs, as if dancing with some unseen entity.

One of the policemen grabbed for me. I dodged, allowing my forward motion to carry me into the other cop's line of fire. He got off a shot before I tackled him headfirst. He landed on the bare wood floor, and I landed on him.

I had no time. The pitch and timbre of Goutard's chant changed, becoming less organized and more powerful. I'd never been present for the calling of a demon, but the very air tingled with foreboding. The dynamic current swelled impossibly large. I could barely draw a breath.

Something crashed into me, a dense weight pinning me with fists and knees. The first policeman. I had no time. I needed to reach Sara before the worst happened.

I fought, throwing a vicious series of punches to the midsection of the one beneath me. Would that I had Sara's dagger. I could have made short work of both of them. The policeman curled up, and I rolled to the side. I landed in a crouch, but before I could regain my feet, a pair of demon hands wrapped around my throat.

No time. I reached behind, jabbing my fingers into soft tissue, maybe an eye. I gouged harder, and blood ran over my hand. Goutard continued his macabre dance, spiraling around Sara without coming close enough to touch.

Despite the wound to his face, the demon policeman dug his fingers into my flesh and yanked, as if he wanted to tear the head from my body. This had to end. I took hold of his wrist and squeezed until the bones crunched in my grasp.

He wailed, and his hold on my neck weakened. I pushed up to standing, yanking him around so I could grasp his head and snap his neck. He fell with a heavy thud, but before I could move, his partner forced the blunt end of a service revolver into my face.

"Wait a minute." Goutard's command brought everything to a halt. "I've got a better idea."

Gesturing with the revolver, the policeman brought me closer to Goutard. The gray haze of a demon's essence surrounded them, and Leo hovered behind, his face a mask of glee.

"He's so pretty." Goutard stepped closer to Sara. "The demon will take over in just a minute, and then he'll be all mine to play with. Well, his body, at least. It seems a waste, doesn't it, that he won't be here"—he tapped the knife against Sara's temple—"to enjoy the fun?"

I did not reply, because the image he evoked sent a further surge of dread through me.

"But you know what? Maybe there is another option." His smile stretched slow and bright and evil. "You know, Brother Thaddeus, you could save him." He chewed on his lower lip hard enough to draw blood, his eyes still black as if the demon had already taken him over. "Drain him. Just suck all the blood out of his body till his heart stops beating."

My mind flinched at the idea, though I schooled my face into impassivity. Not once since the day I'd been turned had I drained all the blood from a human. I'd refused to contemplate such gluttony. But now, knowing Sara would otherwise die after being tortured by a demon…

"Oh yeah. You've got that sullen-monk thing going on, but your eyes ain't lying, vampire. You wanna do right by your boyfriend, even if it sends you straight to hell."

I was already there. Lowering my hands, I bowed my head.

"Hey buddy, go get the lasso, okay?"

The demon policemen crossed the room, and moments later, the circle of silver fell around my shoulders. My body's weakness was nothing compared to the anguish in my soul.

"Come on over, Brother Thaddeus." The haze of demon essence coalesced between Goutard and Sara, and he stroked Sara's skin with the blade. "Which is it? Let the demon in or kill him yourself?"

Maybe those weren't my only choices. I took a step toward the two of them, and when Goutard didn't stop me, I entered the circle.

The madman stepped back from Sara, allowing me access. Did Sara have to die? I crossed my arms, attempting to calm myself. His heartbeat fluttered, a rapid staccato beat against my slow, undead pulse. I did have a third option, one that cut through my soul like a cry of anguish in the dark. Abhorrent, untenable, but possible.

I could turn him.

This black gift, which I had refused to give to anyone else, could sustain Sara's life indefinitely. Once I'd broken his skin and started the flow it would be a simple thing to cut myself and allow him to taste just a few drops of my blood. Goutard was so deranged, he might not even notice, and if he did, and if he killed us both, then our fate would be in the Lord's hands.

If contemplating this act didn't remove me permanently from his sight.

"Careful, Thad-dee. You're taking too long." His light tone didn't disguise the menace in his voice. "You behave, or"—he shrugged, a move that was more of a spasm—"I can settle for a pretty body."

So many innocents had died because of me, and though Sara might hate me for it, I could not add him to the list.

I wrapped my arms around him, fitting his body to mine. To hold him so intimately in this setting was painful. Every gesture took on tremendous importance, for we stood on the edge of a precipice. No light shone from his eyes. If I did this thing, he may never look on me kindly again.

But he would not die.

For a moment, sadness transcended my fear, and his salty-sweet scent overcame the demon fug. Eighty years ago, I had denied Leo this thing, but now I bent my lips to Sara's throat. "I'm sorry, Sara. *J'en suis désolé.*"

*W*AS THIS DYING?
    Sara's mind caught on something, and the images slowed.

The image of Durga. The altar. The few minutes of clarity he had felt after performing the puja. He needed clarity now. Peace to clear his mind of the foulness pouring into it. He reached for the memory—his room in Thad's home, performing the puja. He imagined picking up the copper vessel and pouring water into his right hand for the purification of body, speech, and mind. He could almost feel the cool water on his lips as he sipped and then began the mantra his grandmother had taught him.

Aum aeem bhreem hanumate, shree ram dootaaya namaha.

The entity still battered. It still ripped and stabbed.

Sara ignored it. He made offerings to Durga.

Turīya guṇa sampannam nānā guṇa manoharam ānanda saurabhaṃ puṣpaṃ gṛhyatām idam uttamam. He lit incense, then the lamp.

Seething malevolence flung itself at the walls of his mind.

He finished with the Gayatri Mantra.

Did the cracks seem smaller?

He began again, holding the image of Durga in his mind. *We do not pray to the statue,* his grandmother had told him, *for God is everywhere, in everything. The image is only to help us focus so the Lord can manifest to our conscious mind.*

SO MUCH DESPAIR.

Goutard would torment me, the Church would destroy me, and the Lord had tested my faith beyond my capacity to endure. I ran my hands over Sara's back, as if I could absorb humanity through his skin. I had but one choice, really, and I would rather die than cause him any pain.

"Come on, now. I wanna see you drain him." Goutard's voice cut through the air.

A scuffle drew my attention. Nohea, wrestling with the demon cop. "Don't do it," she gasped. "Don't, Thaddeus."

I turned back to Sara, whose warmth stilled my soul. Leo caught my eye, his expression impassive, his eyes a window to the endless night of the abyss. Goutard must have used the *Daemanun* to drag his soul back from Purgatory. To see his essence trapped by evil troubled me.

To know the same evil had injured Sara disturbed me beyond tolerance. I pressed him closer, and with the greatest, utmost care, I made a cut with my incisors. Blood beaded it up, rich and salty. I sucked those drops away; one mouthful, then another, enough to draw strength.

Not the draining gush Goutard wanted, and not enough to rob Sara of his humanity.

For if I'd learned one thing in my long, long life, it was never to give up hope.

I would fight, because defeating Goutard was the only way to set all of us free. Sara's life force infused me, and I reached for the silver chain. Silver weakened me but did not cause paralysis. I tore at it, and the links burned into my palms.

ON THE THIRD REPETITION OF the mantra, Sara stood before the altar in his room on First Street. According to the sun streaming in the window, it was noon.

He took a deep breath and opened his eyes.

A gleaming blade arced toward his face.

Sara screamed.

SARA'S EYES OPENED. BROWN, NOT black. Not a demon.

Yet.

The circlet of silver snapped.

Free of its power, I felt rather than saw Goutard raise his athame. I caught his hand on the downswing, squeezing till he screamed. He broke from my grasp, flailing with both fists. I shoved him away from Sara, but not before Goutard's blade struck him hard enough to bring forth a cry.

The noise of our battle must have drawn the demonic essence, for it surrounded us both, a murky fog burning my skin like poison. I'd read that a demon needed a crack in someone's soul to enter, and while my own had many imperfections, I had to believe Goutard's was rent by crevasses.

I stalked him, and he ran, scuttling away. This must end. Any bit of humanity leached from my soul, and my own monster took full control. My vision shifted, colors fading, my opponent's every weakness highlighted.

"Back off." The cocky edge had left his voice. He scooted away, stopping only when he hit the wall.

The demonic miasma swirled between us, tightening its grip as if seeking a way in.

"This is over."

"Shoot." Marc sniffed and rubbed his mouth. "We could have been something, Thaddeus Dupont, but you know what? I haven't met a demon yet I couldn't control." He stiffened, throwing his arms out wide. "All I have to do is let this one in."

His scream exploded, loud enough to shake the walls.

Within a heartbeat, a demon stared at me through Goutard's eyes. The being rubbed his hands over his face and hair as if overcome by the exhilaration of touch. Incorporating Goutard's innate ability with a true devil made him the most powerful being I'd ever faced.

I leapt for him, diving through the weak remains of the circle. He may have been faster and stronger, but I was more desperate. Our initial impact cracked the windows. I grappled with him, shoulder to shoulder, both of us straining. He got a hand on my jaw, forcing my head back. I tore at his ear.

He forced me down on one knee, then called a jewel-hilted dagger from the ether. More silver. Just its proximity weakened me. He raised his arm, and I saw death in his eyes.

With a sharp crack, the tip of Nohea's whip stung his arm. Surprise gave me a millisecond's advantage. I rose, shouting, "*Vade ad infernos*," and with heavy blows, I forced him out of the circle of power.

Vade ad infernos. *Go to hell.*

The being fought me, tearing at my skin and my hair. It might have underestimated my ability or maybe it was overwhelmed by simple human sensation. Either way, I found a moment of vulnerability. Though the spirit was more powerful than anything I knew, the body was made of skin and bone. I stiffened my fingers, reached in, and tore out its heart.

Blood ran over my hand. Flesh caught in my nails. I wiped my palms on my trousers, stepping away to let the body slide to the floor. The shoulders curled, and the head dropped forward.

But it did not fall.

I took another step back, confusion turning to frank horror. Goutard's body straightened, hands hovering on either side of the gaping wound.

"While I admire your intent"—the thing reached for me, dragging me close—"you'll need to come up with an alternative solution."

Fear seized my muscles, nearly shattering my will. I dropped the heart and tried to break free. The creature tightened its grip, and in a spray of blood and foul invective, threw me against the wall.

I hit the wall hard with my shoulder and head. My own weapons were too far away, but Sara's belongings lay within reach. The being slammed me again from behind, and I stumbled to my knees. Crawling, terrified he would guess my intent, I did not stop until my fingers wrapped around the leather sheath of the one blade in existence that could separate a demon from its host.

Sara gave a low moan, distracting me for a moment.

"You're quite accomplished." The rancid sound of the demon's voice tore my attention away from my lover.

"And when I am done," I said, "you will return to hell."

"I do not believe you." The demon launched himself at me, and with a single sweep, I planted the blade deep into his belly. I met his foul black gaze. With a low hiss, the darkness in his eyes faded to a human brown. They glazed over, fading to gray. The lids closed, and the body sagged against me.

Dead.

SARA WAS STILL ALIVE. FOR now. Someone had cut him down. Thad crouched over him, fear and guilt radiating off him in waves that required no mystical connection to read.

Sara tried to smile, but his face didn't want to move right.

Something wet and sticky obscured the vision in one eye. He still couldn't feel his hands. And he felt weak. So weak. It was hard to keep his eyes open. He struggled to do it anyway. He had to tell Thad… His eyes drifted shut, and he forced them back open.

MAYBE HIS EYES HAD BEEN closed longer than he thought, because now he was in Thad's arms. Thad sat on the floor, rocking him gently and murmuring brokenly in French. Sara turned his face into the scent of cypress, letting it clear away some of the stench. "Sorry," he managed, before his eyelids drifted down again.

HIS EYES WOULDN'T OPEN. HADN'T he just done this?

MOLTEN COPPER IN HIS MOUTH.
"Swallow, *cher,* you must swallow."
But he didn't have to. The fire already raced through his veins. He could feel his heart beat in time with Thad's.

"AGAIN." THE VOICE COMMANDED HIM up out of the darkness. Hot liquid against his lips.
Sara jerked awake.
"No." He turned his head, spitting out as much of the blood as he could and scrubbing at his mouth. "No-no-no-no." Confusion flashed over Thad's face, then comprehension.
"It is only to help you heal."
"I won't be…?"
"*Non.* You will not be like me." Some dark emotion crossed his face at the words, gone before Sara could catch it. "You were near death, but not so far gone I could not bring you back whole."

Oh. He did feel better. Thaddeus however… Sara reached for his face, then let his hand fall back, afraid any touch on the burned skin would be painful. They were alive, but his vampire was hurt. Because of him. Sara glanced around the room. They were surrounded by destruction and death. He looked back up at Thad, seeking comfort in storm-cloud eyes. "Can we go home?"

"*Oui.*"

Another thought occurred to him as Thad stood, lifting him effortlessly. "Nohea?"

"In better shape than you are, but thanks for asking." Nohea's voice came from somewhere behind him.

Sara let himself sag against Thad's chest. The vampire blood sang through his veins, working its magic. Sara thought maybe he could stand up and walk out on his own. He didn't mention it. Instead, he let Thad carry him and listened to their hearts beat together.

CHAPTER TWENTY-SIX

NOHEA DROVE US HOME.

She had been injured, though her ability to heal allowed her to deny the extent of her hurt. I rode in the rear seat with Sara. He had passed from semi-consciousness to a restless sleep, and more than anything, I wanted to keep him close.

"Brother Michael says they'll have a crew out to the house within the hour," she said.

I found I did not want to think about the brothers or the priests or the Church. "You will both need food."

Nohea glanced at me over her shoulder and signaled to turn into the driveway alongside my First Street house. "I think your boy likes pizza, and quite frankly, I am not in the mood to bang around in your kitchen for anything more than a bottle opener for my beer."

"Not Domino's." Sara straightened, shifted, then settled in against me.

I adjusted my arm to pull him closer still. "Put it on my account."

Nohea pulled the car into the garage. "It's all on your account, Thaddeus Dupont."

I told her to take care of herself, and she left me on my own to assist Sara. I would not have accepted her help, even if she'd offered. Sara could stand, though I kept an arm around his waist, pretending he needed the support.

In truth, I needed to feel him, warm with life. I needed his velvet skin and his honey-spice scent. His breath. The beat of his heart.

Slowly, we made our way upstairs. My wounds had healed for the most part. The burns caused by the halogen lights had subdued, and the canyons carved by the bindings on my wrists were filling in with tissue, covered by raw, pink skin.

At the top of the stairs, Sara would have veered toward his room, but I restrained him. "In here." I tugged him toward the bathroom.

"Need sleep…"

I kept my hands on him. "Soon."

The tub was large and deep, and I set the tap running hot. Sara shivered in the rising steam. Caring for him became an imperative. "Here." I gently lifted the shirt over his head, baring my teeth at the slashes marking his chest. "Let me."

The tub took several minutes to fill, and I spent the time undressing my young assistant, stroking his warm, bronze skin. His shivers slowed, and his breathing mellowed under my touch. I made note of each bruise, each scuff mark. He was healing, yes, and I swore he would never again suffer such injuries in my service.

"What are you doing, Mr. Dupont?"

"Thaddeus," I murmured. I knelt to remove his shoes, shushing his protests. "Let me take care of you."

He braced himself with his hands on my shoulders. "You don't need to."

"Sara." I tipped my head up, forcing him to meet my gaze. "You were not meant to be here as my assistant, nor were you intended to be the focus of a demon's attack. Yet you are, and you were, and somehow you fought it all off. This"—I gestured to his shoes and the bath—"is the very least I can do."

I stood next to him while waiting for the water to reach a decent depth, still lightly stroking his skin. He moved closer and rested his head on my shoulder. I wrapped an arm around him, emotions running riot. Pride, affection, even, possibly, love.

Love.

Not an emotion I'd expected, yet there it was. This young man had folded himself seamlessly into my life, bringing with him a vibrant joy, and yet he had the inner steel to defeat a demon possession. I suspected I'd never say the word out loud. If I could show him, I would.

Determining the water to be an adequate depth, I assisted Sara into the tub. He sank down with a sigh, and I wished I could add rosewater or lavender to the water, as if the addition of such a tiny detail would demonstrate my feelings.

"You don't need to go to all this trouble, Mr…um, Thaddeus."

Sara's cheeks were rosy from the heat, and also likely from the infusion of vampire blood I'd given him.

"No trouble." I'd spend all night here if Sara needed me. I'd lost track of time, missed several of the hours. I didn't care.

If I could rectify the damage done by the demon, I would.

Lifting one of his feet above the water, I soaped it, massaging the arch, gently flexing his toes. He hummed in response.

I did the same with the other foot, and when I had it cleansed, I propped his heel against my chest and massaged his calf muscle.

After massaging both calves, I ran my fingers up his thigh, stroking his hamstring.

"Be careful." He smiled, though his eyes were closed. "You're going to start something if you go much higher."

I hadn't intended to *start something*; no impulse could have been further from my mind. Yet my hands continued their journey, kneading Sara's thighs, thumbs skimming over the tender skin of his groin.

"Hoh-oh-oh," he shivered, his arousal apparent. My blood would have cured his physical hurts, but I could take no credit for his emotional fortitude.

"I want…" I started, stopped, unable to articulate my true intention. He lay soaking in the steaming water, his semi-erection the singular evidence of tension. Otherwise, his muscles had gone soft, his eyelids heavy. "Let me clean you." I stalled, afraid of what I really wanted.

His grin provided pure encouragement. "Do your worst."

I reached for the soap, made a lather. He shifted so I could wash his back, and he allowed me to lift his arms, his legs. I confess I paid particular attention to his chest, teasing his nipples, pleased by his soft gasps.

When every other part of him was clean, I attended to his balls and then his cock. Our previous encounters had been rushed and desperate things. This time, our last, I savored him.

I swirled my fingers through the water to cup his balls. His injuries had been the result of my weaknesses, my sensitivity to light and inability to break the bonds that held me. Through my touch, I begged forgiveness.

I made him wait, reducing him to a whimper before I finally took hold of him. I rubbed my thumb over the head, his slickness palpably different from the surrounding water. I didn't so much stroke as worship him, my grip tight, my attitude humble.

Shifting higher up on my knees, I held his balls in one hand and his cock in the other. To my pleasure, he began to give me direction. "Open me up," he whispered. "I want to feel you."

What could I do but honor his request? Touching his puckered ring with my fingertip was more of a promise than anything else. My balls turned heavy and my cock hardened, while I teased him with one finger, dipping in no farther than one knuckle.

I'd long since lost track of time, though instinct told me

I had hours before the sun rose. Sara's shivers returned, and his head drifted, damp dark hair clinging to his cheekbones, eyes closed. His muscles clenched, and I judged him close to his peak. "Here," I whispered. "Let us go to bed."

Wrapping him in a towel, I carried Sara to the guest bedroom. My own room had too many ghosts. Any reticence on my part had been washed away with the soap and water. Soon I would face judgment. For now, I would endeavor to show Sara the depth of my feelings for him.

I laid him on the bed and pulled up the comforter, so the only chills would be the ones I caused.

"There's lube over there." He pointed across the room. I retrieved it from the dresser and stripped off my clothes.

"Fuck, you're gorgeous," he said.

"Language," I mock scolded. Then, shoving aside the blankets, I climbed between his knees. Without my invitation, he spread his legs, pulling his thighs up. Squirting a palmful of lube, I stroked my own cock. With lubed fingers, I brushed down his taint to his hole, watching closely for signs he was ready.

"What are we doing, Thaddeus? This feels—"

I added a second finger, reaching for his pleasure spot. Curled and flexed and stroked him until his back arched and he groaned in response.

"This feels…"

I lined the tip of my member up with his hole. Exhaled a silent word of grace. Flexed my hips. He hissed as I pushed through the ring. I paused, and at his nod, I thrust deep into his warmth.

When I had myself seated fully, he tried again.

"This feels real, Thaddeus."

Afraid to admit to myself the truth in his words, I buried my face in the sweetness of his neck and began thrusting.

"This feels—"

I claimed his mouth in a kiss, thrusting harder. He wrapped his hands in my hair and tugged till my eyes watered. The high keening of desire spurred me, turned my movements rough and jerky. His scent and the sound of his cries overwhelmed me, drove me on.

I was close, skating on the edge of my release, so I took him in hand. His groans deepened, and soon he stiffened, clamping down on my cock. He shot, warm and thick, over my hand and across his belly, the joy in his smile driving me higher.

Shifting his legs so they rested on my shoulders, I lifted his hips in my palms and pounded into him. Four thrusts, five, and then I cried out, transported by my release.

His laughter carried me to earth.

I found his mouth again in a kiss as soft as the other had been frantic. I relished his taste, the mellow burn of his late-day shadow, and the density of his muscles under my hands. Calming further, our kisses turned into gentle nips. I settled beside him, and he rested his damp head on my shoulder. We used the towel to clean up, and I pulled the comforter over both of us.

"You spoke the truth earlier," I said, my body sinking into the languor of the moment. Despite the incongruity of the idea, I felt compelled to speak it aloud. "Though it may be impossible, what we share is real."

CHAPTER TWENTY-SEVEN

"THADDEUS?" NOHEA TAPPED ON THE door of the guest room and cracked it open. "There's a room full of priests downstairs. You better come."

I rolled over, stifling a groan. At a guess, they'd given us all of twelve hours since we'd defeated Marc Goutard. "A moment, please."

"I'll tell them you'll be right down." She spoke just above a whisper. If I wondered how she'd known to find me in this room, I didn't waste time worrying. A week ago, I would have dreaded these circumstances. Now I hardly cared.

The door closed with a soft click. I lay still and allowed myself to experience the luxurious bedding, the shimmering twilight, and the warmth of the man snoring quietly beside me.

Sara.

I brushed a dark curl away from his face to better marvel at the beauty of his cheekbones and the soft curve of his lips. I cringed at the scar on his brow left by Goutard's violence. For once, though, the pleasure outweighed the guilt.

Unfortunately, my newfound spiritual openness made it impossible to keep from touching him, and soon he stirred.

"Shouldn't you be chanting or something?" he murmured, his tousled hair and sleepy eyes further establishing his place in my heart.

"Apparently, Brother George and some of his cohorts are here, ready to be apprised of our activities."

He rolled, trapping me beneath his chest. "I can think of a lot better ways to have fun than talking to a bunch of priests."

"Well, yes." I ran my knuckles along the curve of his jaw. "But they will not be deferred." My mood sobered in anticipation of the coming confrontation. "You should know…" Words escaped me. How to explain this agreement I'd made so long ago?

"When I agreed to work with the White Monks"—I searched for a way to make him understand—"they promised to provide me with the services of a business manager and an assistant."

He interrupted by kissing my palm. "Bonus."

"Certainly." I smiled, caressing his face. The ease with which he gave of himself shamed me. "They included a provision stipulating I wouldn't engage in, well"—the blush almost locked down my tongue—"carnal relations."

"Oh." He stretched into a yawn. "It's a monk thing."

"Not exactly. I'm not a monk, after all—"

"I won't say anything if you don't." Sara settled on his side and slung a leg over mine. My silence brought him up on an elbow. "You didn't say anything, did you?"

I held his gaze for as long as possible.

"Well, shit, of course you did." He dropped onto the mattress. "So now what? Are they going to excommunicate you or something?"

The delay in my answer had him shaking his head. "I do not know," I finally said.

He sat, roughly tugging on the comforter. "Right. They're going to stake you instead," he teased. "Ha! Like they could. Hey, if they excommunicate you, we can go into business for ourselves. We don't need a bunch of badly organized celibate dudes to fight demons. I bet there are people who would be willing to pay us pretty well for our unique skills."

He did not really believe they would attempt to harm me, and I would not burden him with the possibility. I sat, mirroring his position as he talked. Not long ago, if the monks had attempted to exterminate me, I might have let them. Leaning forward, I rested my forehead against his. Now I would do what it took to survive.

My urges were, if anything, more depraved than they'd been before I met Sara, but knowing him had made questions of morality irrelevant. I would resign myself to an eternity in hell if it meant a single lifetime with him.

Pressing his knuckles to my lips, I smiled. "Meantime, let us get dressed and face the inquisition."

NOHEA'S *ROOMFUL OF PRIESTS* TURNED out to number three. Brother George, of course, because he was always involved in any dealings with me. Father Patrick, who might be the closest thing I had to an ally, though I still could not bring myself to trust him. If his theory was correct, and the evil we'd faced was linked somehow to events in California, then perhaps he'd argue to preserve my existence long enough to establish the connection.

The third was Brother Michael, who usually presented himself when Victim Services were called for. His presence unsettled me, since I couldn't identify his role in the current circumstances. Who would need the comfort he excelled at providing?

All three of the clergymen rose when we entered the formal living room, another gesture I had difficulty understanding. The windows looked out into the velvet night, and someone, maybe Nohea, had turned on every lamp in the room.

"Thank you for meeting with us, Thaddeus." Father Patrick settled into the channel-back loveseat, which cued the others to sit. "I understand you had a bit of a dustup last night."

"We did." Keeping my expression benign, I explained the circumstances leading us to the Perrier Street house, how between us we'd deanimated the possessed policemen, and how with Goutard's final death, Leo had disappeared. I made it very clear the success of our endeavors had depended on Nohea and Sara, because they were each an integral part of the team.

"So this *De Praestigiis Daemonum.*" Brother Michael rested his hands on his knees, a thoughtful frown creasing his brow. "Did you ever actually see it?"

"No, but I'm pretty sure Marc Goutard had it." Sara's comment got everyone's attention.

"The one you killed." Brother George made little effort to contain the judgment in his tone. All these years, this man had tolerated my presence when he so clearly abhorred my being. I must have been a daily penance for him.

"The one who was already possessed by a demon and would have killed all of us," Nohea growled from the corner.

"Absolutely." Father Patrick nodded with enthusiasm. "This man, Goutard, appears to have been a credible threat, though I'm not one hundred percent convinced he's the one I came here after." Patrick gave me a speculative glance. "Are you willing to keep looking?"

Surprise held my tongue, an opening Brother George took advantage of. "Wait a minute. It's obvious what these two have been getting up to. We can't—"

"Your concern is noted, George, but honestly, if the Catholic Church got rid of gay men, we'd lose half our choir directors and most of our tenors." Father Patrick's white clerical collar bumped against the soft skin under his jaw. "That's why I invited Michael along for this discussion."

Patrick's attitude sent off a warning chime. "*Quoi?*" If a thing sounded too good to be true, I had learned to be suspicious.

Brother Michael grinned. "I practiced law before joining the White Monks."

"And we need a lawyer to rework your contract." The finality in Father Patrick's tone shut down any other discussion. "I suspect your Mr. Goutard wasn't flying solo, and getting hold of the grimoire is going to be key to finding who's really behind things."

"I can't say I agree with this." Brother George stood and strode over to the window, arms crossed as if he wanted to throw me out into the fading daylight. "But if you're determined"—he glanced at the priest—"then let's send the others away and settle things."

Send the others away?

Nohea grasped his meaning before I did. "Oh hell no." She jumped out of her chair. "No disrespect, but you need somebody here to keep you from signing something stupid."

"I beg your pardon?" I blinked at her, aware of Brother George's grimace and Brother Michael's barely stifled laugh.

"She's right," Sara said, shrugging with open palms in response to my glare. This conversation had progressed faster than my thoughts could assimilate.

Brother Michael leaned forward, resting his elbows on his knees. "Look, unless I've misunderstood Father Pat, I'm just going to refine the language in your contract, Thaddeus, to allow you more leeway in how you choose to make your life." He looked to the other priest and received a nod of confirmation. "I'm changing one line, maybe two."

Brother George muttered something from the window. The others ignored him, and Brother Michael brought a small laptop out of the case at his feet. While he was typing, Father Patrick continued the discussion.

"We could make certain changes to his contract, too"— he nodded at Sara—"as long as we're doing this." I did not want him bound to me by a sheet of paper or the strictures of the Church. Sara should have an escape clause if he ever wanted to return to his old life.

"Yes." I nodded. "If you can release—"

"No." Emotions crossed Sara's eyes faster than I could track. Confusion. Anger. Embarrassment. "I don't want out of the stupid contract." Sara glared at me. "Why?"

"Because you're young, and..." The hurt in his eyes shredded my resolve. My feelings for him came from a place of deep certainty. Possibly I'd underestimated him in some way.

"See? This is what I'm talking about. Thaddeus, do yourself a favor and shut up before you get into more trouble." Nohea moved so she could read over Brother Michael's shoulder. She pointed to something on the screen. "I don't suppose...?"

"I am sorry." Brother Michael sounded sincere. His eyes shifted to Brother George. "We are only authorized for certain changes, and we all must agree."

Nohea frowned before giving him a grudging nod. "This will have to do, then."

"Ready?" Father Patrick asked Michael.

The brother tapped at his laptop screen and nodded.

"Then if Sara and Nohea would be kind enough to leave us, we'll finish up with Thaddeus alone."

Father Patrick held up his hand, forestalling Sara's argument. "The contract we have with Thaddeus requires certain blessings and consecrations. Since you are not a member of our Order..." He trailed off.

Nohea rounded on Father Patrick as he tried to usher her out. "Before I go, we need to discuss Angelique."

The clergymen shared a quick glance, and Patrick put his hand on Nohea's shoulder. "I'm very sorry, my dear. I know I promised to look into this, but things are...complicated."

Nohea planted a finger in the center of his chest. "You

get me my baby back, or I will show you complicated."

With a graceful nod, Patrick wrapped her hand in his. "I think we all believe things will calm down, and in a very short while, I'll make arrangements."

Nohea subsided, though the tension in her jaw suggested she'd follow up with him on this issue very soon. Perhaps daily.

"Oh, and Nohea?" Father Patrick's smile grew more formal. "We should make a visit to the police detective who is investigating your sister's murder."

"Fine." She snapped the word and dragged Sara through the door.

The rituals surrounding my service were completed in short order, and with their completion came an unexpected relief. Sara might have regarded me with ill humor, but for the first time in some eighty years, a twinge of hunger brought forth something like anticipation.

"DO YOU NEED ME DOWN here? Because you two may have slept, but I've been dealing with the Church all day."

"Shhh." Sara sat with his back to the wall, next to the closed door.

"Don't *shhh* me. You had your ear up against the damn door for an hour. You couldn't hear anything then, and you can't hear anything now. Father Pat isn't wrapping him in silver chains or trying to stick a stake through his heart. I'm going to bed."

True. If they were going to do any physical harm to Dupont, they would have attempted it before Brother George and Brother Michael left half an hour ago. And they would have brought more monks. And God, he wished the idea they might try to stake Thaddeus had never occurred to him. When Sara had brought it up, he had been joking. But Thad hadn't joked back. He had gone all quiet and evasive. Like maybe it was an actual *possibility*. And then

Thad had tried to end his contract and get rid of him.

Sara drummed his fingers against his thighs, trying to relieve some of the residual stress. Nohea was right. If they were going to do anything horrible, they wouldn't have left Father Patrick to do it alone.

Or maybe they would have. Probably Dupont would lie down and bare his chest if he thought God wanted the stupid monks to stake him.

No. That was silly. They had just modified his contract. Thad was safe. For now, at least. Unless the monks had some other reason they wanted Sara and Nohea out of the room before they finished.

He rubbed his own chest, trying to make sure the anxiety was all on his end. Big extra shot of blood earlier. Seemed he ought to be able to read every thought in Dupont's head and maybe see out of his eyes, too. Instead, the connection was just as vague and gimpy as always. As far as he could tell, Dupont was as close to complete peace as he ever got. Locked in a room with a freakin' priest after an act Thaddeus considered immoral.

He rubbed his chest again. He had to be reading that wrong.

Footsteps sounded on the other side of the door. Sara scrambled to his feet just in time to keep Father Patrick from tripping over him. He ignored the priest, shoving past him to stand next to Thad, who looked calm and relaxed. Asshole. If things were all hunky-dory, why had he and Nohea been evicted? He wasn't buying the super-secret-monk-stuff excuse.

He opened his mouth to ask what was going on, but Thad touched his arm and gave a barely perceptible shake of his head. Great.

He turned his attention to Father Patrick, who seemed impervious to the stink-eye he was getting.

The priest just smiled at both of them. "Well, I think we've covered everything. Thaddeus, I'll let you know if we get any new intelligence. For now, I think it best if you and your team spend some time recuperating."

Your team. The words hooked into Sara's brain. That was him. He was part of Thad's team. Or at least he hoped so. He hadn't let them modify his contract. They were stuck with him for at least a year, right?

Before he could think of any coherent questions, the priest was gone.

He turned to Thad instead. "So, you aren't excommunicated or whatever?"

Thad's mouth twitched up at the corner. "I am a vampire. I suppose you might consider me excommunicated by default."

"Oh. But you're not *more* excommunicated?"

"No. My status with the Church and the White Monks has not changed, although we have modified certain details of our agreement in keeping with the fact that I never took vows as a monk."

"Huh." Yeah, he just bet the monks didn't want to lose their pet demon hunter. He thought about what details they might have changed. The way Brother George had high-tailed it out of the house earlier with his face all pinched up, he had a pretty good idea. He stepped closer to Thad, slipping his arms around his waist. To his surprise, Thad didn't push him away.

"I was serious earlier. We could still hunt demons if you didn't work for the Church anymore." Because no matter what concessions they had made, he didn't think the monks had Thad's best interests at heart.

"We could," Thad said. "But despite my transgressions, they yet offer the return of my soul."

Is *that* what they had told him? *Bastards.* Sara opened his mouth to tell Thad that was bullshit, then shut it. He didn't know if he even believed in a soul. If such a thing existed, the monks certainly didn't have any authority over Thad's. They were just using him and torturing him with their contracts and rules while they did. But if he were to convince Thad… *I am vampire, an unholy creature. There can be no end to my penance.* Thad believed in souls. He believed his own had been lost and the monks could return it to him. Could Sara take hope away from him?

"What were you doing in there with Father Patrick for so long?" he asked instead.

"He heard my confession."

"Oh. What were you confessing?"

Thad blushed.

"Great. I suppose that's the end of that, then." Because Thad considered their union a sin. He stiffened as he remembered Thad's bloody back. When he could force himself to speak, he barely recognized his own voice. The anger closed his throat until his voice was so guttural, it became almost a growl. "What did that damn priest tell you to do?"

"Language," Thad replied mildly. "He is a man of God."

Sara ignored him. He could decide how godly Father Patrick was on his own.

Thad relented and continued, "I am to chant the hours. I am to be mindful of the infallibility of Our Father. I am to seek guidance through prayer until God's will is made clear to me. I am to continue to make confession whenever I believe I have sinned." He paused. "I suppose I shall do so regularly."

"That's all?" He was afraid to hope, because that sounded almost like… "Hey. Hold up!" He wasn't ashamed of the things they did together, but… "You mean you're going to blab to the Church every time we…?"

"Just to Father Patrick, and I will not go into any details." Sara hadn't known Thad's face could get so red.

Prude. But his prude. His prudish vampire who intended them to sin and do very non-prudish things together.

Sara grinned. "Come upstairs. We should get our money's worth for all these confessions you're going to be making."

~THE END~

Want to know when the next
Hours of the Night Book is out?

Keep in touch with Liv and Irene!

www.IrenePreston.com
www.LivRancourt.com

BONFIRE

(HOURS OF THE NIGHT 1.5)

Silent night, holy hell.

Thaddeus and Sarasija are spending the holidays on the bayou, and while the vampire's idea of Christmas cheer doesn't quite match his assistant's, they're working on a compromise. Before they can get the tree trimmed, they're interrupted by the appearance of the *feu follet*. The ghostly lights appear in the swamp at random and lead even the locals astray.

When the townsfolk link the phenomenon to the return of their most reclusive neighbor, suspicion falls on Thaddeus. These lights aren't bringing glad tidings, and if Thad and Sara can't find their source, the *feu follet* could herald a holiday tragedy for the whole town.

Available Now!

ACKNOWLEDGEMENTS

FOR ALL THAT WRITING IS a solitary activity, it sure does take a village to publish a book. I'd like to thank everyone we worked with on this, especially our tough-minded beta readers, Alexis Hall, Ellen Gregory, Pixie Henry, Synithia Williams, Nan Holcomb, and Amanda K. Byrne. Our editors Linda Ingmanson and Michael Valsted did a fantastic job, and our cover artist Kanaxa is absolutely brilliant. It was a pleasure to work with all of you, and I'd do it again in a heartbeat.

Vespers is the first book Irene and I have worked on together, and I'm grateful for the day she poked me and said, "you really need to write another vampire story". Vespers is the most ambitious project I've ever been involved with, and I can honestly say it's my best book yet, primarily because of Irene's involvement. Not only is Irene a fabulous writer, but her knowledge of the business end of writing far exceeds mine, and her organization and attention to detail continues to amaze me. I can't even tell you how many continuity errors she caught...and yeah, sometimes a space is just a space.

I want to say something about Amanda Byrne, who passed away unexpectedly July 5th. She was only thirty-five, and my go-to beta reader, critique partner, and friend. She was the one I bounced ideas off of, who held my hand when I sent off queries, who cheered me up when the inevitable rejections came in. I could send her a paragraph or a couple pages or a whole book and ask, "does this even work?" and she'd tell me. She was funny and snarky and smart, and I miss her every single day. She thought self-publishing

Vespers was a great idea, and I know she'd be cheering us on.

As always, I couldn't do this without the home team. Kent, Ruby, and Matt, you guys are my center. Thank you so much for your patience and understanding. I promise I'll get up from the laptop…in just one more minute…And to you readers, thank you. Irene and I wouldn't get very far without your support and enthusiasm.

UMMM, WOW – LIV SAID most stuff, so *ditto* (except sub in Bones and Kiddo for the final paragraph – No offense to K, R, & M, but I gotta prioritize).

Special thanks to Gene Smithson and Anindo Chatterjee. Gene endured my random messages about cross-bows and other items of interest. If you ever need to escape from zip-ties (or most anything else), Gene's your man. Anindo patiently answered my questions about gods and pujas.

Also – I apologize for completely pulling the wool over Liv's eyes in regards to almost all my abilities. Liv's the one who got me to *actually write words* and also managed to move the story along so Sara isn't still stuck out in the swamp trying to figure out why his memories are fuzzy. If you wonder where Thaddeus and Sara came from, thank Liv for the original concept. Also, she has *(almost)* convinced me that the world won't implode if I change a plot point or reimagine a character trait occasionally. This is a good thing.

And to you, thanks for picking up the crazy book about the gay-Catholic-vampire-monk. Liv and I hope you'll join Thaddeus and Sara as their adventures continue.

Irene

CHANGE OF HEART
AN HOURS OF THE NIGHT STORY
BY LIV RANCOURT

Preacher always said New Orleans was a den of sin,
so of course Clarabelle had to see for herself…

A body reaps what they sow, and Clarabelle's planted the seeds of trouble. The year is 1933, and not much else is growing in the Oklahoma dirt. Clarabelle's gone and fallen in love with her best friend, so she figures it's time to go out and see the world.

If she's lucky, she'll find the kind of girl who'll kiss her back.

Clarabelle heads for New Orleans, and that's where she meets Vaughn. Now, Vaughn's as pretty as can be, but she's hiding something. When she gets jumped by a pair of hoodlums, Clarabelle comes to her rescue and accidentally discovers her secret. She has to decide whether Vaughn is really the kind of girl for her, and though Clarabelle started out a dirt-farming Okie, Vaughn teaches her just what it means to be a lady.

A Taste of You
By Irene Preston

Hell's Kitchen has nothing on the flames Giancarlo
and Garrett ignite at Restaurant Ransom...

Garrett Ransom is America's hot chef du jour. He has a Michelin-starred restaurant in New York City, a hit reality TV show, and a new man in his bed every week. Yes, he secretly thinks his business partner, Giancarlo "Carlo" Rotolo, is hotter than a ghost pepper, but he would never jeopardize their friendship with a fling. Then Garrett overhears some juicy gossip among the crew and realizes he'll have to break Giancarlo's cardinal rule, no banging the staff - for Carlo's own good, of course. Just a taste of Carlo should be plenty. Long-term relationships aren't on Garrett's menu.

Giancarlo's been in love with Garrett forever. He's sure Garrett will eventually realize they are destined to be more than business partners. But when Garrett installs his latest boyfriend as their new chef d'cuisine and announces plans to leave Carlo in New York while he opens a second restaurant on the west coast, Carlo is forced to re-evaluate his life.

Can a high-strung British chef and a nice Italian boy from Brooklyn find the perfect fusion of fine-dining and family-style?

ABOUT THE AUTHORS

IRENE PRESTON HAS TO WRITE romances, after all she is living one. As a starving college student, she met her dream man who whisked her away on a romantic honeymoon across Europe. Today they live in the beautiful hill country outside of Austin, Texas where Dream Man is still working hard to make sure she never has to take off her rose-colored glasses.

Visit Irene at:
www.IrenePreston.com

LIV RANCOURT WRITES ROMANCE: M/F, m/m, and v/h, where the h is for human and the v is for vampire…or sometimes demon. She writes funny. She doesn't write angst. When not writing, Liv takes care of tiny premature babies or teenagers, depending on whether she's at work or at home. Her husband is a soul of patience, her dog is the cutest thing evah(!), and she's up to three ferrets.

Visit Liv at:
www.LivRancourt.com